Praise for Blessings

Also by Sharon Sala

FOREVER *my* HERO

SHARON SALA

sourcebooks
casablanca

Published by Sourcebooks Casablanca, an imprint of Sourcebooks, Inc.
P.O. Box 4410, Naperville, Illinois 60567-4410
(630) 961-3900
Fax: (630) 961-2168
sourcebooks.com

Printed and bound in the United States of America.
OPM 10 9 8 7 6 5 4 3 2 1

*Life is in a constant state of evolution. As
long as we're breathing, we're changing.*

*Life is also a journey with lessons. How we react
to the changes are the lessons. Do we let the
changes destroy us, or do we figure out another
way to incorporate the change and move on?*

*This sweet story, about two people trying to figure out
where they belong, is a story of hope, perseverance,
and the revelation that love is fluid and never-ending.*

*We don't lose love. It just moves to another
place and waits for us to catch up.*

Chapter 1

THE MORNING SUN WAS STILL WET BEHIND THE EARS AS Danner Amos walked out of his house to get the Sunday paper. As he bent over to pick it up, he heard the sound of a car engine rev up and noticed his neighbor, Elliot Graham, was backing from his drive. It was obvious from where he was standing that Elliot was on a collision course with one of two small shrubs at the end of his driveway, but he was going too fast for Dan to warn him.

Sure enough, Elliot rolled right over it, then braked, put the car in drive, and rolled over it again as he went back up his driveway to try again.

Dan was trying not to laugh, but when Elliot put the car in reverse and took another try at backing out, he rolled right over the one on the other side instead.

Dan laughed at the expression of disgust on Elliot's face. Then Elliot saw him, rolled down his window, and yelled, "I meant to do that!" Then he smiled and waved before zipping off down the street.

Dan was still chuckling as he headed back inside. His plan for the day was food and watching football on TV. If the renters he was responsible for didn't have any issues, it would be great.

Elliot's plan was completely different. He'd had a dream last night about Gray Goose Lake, which made him remember the overlook where he and his wife, Helena, had always picnicked. Today, he was going back to that overlook to paint the scene from that viewpoint. It would be a wonderful reminder of happier times that he could frame, and he had the perfect place to hang it.

His drive out to the lake was relaxing, and when he parked and got out, he put on his painting hat—an old, paint-stained Panama hat with a wide, floppy brim—then began to gather up what he wanted to take with him.

It had been a few years since he'd been to the lake, and the hiking trail was a bit overgrown. Elliot stumbled once and dropped his paint box, then had to gather up the tubes of oil paint that fell out. Even after all that, he reached his destination only slightly out of breath. Once he set up his folding easel and the little portable folding stool, he opened his box of paints, prepared his brushes, and then sat for a few moments, just enjoying the view and talking to his long-deceased wife.

"Look, Helena! There is an eagle perched at the top of that big pine straight across the lake. Oh, how magnificent. I must remember to put him in the painting… just for you."

He felt a slight breeze against the back of his neck and smiled. There was no wind today. Only his love.

Without any further delay, he picked up a piece of charcoal pencil and began to rough in the scene, delineating the horizon, then where the tree line would be. He sketched in the shape of the shoreline, and then the boat ramp just to the left, and tossed the charcoal back into the box.

His first choice of paint was to mix what would be the

darkest colors in the lake. Dark was depth, and a painting was nothing without depth—like a person was nothing without depth of character—and he applied the paint to the canvas with a palette knife, giving contour and texture. The lighter colors would come in later on top of the darker, and then the lightest color, which would be glints of sunlight on the ripples, would be added last.

The sun rose higher, but Elliot's hat kept the sun from his face. He was totally into the work, oblivious of everything around him.

While most of the people this morning were just sitting down to breakfast, Junior and Albert Rankin had headed straight to their granny's old cabin at the back side of their land. Today was sale day, and they were ready to load up their latest marijuana harvest, which they'd let cure at the cabin. They wasted no time loading the boat they were pulling, and as soon as they were finished, they covered it with a tarp, and then drove off their property and headed for the woods around Gray Goose Lake to check their grow patches before heading down to the lake to meet their buyer.

They'd been growing weed under their daddy's nose for two years now. They might be accused of being too confident, but Big Tom Rankin had a girlfriend, and when he wasn't at his job at the local feed store in Blessings, his spare time was taken up with her.

Big Tom's wife, Lillian, had died when her sons were twelve and fourteen, leaving Big Tom in grief and his sons on their own too much. By the time both boys were in high school, they were raising a small patch of tobacco on the farm to help subsidize their dad's small paycheck.

Many years later, they were still growing tobacco, taking care of the family's small herd of cattle, and keeping everything in running order. But the dividends they received as small-time farmers weren't enough to suit them anymore.

Once they were satisfied all was well at their grow sites, they headed for the lake to their usual boat ramp, unloaded the boat into the water, then started the outboard motor and headed out to the middle of the lake to fish while they waited for their buyer, Oscar Langston, to arrive from Savannah.

Oscar used the same cover that the Rankin brothers used to meet his suppliers, by arriving with his boat and fishing gear. Once he reached the lake and got his boat out on the water, he would meet up with the Rankin brothers and go to their boat ramp, where they unloaded the packaged products from one boat to the other, exchanged money, and then went their separate ways.

They were still out on the lake fishing when Oscar arrived, but he didn't head for the boat ramp as usual. He was red in the face and angry, which made them nervous. Then Oscar circled their boat, making them bob in the wake of his larger boat as he pulled up beside them.

"What's going on?" Junior asked.

"I'm in a hurry. One of my other suppliers shorted me, and I have pissed-off buyers waiting for product. I don't have time to follow you to shore. Start passing me the goods. Here's the money," he said, and handed over a large envelope.

Albert counted the pay while Junior pulled the tarp

aside and started handing over package after package of weed. They were down to the very last packages when Albert noticed someone up on the cliff on the west side of the lake. Someone who had a ringside seat to what they'd been doing.

"Junior! Someone is on the cliff!"

Junior Rankin looked up, saw a man sitting on the cliff looking straight at them. "What the hell?"

Oscar's voice deepened in anger. "Hurry up. Unload those last two packages ASAP. I'm outta here!"

Junior tossed the last two packages into the boat.

"You don't leave witnesses. Get rid of him!" Oscar said.

Albert gasped. "We don't kill people!"

Oscar pointed a finger straight at Albert's face. "Well, I do."

Junior paled. He got the message. If they didn't get rid of the witness, Oscar would get rid of them.

"Don't worry, Oscar. I'll make sure we're in the clear," he said.

Oscar glared, started the engine, and took off across the lake, then soon disappeared from view.

Junior glanced at the man up on the overlook across the lake. "Well, hell."

Albert was already shaking his head.

"Just come with me to keep watch. I'll do it," Junior said.

Albert was a grown man, but he started to cry. "I won't have a part in this. Not even to keep watch. You take me back to the shore. I'll walk home."

Junior frowned. "Dammit, Albert! You're just as much a part of this as I am."

"No! No, I'm not!" Albert shouted. "I help you grow weed...but I don't help anybody commit murder."

"Well, you're coming with me, so shut the hell up and—"

Before Junior knew what was happening, Albert kicked off his shoes and went headfirst out of their boat and started swimming for the opposite shore.

"Shit," Junior said. He knew his brother. When he said no, he meant it, regardless of the reason, so this was definitely left up to him.

He started up their outboard engine and headed for a spot farther down on the west shore.

He reached shore out of sight of his target, pulled the boat up far enough that it wouldn't float back out on the lake, then started running up through the trees. The closer he got to the man, the more anxious he became. Could he really do this? Could he kill another human being?

But if he didn't, what was going to happen to him and Albert? What if Daddy found out? What if the law found out and arrested both of them? He would never get over the shame of going to prison. It would kill Daddy. He and Albert would be the first Rankins ever to be in trouble with the law. All the generations before them had been honorable men, and he and Albert would be the ones to ruin their name. And while he was berating himself for the mess they were in, he walked right up on the man he'd come to kill.

What the hell? He's an old man, and he's just painting a picture. I don't have to do this. I'm not going to do this.

But as he stood there, unobserved, his focus shifted

from the man to the picture he was painting, and he stifled a groan. The man was painting the scene before him, and squarely in the middle of the lake, he'd painted the two boats and men loading packages from one boat to the other.

Of course no one would ever know who it was in the boats. He'd painted them very small and hardly more than blobs of color, but people in Blessings would wonder, and if asked, the old man could obviously elaborate on what he'd seen. People in Blessings would question what possible reason men would have to be loading goods from one boat to another out in the middle of Gray Goose Lake.

Junior felt like crying. God, he just wanted to be a kid again. This wasn't something he could let go after all. He looked all around beneath the trees for a weapon before taking a step because he knew the sound would give him away. There were dead limbs beneath a tree to his left, so he focused on one and picked it up as he came out of the trees, swinging as he went without giving the old man time to react to the sounds behind him.

The limb made a solid *thunk* against the old man's head, somewhat reminiscent of the sound a watermelon makes as it bursts apart. The sound startled Junior, but not as much as the sight of the old man sliding off his stool and crumpling onto the ground.

For a heartbeat, Junior was frozen in place, and then he thought about what he'd just done and ran over to make sure it was a one-blow deal. He felt for a pulse, but was shaking so hard he couldn't tell if the man was dead or alive. He thought about tossing him over the cliff and down into the water, but couldn't do it. He looked down at the painting and without thinking, jammed a hole in the canvas where the old man had painted the two boats. Then he broke a limb off a nearby bush and used it to scrub out his footprints as he backed away, and kept brushing them out until he was a long ways away.

At that point, he dropped the limb and ran the rest of the way back to his boat. He fell twice trying to push the boat back into the water and was soaked by the time he got it far enough offshore to float. He crawled in, tripped and stumbled all the way back to the outboard motor to start the engine, then left a rooster tail of water in his wake.

He couldn't get the sound of breaking the old man's skull out of his head and was crying by the time he finally reached the other shore. He loaded the boat back up on their trailer, jumped in the truck, and headed for home.

But the thought of home reminded him of Albert. Was he already there? Did he call Daddy and tell him what they'd done, or would he just keep quiet about everything? Junior wasn't sure. All he knew was this shit was far from over. If he was still alive when day broke tomorrow, he was going to destroy every grow patch they had and call it quits.

~~~

Albert had his own tribulations getting to shore, and there was a time or two he wasn't sure he'd make it. By the time he felt solid ground beneath his feet, he was neck deep in water and as exhausted as he'd ever been as he walked the rest of the way to the shore.

He was shaking from the chill of the water when he

started toward home, which was a good three miles as the crow flies. Even though he was going to do this barefoot, he started running, taking the crow's route, which was for him a shortcut through the woods.

The ground was covered in fallen leaves and brambles, hidden rocks and broken limbs, but he was so scared he barely felt the pain. By the time he reached the fence around the pasture behind their house, there was a sharp pain in his side and he was gasping for breath. The muscles in his legs were shaking so hard that he was afraid if he stopped, he'd pass out where he stood.

Thank God his daddy had gone to church with his girlfriend that morning. He'd have the house to himself to get cleaned up. But his feet were going to be another matter. They were beginning to burn. He was afraid to look at how many cuts and thorns were likely in his feet, and God knows when he'd be able to put shoes on again.

He didn't know yet how he was going to explain that away, but he'd think of something. These days, their father-son relationship was down to hellos and goodbyes.

He was still moving as he stumbled through the cow lot, and beginning to hobble as he reached their backyard. The familiar sight of the old two-story home made his vision blur. He and Junior had ruined everything. Almost two hundred and fifty years of the Rankin family living on Georgia soil, and look what they'd done. There wouldn't be any others born to take over if he and Junior were in prison.

Albert choked on a sob when he couldn't go any farther and dropped to his hands and knees, crawling the rest of the way to the house, then up the back steps and straight into the kitchen. He crawled all the way through the house and up the stairs to the bathroom, grabbed some tweezers and a bottle of alcohol, and sat down with the bathtub at his back and finally looked at his feet. They looked like raw hamburger.

"Oh man...I'm gonna need stitches," he muttered, then leaned back against the tub and passed out.

———∿∿∿———

Junior got home, grabbed Albert's shoes out of the boat, and headed for the house. When he saw a blood trail on the back porch, he panicked and started running as he followed the trail upstairs, trying to imagine what had happened to Albert to have caused it. He found his brother passed out on the bathroom floor, saw the bottoms of his feet, and started crying all over again.

"Albert! Albert! Can you hear me?" he asked as he tried to shake his younger brother awake.

Albert moaned, then slowly opened his eyes.

"It's you!" he said.

Junior nodded.

"Did you do it?" Albert asked.

Junior nodded.

Albert moaned and covered his face.

Junior sighed. "You 'bout ruined your feet. I need to get you to the doctor."

Albert swallowed back tears. "I can't walk on them anymore."

"I'll carry you," Junior said.

"How will I explain this?" he asked.

Junior shrugged. "Tell them you fell in the lake and took your shoes off to dump out the water. Tell them you were spooked by a black bear and took off running."

Albert was still choking back tears as he nodded. "Yeah, that would work. Okay. That's my story. And you were way out on the lake fishing and didn't see any of it. You found my shoes, saw my footprints heading for home, and found me here."

Junior patted his brother's head. "Yeah, that's how it went down," he said. "Now let's get you up. I need you to get on my back. I can carry you piggyback easier than I can tote you any other way."

"You'll have to help me get up," Albert warned.

So Junior lifted him to an upright position. As he did, they caught sight of their faces in the mirror.

They were still big, redheaded men with green eyes and broad shoulders. But they didn't look so much alike anymore. Albert's face was twisted in pain, and Junior looked like he'd aged ten years. When you made deals with the devil, it showed on your face.

"Okay now," Junior said as he turned around. "Put your arms around my neck, and wrap your legs around my waist."

"I'm gonna be too heavy," Albert said.

"Naw, you'll never be too heavy, Albert. You'll always be my little brother. Now hang on tight. We've got to get downstairs before we can go anywhere."

Just like they'd done since they were children, Junior shouldered the load of his brother's body and made it down the stairs, then outside to the truck. He got Albert into the seat and took off out of the driveway faster than he'd run from the old man's ghost, heading straight to the hospital in Blessings. Albert saw his cell phone in the console of the truck and put it in his pocket. He was wishing for a bottle of water when he fell asleep.

Their arrival caused quite a ruckus in the ER, but Albert was so relieved by the doctor's decision to put him to sleep to repair the damage that he happily passed out on cue, leaving Junior to call their daddy.

———

It was the acknowledgment of pain that brought part of Elliot back to consciousness. He wasn't awake enough to open his eyes, but he did roll over onto his back, which sent a shock wave of pain rocketing through his body. He passed out again, oblivious to the sun beaming down on his face.

After the sun had done all the damage it could do, it sank below the horizon and the night animals came out. An owl swooped across Elliot's body, snatching up a snake in the nearby grass, and flew away with it still dangling from its talons.

Around midnight, a lone coyote out on the hunt caught the scent of blood and went to investigate. But when it got there, the scent of man was stronger. Hesitant, it slipped closer, and then something crashed nearby, and the coyote took off running through the woods.

A possum sauntered past Elliot's body, sniffing around him without interest before moving away. Later on, a raccoon did the same, staying far enough away from the human scent to feel safe.

Later, a young buck that had been spooked by hunting dogs ran through the trees just beyond where Elliot was lying.

Twice in the night Elliot surfaced, but each time the pain of his wound and his deteriorating condition quickly pulled him back under.

Then night passed, and the sun rose on the new day.

———

Alice Conroy woke up in a cold sweat with the echo of Marty's screams still in her head.

Nightmares! Would they be with her for the rest of her life? God, she hoped not. But she still had secrets from the day her husband died and never intended to share them.

To this day, no one knew her side of what happened— that Marty was in their house, high on the same meth he was making in the old shed down by the barn. She'd known it since daylight. He kept muttering about starting over and needing to wipe the slate clean. He kept saying he was going to set everything on fire and walk away from that life. He kept promising and promising he would fix things. But she'd ignored him because he always talked crazy when he was high and had gone outside to the garden she was working, getting it ready to plant in a couple of months when it warmed up. And that's why she was in the garden when her house exploded behind her, knocking her facedown into the freshly tilled earth.

She sat up in bed and covered her face. When she did, the whole nightmare came back in detail.

Burning debris was still drifting down around where Alice was lying. Thrown several feet forward, she was facedown in the garden, unaware it was their house that had exploded until she heard Marty screaming. She rolled over, saw the blaze and the smoke, and in seconds was up and running toward the house, shrieking for help.

But it was too late for Marty. She watched him stumble out the back door, on fire from head to toe. He swayed forward, then fell backward just as the roof of the porch collapsed on top of him.

She needed her cell phone, but it was in the car parked under the blazing carport. And the car was on fire.

They still had a landline.

But it was inside a burning house.

The only saving grace about the whole day was that her children were at school.

She turned around and ran the three miles to her mother-in-law's house, screaming all the way.

Thank God for alarm clocks, Alice thought as she threw back the covers and headed to the bathroom. She made a face at herself in the mirror as she washed away the last of the bad dream. She needed no reminder of how much she had to be grateful for now. Waking up in Hope House every day, and knowing she and her family were living here rent-free for as long as they needed, was nothing short of a miracle.

The last five months since Marty's death were behind them, and there were no tears left to cry for his absence in their lives. She had grieved his loss three years ago when he started making and selling meth, and kept the relief of his death to herself.

Today was Monday, and the beginning of the second week of September. She had a job to go to, for which she was grateful, and school for the kids. It was time to wake them up. She turned the heat up a bit after she came out of her bathroom and crossed the hall to her son's door.

Charlie had just turned thirteen and was now in seventh grade. Not only was he a head taller than she was, but the last year of their life had turned him into a man far too young.

Her seven-year-old daughter, Patricia, who went by Pitty-Pat, was still young enough that she would forget the hell her daddy had put them through before he died—but Charlie never would.

Alice knocked on Charlie's door.

"I'm up, Mama," Charlie said, and came out into the hall smiling. "It's gonna be a good day," he said, and hurried to the bathroom.

"Thank you for him, Lord," Alice murmured, then went next door to wake her baby. Pitty-Pat always slept with her head under the covers, so Alice had to unwrap her first. "Good morning, Pitty-Pat. Time to get up."

"Not now," she whined.

Alice pulled the covers back. "Yes, now. Charlie is in the bathroom, so you can come to my room and use mine."

Pitty-Pat rolled over, yawning. Magic words. Mama's bathroom was so shiny and beautiful.

"Brush my teeth in there, too?" she asked.

"Yes, but bring your toothbrush this time. You may not use mine."

Pitty-Pat swung her legs off the side of the bed and got up. "Mama, I'm too big to be Pitty-Pat now. I am just Patty, okay?"

Alice blinked. It actually hurt to hear her daughter say this, although raising children to be independent and think for themselves was what Alice's parenting style was all about.

"Of course it's okay…Patty."

The little girl nodded. "Gettin' my toothbrush now."

"I'm going to start breakfast. Don't dawdle getting dressed, or Charlie will eat all of your eggs and toast."

"No! Don't let him!" Patty cried, and ran to get her toothbrush.

Alice grinned. It worked every time.

—∿∿—

Lovey Cooper was already at Granny's Country Kitchen feeding the early risers in town. Mercy Pittman, the police chief's wife, was in the kitchen at Granny's, baking biscuits by the dozens.

Mercy's sister, Hope, who was a nurse at Blessings Hospital, was going off duty after a long night spent in the ER. Hope thought of her husband and brother-in-law out on the farm, already up and feeding cattle by daybreak. She was so tired, the thought of getting home and then making a big farmhouse breakfast before she got to go to bed was overwhelming.

But there were always Mercy's awesome biscuits, so she stopped by Granny's long enough to say hello and take a dozen sausage biscuits home. She thought to herself, as she headed for the farm, that she might have just enough energy left to scramble some eggs for the guys to go with them before she crawled into bed.

—∿∿—

Fred Bloomer, who owned the hardware store where Alice Conroy worked, was shaving before going downstairs to breakfast. His wife wasn't much of a cook, but she did do breakfasts, adhering to the belief that one needed a solid meal to begin each day.

Larry Bemis, the night dispatcher at the police department, was clocking out to go home, while Avery Ames, the day dispatcher, was already on the job.

Chapter 2

Local lawyer Peanut Butterman was sitting at the kitchen table watching his bride, Ruby, make breakfast. He'd had a smile on his face ever since she'd said "I do," and was still considering himself the luckiest man in Blessings.

Ruby took the last stack of pancakes from the skillet and turned off the burner before carrying the food to the table.

"That smells so good," Peanut said, and slid a hand across the small of her back.

"But not as good as you and that aftershave," Ruby said before sitting down.

Peanut sighed. "You bless me in so many ways," he said. "Have I told you how much I love you?"

Ruby smiled to herself, thinking about how it felt to make love with him. "Not in the last five minutes, and for the record, I love you more. Pass the butter."

Peanut laughed and slid it toward her.

After finally getting Peanut off to work, Ruby began going through the list of things she needed to do today. Her beauty shop, the Curl Up and Dye, was closed on Mondays. But she always had more than enough to do.

There was laundry for home and laundry for her shop, a list of groceries to buy, and clothes to pick up at the cleaners.

She paused as she passed a mirror to check her hair and makeup. She was still happy with her hair being this shade of black and intended to keep it for a while longer. It had grown much longer during the past three months, but instead of cutting it to chin length as she normally wore it, she was letting it grow. Right now, it brushed the tops of her shoulders, and the bangs she was wearing were just above her eyebrows. It was the most daring look she'd ever worn, but she was a woman who dared, so it fit.

While Blessings was readying for the new day, Danner Amos was still asleep, lost in the never-ending nightmare of his past, and it always started in the same place.

He turned away from the sink as Holly came hurrying into the kitchen. "I thought you and Blake were already gone," he said.

"My car won't start, and Blake is going to be late for school."

"Take mine," Dan said. "I'll call the garage to pick yours up, then take a cab to the office."

"You're the best," Holly said, and blew him a kiss.

Dan followed her to the front door and then stood in the doorway waving as Holly buckled their seven-year-old son into the back seat, then jumped into the car.

Dan's heart was beginning to pound. He knew what came next and was trying so hard to wake up, but the dream would never turn him loose until he rode it all the way to the end.

The early-morning sunlight reflected on the hood of his Lexus as he watched her check her makeup in the rearview mirror. He smiled. She always looked good to him. Then he saw her reach toward the ignition. Blake was waving at him from the back seat.

He stepped out of the doorway and into the sunlight, his hand lifted to wave back, when the world exploded before his eyes.

Pieces of the Lexus went airborne. All of the windows in the front of their home shattered. Something hit the side of his face as the car burst into flames.

He screamed.

And then he was sitting up in bed, awake and shaking. He touched the scar on the right side of his face and felt tears.

Nothing ever changed.

He threw back the covers and got out of bed. After a quick shower, he dressed for the day and went to the kitchen. Discovering he was out of milk ended the idea of another bowl of cereal at home, so he opted to go to Granny's for breakfast.

The food there reminded him of home, from the chicken and dumplings on the Sunday menu to the biscuits and sausage gravy on their breakfast menu.

He did not regret taking on the manager duties for Aidan Payne's rental properties and was seriously considering buying him out. Right now, he was still learning the routine and building a relationship with the renters. He sent Aidan a monthly statement of repairs, including names of the people moving in and out, and the running total of received income, along with paying himself.

There was no pressure, no worries, and as low-key a life as he wanted.

He was wearing a long-sleeved shirt, Levi's, and boots as he left the house. He jammed his old cowboy hat on his head before he got in the truck and headed uptown. It was a little after 8:00 a.m., and he was thinking about the biscuits and gravy as he drove. He braked at a stop sign, waved at the woman walking her dog, then accelerated through the intersection.

The parking lot at Granny's was more than half-full as he parked and got out. He met one of his renters exiting the café, carrying a to-go order and a cup of coffee.

"Good morning, Frank. How's your wife feeling?"

"Morning, Dan. She's better. Pneumonia is almost cleared up. Doctor will release her to go back to work soon, but I'm still babying her a bit." He held up the to-go order to make the point.

"Give her my best," Dan said.

Frank grinned. "I sure will," he said, and got in his car as Dan went inside.

Lovey was at the register. She still hadn't gotten used to seeing a cowboy in Blessings, but it was beginning to grow on her. The man was seriously good-looking, even with that scar.

"Morning, Dan. Are you joining anyone?"

"No, just me today," he said, and took off his hat.

She picked up a menu and led him toward a small booth.

"Your waitress will be with you shortly," Lovey said. "Enjoy!"

"Yes, ma'am. Thank you," Dan said, and laid his hat on the seat beside him. But before he could open the menu, Shelly Mayberry, the newest waitress, was at his table with a pot of coffee and a glass of water.

"You take it black, right?" Shelly asked.

Dan looked up in surprise. "Yes, thank you."

"Welcome," she said as she filled the cup. "Do you need to study the menu a little longer, or do you know what you want?"

"I know what I want. Biscuits and sausage gravy, with a couple of scrambled eggs on the side."

"Coming up," Shelly said, and left to turn in the order.

Dan spooned an ice chip into the coffee to cool it enough to drink, then added one more for good measure. He was still waiting for his food when Lon Pittman came in. Dan could tell by the look on the police chief's face that something was wrong. He watched, curious as to who he was looking for, then saw the chief make eye contact with him and head his way.

"Morning, Dan. Sorry to disturb you, but I'm doing a welfare check on your neighbor, Elliot Graham. He isn't answering his phone, some of his landscaping has been damaged, and his car is missing. I was wondering if you remember when you saw him last?"

Dan frowned. "I saw him early yesterday morning, and I actually witnessed the shrubs going down. Elliot did it. He took one out the first time he tried to back out of his drive, then took the other one out when he tried it again. But he made a joke about it as he drove away. I haven't seen him since."

"Was he going toward Main?" Lon asked.

"Uh…no, toward the park."

"Okay, sorry about interrupting you. If you happen to see him, give me a call."

"Sure thing," Dan said.

Shelly brought his breakfast as the chief left the café, and he forgot all about the moment as he settled in to eat. The food was hot and seasoned perfectly. He ate with gusto, downing two cups of coffee with it, and was waiting for the waitress to bring his bill when his phone signaled an incoming call. He glanced at the caller ID and frowned. It was one of the renters.

"Hello. This is Dan."

"Dan, this is Margie Wilson over on Lee Street. My shower won't drain."

"Okay, Margie, I'm just leaving Granny's. I'll run by the house and pick up some tools and be right over."

"I'm already late for work, so bring your passkey and come on in."

"Will do," Dan said. "Sorry for the inconvenience. If I can't fix it easily, I'll get a plumber over there today."

"Thank you so much," she said, and disconnected.

Dan waved Shelly down, got his bill and his hat, and paid Lovey on the way out.

"Thanks for breakfast," he said.

She grinned. "Any time, cowboy."

———

Lon Pittman wasn't really worried about Elliot—yet. What was odd was how the old man had flown under the radar in Blessings for as long as he had. He'd lived across the street from Preston Williams for years, but spent a lot of that time traveling. But after Elliot's wife, Helena, passed away, he'd given up everything and turned into something of a hermit.

It wasn't until Mercy Dane had come to Blessings that he'd come out from under the shadow of loss. When Mercy became the renter of the apartment over Elliot's garage, it was her indomitable spirit that, once again, pulled him into the flow of life.

Even though Mercy and Lon were married now and living in Lon's home on the other side of Blessings, she'd stayed in touch with her old landlord, and it was Mercy who'd called attention to the damaged shrubs and then to his absence yesterday evening when she'd stopped to check on his welfare. When she went by again and he still wasn't there, she alerted Lon to the fact.

He'd started out thinking this welfare check would amount to nothing, but he wasn't so sure now. The longer he looked and the more people he talked to, the more concerned he became.

Elliot Graham was no longer in Blessings, of that he was certain. But where did he go? When was he coming back? Or had something happened? Was he lost? Had he become the victim of a crime? The possibilities were endless, and the longer he stayed gone, the less chance Lon felt he had for a positive resolution.

Lon was cruising the perimeter of the park when his cell phone rang. It was the police dispatcher.

"What's up, Avery?" Lon asked.

"Just got a phone call from Millie Powers. Said there's a car parked out at Gray Goose Lake that's been there for two days now. She saw it yesterday and didn't think anything of it, but when she went back today and saw it was still there, she felt something was wrong. It was unlocked, so she checked inside and found mail in the passenger seat addressed to

Elliot Graham. That's why she called us instead of the sheriff."

"Did she give a location of the car?"

"Do you know where Millie lives?" Avery asked.

"Yes," Lon said.

"So, she said take the first turn west past her place, and it's parked near boat ramp number two."

"Notify County what's going on, and let them know I'm already en route. I'll stay in touch."

"Will do, Chief."

Lon hit the lights and siren, then made a U-turn before heading out of Blessings. He was already planning to get Charlie Conroy and that bloodhound again if he couldn't locate the old man in a timely fashion.

The closer Lon got to the lake, the more anxious he became. By the time he passed Millie Powers's home, he was sick to his stomach from thinking about what might await him. He braked as he arrived at the turn and took the gravel road.

He saw Elliott's car just after he pulled up. He was thinking of the snakes, big cats, and occasional black bear that might be around the lake. Animal attacks were rare, but they were a possibility.

He grabbed a handheld radio and popped the trunk to get a rifle. After checking to see if it was loaded, he pocketed some extra rounds, shouldered his backpack, and headed toward the car. He knew Millie Powers had been inside it looking for a clue as to who owned it, but he looked inside to satisfy himself before striking out. After circling the car a couple of times, he finally found a set of tracks leading along the shore and followed them.

About two hundred yards from the car, he found his first clue. It was a tube of oil paint—burnt umber. That was when he remembered that Elliot was an accomplished artist, so he took a picture of the tube of paint, put up a marker to indicate where he found it, then dropped the paint tube in an evidence bag and kept moving.

Lon paused a moment along the shore to look around and slowly became aware of what might have led Elliot out here. The views from any direction were stunning. He turned back to the footprints and kept walking. About fifty yards farther, the land began to slope upward, forming a cliff about thirty feet from the water below. It was the high point at the lake, and the place people referred to as the overlook.

He started up the slope in long strides and, only seconds after breaching the crest, saw a folding easel on its side, a canvas lying in the grass, and a little folding chair still sitting in its upright position. Elliot was flat on his back on the ground beside the chair.

"Oh no," Lon muttered, and started running. The moment he reached the body, he dropped to his knees, all but certain Elliot was dead.

But when he checked for a pulse, to his great relief he felt one. However, having been faceup with the sun beaming down on him all day yesterday, and no water to drink, the old man was in bad shape. His eyelids were burned and crusted shut. His skin was red and blistered, and his lips were swollen and cracked to the point of bleeding and peeling. Lon began to check for injuries and almost immediately found a bad wound on the back of Elliot's head, but nothing to explain how he'd gotten it.

Elliot could have had health issues that caused him to lose consciousness and fall onto a rock, but there was nothing anywhere close to him that could have caused that wound, which made him suspicious. If there were no rocks behind him, then passing out and falling backward would not cause this huge wound on the back of his head.

Lon reached for his radio to call it in, then changed his mind. The fewer people who heard this call, the better for all concerned, so he used his cell phone instead and called the dispatcher.

Avery answered on the first ring.

"Dispatch. Avery speaking."

"Avery! I found Elliot Graham. Notify County to go due north along the shore past his car. He's on the ridge, he's alive, and I need a Medi-Lift chopper, ASAP."

"Will do, Chief. Anything else?"

"Tell them to hurry," he said, then shrugged off the backpack.

Before he moved anything at the scene, he needed to record it as he found it, so he began taking pictures. When he saw the canvas with a hole punched right in the middle of it, his skin suddenly crawled. Elliot saw something he wasn't supposed to see and it nearly got him killed. He took pictures of that, and then the entire area around his body before he set his camera aside and grabbed a couple of water bottles from his pack.

"Elliot, can you hear me? It's Chief Pittman. I have water."

Because of the wound on Elliot's head, Lon was afraid to move him, so to keep him from choking, he dug through his pack again, found a clean bandanna, soaked it with water, then squeezed the tiniest bit between Elliot's lips. He repeated that several times, then switched to Elliot's face and poured a small but steady stream across his forehead, letting it run across his burned and crusted eyelids. As he did, Elliot moaned.

The sound was encouraging. "Elliot! This is Chief Pittman. I have water. Can you open your mouth a little?"

Elliot tried, then cried out in pain when movement made the cracks in his lips begin to bleed.

"It's okay, it's okay," Lon said. "I'll squeeze some more between your lips. I won't let you choke. You're safe now. A medical chopper is on the way. We'll get you to the hospital ASAP."

Elliot moaned and lost consciousness again.

Lon continued to pour water on his face and around his eyes. He found some Vaseline in his backpack and rubbed a tiny bit on the cracked and bleeding places on the old man's lips. By the time he was beginning to hear the voices of the county officers, he also heard the sound of an approaching helicopter.

"Elliot! Can you hear that chopper? Help is coming," Lon said, then looked up.

County officers Butler and Treat were coming up the slope on the run. Lon knew both of them.

"Chopper's here!" Butler said, pointing as he ran, but the warning was unnecessary. The downdraft from the rotors was stirring up everything loose on the forest floor around them.

"They're sending down a litter and a medic," Treat added.

Lon looked down at Elliot and checked his pulse again, reassured by the faint throb of a heartbeat.

In less than fifteen minutes, the medic had assessed Elliot's condition and stabilized him enough to be moved.

Lon and the officers watched, unable to take their eyes off that basket swinging in midair until Elliot and the medic were safely inside the chopper.

As soon as the chopper headed back to Blessings, Lon grabbed his backpack.

"I'll leave the scene to you guys. I assume you'll be treating it as a crime scene, considering the hole someone punched in the canvas and the wound on the back of his head. Note that he's lying in nothing but grass and dirt, so there's nothing here that would have caused that wound had he fallen. Oh, I found this tube of paint on the trail, and I took a picture and left a marker before I bagged and tagged it for you. I also took photos of the scene as I found it before I tended to Elliot. I'll email those to the sheriff's office when I get back to the precinct."

"Yes, sir. All scenes are crime scenes until proven otherwise. It's protocol. We'll enter the tube of paint into evidence and tell Sheriff Ryman to look for the photos. If I learn anything new, you'll be notified, and by the same token, a copy of whatever information Mr. Graham is able to share will be appreciated."

"Of course," Lon said, and headed off down the slope as fast as he could go, then ran all the way back to his cruiser.

The first thing he did was send Mercy a text. If it hadn't been for her, Elliot Graham would surely have died.

Mercy was up to her elbows in piecrusts when she heard the phone in her pocket signal a text. Lon had promised to let her know what was up, and she quickly cleaned her hands before reading it. Her reaction was one of pure shock.

"Oh my God!"

Lovey was on her way back into the dining area when she heard Mercy. She stopped and turned around.

"Honey! What's wrong?" Lovey asked.

Mercy was shaking. "Lon found Elliot unconscious at the lake. He'd been there since yesterday. He's in bad shape, and his injuries don't add up to an accident. They're bringing him into the ER here by chopper."

"What on earth?" Lovey asked.

"I don't know," Mercy said, but she was in tears. "Lon will keep me updated. All I can do is pray."

Elvis, the fry cook, was frowning. "Can't imagine anyone hurting an old man like that, but there's no accounting for how people behave these days."

Mercy shuddered. "I can't bear to think of him being attacked in some way!"

Elvis shrugged.

"Keep me updated," Lovey said.

Mercy nodded, then sent a text back to Lon to keep her informed of what was happening before going back to work.

The news quickly spread from Granny's to the rest of the Blessings residents. They were horrified, thinking of Elliot out there alone overnight, the victim of an attack.

Dan Amos was on his way to Bloomer's Hardware to get a part to fix Margie Wilson's shower. He'd forgotten the shower was a tub/shower combination until he'd gotten to her house, but it soon became obvious the problem wasn't with the actual drain. It was the part that released water in the tub so it could run out.

He didn't know exactly what it was called, but he'd taken a picture of it and watched a YouTube video of how to fix it. If Bloomer's had the part, he was good to go. If they didn't, the plumber was about to get a call.

As he pulled up in front of the store, he smiled. He would get to see Alice Conroy again. She was pretty to look at, but it was her manner that was so engaging. And she was smart. And there was that brief kiss they'd shared about a month ago as she was helping him find some gaskets. She'd been talking and smiling and pointing out the sizes he needed when he just leaned over and kissed her.

It was hard to say who was more shocked, Alice or him.

He immediately apologized over and over. She was never upset or angry, but he'd obviously embarrassed her and he regretted that, even as he was breathing a sigh of relief that she'd given him an out. But ever since then, there was that spark of knowing what had happened between them, and the wondering if it would ever happen again.

And today was no different. He was thinking about her as he walked into Bloomer's. Then he heard Alice and the customer at the counter talking about Elliot, and it didn't sound good.

"Excuse me," he said as he approached. "I don't mean to intrude, but Mr. Graham is my neighbor. Did I understand you to say he'd been found?"

"Yes," Alice said. "They found him unconscious out at Gray Goose Lake. It appears he'd gone out to paint because his things were there beside him, but they don't know what happened to him."

Dan was immediately overwhelmed with guilt. He should have paid more attention that Elliot hadn't come home.

"That's terrible," he said, and quietly walked away, moving down an aisle to distance himself so they could finish their conversation.

He kept imagining the old fellow exposed to the weather, alone, and unconscious. It was nothing short of a miracle that he was alive. Dan was so upset that he forgot what he'd even come for, and then Alice found him standing in front of pipe fittings, staring off into space. He felt a gentle, tentative touch on his arm and turned around.

"Is there something I can help you with?" she asked.

He nodded, then pulled the picture up on his phone and pointed to the part he needed. "This isn't working anymore. At first I thought something had just come loose, but after unscrewing it for a better look, I discovered it was broken." He showed her yet another picture and then watched her frown.

"I'm so sorry. This is a little bit beyond my expertise. If you'll wait a moment, I'll go get Mr. Bloomer to help you."

He nodded, and within a couple of minutes, Fred Bloomer was on the computer with Dan at his side, checking for the proper part number, then checking his online inventory to see if he had one. And he did. Dan was happy his renter wouldn't have to wait for a part before he could fix the shower, and carried the part up front to pay.

Alice was waiting at the register. She kept glancing

at him when she thought he wasn't looking. She might as well have been staring, which would have given him an excuse to stare back, because he was aware of everything about her. He'd seen her kids, and he'd seen her with her kids. He knew her husband was dead, and that she had tasted like peppermint when he had kissed her.

Alice rang up the parts and then paused and glanced up at him. "Do you have everything else you'll need?"

"I think so. If I don't, I'll be back," he said, and grinned.

Alice sighed. Dan Amos was a very handsome man. She did not want to be attracted to any man. She'd had all the disappointment in her life that she could handle. And yet there was that kiss, and here he was, smiling at her, making her heart flutter.

She smiled shyly. "Not wishing you any bad luck, but we're always happy to see you." The moment that came out of her mouth, she flushed.

Dan grinned. "Well, thank you, ma'am."

"Considering the fact that you stole a kiss from me once, the least you can do is call me Alice," she said.

He blushed. "Yes, I did, and while I should apologize again, the truth is that I am not one bit sorry it happened."

She laughed.

"And I'm Dan. Never Mr. Amos to you. In the meantime, I'm off to make Margie Wilson's evening better than her morning," he said, and headed out the door with the parts.

He didn't know he was still smiling until he got in his truck and caught a glimpse of himself in the rearview mirror.

Instead of shifting into a scowl, he just shook his head and drove away.

Chapter 3

ALBERT RANKIN HAD SPENT THE NIGHT IN THE HOSPITAL after the ordeal with his feet, and he was being released today with the understanding that he could not put weight on them until it was time to remove his stitches, which meant at least a week.

Yesterday, as soon as Junior headed to Blessings with his brother, he had called their daddy to let him know what had happened. Big Tom left work and was there waiting when they arrived. Then, to their surprise, Big Tom stayed with Albert all night, sleeping in a chair beside his younger son's bed.

Junior went home to feed the livestock and was alone in the old house all night. Usually, he liked sleeping with ghosts, but not last night. He'd felt their judgment as surely as if they'd appeared before him. Albert's sleep wasn't much better, but going home gave his day a brighter outlook.

Albert and Big Tom were on the way out of the hospital, with Big Tom walking beside the orderly who was pushing Albert's wheelchair toward the exit. They came out of the hospital just as the chopper arrived with Elliot Graham inside.

Big Tom looked up as the helicopter came down onto the landing pad. "What's all that about?" he asked.

Albert shaded his eyes against the sun to watch the

descending medical helicopter as the orderly stopped the wheelchair at the curb.

"They found an old man out at the lake and are bringing him in. Whatever happened, they said he was in bad shape and was out there alone all night," the orderly said.

"Who is it? Someone from Blessings?" Big Tom asked.

"Some old man named Elliot Graham. I heard them talking about it down in ER when I went to get a wheelchair. Supposedly he's some famous painter from back East who retired in Blessings several years back."

Albert was stunned, and then relieved. The old man was alive! Junior hadn't killed him after all. And then he wondered if the Graham fellow had seen Junior before he was attacked. This mess continued to wind itself into a tighter knot.

Then they helped Albert into the front seat of his daddy's truck and put the wheelchair he'd rented from the hospital pharmacy in the truck bed.

"Ready to go home, Son?" Big Tom asked as he slid behind the wheel.

"Yes, sir," Albert said.

Big Tom drove straight to the pharmacy to get the pain prescription filled before they headed out of town.

"Son, will you be okay sitting here for a bit?"

"Yes, sir, I'll be fine. I don't want to go home without those pills, either."

Big Tom patted him on the shoulder. "I won't be long," he said, and hurried inside.

The moment his dad shut the door to their pickup truck, Albert reached for his daddy's phone that he'd left in the console and called his brother.

Junior was in the barn when his phone rang. He recognized his daddy's number. "Hello, Dad. How's Albert?"

"Albert is fine and on his way home," Albert said.

Junior recognized his brother's voice. "Albert! How are you feeling?" he asked.

"Oh, it hurts like hell, but Daddy is in the pharmacy getting my pain prescription filled. Listen, I have news about the man at the lake. He's not dead."

Junior groaned, and then his voice started shaking with emotion. "Oh sweet Lord, what a blessing!"

Albert frowned. "So this makes you happy? I assume you are saying he can't identify you?"

"He never saw me. Who is it?"

"So you didn't know him at all? Never even seen him before?"

"No," Junior said. "What's his name?"

"An old man named Elliot Graham. Some famous artist who retired in Blessings."

"I'll be praying for a complete recovery. I have already accepted that my life from this point on doesn't matter. If I escape discovery, I'll spend the rest of it doing the good Lord's work."

Albert was surprised by Junior's vow, and at the same time relieved that his brother obviously regretted what he'd done.

"Don't go back to the grow patches," Albert said.

"I was gonna destroy them myself," Junior said.

"No. Leave them be. If they figure out he was the victim of an attack, the law will be everywhere around that lake looking for someone to arrest for his injuries. It won't matter none if they find the weed. They can't tie it to us. But what you should do is go to Granny's old cabin and make sure there isn't a trace of weed left there or in the boat. Take some square bales of hay up to the cabin and store them in there. Wash that boat out from top to bottom and then cover it with a tarp and pull it into the old machine shed."

"Good thinking, Albert. I will do that, and I will not go near the grow patches ever again. I promise. I'm sorry I didn't listen to you," Junior said.

Albert sighed. "So am I, because you did something I never thought you'd be capable of doing. Just because the old man is still alive is not because of anything you did to save him.. You tried to kill a man, Junior. Don't ever forget that."

Albert disconnected before his brother could reply. He didn't want to hear anything more. There would never be a reason good enough to make that knowledge go away.

Dan finished repairing the plumbing problem at Margie Williams's house, went home and unloaded the tools, then hurried into the house to call Aidan Payne.

Aidan was in his office at the restaurant when his cell rang. When he saw it was Danner Amos, he immediately assumed something was wrong with the rental properties.

"Hello."

"Aidan, this is Dan. Something happened here in Blessings that I knew you would want to know about."

"What happened?" Aidan asked.

"Elliot Graham went missing yesterday. It appears he'd gone to the lake and something happened to him there. He was out there all night, and no one knew. Chief Pittman did a welfare check this morning, then began the search and that's where they finally found him."

"Oh my God!" Aidan said. "Do they know what happened?"

"I haven't heard details other than his injuries don't line up with an accident. All I know is that they found him alive but in critical condition. They airlifted him to the hospital here in town. I'm on my way up there in a few minutes to check on him. I'll fill you in with more details as I learn them."

"Please do," Aidan said. "I dread breaking the news to Phoebe and Lee. They were very close to him because he and my grandfather, who owned the house you're in now, were best friends."

"I remember that," Dan said. "So, I'll let you go and text you if I hear anything more."

"Take care, and thanks for calling," Aidan said.

Dan pocketed his phone and left the house to go check on Elliot's condition.

Alice was unpacking a new shipment of parts between waiting on customers. She'd just emptied and shelved the contents of all of the boxes but one. She broke down the empty box and carried it to the back room, then returned to the front of the store to finish up. She reached for the box cutter without looking, then screamed and yanked back her hand in horror. She'd accidentally left the blade exposed, and now her hand was gushing blood from the cut in her palm.

She put pressure on her wrist as she ran to the back,

calling Fred's name as she went. He was frowning when he came out of his office, and then he saw her hand and all the blood and gasped.

"Sit down!" he shouted, and ran for a package of paper towels, tore it open, and handed it to her. "Press your palm against this roll as hard as you can. I'm calling 911."

Alice moaned. It was beginning to hurt, and she was feeling faint from the shock. "I'm so sorry," she mumbled, but Fred didn't hear her. He was in his office on the phone.

By the time the ambulance arrived, Alice was sitting with her head between her knees to keep from passing out. The EMTs packed the cut to stifle the blood flow and loaded her on a gurney. She was in the ambulance before she finally fainted.

Dan was almost to the hospital parking lot when he heard an ambulance siren. He looked in his rearview mirror, saw it coming up fast behind him, and pulled over to the curb to let it pass, then followed it in.

He was circling for a place to park when he saw the EMTs pulling the gurney out of the ambulance. It was curiosity that made him slow down and look to see who it was, and when he recognized Alice Conroy, the skin crawled on the back of his neck. What in the hell? He'd just seen her a couple of hours ago and now this? His reaction was knee-jerk. He didn't think about why he was getting himself involved as he parked and ran inside.

The receptionist looked up as Dan stopped at her desk.

"Alice Conroy. Where is she? They just brought her here by ambulance," he said.

"Are you family?" she asked.

"A friend."

"I'm sorry, but you can't go back."

"I just saw her a couple of hours ago, and she was fine. Was she in an accident? Is she ill?"

The receptionist sighed. She wasn't supposed to divulge information, but this wasn't exactly personal.

"She accidentally cut her hand is all I know."

Dan felt the panic in his gut dissipating. "Okay, and thank you. I just saw her unconscious on the gurney and…" He stopped. He didn't have an explanation for why he had panicked, or why he felt the need to check on her. "Uh…I think I'll just sit here and wait. If you can just let her know Dan Amos is in the waiting room, and if she needs anything, I'm here to help, I would appreciate it."

"Yes, I can do that," she said. "Dan Amos, you said?"

"Yes, ma'am," he said, and found a place to sit out of the way.

Dr. Quick was assessing Alice's vitals as one nurse was hooking up an IV and another was already preparing the cut hand for stitches. After satisfying himself that all of the readings were normal, he began trying to wake her.

"Alice! Alice! Can you hear me? You're in the emergency room."

"What happened?" she mumbled, then felt the burn of the wound on her palm. "Oh…my hand. I cut my hand."

"Yes, ma'am, you sure did. How did this happen?" he asked.

"A box knife. I was unpacking inventory and accidentally cut myself."

"The EMTs said you lost a lot of blood. Do you have a problem with blood not clotting?"

"A little," Alice said. "Mama always said I was a free bleeder…whatever that means. How long will this take? I need to get back to work. Mr. Bloomer is—"

"Mr. Bloomer is going to be on his own for the rest of today. We're going to disinfect the area, then there will be some shots to deaden it before I stitch you up."

Alice moaned. "This is such a mess. I can't believe I caused all this trouble."

The nurse patted her shoulder. "Don't fuss, honey, accidents happen."

They were getting ready to deaden the wound when the receptionist knocked and then entered the room. "Excuse me, Doctor, but I have a message for your patient."

"Certainly, go ahead," Dr. Quick said.

"Ma'am, you have a visitor in the waiting room. He asked me to tell you that he's there, and if you need help, he's offering his assistance."

Alice was shocked. She didn't know anyone who would do that. "Who is it?" she asked.

"He said his name is Dan Amos."

Alice's eyes widened. "Seriously?"

"Yes, ma'am. He wanted to be here with you, but since he wasn't family…"

Alice didn't know what to think, but having the company would be comforting. "If he still wants to be here with me, I would appreciate it."

Dr. Quick smiled. "I think a little company would give you something to think about besides what comes next. Send him back," he said.

"Yes, sir," the receptionist said, and left the room.

A couple of minutes later, they heard rapid footsteps coming down the hall and then Dan Amos was in the room, a bigger-than-life cowboy coming toward her with purpose.

For just a second, Alice thought about that kiss, and how close she'd come to kissing him back, then reminded herself of the vast gap between their lives. However, his appearance seemed to change the energy from tears and pain to a quiet calm as he approached the bed.

"Alice, forgive me for intruding, but I have been where you are, and I was also alone." He ran a finger along the scar on his face to punctuate the statement. "I'll do whatever you want, whether it's sitting in the room just for moral support, or offering a hand to squeeze if the pain gets too rough."

Her voice was shaking. "I'll take your company and your hand."

"Done," he said, and moved beside her, reached for her good hand, and threaded her fingers through his.

Feeling her nervousness as they touched, he winced at the sight of the cut. "You did a job on yourself," he said.

Alice glanced up at him and grimaced. "This is so going to mess up my routine," she muttered.

"Routines are meant to be changed. If they weren't, they'd be called ruts," he said.

Alice sighed. "Well, that's one way of looking at this mess."

He patted her shoulder.

A nurse had everything out on the tray that Dr. Quick would need and was standing by to assist. "Ready when you are, Dr. Quick."

He nodded and picked up the loaded syringe to deaden the area to be stitched. "Alice, I'm going to begin deadening the area now. It will have a pretty good sting. I'm going to apologize ahead of time, okay?"

She nodded, then closed her eyes.

Dan was watching, remembering, and knowing it was going to hurt like hell.

The first stick of the needle was both shocking and excruciating. Alice cried out from the shock and then tightened her grip on Dan's hand. Even then, she couldn't stop from moaning each time the doctor injected. Tears were running down her cheeks, and she was shaking all the way to her toes by the time he'd finished.

"I'm so sorry," Dr. Quick said. "We'll wait a couple of minutes before we start just to make sure the area is numbed enough. You rest."

Dan patted her head. "You're doing great," he said.

"I cried," she muttered.

"I cried through the whole thing on my face," he said.

She blinked away tears. "You did?"

He hesitated to elaborate, but hard times often called for hard stories. "I did. Most of the tears were from watching my family die in an explosion, and the rest were from the pain on my face where I'd been hit by debris."

Alice gasped. "My husband was high on meth. I was outside when the explosion occurred in our house, but he set our house and car and himself on fire. I saw it all."

They stared at each other in disbelief. The odds of them both losing their partners in deadly explosions was random and shocking.

The nurse set another tray nearby containing needles

and sutures and everything else the doctor might need to close up the wound.

"Here we go again," Dr. Quick said. "You should not experience any pain, and if you do, let me know and I'll stop and deaden it some more, okay?"

"Okay," Alice said, and glanced down at the gaping wound on her hand.

Dan felt her tensing up again and brushed a finger down the side of her cheek to get her attention, then gently turned her head. "Look at me, not the needle, okay?"

She fixed her gaze on the curve of his lower lip and then glanced up at his eyes and was instantly lost in the empathy she saw and felt.

"Tell me about your kids," Dan said.

It was the perfect subject, as Alice's whole face lit up. "Charlie turned thirteen this past summer. He is an official teenager, but he had already taken on the role as man of the family. I hate it for him. He needs to be a kid now, but life isn't always fair."

"How old is your little girl?"

"Patty is seven. One minute she's all little and in my lap, and the next she's worrying about what to wear. And I can't forget Booger. He's part of the family, too."

Dan grinned. "Who's Booger?"

"Charlie's bloodhound. His tracking skills are something."

"Oh…right!" Dan said, and glanced at her hand to see how much more the doctor had left to stitch. At least it wasn't paining her now. "So, did you grow up here?"

"No. I grew up in the hills about twenty miles south of here. Marty, who was my husband, grew up just down the road from me. We were the same age and in the same class."

"Do you have parents you want to call?" he asked.

She shook her head. "My parents are dead, and after Marty died, for whatever reason, his family didn't want anything to do with us anymore. Not long after Marty's funeral, at his mother's orders, one of his brothers brought us to Blessings, dumped us out on a street corner like unwanted puppies, and drove away. All we had were the clothes on our backs and the money he'd given me. It was just over four hundred dollars, most of which went to the place I rented for us to live in."

Dan was horrified and it showed. "Wow, not much family unity there."

All of a sudden she winced a bit and looked at the doctor.

"Did that hurt?" he asked.

"It stung a little, but not bad," Alice said.

"That was the deepest part of the cut. The rest shouldn't be that sensitive," he explained.

"Okay," Alice said, and then once again leaned back and closed her eyes.

Dan took advantage of the moment to really look at her. She had a fragile appearance, but looks were deceiving. Alice Conroy was a tough little thing, but she had thick, glorious hair the color of hot chocolate, and she was pretty.

Finally, the doctor tied off the last stitch.

"That's it!" he said. "We'll bandage this up, and you'll be good to go. I need you to keep it dry and bandages on. Come back in three days. I want to take a look at it and change the bandages. They will stay on until you come back to get your stitches out. I'll send a pain prescription with you when you leave. Get it filled and follow the directions on how to take it."

"Yes, sir," Alice said.

The nurse proceeded to bandage her hand, and when she was finished, she left to get the paperwork for Alice to sign and came back with papers showing she was being released, along with the prescription.

"I'm right-handed," Alice said, holding up her bandaged hand.

"With you witnessing, I'll sign it," Dan said.

The nurse nodded.

"Thank you," Alice said, and started to get down from the bed.

"I need to take you out in a wheelchair," the nurse said. "Hospital rules. Be right back."

"Oh. Okay," Alice said, then glanced up at Dan. "My car is at the hardware store. If you could give me a ride to get it, I would appreciate it."

Dan frowned. "I'll take you to the hardware store to get your purse and car keys. Then I'll take you to the pharmacy in your car to get the prescription filled, then I'll take you home."

"But how will you get your truck?" Alice asked.

"I can call any number of people for a ride, okay?"

She sighed. "Yes, okay, and much appreciated."

Without thinking, he reached out and cupped the side of her cheek. "You're welcome, and thank you for letting me help."

His hand on her face was warm. His touch was gentle. The urge to lean against him was strong. Instead, she managed to keep her composure.

An orderly came back with the wheelchair and seated her in it.

"I'll drive my truck up to the exit," Dan said, and took off at a lope.

"Nice guy," the orderly said, as he began pushing Alice down the hall.

"Yes, he is," Alice said, and tried not to think about facing her boss with the news that she was ordered to go home.

By the time the orderly wheeled her out the exit, Dan was waiting for her arrival. He opened the passenger door as the orderly pushed her all the way to the truck. But when Alice stood up, Dan scooped her up in his arms and set her in the passenger seat.

"It's too tall for you to climb in."

Alice was still trying to process the fact that she'd been kissed by him, and now he'd held her in his arms. "Uh, yes...I can see that. Thanks again."

He grinned, then leaned across her to fasten the seat belt, which put his cheek within kissing distance. She closed her eyes and tried not to think about that, then heard a click.

"There you are. Good to go," he said. "Do you feel sick at your stomach? The seat reclines. I can fix it so you're lying back some if you want."

"No, no, I'm okay," Alice said.

"Awesome," he said, and shut the door, then circled the truck and got in behind the wheel. "First stop, giving your boss the news."

"I don't want to make him angry. I really need this job."

Dan frowned. "I can't imagine any part of this making him angry. Don't worry. I got your back."

Alice's eyes welled.

"What's wrong? Was it something I said?" he asked.

"I haven't had anyone backing me for a very long time."

Dan gave her a thumbs-up, then put the truck in gear and drove away. But he was moved by what she'd said. His rap sheet was nothing but a long list of him rescuing people in need. He had ridden a lot of white horses in his life, minus the shining armor. But this felt different. He was becoming invested in far more than her physical welfare. The unknowns were still an issue with him. Could he handle becoming friends, really good friends, with a woman and her kids? Even more to the point, would she be receptive to the idea?

He sighed. Okay, so his emotional starvation was finally being fed, but he reminded himself: *Small servings of empathy, Danner, and small bites.*

Chapter 4

DAN DROVE STRAIGHT UP MAIN TO BLOOMER'S HARDWARE and parked right beside Alice's car.

"I need to get my things and talk to Fred," she said.

He nodded. "Hang on, I'll help you out and walk in with you, just in case you get a little light-headed."

"Thanks," she said, and watched as he circled his truck on the run, then opened her door. Before she had time to even try getting out on her own, he grabbed her by her waist and lifted her out with ease.

Alice sighed. *Good-looking, kind, and he's strong, too? Almost too good to be true.*

"Are you okay?" he asked.

She nodded.

"If you need to steady yourself, grab hold of me. I won't let you fall."

Again, her eyes welled with tears, but she looked away, unwilling for him to see how weepy she was. It was all because of the shock and the pain. That was why. Not because the thought of having someone to depend on made her wish it was him. The only thing they had in common was the way their spouses had died, and that wasn't a connection on which a relationship might be built. It was just a horrible reminder of the worst days of their lives.

Her legs felt a little rubbery as she stepped up onto the sidewalk, but she made it inside without incident.

Fred Bloomer saw her coming in and, to her surprise, hurried toward her and gave her a hug.

"Alice! You scared the life out of me! Are you okay?" he asked.

She held up her hand. "The doctor told me to go home today, but I'll be back here tomorrow, I promise. I'm so sorry this happened. I didn't intend to put you in a bind."

"Don't talk nonsense!" Fred said. "Accidents happen to all of us. Of course you're going home. And I want you to stay there tomorrow, too, and if you're still in too much pain after that, just call me. We'll figure it out. My wife has already volunteered to come in and help out. All we want is for you to heal."

Alice cried again, but this time they were tears of relief.

"Thank you, Fred. I need to get my things. Dan is going to drive me home in my car so it will be there when I feel good enough to drive it."

"You need a ride back?" Fred asked. "I can call a friend."

"I've got it covered, but I appreciate the offer," Dan said.

Alice pointed toward the back of the building. "I need to get my purse out of the locker. Will you work the combination lock for me?"

"Absolutely," Dan said. "Lead the way."

They had to walk single file through the aisles to get to the back room, which gave Dan an interesting view of Alice and one he hadn't seen before. Finding out that the sway of her hips moved in opposite juxtaposition to the sway of her ponytail was fascinating.

Science was a wonderful thing.

And when he thought about it, so was biology.

"This is my locker," she said, pointing to number ten. "I need to sit down," she added, and plopped down on the bench in front of them.

Dan eyed the white circle around her mouth and the beads of sweat across her forehead and knew she was alternating between dizzy and nauseous.

"What are the numbers?" he asked.

"Right ten, left four, right eight, left one."

He spun the lock to clear it, then repeated the steps. When it popped open, he put the lock on the top of the locker and opened the door.

"Here's your purse," he said, and set it on the bench beside her. "And here's your jacket. Want to put it on, or do you want me to carry it?"

"Just carry it, please."

"Are these your car keys clipped to the purse handle?"

She nodded, then leaned forward and put her head between her knees again.

"Bless your heart," Dan muttered. He hung her purse on his arm, threw the jacket over it, and scooped her up in his arms.

"Oh my God, you don't have to do that," Alice said.

"You are as white as a sheet and about to face-plant. I do not want to take you back to the ER with a broken nose, okay?"

She leaned her head against the strength of his chest. "Yes. Okay."

Dan carried her back through the hardware store as easily as he'd carried his sack of plumbing parts earlier.

Fred looked a little startled, then saw how pale she was and rushed ahead to open the door.

"Hey, Fred, these are her keys," Dan said, jingling them on the end of one finger. "Open the passenger door for me."

Happy to be of help, Fred had the car unlocked and the door open in no time. He watched the gentle way Dan Amos had of settling her in the seat and buckling her in, then putting her release papers in her lap before shutting the door.

Fred handed him the keys. "Don't know how you happened along to help her, but on her behalf, I thank you," he said, and shook Dan's hand.

"It's all good," Dan said. "Happy to help." And then he got in the car. Within moments he backed up, then took off up the street.

Fred sighed and went back inside. It was almost four o'clock. Only a couple of hours until closing.

Fred wasn't the only one ready for this day to be over. Alice was emotionally spent. But she would have been feeling much worse if she'd had to cope with all this on her own.

Dan glanced at the papers in her lap. They needed to get that pain prescription filled.

"Alice, I saw a prescription on your release papers. Do you see it in the papers I laid in your lap?"

Alice shuffled through the stack and saw it paper-clipped to one of the pages. She pulled it loose. "Yes, it's here," she said.

"Hang on to it, and we'll get it filled at the pharmacy before I take you home."

Alice reached for her purse on the floor by her feet. "I'm not sure if I have enough cash to—"

"I've got it covered," Dan said.

She ignored her. "I don't like owing people."

He frowned. "I'm not 'people.' I'm your friend Dan. Can you make pie?"

"Yes, but what does that—"

"When you get well, make me a pie. That'll be the best payback ever."

She sighed. "Yes, well, okay," she said, too weary to argue.

A few minutes later, he pulled up to the curb at the pharmacy and parked.

She handed him the prescription.

"I'll be as quick as I can," Dan said, and hurried inside.

Alice leaned back and closed her eyes. Her hand was beginning to throb. It was evident those pain pills were going to come in handy. She took a deep breath and then exhaled slowly, willing away the ache.

All of a sudden, someone was knocking on her window. She opened her eyes, saw Ruby Butterman standing by her car, and rolled down the window.

"Hi, Ruby," Alice said.

Ruby's expression was total empathy. "Honey! I was running errands when I heard the ambulance and saw it backed up to the hardware store, then saw them carrying you out. What happened?"

"I accidentally cut the palm of my hand with a box cutter. I guess I passed out."

"Do you need help? Who's with you?" Ruby asked.

"Dan Amos happened in on the incident and is helping to get me home. He went inside to fill a prescription for me."

Ruby patted Alice's shoulder. "Bless your heart.

Don't worry about a thing. I'll bring supper to your house this evening. Around six? I know your kids are probably too hungry from school to wait any longer."

"Oh, Ruby, that's so sweet, but you don't—"

"I am well aware I don't have to. But I want to. Is that okay?"

"Oh Lord, I'm going to cry again," Alice said as tears welled.

Ruby frowned. "It's going to be okay, honey. You'll heal up before you know it. In the meantime, take all the help you can get."

"Yes, ma'am," Alice said.

"That's that, then," Ruby said. "See you later." She smiled and waved.

Alice watched her hurrying down the street to where she was parked, and then she drove away.

"That woman never walks when she can run," Alice said, then held her hand up against her chest and closed her eyes again.

A few minutes later, Dan was back. "You're hurting, aren't you?" he said as he scooted behind the steering wheel.

Alice nodded.

Dan pulled a bottle of water out of the pharmacy sack, along with the bottle of pills, and opened both. "It says take one every four hours or as needed," he said, and dropped a pill in her hand, waited until she put it in her mouth, then handed her the water.

Alice took it gratefully and swallowed it down, then drank more before she gave it back.

"Thank you, again," she said as he screwed the cap back on the water and set it in the console.

"You're welcome, again," he said, then grinned, then backed up and headed down Main. "You live in Hope House, right?"

Alice was praying for that pain pill to kick in and glad to have something else to think about. "Yes, we do, thanks to Phoebe Ritter. I guess she's Phoebe Payne now," she added. "She gave me this car, too, did you know that?"

Dan looked surprised. "Really? Just gave it to you?"

Alice nodded. "This town is full of good people, and you're one of them. Your presence today was so unexpected and, at the same time, absolutely God-sent. I have no words to express how much I appreciate it, and you, except to say thank you. When my hand gets well, I owe you dinner *and a pie*, okay?"

"Absolutely okay," he said. "I never turn down home cooking, and like I told you before, I knew what you were going through. Didn't seem right you had to do it alone."

"You are a good man," Alice said softly, and closed her eyes.

Dan glanced at her profile, then swallowed past the lump in his throat as he drove. She was getting under his skin without even trying.

A couple of minutes later, Alice opened her eyes to see where they were and was relieved to see they were almost home.

Dan pulled up into her driveway and parked under the carport.

"Which one unlocks your front door?" he asked, holding up the keys.

"Thanks to Patty, it's the one with pink fingernail polish on it," Alice said.

Dan grinned. "Perfect." He sorted out the key, and when she started trying to unfasten her seat belt, he jumped out. "Wait. Let me help you," he said.

She had already overdone it at the hardware store, so she gathered up her things and didn't argue. When he opened the door and leaned in again to unfasten the seat belt, she got another whiff of his aftershave and an up-close look at the scar on his face. A vivid reminder every day of what he'd lost when it happened. *Sweet Lord.*

"Okay, now easy does it," he said as he helped her out, then gripped her arm until she was steady on her feet. "Feeling okay to walk?" he asked.

"Yes," she said.

They were halfway up the steps when Alice groaned.

"What's wrong?" Dan asked.

"There come my children. They've already spotted the bandage on my hand, and from the look on Patty's face, she's on the verge of tears."

Dan saw the kids coming up the sidewalk, his gaze lingering longer on the long-legged boy holding his little sister's hand. His son would have been this age… if he'd lived.

"Looks like your son is giving me the stink-eye," Dan drawled.

Alice laughed, and the delight in her voice rolled through him. "I didn't think about that," she said. "He'll be fine once he's sure you think I'm short and ugly."

"Well, hell," Dan drawled. "Then he's in for a belly-ache, 'cause that's not possible. You are, as my grandpa used to say, 'a fine figure of a woman.'"

Alice was too shocked at the compliment to respond, and then the kids were running up the drive, talking as they ran. Dan unlocked the door and stepped aside, letting Alice calm her children. As soon as they were assured she wasn't mortally wounded, she introduced them to Dan.

"Kids, this is Mr. Amos. He's a regular customer at the hardware store, and helped me at the hospital, and then helped me get home. Dan, this is my son, Charlie, and my daughter, Patty."

"Hi," Patty said, and hid her face against Alice's belly, but Charlie turned around, looked Dan square in the eyes, then smiled and offered his hand, one man to another.

"I sure thank you for helping Mama, and for getting her and our car home."

"You're welcome," Dan said. "Your mama is a friend, and friends help each other, right?"

"Yes, sir." Charlie nodded, then turned into the man Alice claimed him to be. "Mama, you're pale. You need to get inside and sit down. Patty, turn loose of Mama so she can walk. Mr. Amos, you're welcome in our house," he added.

"Thank you, Charlie, but I'm gonna call my ride and get on home." He took a card out of his wallet and handed it to Charlie. "If anyone in this house needs help at any time, I am always available."

Alice was already settled in the recliner when she realized Dan wasn't coming in.

"Dan, don't sit out on the porch to wait for your ride. Come in."

"Not this time," he said. "You've had enough excitement for one day. Just settle in and let that pain pill kick in. Charlie has everything under control."

Charlie beamed. "Yes, sir, I do."

Dan waved and then took out his cell phone as he started down the steps.

Alice watched out the window for a few minutes, and when she saw a police car drive up, she realized the chief was giving Dan a ride back and then closed her eyes. But she could still see him in her mind, striding into the ER, holding her hand during all the pain and not getting all weird about her constant need to weep.

And hearing the lack of emotion in his voice when he talked about the explosion that killed his family. She knew what that meant. She knew what that felt like. How a body can go numb from the shock. How the story of why you are no longer married becomes the new you. How you became the widow or the widower. It is your new identity. That's how you go numb. Because if you feel too much, you know you'll die.

She fell asleep thinking about that scar on his face, and the next time she woke, Ruby Butterman was knocking on the door with their supper.

~~~

Junior Rankin was in the barn doing evening chores when his cell phone rang. When he saw the number, his gut knotted. He wasn't surprised by the call, but he was about to put an end to the relationship. He cleared his throat, then answered. "Hello."

"It's me," Oscar said.

"Yes, I know. What do you want?" Junior asked.

Oscar was taken aback by the timbre of Junior Rankin's voice. "I want to know if you did what I told you to do."

"I tried and failed. The old man is still hanging on, and I pray to God he lives. This has taught me something about myself. We're done doing business with you. Don't come back. Don't show your face in this place again, and count yourself lucky."

"You don't threaten me!" Oscar said.

"That wasn't a threat," Junior said. "We're out of the business, so we have no need to ever cross paths again, understand?"

"You're really quitting?" Oscar muttered.

"It's already a done deal. I nearly killed a man, and my brother's hurt bad, and that's all the reason I need."

"Well then," Oscar said.

Junior disconnected, then finished feeding the pigs before heading back to the house. He felt old. Old and used up before his time. By the time he got to the back door and cleaned his feet, he was fighting the urge to cry. Men didn't cry. But he didn't feel much like a man anymore, either.

Jesus Lord, I can't find a way to forgive myself.

And with that, he opened the door and walked into the kitchen. His daddy was heating up stew at the cookstove, and he could smell corn bread baking in the oven.

"Smells good, Daddy," Junior said.

Big Tom smiled at his elder son. "Just stew and corn bread."

"Nothing better," Junior said. "Soon as I wash up, I'll help you. Is Albert asleep?"

"Not sure. Go check on him. If he's awake, I'll take him a tray."

"Yes, sir. Be right back," Junior said, and hurried down the hall to his brother's room.

Albert was awake and watching TV when Junior came in.

"Daddy sent me to see if you were awake. He's gonna bring your supper."

Albert nodded. "Yes, I'll eat some. Maybe food in my belly will help settle those pain meds. They make me have crazy dreams."

Junior's voice was shaky. "Sorry about your feet, Brother."

"No worries. I did it to myself. Tell Daddy to put some sorghum molasses on one piece of that corn bread for me, will you?"

Junior gave him a thumbs-up and left, taking long, hurried strides as he returned to the kitchen.

"He's awake, Daddy. He asks if you will put some molasses on one piece of his corn bread."

Big Tom grinned. "I already knew that. You go ahead and dish up some food for yourself while it's good and hot. I'll be back soon."

Junior nodded, but his appetite was poor. Food seemed to stick in the back of his throat, or if he did manage to swallow it, it sat in a knot in his belly. Still, Daddy would know something was wrong if he skipped a meal, so he dished up a little of everything and sat down, then reached for the salt.

He didn't have to taste it to know Daddy's stew always needed salt. He was buttering a piece of corn bread when Big Tom returned, and then he managed to put worries aside as he and his dad shared the food and their day.

—◆◆—

Chief Pittman was more than happy to take Dan back to get his truck, and as they rode, Dan questioned him about Elliot Graham, since he never did get the chance to check on the old man himself as he'd planned.

"The doctor told me he has a severe concussion, but there was nothing around his body that would have caused that wound. The sheriff is investigating under the assumption that he was attacked because the painting he'd been working on had purposefully been destroyed. His wallet and money were still in his pocket, as well as the keys to his car. I think he saw something happen out on the lake, and innocently painted it into the scene. Someone saw him, found him, and destroyed the painting, but that's all supposition."

"That's a reason," Dan said. "I spent too many years in court to ignore that truth. I wouldn't mind taking a look at those photos. Not that I think I'll see something others don't. Curiosity, I guess." Dan frowned. "If there was something in the painting someone didn't want seen, it must have been illegal."

"Agreed," Lon said, and then pulled up to the curb beside Dan's truck.

"Thanks for the ride," Dan said.

He was unlocking the truck when the chief drove off, and for a few moments he paused beside the door and looked down the main street of Blessings.

Small businesses run by good people. Granny's Country Kitchen. The courthouse. The office building where P. Nutt Butterman, Esquire, spent his days in and out of court. Phillips Pharmacy. The florist. The gym. And farther down, the Curl Up and Dye and the bank.

Behind him there was a dress boutique. The

feed-and-seed store, the quick stop/gas station, and the Blue Ivy Bar.

It wasn't unique as small towns go. But the people in it—people like Alice Conroy—made it remarkable. He'd wondered about his decision to come here at first, but no more. No more. For better or worse, this was where he belonged.

Satisfied, he drove by the Piggly Wiggly to pick up a few things, including milk for breakfast cereal, then headed home. He had a little juggling to do financially, but he was going to make an offer on the rental properties, including the house in which he was living. It was time to put down roots again.

Elliot was hooked up to all manner of machines, and it was the incessant beeping that finally locked him into a sound to follow back to waking up. When he realized he was in the hospital, he frowned. *How did this happen?*

He started to call out, then felt the skin pulling on his burning lips and decided against it and lay there, waiting for someone to come in. He'd almost fallen asleep again when the door opened, and he heard the squeak of rubber shoes against a tiled floor.

A nurse!

He opened his eyes again, saw the woman adjusting his IV, and got her attention. "Hurt," he said, pointing to his lips, then his head.

"I'll get something for your lips," she said. "You hurt the back of your head. Do you remember how you did it?"

"No," Elliot said, and closed his eyes. He didn't want

to talk to her anymore. He wanted her to go get something to put on his lips.

She left quickly, and when she came back, a doctor was with her. She put the ointment on his mouth and then stepped aside so the doctor could examine him.

"Good afternoon, Mr. Graham. My name is Dr. Hastings. How do you feel?" he asked.

"Hurt."

"You have a serious head injury. Do you know how it happened?"

"No," Elliot said.

"Why were you at Gray Goose Lake?" Hastings asked.

Elliot frowned. He had to think about that. He didn't remember being there. Oh…wait…

"Painting," he said.

"Did you see anyone there?"

"People in boats," Elliot said.

"But no one around you?"

"No. Head hurts. Talked enough. Medicine."

"Yes, I'll order you some pain meds. I have to notify Chief Pittman that you're awake. He wants to talk to you."

"No talking. Medicine."

"Nurse will bring you medicine shortly."

"Go home?" Elliot asked.

"Not yet. Just rest for now."

Elliot sighed, trying to remember if he had any animals depending on him for food, then decided he didn't. He closed his eyes again, and this time his sweet wife, Helena, was there waiting for him. It didn't seem weird to him to see her, although she'd passed away some years back, but when she put a finger to her lips to indicate quiet, he relaxed and drifted off to sleep.

The nurse came back with her laptop trolley, injected pain meds into his IV, and then ran his vitals. She made note that he still had quite a bit of fever, and then a personal observation that his poor face was so going to peel from the sunburn. She checked all the readouts on the machines, entered them into the laptop, and then wheeled it out, letting him sleep.

After Chief Pittman got the phone call from Elliot Graham's doctor, he decided not to question him at all until tomorrow. According to Dr. Hastings, Elliot didn't know how he'd gotten hurt, and his mouth was hurting too much to talk anyway.

Dan was in the kitchen frying up a slice of cured ham, and there was a pan of biscuits in the oven. They were the pop-out kind from the Piggly Wiggly, but eaten hot, they made good fried ham sandwiches.

He had just turned off the stove and was about to take the biscuits from the oven when the doorbell rang. Frowning, he turned off the oven and set the pan of hot biscuits on the stove to keep them warm as he hurried to answer.

When he saw the chief's patrol car through the window, he couldn't help but wonder why he was here. But he was about to find out. He opened the door with a smile. "Hey, Chief! Come in."

"I won't stay," Lon said as he stepped over the threshold and came in just enough that Dan could close the door. "I had the sheriff send me photos of the crime scene, including the canvas Elliot was working on. Still want to see them?"

"Yes, very much so," Dan said.

Lon pulled the photos up on his cell phone, then

handed the phone to Dan and watched him slowly scanning the array.

"See anything suspicious?" Lon asked. "I can't see anything out of place."

"It looks like he was painting a boat on his canvas. Was there a witness?"

Lon shrugged. "Not that we know of. The lake isn't used for water sports, just fishing."

Dan looked and looked at the photos, even enlarging the screen on the cell phone for a closer look. Finally, he shrugged.

"I don't see anything specific," Dan said. "Sorry I bothered you."

"No bother at all," Lon said. "Always willing to do anything that might help solve a case."

"So, are you opening an assault case on Elliot?" Dan asked.

Lon nodded. "The sheriff is, with the understanding it might turn into attempted murder if I learn anything new."

"I'll pass the message on to Aidan and Phoebe Payne," Dan said, then added, "I have some biscuits and ham for breakfast. They're canned biscuits…nothing like your Mercy makes, but if you're hungry, I'll gladly share."

Lon smiled. "She is something of a magician in the kitchen, isn't she? And I'll pass on the offer, but I thank you."

Moments later, the chief was out of the house and on his way back to his car, while Dan was in the kitchen, filling his plate. He added butter and jelly to the table, poured himself a cup of coffee, and sat down to eat.

As he did, he thought about Alice. Did she get any sleep last night? Was she in pain? Did she manage to get her children off to school? And then he let that one go, because he knew if she was unavailable, her son, Charlie, had it handled. She'd mentioned something about Charlie having to grow up too soon. And maybe he had, but he was doing a damn fine job of it.

Dan made himself a second biscuit and ham and added strawberry jam. "Umm," he said as he took a big bite. It was like adding cranberry sauce to a Christmas turkey.

He took his time eating, but when he was finished, he stayed at the table long enough to make that call to New Orleans.

Aidan was up and on his way to the restaurant when he got Dan's call. He answered with trepidation, afraid the news would be bad. "Hello?"

"Hey, Aidan. I have some news, most of which is good. Elliot woke up in a better-than-we-expected condition. He didn't know how he got hurt. Unless someone comes forward with new info, or he recovers some memory, we may never have answers."

"Well, hell. I don't like to think of someone getting away with attempted murder," Aidan said.

"It's early days," Dan said. "Don't give up on it yet."

"You're right," Aidan said. "But keep me in the loop."

"I will," Dan said. "And now that news was delivered, I have a bit more."

"Oh? About what?" Aidan asked.

"Your property…the family home, the rentals. I want to buy them."

Aidan grinned. "Seriously? That's wonderful. I had a feeling that might be a good fit for you. Do you intend to practice law again? I would imagine Peanut Butterman would be glad to add a partner like you."

"No to the law practice. I don't have the heart for it anymore, and I like what I'm doing."

"Well, make me an offer, and we'll go from there."

"Yes, I'll get the papers drawn up with an official offer and have it faxed to you. And now I'm going to change the subject again. I assume Lee is back in college?"

"Yes, but he transferred from Savannah University to Loyola University here in New Orleans."

Dan smiled. "That's awesome. So that takes care of son #1… What's the scoop on baby #2? Is Miss Phoebe well? Do you know if it's a boy or a girl?"

Aidan's voice echoed the joy in his life. "Phoebe is fabulous. Our baby girl is healthy, and with a delivery date that will be here before we know it."

"That's great," Dan said. "I'll tell you from experience, enjoy every moment."

Aidan knew what Dan had lost, and what it must take for him to celebrate family when his was gone.

"Yes, I will do that," Aidan said. "In the meantime, I'll be waiting for your offer."

Dan was smiling as he disconnected. It felt good to have a plan.

Chapter 5

ALICE'S SLEEP WAS RESTLESS. EVERY TIME SHE GOT OFF TO sleep, she would bump her hand turning over. She was relieved when the alarm went off to begin another day.

She got up to get the kids off to school, but Charlie took over and made their lunches while Alice set cereal and milk on the table.

Patty came into the kitchen in tears, carrying a hair-brush and an elastic band for her ponytail.

"What's wrong?" Alice asked when she saw the tears.

"I can't do my hair, and your hand can't do it, either."

"Stop crying, Patty. I'll do it," Charlie said. "Now sit down and eat. We're walking to school this morning because Mama doesn't need to be trying to drive."

Patty minded Charlie just like she minded her mother and did as she was told.

"Do you want some banana on your cereal?" Charlie asked.

Patty nodded, watching him slice half a banana on her cereal and the other half on his. He poured milk, then scooted her up closer to the table.

"Don't dribble any on your dress," he said.

"'Kay," Patty said, and politely ate her whole bowl of cereal with her chin over the bowl.

Alice stifled a grin and winked at her son. "You do know that you rock?" she said.

He grinned as he picked up the hair band and brush

and quickly put his little sister's hair up in a ponytail, then sat down to eat his cereal, too.

"Oh…Mama, I have football practice after school."

"No problem," Alice said. "I'll have all day for my hand to rest, so I'll pick Patty up when school is out. Patty, did you hear that?"

Patty nodded, still chewing. "I wait for you at school," she said.

"That's right," Alice said.

"Goody. I get to ride home this afternoon," Patty said.

"Charlie, will you be very late?" Alice asked.

"I don't think so. We have a game on Friday. I think Coach just wants to make sure we know the plays. If we are going to be late, I'll borrow a phone and call."

"Thank you. Do you have milk money?" she asked.

"Yes, ma'am, enough for me and Patty. Don't worry. Just rest today and don't try to do anything."

"Yes, sir," Alice said.

Charlie sighed. "I just want you to feel better, Mama."

"I know, sweetheart. I was just teasing you," she said, then glanced at the clock. "You both need to leave or you'll be late."

"Yes, ma'am," Charlie said. "Patty, go get your jacket and backpack."

"Okay," she said, and ran to her room, then back to the kitchen.

Charlie put her lunch inside her backpack and put a quarter for her milk in the zippered pouch on the outside of the backpack, and then patted the top of her head.

They hugged their mother goodbye, and then they were gone. The house was immediately quiet. Alice didn't know whether to feel lonesome or relieved, but her hand was hurting enough she'd already decided to take a pain pill and go lie back down. She rinsed the cereal bowls and drinking glasses, then slipped them into the top shelf of the dishwasher.

She wasn't hungry, but she knew better than to take pain pills on an empty stomach, so she toasted a piece of bread and, when it popped up, smeared on some butter and ate it while she finished her coffee. She had just swallowed the pain pill when there was a knock at her door. She wiped her hands and went to answer, but when she opened the door, she smiled. Seeing Dan Amos this early in the morning was a good way to start a day.

"Hi," he said. "I wanted to stop by and check on you before I got busy today."

"That's really sweet of you," Alice said. "Come in. Would you like a cup of coffee?"

"Sure, but I'll follow you and pour it for myself."

"Kitchen is this way," she said, then once they were there, she opened a cabinet door for him to get down a coffee mug, then stepped out of the way. "Do you need cream or sugar?" she asked.

"No, black is good," he said. "Did your kids get off to school okay?"

"Yes. Charlie is a whiz. But I have to pick Patty up when school's out this afternoon because Charlie has football practice."

"I can drive you," Dan said, eyeing the way her cheeks turned pink when he offered.

"Oh, I think I've already bothered you enough," she said.

"If it was a bother, I wouldn't have offered," he said,

and then took a quick sip of the coffee without taking his eyes off her.

He didn't realize he was doing the thing he used to do in court before approaching a witness on the stand. He always knew if the witness was going to cooperate or not just by the way they were sitting, or if they wouldn't look him in the eyes.

Alice was looking straight at him. He liked that. A woman who did not play games.

Alice wanted to see him again, and she wasn't looking forward to driving, and she liked him. He was a nice man. A good-looking man. *Admit it*, she thought. *A nice, good-looking man*. And just like that, she'd sold herself on saying yes.

"Since you put it that way, I'll take you up on the offer," she said. "You'll have to pick me up about a quarter to three. School is out a bit after three, but if you don't get in line to get your kids, you'll get stuck in bus traffic."

"No problem," he said. "I'll be here. Is there anything you need today? Like groceries or medicine from the pharmacy?"

"No, thank you. I have everything I need," she said. "I'll see you this afternoon, then."

"Yes," he said, then finished his coffee and set the cup in the sink. "So, I better be going. See you later?"

"Right, see you later," she echoed, and followed him to the door.

He turned around to say goodbye again, and then got lost in her wide-eyed gaze.

The smile on Alice's face stilled, then faded. For one long, silent moment, she forgot to breathe.

Dan felt the strongest urge to kiss her again, but that wasn't happening until he knew she was a willing recipient.

"See you," he said suddenly, and was out the door and almost running to his truck.

Alice stood in the doorway, watching as he drove away. She didn't know what was happening between them, but she was woman enough to recognize that whatever it was, he felt it, too.

As soon as he was gone, she locked the front door, then went back to her bedroom. Glad she'd left the bed unmade, she kicked off her shoes, crawled in between the covers, and closed her eyes. The last thing she remembered was hearing a lawn mower somewhere on the block.

Beulah Conroy had just finished raking the leaves from Marty's grave. She was heartbroken about her oldest son's absence from her life and wasn't anywhere close to getting over it. Her other two sons were from her second marriage. She made no excuses for the fact that she loved Marty more than she loved her sons, Moses and J. B., from her second marriage to Ike Gatlin. That's just how she was.

She leaned the rake against the iron railing around the family plot, gathered up the armful of leaves, and carried them out of the plot, stringing them behind her as she walked. By the time she got to the barrel where they burned their trash and dumped them in, half of them were gone. She didn't care. As long as they weren't on Duke's or Marty's graves.

She heard hinges squeaking and then the slam of the kitchen door behind her. The boys were obviously home, and she hadn't even heard them drive up.

Then Moses was at her elbow and sliding a hand across her shoulder. His touch was as gentle as his voice. "Hey, Mama, I was driving past Marty's old place and saw some chanterelles. I know how much you like them. Want me to go back and get you some?"

Beulah frowned. "I don't know that I want to eat anything from that place. It took Marty away from me."

Moses Gatlin resisted the urge to roll his eyes. "No, ma'am. That land had nothing to do with Marty being high on meth and setting everything on fire, including himself. Now do you want the mushrooms or not?"

Beulah glared. Moses was in his late twenties, but had been taking care of her after Marty lost his mind doing meth. She didn't have it in her to say aloud what she knew to be true. It was Marty's fault that he was dead. She glanced over Moses's shoulder rather than at him.

"I guess some chanterelles would be tasty at supper tonight, but I want to go with you," she said.

"I was gonna walk up, but since you want to go, we'll drive up, Mama. J. B. is going, too. He's hoping to get a mess of squirrels for supper."

Beulah looked down at her clothes and brushed off some debris. "Give me a bit to get my things."

"Take your time. I'll get the baskets and knives. We'll be waiting in the truck."

She already had on her work clothes—a pair of Ike's old overalls and one of Duke's long-sleeved shirts—but she wanted a hat. With fall coming on, spiders were more frequent in the woods than usual, and she did hate to walk into a web and have to pick the spider out of her hair.

A few minutes later, she emerged from the old two-story house that Duke Conroy had inherited from his father and got into the passenger seat. J. B. was already sitting in the truck bed, and Moses was behind the wheel. As soon as Beulah shut the door, they took off at a slow but steady pace.

The day was nice. The leaves on some of the trees were just beginning to turn, and the windows were down on both sides of the cab, keeping a tunnel open for the air to circulate.

Moses and J. B. had taken after their daddy and were average in height, stocky and raw-boned men with their mama's brown hair. This past year had put more gray in Beulah's hair than all the years before, and Moses was surprised she had wanted to come, because she hadn't been to the scene since the day Marty died.

Moses still had nightmares about hearing Alice screaming before she even reached their house. And then when she did, they were all in panicked disarray. By the time they had called an ambulance and the volunteer fire department, Alice had gone from hysteria to total silence.

Mama read that stony expression on Alice's face as a woman who didn't care her man was dead, but Moses knew she'd just gone into shock. And when they all went back and saw what was left of Marty's body beneath the burned-out roof of their house, they were in shock as well.

They were all still at the site when the school bus came and let the kids off. The moment the kids saw the smoking ruins, they began crying. But finding out their daddy had died in the fire was the worst thing Moses had ever witnessed. It was their panic that brought Alice back to the reality of their life, and it was Moses who took her and the kids, and Marty's dog, Booger, back down to Beulah's house. They tied Booger up outside, then Moses had helped them settle into the spare rooms upstairs.

During the days that followed, every time Beulah laid eyes on Marty's wife and kids, she glared at them as if they were responsible for her son's demise and refused to talk to any of them.

A few days after Marty's funeral, Beulah woke up and told Moses to take them and that dog down to Blessings, that she didn't want to see them again because they reminded her of losing Marty.

Moses shuddered, remembering how scared they'd looked being dumped out on the street, and how Charlie had clung to the dog with one hand as tightly as he was holding his mama's hand with the other. Alice was holding Pitty-Pat when he gave her all the money he had and then left without looking back. It was, to date, the worst thing he'd ever done. He regretted it. He wondered how Mama felt now, since time had passed.

"Hey, Mama…"

Beulah was riding with her eyes closed until Moses spoke. "Yes?"

"Don't you miss Alice and the kids?"

Beulah's jaw jutted in anger. "I don't care to talk about them," she muttered.

"But they're our kin!"

Beulah didn't answer and stayed silent up to the time they arrived. She acted as though Moses hadn't even mentioned them as she leaned forward, pointing at the pale-yellow fungi growing around a fallen tree.

"You were right! Those are some fine chanterelles," she said as Moses parked. They got out, carrying their baskets and knives, as J. B. shouldered his rifle and headed into the woods. Beulah eyed his departure without complaint and began issuing orders to Moses instead.

"Don't forget, if there's two chanterelles growing together, leave one, and make sure you only gather the mature ones. And watch where you walk. Don't stomp around all over the place. Some of them will have already shed their spores."

"Yes, ma'am," Moses said, even though she had said the same thing every year since he had been old enough to go with her.

They went straight to the fallen tree she'd seen from the truck and began harvesting the mature mushrooms.

"Cut them level to the ground, and trim them up out here," Beulah said. "I don't want to be carting dirt home and making them twice as hard to clean."

Moses gave her a thumbs-up and kept working.

Twice while they were there, they heard gunshots. J. B. was either wasting ammo or setting them up for some fried squirrel and buttered mushrooms tonight.

When they were done, they moved around the old home place until they found another patch of chanterelles growing beneath some trees at the edge of the woods.

Beulah heard more gunfire as she dropped to her knees and, as she did, noticed something red beneath the leaves. She was brushing them aside when she stopped, staring down in disbelief. It was the rag doll she'd made for Pitty-Pat two Christmases ago. She picked it up, clutching it against her chest as her eyes blurred with tears. How did this doll get way out here? She knew her little granddaughter would never have thrown it away. Then she remembered that the house had exploded. She looked back to where the house used to be. Yes, it could have wound up out here from the blast.

But it was the reminder Beulah didn't need or want to see.

Marty's babies. I threw them away.

"Mama? Are you okay?"

Beulah wiped her eyes with the backs of her hands. "Yes, I'm fine," she snapped, but she laid the rag doll in her basket beneath the fragile flutes of the chanterelles, then methodically moved through the scattered mushroom patches, adding more and more to her basket until it was full and brimming over.

"Nice ones, Mama," Moses said as he caught up with his mother and sat down beside her.

Beulah looked at his basket. It was equally as full as hers. "We have ourselves plenty to eat now, and I'll string the rest of these up to dry," she said.

Before Moses could comment, J. B. came walking through the woods with five squirrels tied together by their tails.

Moses looked up and grinned. "Good hunting, Brother."

"And you two as well," J. B. said. "We'll be eating good tonight. Are y'all done?"

Beulah stood, brushing leaves and dirt from her overalls. "Yes, we're ready," she said.

Moses reached down to get her basket as well as his own, but she shook her head.

"I'll carry mine," she said, and headed back to the truck.

Even though charred rafters had fallen in on the house when it burned, Beulah saw it as it had been when they passed it by. Remembering how neat and clean Alice always kept the house, and the big vegetable garden she always grew. The house had been needing fresh paint when it burned. Just as well they didn't go to that trouble. It would have been a waste of money.

She got into the truck, put the basket of mushrooms on the floorboard between her legs, and then laid her hat in her lap.

"Here's some water," Moses said, and handed her an unopened bottle as he slid into the driver's seat.

"Thank you," she said. "You are a good son."

Moses smiled. The praise was rare and treasured. "Why, thank you, Mama." Then he glanced up into the rearview mirror, waiting until J. B. was in the truck bed and settled. When J. B. gave him a thumbs-up, it was Moses's signal to move. They headed down the hill to their house.

As they rode, Beulah kept glancing out of her window at the trees they were passing and caught a glimpse of a bobcat hunkered down in a thicket. She thought of Alice running all this way for help. She must have been scared out of her mind.

An ache settled in the middle of her chest, then spread into a knot in her belly. She opened the water bottle and took another big drink, then handed it to Moses.

"I've had all I want. It's yours if you're thirsty," she said.

"Yes, thanks," Moses said, and finished it off as he

drove. He kept eyeing his mother, wondering why she was so quiet, and then chalked it up to going back to where Marty had died and let it go. When they got home, Moses left his mushrooms in the kitchen with Beulah.

"I'm gonna go help J. B. clean the squirrels," he said.

She nodded without looking up, but the moment the back door slammed, she was emptying her basket onto the counter to get to the doll. She grabbed it and took off to her room, hid it in the back of her closet, and went back to finish working up the chanterelles.

Later that night, long after both her boys had gone to bed, Beulah was tossing and turning. When she finally fell asleep, she dreamed Duke and Marty were standing at the foot of her bed, praying for her salvation.

She woke abruptly, then groaned. It was about three more hours before daylight, so she went to the bathroom to take something for her headache. When she came back, she sat down on the side of the bed. It had been a long time since she'd said a prayer. Part of it was because she was mad at God for taking both of her husbands and her firstborn son, and the other part was because she didn't think prayers really worked.

Beulah thought about going all the way to Blessings and looking Alice up just to check on her and the kids, but she was afraid to face her daughter-in-law. They had basically been abandoned—left to fend for themselves. Almost anything could have happened to them, and not once until today had Beulah given them or their welfare a second thought. She didn't want to know they might have been hungry and homeless. Truth was, she didn't have the guts to go. Without saying a prayer, she got back into bed and turned to face the wall, which was typical Beulah. When something happened she didn't like, she had a tendency to ignore it.

By the time the sun rose, she was up and busying herself with daily chores. The idea of finding out what had happened to her kin was shoved to the back of her mind.

Alice woke up again just before noon. The thought of food made her stomach turn, so she poured herself a glass of sweet tea, grabbed a dog treat, and went out onto the back porch and settled on the top step with her drink.

The old bloodhound had been asleep under the trees but woke when she came outside. He greeted her with one deep *woof*, and when she sat down, he ambled over and lay down on the step just below her feet.

"Good old Booger," Alice said, and held out the treat.

The dog took it gently from her fingers, crunched it once, and swallowed.

Alice laughed. "Did you even taste that?" she asked.

Booger gave her a soulful look, and when there were no more treats forthcoming, laid his head back down on the steps and closed his eyes.

And so they sat, Alice with her tea and Booger with his dreams of the old days, chasing rabbits out of the garden.

By the time her tea was gone, she was beginning to get hungry. She gave the old dog a quick pat on his head and then got up and went back inside to make some lunch.

Unfortunately, it took less time to eat her sandwich than it had making it. It worried her, wondering how work was going to play out. She could probably work the register with one hand, and she could certainly deal with money and customers, but Fred was going to be stuck with all of the lifting and shelving until she was well.

Life was a series of ups and downs. This little setback was just a reminder of how tenuous her hold was on the new way of life. But Alice liked how it felt to be a strong and competent woman. She'd be well soon and beholden to no one—except maybe Danner Amos. His help had been unexpected but welcome.

She set her dirty plate in the sink, put some dry beans on to cook in her slow-cooker, added a chunk of cured ham hock, and seasoned it all up. This would be supper, along with a pan of corn bread.

Alice Conroy's world was on the upswing, but she took nothing for granted. She'd already learned the hard way how quickly life could change.

Chapter 6

Dan worked around the house all afternoon, but with one eye on the clock. To say he was looking forward to seeing Alice Conroy again was an understatement and due entirely to the length of time he spent thinking about her. In a way, these feelings he was having were something of an awakening.

For the longest time after Holly and Blake had died, his entire purpose in life had been to track down the man who'd rigged Dan's car to explode. He'd wanted revenge but had to settle for justice. After that, he went numb. Life had no purpose, and the thought of practicing law again made him sick to his stomach. As for the thought of having anyone else in his life, it was not only foreign but repugnant.

But time passed, dragging him along with it, and the sting of hearing Holly's name lessened to a tug of longing. Seeing little boys that would have been Blake's age growing up into young men slowly changed from brutal pain to a sense of sweet regret.

He hadn't been looking for love when he came to Blessings, but this was the closest he'd been to it in years. He didn't know what would come of this attraction he felt for Alice and her kids, but he was finally willing to find out. Maybe it had to do with learning that their marriages had ended in the same brutal tragedy. If she was willing to give him a chance, he might be ready to give this a try. It would be his first venture in dating, but maybe this was how life worked. Maybe this was how you went about healing a broken heart.

When the time came to go get Alice, he became anxious all over again, then reminded himself he was just the taxi she needed. There was no pressure in that.

―⁂―

Alice was standing in her closet, staring at the few outfits she had and trying to manifest herself a little miracle from the clothes she'd been given by the good people of Blessings—something that might catch Dan's eye. Something bordering on sexy, but not. Something that turned her into Cinderella.

Only they weren't going to a ball, just Blessings Elementary. She wasn't going in a sparkling coach pulled by four white and prancing horses. She was hauling herself up into a work truck wearing what she had on, with no makeup and her hair hanging down around her shoulders. It was nothing more than a ride to pick up Patty, then bring her home. She wasn't even sure there was a man who could heal what life had done to her. She'd lost love, happiness, and trust when Marty turned to drugs—and what was left of her family when they'd thrown her and her children away.

Sighing, she turned off the closet light and carried her purse into the living room and set it beside her jacket. The television was on, and as she sat down to wait, she caught the tail end of a weather report and the words *tropical storm*. They'd been talking about that storm for days now, but something the weatherman said was enough to make her turn up the volume.

According to him, Tropical Storm Fanny was, at the moment, on a dead-on course with the Georgia coast. Alice knew hurricanes happened, but they rarely stayed on one course, especially after the storm began nearing a coastline. She was counting on this storm changing course, too.

Then she heard Dan's truck coming up the drive, turned off the TV, and was struggling to get into her jacket as she hurried out the front door. She only had one arm in the jacket when she got to the truck, but Dan was ready for her. He helped her put it on, lifted her into the passenger seat, and reached to buckle her up. Before she could get over the feel of his hands around her waist, he shut her door and jumped in on the other side.

"Did you get some rest?" he asked as he backed out of her driveway.

"Yes. I feel pretty good. As long as the pain pills don't wear off," she added.

He grinned. "Ah, yes…blessed oblivion is often a good thing—if it doesn't last too long."

"Right," she said.

As soon as he neared the elementary school, Alice directed him to the proper lane.

"This is it," she said. "Now we wait, and let me say how much I appreciate this help. Once before, I mashed my finger in the car door. It took forever to heal, and of course the fingernail eventually came off, and then it was ugly. Took most of the year for my finger to heal and the nail to grow back."

Dan was partly listening, but mostly watching the different expressions coming and going on her face, fascinated by the way her eyes almost closed when she laughed. In the middle of her story, he realized he needed to move up with the rest of the cars in line.

"Oops, it appears I'm holding up the process here," he said, and eased forward.

"It's pretty much stop and go," Alice said. "Nobody gets out of line, and the children are loaded up in parents' cars in order. It's a bit of a hassle waiting for some kid to come out of the group to get in his parents' car, but it is certainly a safe way to make sure no kids are darting out into traffic."

Dan looked again, seeing the procedure from a different perspective. She was right. This was a foolproof way to get kids in the cars without having to move them in and out of traffic.

And then he saw something that made him frown. "Those two big dogs just ran out of the alley. I didn't think dogs were allowed to run loose in Blessings."

"They're not," she said. "That's why I'm so grateful for the fenced-in backyard at our house. It gives Charlie's dog plenty of space, and if it happens to be a rainy day, he has the whole covered back porch for shelter until we get home."

Before Dan could comment, Alice pointed. "Oh no, those dogs are heading straight to the schoolyard, and the kids are going to come running out of the school. They're usually squealing and talking loudly. What if that incites the dogs to attack?"

"This isn't good," Dan said. "Did you bring your phone?"

She nodded.

"Then call the school. Tell them to keep the kids inside and not ring the bell. I'm going to call the police chief. We need to get these dogs rounded up so it's safe for the kids to come out."

Alice's hand was shaking as she quickly made the call. Dan could hear her explaining what was happening as he got out of the truck to make his call. It rang a couple of times and then Avery, the dispatcher, answered. "Blessings PD."

"This is Dan Amos. There are two big dogs loose on the front grounds of the elementary school, and it's almost time for the kids to come out. I think these dogs need to be caught before it's safe to let the children out of the building."

"Thank you, passing on the message," Avery said, and began dispatching officers to the scene.

Chief Pittman was in his cruiser when he heard the broadcast. He immediately responded to the call and headed for the school, along with two more officers coming from different parts of town.

Dan started to get back in the truck with Alice when he saw a bus driver get out of the bus and walk all the way to the back of it, unaware of the dogs' presence.

Alice saw him, too. "The driver! He doesn't see the dogs!"

"Stay in here and don't get out," he said.

"Be careful!" Alice said as he shut the door.

He was still watching the dogs, and when they stopped what they were doing to suddenly focus on the driver, the hair rose on the back of Dan's neck.

He knew, even before he yelled, that they were going after the man. He grabbed a rope and a crowbar from the back of the truck bed and started running, yelling at the driver to get back in the bus.

The driver heard someone shouting, but before he could turn to look, he caught movement from the corner of his eye. When he saw the dogs coming at him in a dead run without making a sound, he knew he was in trouble. He started running, desperate to get back on the bus and close the doors, but they were faster.

The bigger dog leaped and took the driver down in midair. The man's bloodcurdling screams excited the dogs even more as they began snapping and snarling, trying to get to his throat.

The driver had his arms over his face as he began to roll, trying to get beneath the bus. He was almost to safety when the dogs began biting at his ankles and legs, pulling him backward to get him out.

Alice was inside the truck, watching in horror and praying over and over: "Keep them safe…keep them safe… Please God, keep them safe."

Dan was yelling and shouting as he ran, trying to get the dogs' attention, but they were in for the kill and blind to everything but the bloodlust.

Parents began getting out of their cars and screaming at the dogs, too. A couple of men were running toward the dogs, but Dan got there first.

He took down the bigger one with the crowbar. It dropped without a sound. When the other one came at him, he swung at that one, too, hitting it hard enough that the dog turned tail and started to run away.

Dan loosened the rope into a lasso and threw the loop, yanking it so tight that it pulled the dog backward off its feet. Before it could get up again, Dan had the rope around the muzzle and the dog tied, one front foot tied to a back foot, like roping a calf in a rodeo.

Chief Pittman rolled up just as Dan was pulling the bus driver out from under the bus. The chief called for an ambulance, then jumped out of his cruiser as two other officers rolled up behind him. "Secure the scene!" he yelled, and ran toward the bus and the driver who'd been attacked.

Alice leaned back in the seat, shaking. "Thank you, Lord."

She could only imagine what was going on inside the school and hoped Patty wasn't scared.

—∿—

The middle school was unaware of the ongoing drama at the elementary and proceeding as usual. School had been dismissed, and the football team was already taking the field for practice when the coach got a phone call about the dogs.

There were other students sitting in the bleachers who'd come to watch practice, and they were getting similar calls. Before long, word had spread to the players as well that two stray dogs had attacked a bus driver at the elementary school. And, as gossip would have it, someone suggested the kids had been in danger, too, which morphed the story into kids also being injured.

When Charlie heard about it, his first instinct was for his family. He ran to the coach, begging to be excused from practice.

The coach frowned. "You know you're putting your chance to start with the team in jeopardy by doing this?"

Charlie was struggling to maintain his emotions.

"But, Coach, this is my family. They depend on me for everything. I have to know if my mom and little sister are safe."

"Oh…right," Coach said. "How about I let you borrow my phone to check on them?"

"Yes! Yes, thanks, Coach." Charlie took the phone and quickly called his mom.

Alice saw the name and number pop up and frowned. Wasn't this the football coach? Oh no! What if Charlie got hurt?

"Hello?"

"Mama? Oh, thank goodness," Charlie said. "Are you and Patty safe? We just heard about the dogs attacking one of the bus drivers. Were any kids hurt?"

"No kids were hurt, honey. Dan brought me to pick Patty up so I wouldn't have to drive today. We were talking, waiting in line when he saw the dogs. The principal kept the kids inside until it was safe. The police were on the way when the dogs attacked one of the drivers. Dan grabbed a crowbar and a rope from the back of his truck and ran to help."

"Oh man! Is he okay? How bad is the driver?"

"I don't know about the driver. The ambulance just arrived, but Dan was the hero of the day, for sure! He took the biggest dog down with the crowbar, and when the other one tried to run away, Dan roped it and hogtied it like a calf at a rodeo."

"Seriously?" Charlie asked.

"Yes, seriously," Alice said.

"Okay, Mama, I've got to go back to practice. I'll be home later. Love you, and you and Patty take care. I'll make supper after I get home."

"Okay, love you, too."

Charlie ended the call and handed the phone back to his coach. "Thank you, Coach."

"Is everyone okay?" he asked.

"My family is fine. The only person who got hurt was a bus driver. Do you know Mr. Amos? Dan Amos, who is handling Mr. Williams's rental properties for Mr. Payne?"

"Oh…the cowboy!" Coach said.

Charlie grinned. "Yes, sir. And I guess he proved it today. Mama said Mr. Amos saw what was happening, took a rope and a crowbar from his truck, took one dog out with the crowbar, then roped and hog-tied the other one like a calf at a rodeo."

Coach grinned. "That would have been something to see. Now get yourself back out on the field."

Charlie nodded. "Yes, sir. Thank you again," he said, and took off at a lope.

Back at the elementary school, the ambulance left for the ER. The chief called one of the men from the city barn to bring a truck to pick up the dogs. They needed to find a place to lock them up and find out who they belonged to. As soon as they were removed, the principal got the go-ahead to ring the bell.

School was officially out for the day, and parents were standing outside their cars, making sure they were in plain sight today so that their children would not be afraid.

Dan was on his way back to his truck when Alice got out. She waved at him, then stood out on the sidewalk so Patty could see her. She would be looking for their car, not Dan Amos's truck.

Dan jogged over to where she was standing and tossed his crowbar into the truck bed.

"You were amazing," Alice said. "I was afraid you would get hurt, too."

He grinned. "It appears I haven't lost my roping skills."

Alice's eyes widened. "I thought you were a lawyer before you came here."

"I was once, but I grew up on a ranch in Texas. My parents still live on it, but both of my brothers run it now. When we were kids, we all worked the ranch," he said.

"So I guess you ride horses, too?" she said.

Grinning, Dan pointed to his boots and belt buckle. "Yes, ma'am. This stuff's not for show."

Alice laughed and then heard the bell ring and turned toward the school. Within moments, kids began emerging through the front doors. "Here they come," she said.

Dan was still trying to get past how her laugh made him feel when the children began coming outside. To his surprise, there was actually a kind of order to their exit. Teachers walked with part of the students toward buses, while other teachers walked with the in-town riders. He was wondering who would be driving the injured driver's bus when he saw a man come jogging out behind some of the kids and head that way.

"That's the PE coach. I'll bet he's going to be the substitute driver," Alice said, and then pointed. "There's Patty! Oh…she doesn't see my car."

"We'll fix that," Dan said, and once again, he picked Alice up by the waist and swung her up and into the truck bed. Now she was heads above everyone. "Wave! She'll see you," Dan said.

Alice's heart was hammering as she turned and waved, and then kept on waving until suddenly Patty saw her, smiled, and waved back.

"She saw you, right?" Dan asked.

"Yes, she did! Thank you so much."

"Ready to get down?" he asked.

She nodded.

This time, he let the tailgate down and then held out his arms. She sat down on the tailgate, then he lifted her off and set her on her feet.

"We should have driven my car. Then you wouldn't have to be helping me up and helping me down," she said.

"What's the fun in that?" he asked, grinning as he set her back into his front seat.

She was a bit taken aback by the teasing, then laughed. Moments later, they began moving up in line along with everyone else. Within a couple of minutes, they were at the loading zone. Dan jumped out and opened the back door of his truck.

"One more Conroy girl to load up, and then we're good to go," he said as Patty came running.

As soon as she was buckled in the back seat, she started talking.

"Mama, a girl named Shirley threw up on teacher's shoes at lunch. I got a happy face on my workbook page and skinned my knee at recess! Did you know there were mean dogs at our school? Will they come back? I might be a'scairt tomorrow."

Dan was grinning. "Does she ever stop to take a breath?"

"Rarely," Alice said, then turned around to look at Patty. "Good for you for getting a happy face. That makes Mama's face happy, too. We did know about the dogs. Mr. Amos saw the dogs and ran to help the bus driver. He stopped the dogs, and the police came and took them away. You don't have to be scared about anything, okay?"

"Okay, Mama. Thank you, Mr. Amos."

"You're welcome, Patty." Then he glanced at Alice. "Do you need anything before I take you home?"

"No, thank you. We have all we need," she said.

"Okay then," he said, and turned left at the stop sign by the school.

"Mama, is Charlie gonna have to walk home by himself? Won't he be a'scairt, too?"

Alice shook her head. "Charlie walks home every day, and no, he won't be scared. Charlie is a big boy, remember?"

Patty nodded.

Dan smiled as he drove, enjoying the little girl's chatter and Alice's calm demeanor. He was actually disappointed when he reached their house and pulled up into the driveway.

"Well, ladies, you're home. Alice, if you will bear with me one more time, I'll help you two out and see you to the door like the gentleman my mama raised me to be."

He circled the truck, helped Alice down first, and then Patty. Once Patty's feet touched the ground, she was running toward the house and already on the porch, airing her cheerleader skills by running from one end of the porch to the other, cheering as she went.

Dan laughed out loud at the surprised expression on Alice's face.

Alice sighed. "Don't encourage her."

"Is that even possible?" he asked, as he helped her up the steps. "House key?"

She handed it to him. "It's the one with the pink nail polish on it, remember?"

"Got it," he said, unlocked the front door, and then stood back out of the way as Patty danced through the doorway and into the house. Dan was still grinning as he dropped the key ring into Alice's palm. "It has been a pleasure to spend this time with you and your mini me, Ms. Alice. Maybe we could do this again sometime when there's nothing else calling your attention."

Alice was so shocked by the invitation that she forgot to answer.

Dan hesitated. That wasn't the response he was hoping for. "Uh…so, is that a silent yes, or a silent no?"

She blinked. "Oh. I'm sorry. Uh…it's a yes, and thank you?"

His heart skipped a beat. Here he was, wanting to kiss her again. He settled for a touch on her forearm. "Take care of that hand," he said, and left before he made a bigger fool of himself or she changed her mind.

He was on his way home before the shock of what he'd done finally hit. "I cannot believe I asked her on a date." He drove a whole block farther. "I can't believe she said yes," he added. He got home and all the way inside his house with one last question yet unasked. Was tomorrow too soon?

The next morning dawned with an overcast sky and a repeat of the previous day's update about the tropical storm still out at sea.

Elliot Graham was healing well from the sun burns, but he was still suffering the aftereffects of the concussion. The staples they had put in his head made it sore, and since he lived alone, he was forced to stay in the hospital until the dizziness and headaches completely subsided.

Bored out of his mind and concerned about his home and the accumulating mail, he began pacing in his room, then up and down his hall, then circling the whole floor.

As he did, he took it upon himself to visit with other patients and began calling the nurses' attention to a dinner tray needing to be picked up in one room, and another patient's request for pain meds yet to be delivered.

At that point, he was banned from leaving his room again. A penned-in Elliot Graham was proving to be something of a pain in the neck, so when the county sheriff came by just before noon, Elliot was glad to see him coming.

"Mr. Graham, I'm Sheriff Ryman, but you can call me Joe. Are you up to answering a few questions?"

Elliot eyed the heavy-set, middle-aged man with pure relief. "Gladly. I am thoroughly sick of my own company," he said, and gestured toward a chair. "Pull it up and have a seat."

Sheriff Joe grinned. "Thank you, sir, but I won't be here long, so I'll stand."

"Suit yourself," Elliot said, but he was less pleased with the company than he had been.

Sheriff Joe pulled out a notepad with the questions he intended to ask. "First of all, what is the last thing you remember before being attacked?"

Elliot raised the head of his bed a little so they were on a more even line of sight.

"I don't remember any attack. I haven't remembered much of anything, and that's still the case. I know I was on the overlook, painting the scene directly in front of me. My wife and I used to picnic there before she passed, and I wanted to paint the scene and frame it to hang in my house."

Sheriff Joe nodded and made a couple of notes. "The canvas we recovered at the scene had a hole punched in the middle of it, although it appears you were in the act of painting a boat out on the lake. Did you know who it was?"

Elliot shrugged. "I don't remember seeing boats right now."

The sheriff frowned. "Okay, then moving forward a bit in time... When did you become aware someone was walking up behind you?"

"I didn't know. My hearing isn't so good anymore. Sorry."

Joe sighed. "So what you're telling me is that you have no idea who hit you, or why?"

"That's right," Elliot said.

"Do you know any locals you would consider an enemy? Do you have an unresolved beef with someone?"

"No, sir." Then he glanced at the sheriff a little closer. "When was the last time you had your blood pressure checked?"

Sheriff Joe blinked. "Uh…I don't know. Why?"

"You need to pay your doctor a visit, and don't delay. Tell him to check the carotid artery in your neck," Elliot said.

"What would make you say such a thing?" the sheriff asked.

Elliot shrugged. "I know stuff. Go now. Stop down in the ER before you leave."

Joe Ryman was irked and a little unnerved. "Well then," he said. "Thank you for your time. Hope you feel better soon."

"Stop in the ER," Elliot said. "I'm serious."

Disconcerted, the sheriff left Elliot's room in haste. All the way down in the elevator, he kept telling himself to ignore the old fart, but the thought of a stroke or dying scared him. His grandfather and his dad had both died of strokes.

When the elevator doors opened on the ground floor, instead of going out the exit, he followed the arrows to the ER. There, he ran into an ER doctor who had just finished putting a dislocated shoulder back into place and was on his way to the lounge to get a cup of coffee.

Sheriff Joe stopped him in the hall. "Hey, Doctor, I know this sounds weird, but someone just told me I needed to get my carotid artery checked and to do it before I left the hospital. I don't suppose you have time to—"

Dr. Quick reached for the sheriff's neck to check the pulse. It felt slow, so he checked it with his stethoscope. The last thing he expected to hear were bruits—the deadly whooshing sound indicating a severely clogged artery. He turned around, grabbed a wheelchair sitting in the hall, and rolled it behind the sheriff.

"Have a seat," he said.

Sheriff Ryman was startled. "Are you serious?"

"Yes," Quick said, and flagged down an orderly. "Get him to the lab, stat. I'll call in the orders. Stay with him, and when he's through, bring him back here."

"Yes, sir," the orderly said, and turned the chair and the sheriff around.

Dr. Quick moved straight to a phone and ordered the tests. Even though he had to wait for the results, he was already checking for an available surgeon. He was ninety-nine percent sure the sheriff's carotid artery had serious stenosis from a buildup of plaque. To prevent a stroke, he would likely need a stent inserted in the artery to keep it open.

Nearly two hours later, Sheriff Joe Ryman had been admitted to the hospital and was in a bed in the ER, waiting for a surgeon to arrive from Savannah and his wife to arrive as well.

Dr. Quick stopped by to check on him. "I just got confirmation that the surgeon has arrived. We'll be getting you to surgery in just a few minutes."

Joe Ryman had faced down all kinds of perps and even a few mad dogs in his life, but this had him scared. "How will this affect my future?" he asked.

The doctor gave him a pat on the shoulder. "I'd say it should lengthen your life considerably. What you have is like a bomb with no controls. You would most certainly have had a stroke…or even a life-ending heart attack. Out of curiosity, who in the world told you to get this checked out…and what prompted it?"

"We're working a case on one of the patients here… Elliot Graham. I was interviewing him, and he just stopped talking, stared at me weird, and then told me to get down to the ER. I asked him why he would say that, and he said he just knows stuff."

"Really?" Dr. Quick asked.

Joe nodded. "I would have ignored him except for

the fact that both my father and grandfather died from strokes."

"Wow! I might go have a chat with Mr. Graham," Dr. Quick said.

"If you do, thank him for me," Joe said.

Dr. Quick smiled. "I'll be glad to," he said. "Now just relax as best you can, okay?"

The sheriff nodded, and the minute the doctor left the room, he started praying.

Chapter 7

ELLIOT WAS DRIFTING IN AND OUT OF SLEEP WHEN THE phone beside his bed began to ring. He rolled over to pick up the receiver.

"Hello."

"Elliot, this is your neighbor, Dan Amos. Do you feel like talking? If you don't, I can—"

"Oh, for the good Lord's sake, don't hang up!" Elliot said. "I'm bored out of my mind, and it's good to hear your voice."

Dan grinned. "Okay then. Good to hear that. So, first question is... How are you feeling?"

"Quite well, actually," Elliot said. "Of course, my head is still a bit wonky. They're telling me I'm still having some symptoms of the concussion, and they won't let me go home until that passes."

"That sounds like positive progress. I'm so glad to hear that, but I feel the need to apologize. If I'd been a better neighbor, I would have noticed you weren't home, and you might have been found sooner. I promise that won't happen again."

"No! I don't need people feeling the need to keep track of me. It's my own fault for not telling someone where I was going."

"Then we'll make a pact to tell each other. How's that?"

"Works for me," Elliot said.

"On to my second question. Is there anything I can do for you at your home? Do you have plants to water or a pet to feed?"

"No, nothing like that, but I would appreciate it if you'd pick up my mail every day and keep it at your house until I get home."

"Consider it done," Dan said. "I'll go over there in a few minutes."

"Wonderful!" Elliot said.

"Third question… Do you know who attacked you?" Dan asked.

"Unfortunately, I didn't see or hear a thing and have no idea why it happened. My wallet and car keys were still on my person when I was brought into the ER so it doesn't appear the reason was robbery. The sheriff came by to talk to me. Said someone punched a hole in the painting I was working on. Oh…by any chance, do you know what has happened to my car?"

"No, but I would assume they'd tow it to the impound yard at the sheriff's office. It's protocol when a crime victim's vehicle is part of the scene."

"Oh. Well then, I guess I won't worry about that for the time being."

"Can I bring you anything?" Dan asked.

"No, sir, but I sure appreciate the call," Elliot said.

"I'll call again tomorrow to see if you need anything," Dan said.

"I'll look forward to it," Elliot said.

"Yes, sir," Dan said. "Goodbye and rest well."

Elliot was still smiling when another doctor came in and strode to his bedside. The doctor wasted no time in getting to the point of his visit.

"Mr. Graham, I'm Dr. Quick. I understand you sent Sheriff Ryman down to my ER out of concern for his health."

"Yes, I did. Is he in surgery yet?"

Quick was surprised. "Why, yes, as a matter of fact, he is. Could you tell me how you knew of his condition?"

Elliot shrugged. "I just know stuff."

Quick frowned. "You know stuff? Are you saying you're some kind of psychic?"

Elliot's eyebrows arched. "Did you hear me say anything of the kind?" he snapped.

"No, sir, but—"

"My head hurts. I need to rest," Elliot said.

Quick sighed. "Sorry to bother you," he said. "As for the sheriff, you do know you saved his life. He said to tell you thanks."

Elliot shook his head. "I believe the doctor who is operating on him will be the one saving his life. I just—"

"Yes…I remember. You just know stuff."

Elliot sighed. "Exactly."

"Rest well," Quick said.

"Thank you, I shall," Elliot said. "Oh…there's a man out in the ER parking lot who has passed out in the seat of his car. I believe he overdosed on some drug. What you people call meth."

"Are you serious?" Dr. Quick said.

"Of course. Who jokes about things like this? It's a dirty red car…older model," Elliot said.

Quick was already on his cell phone as he bolted out of the room, sending hospital security to the parking lot.

—⁓—

Unaware of the ongoing drama at the hospital, Dan was already on the front step of Elliot's residence, gathering the accumulation of mail from the box. He circled the house, making sure everything was still secure, before going back across the street. He laid the mail on his hall table and then glanced at the time.

He wanted to call Alice but was afraid she might have gone back to sleep after getting her children to school. It was just after 10:30 a.m., so he decided to wait until closer to noon and went back to his office to read over the offer he'd written for the Payne rental properties one last time before emailing it to Aidan in New Orleans.

Unaware she was even a thought in Dan's mind, Alice successfully managed to drive her kids to school. She dropped Charlie off at school and then headed to the elementary. Patty had come home yesterday with a note from her teacher about a missing permission slip for a class trip at the end of the week.

Alice parked in the parking lot at the school and walked Patty inside, then stopped at the office with the note and handed it to Mavis West, the school secretary.

"Patty brought this home yesterday. It seems her teacher is missing a signed permission slip for Patty. She never got home with it and doesn't remember what it was for."

Mavis scanned the note, eyed Patty, and then winked. "Let me check the school calendar." She pulled it up on her computer, then added the teacher's name, and her class schedule popped up. "Oh yes...Mrs. Milam's annual leaf-gathering trip this coming Friday. It's on the Leggitt farm two miles outside of Blessings. They gather different leaves in the morning, have a picnic lunch at the farm, and then are back here around 2:00 p.m. Give me a moment, and I'll find the original note and make a couple of copies. One for you to sign and leave here, and one for you to take home. That way, you'll have all of the information you need."

"Oh yeah! The leaves!" Patty said.

Alice grinned. "Now she remembers. Run on to class, honey. I'll sign your note before I leave."

"Thank you, Mama," Patty said, and left the office with a skip in her step.

"She's a delightful child," Mavis said.

"Thank you," Alice said. But as she waited for the secretary to make the copies, she couldn't help but remember the lack of understanding for their situation when she'd first brought her children here to enroll. Ah well, time changes all things...even people.

"Uh...Mavis, I witnessed the bus driver being attacked yesterday. How is he doing?"

Mavis paused as her expression shifted. "He's doing well, thanks to the good Lord and Mr. Amos. He'll be off work the rest of this week until they remove the staples in his arms and legs." Then she eyed Alice's bandage. "Looks like you have a problem of your own. What happened?"

"Oh, an accident at work. I cut my hand on a box cutter as I was unpacking inventory. I have stitches. Like the bus driver, I'll be fine once they're out."

Mavis frowned. "Goodness. Feel better soon, okay?"

"Yes, ma'am," Alice said. "Did they ever find out who owned those dogs?"

"We were told they were strays that have been in the area for months. People have seen them, but they never caused any trouble and always ran off before anyone could catch them…and then this happened."

"At least they're no longer on the loose," Alice said.

"True," Mavis said, and pulled the copies out of the copy machine. "This is the info letter. You keep it. This is the permission slip that needs to be signed."

Alice read the letter, then picked up a pen. She managed to sign it with her left hand, took her copy of the letter, and left the office. By the time she got back to her car, she was more than ready to get home and take a pain pill. She hadn't taken one this morning because she would be driving, and now her hand was aching.

Taking that pill was the first thing she did when she got back to the house, and then she sat down in the recliner and kicked back until it kicked in. She was frustrated by the fact that she didn't feel quite well enough to spend a whole day at work, but didn't feel bad enough to spend the day in bed, either. So she put a plastic bag over her bandaged hand, wrapped it at the wrist with a piece of masking tape, then put a pork roast in her slow cooker for their supper and started a load of laundry.

She had the television on as she worked about the house and, once again, caught an update on Tropical Storm Fanny. She listened to the weatherman talking about the storm gathering in intensity and frowned. "Listen here, Fanny, you make sure to keep your fanny out in the ocean and leave us land dwellers alone, you hear?"

Then she turned to another station and sat down to watch a game show and fell asleep with the remote in her hand. She was dreaming Dan Amos had thrown a lasso over her shoulders and was pulling her to him when the cell phone in her shirt pocket began to ring.

Startled, she sat up with a jerk and reached for her phone before she remembered her hand, then moaned when she bumped it against the arm of the sofa.

"Dang it!" she cried, then took a deep breath. "Hello?"

"Good morning, Alice. This is Dan. I hope I didn't wake you."

"I've been working around the house this morning. I sat down to rest a few minutes ago."

"Good. Do you need anything? Like a lunch partner or a ride somewhere, or maybe a lunch partner?"

She laughed. "Well, since you inquired so subtly... Mr. Amos, I'm thinking the correct answer is I could use a lunch partner."

"You are correct! The answer is me! I'm thinking something from Granny's on the call-in and pick-up menu."

"Perfect," Alice said. "It's such a dreary day. If she has any gumbo or chili on the menu today, that would be my choice."

"I'm on it," Dan said. "I'll be there shortly, and thank you."

"Why are you thanking me?" Alice asked. "I should be thanking you."

"Because the older I get, the less I like eating alone. See you soon." He disconnected.

The click in her ear made Alice shiver. What was going on here? What were they doing? Was he still being nice, or was it the stirrings of something else? If it was something else, she wasn't going to play coy. She liked him. If it went beyond friendship, that would be icing on the cake of her life.

———

Dan was drinking a cup of coffee as he sat on a bench near the cash register waiting to pick up his order. He was checking emails on his cell when a middle-aged couple walked in. Dan guessed by the way they were looking at each other that they were either newlyweds or newly dating. He watched Lovey approach to seat them.

"Hello, you two. Good to see you again. Hey, Big Tom, how is your son doing? I heard he messed his feet up pretty bad out at the lake the other day, running away from a black bear."

"Yes, it was an unfortunate chain of events. Junior was in the boat out on the lake, and Albert was fishing from the dock when he slipped and fell in. He climbed out of the water and had just pulled off his shoes when the bear showed up. Scared the crap out of him because the bear was between him and the truck, and Junior was too far away to hear him call for help. Albert said he threw the stringer of fish at the bear and took off running."

"Oh my," Lovey said. "Running barefoot through those woods…all those rocks and brambles."

Dan was listening, but the story sounded as fishy as the catch thrown at the bear. And no one with a brain turns his back on a bear and runs. A bear could run a man down within seconds. This man's son would have been safer trying to run to the truck, not running for miles through the woods. And he kept thinking about the pictures the sheriff had sent of Elliot's painting. There was a boat on the lake. What if it was this Junior's boat?

Would the brothers have witnessed anything, or could they have been a part of it?

He watched as Lovey showed the couple to a table, and when she came back, she had his order.

"Here you go, cowboy, and since you said you were taking this to Alice, give her my best."

"Yes, ma'am, I will. Say, I couldn't help but overhear the conversation you were having with that couple you just seated. Who is he? I don't believe I've seen him around."

"Oh, that's Big Tom Rankin and his lady friend, Ethel Shook."

"I heard you talking about the son's injuries. Sounds miserable. When did that happen?"

"Oh, just two or three days ago, I guess," she said.

"Then he's a long ways from healing. Takes a long time to heal up feet. Guess I'd better be going before all this good stuff gets cold."

Dan left the café, thinking about what he'd overheard. He'd pass it on to the chief later. Right now, he had his first official date with Miss Alice and couldn't wait to get there.

~~~

Alice removed the plastic bag from her hand and managed to set the table and make a fresh pitcher of sweet tea and set it in the refrigerator to cool while she was waiting for Dan. When she finally heard a knock at the door, she had to resist the urge to run.

For pity's sake, Alice! You're thirty-four years old. Act like the grown woman you are.

She turned the dead bolt, and when she opened the

door, Dan had a smile on his face and a sack in each hand.

"Umm, that smells good already. Come in," she said.

He followed her to the kitchen. "Okay if I take the stuff out right here at the table?"

"Of course," she said, but when she went to get the pitcher of tea from the refrigerator, he was right behind her. He reached over her shoulder and took it from the shelf and set it on the counter.

"Where are your drinking glasses?" he asked.

"Oh, I have a couple already iced and chilling in the freezer."

He opened the freezer door, got the glasses, and filled them with tea before taking them to the table, then began taking the food out of the sacks.

"Two bowls of chili. Corn bread on the side, and two pieces of Mercy Pittman's coconut cream pie. It's my favorite. Hope it's okay with you."

Alice sighed. She couldn't remember a time quite this special. "Everything is perfect," she said, and dropped into her chair. "Sit. Eat it while it's hot."

"You need a little scoot forward. Hang on," he said, and pushed her and the chair closer to the table, then took his seat. He put a bowl of chili on her plate and opened the foil-wrapped corn bread. "Want butter or anything on it?" he asked.

"No, but it's in the refrigerator door if you do," Alice said.

"Nope. I'm a purist," he said, then reached for her uninjured hand. "Thank you for humoring me. I realized a bit late that this was presumptuous. Forgive me?"

It was the warmth and the strength of his hand that touched her heart. "Don't be silly. There's nothing to forgive. If I didn't want to be doing this, all I would have had to say was no."

Dan looked long and hard into her eyes and then realized he was staring. "I'm not going to apologize for staring. It's hard to look away from a beautiful woman," he said softly, then pointed at the chili. "Want cheese on that? She sent some."

Alice shivered. "Thank you, and no cheese."

He grinned. "I just realized what I said. I called you beautiful and then asked if you wanted cheese on that, as if my attempt at a compliment wasn't cheesy enough. I'm a little out of practice here."

She laughed, and again, his heart skipped. That laugh of hers… If he could just bottle that joy. Instead, he reached for a piece of corn bread and crumbled part of it on his chili.

Alice did the same. Her first bite was the perfect temperature and a little bit spicy, and the corn bread was perfect.

"Goodness…that Mercy Pittman is quite a baker. This is delicious."

"Yes, it is," Dan said, and the tension eased between them as the meal began.

By the time they got to the pie, Alice was stuffed. "It was the second piece of corn bread. I have to save my pie for later."

"I'm eating mine. Want the first bite?"

"Oh, I'm—"

Dan got a clean fork and then cut off the first bite and held it toward her. "Open wide," he said.

She took the bite, rolling her eyes in appreciation.

"Thank you, and oh my Lord, but that's good."

Dan took the next bite and put it in his mouth, well aware they'd just shared a fork. "Ummm, just like the last piece I ate," he said.

She grinned and then got up and brought the tea pitcher to the table and refilled her glass, and then topped his off, too, before she sat back down. "This was fun and so good. Thank you for thinking of me."

"I've been doing a lot of that lately," he said, and kept eating pie without watching for her reaction.

If Dan Amos had a fault, it was that when he saw something he wanted, he wasn't bashful about asking for it, and today he had wanted her company. And it didn't hurt to tell her how happy she'd made him by agreeing.

A short while later, he had her kitchen cleaned up and was getting ready to leave. Alice walked him to the door, and when he turned around, he put his hands on her shoulders, leaned down and gave her a quick kiss on the cheek.

"Thanks for the company. Maybe we can do this again sometime, and include the kids?"

"They would love that," she said.

"Would you love it, too?" he asked.

"Probably, and you don't ever quit, do you?" she said.

"Not until somebody makes me. Get some rest."

He waved as he drove away.

Alice waited until he was completely out of sight before she touched the place on her cheek where he'd kissed her, then closed the door and danced all the way across the living room floor.

———

Dan was still smiling as he headed back to town. Before he started anything else, he needed to pass on what he'd heard Big Tom Rankin say. He drove by the middle school on his way to the police station and thought of Charlie Conroy doing a damn good job of being a man. When he got to Main Street, he turned right and drove straight to the station, grabbed his Stetson as he got out, then put it on and went in.

The dispatcher was eating his sandwich at the desk between answering calls, and he swallowed his bite and quickly wiped his mouth as Dan entered the building. "Afternoon, Mr. Amos. How can I help you?"

"Call me Dan. I wanted to see the chief for a few minutes. Is he in?"

"Yes, sir. Have a seat, and I'll tell him you're here."

Dan took off his hat as he sat down, listening as the dispatcher buzzed the chief's office, then gave him the message. Moments later, Lon Pittman appeared in the doorway.

"Afternoon, Dan. You needed to see me?"

"Yes."

"Let's go to my office," Lon said, and then motioned toward a chair for Dan as he resumed his seat behind his desk. "So, what's up?" he asked.

Dan began to relay the conversation as he'd heard it and ended with one last comment.

"I'm sure it would be simple enough for you to get dates and timelines of when Albert Rankin was taken to the ER, and if it was on the same day Elliot went to the lake. It may not amount to anything, but it is quite a coincidence if it doesn't," he said. "But then there's the lack of motive. Has County found anything out there that would lead to a reason for the assault?"

"Nothing they've shared with me, although I heard Sheriff Ryman just had surgery for a blockage in his carotid artery," Lon said. "But I appreciate this info and will run down the dates before I share this with County. If they jibe, then this may be the break we need."

"Well then, I'll be getting back to work and leave you to yours," Dan said.

Lon walked him up the hall, waved as he went out the door, and then pointed at Avery. "I'll be out for a bit. If you need me, try the police radio first and then my cell."

"Will do, Chief," Avery said, and then reached for the phone to answer a call as Lon went back to his office to get his things.

Back at the Rankin homestead, Junior was doing twice the work every day to pick up the slack from Albert's absence, but he never complained. Even when Big Tom began spending less time with Ethel to get home and help out, Junior would just wave him off.

"I got this, Dad. You can help most by taking care of Albert and doing some of the house chores."

"Sure thing, Son!" Big Tom said. "I'm not much of a cook, but I'm real good at sweeping and mopping. And I'll handle laundry, too."

Initially, Albert's pain sidetracked his concern about being found out, but after a couple of days his feet were feeling better, and as long as he didn't put pressure on them, he was fine. He had a borrowed wheelchair and enough upper body strength to get himself in and out of it and handle whatever else he needed to do. But most of the day he spent flat on his back, and the better he felt, the more his worries returned.

It was now several days since Elliot Graham had been found at Gray Goose Lake. Sheriff Ryman was still in the hospital, recovering from his surgery, when his deputy sheriff, Hunt Terrell, freed up enough officers working other cases around the county to create two investigative teams. And this morning, he'd sent them to Gray Goose Lake outside of Blessings. The teams would search the entire circumference of the lake and hopefully come up with answers or information that would help further this case of attempted murder.

Millie Powers, the woman who'd found Elliot's car, saw all the cars from the county sheriff's department driving past her house and guessed it had something to do with the attack on Elliot Graham. She didn't know what they were going to do, but she had a lakeside view, so she got herself a glass of sweet tea and her binoculars and went out on her back deck to watch.

She wasn't there long before at least a half-dozen officers came out of the woods in front of her house, walking along the lakeshore. Once they passed her house, they fanned out into the woods beyond.

She waved as they passed, and then took herself a big drink of the cold tea and took a gander through the binoculars, watching until they walked out of sight. It was the most excitement she'd had in years.

Meanwhile, out in the woods, the two search teams were being led by Officers Butler and Treat, the two men who'd been on hand when Elliot Graham was airlifted to Blessings Hospital.

They'd seen the brutal wound on the back of the old man's head and would be delighted to find the man responsible and put him behind bars.

The lake was large, but the job had been cut in half by having two teams. And it just so happened that one of the men on Officer Butler's team walked up on the first grow patches the Rankin brothers had planted. He stopped immediately and radioed the searchers. It didn't take long for all twelve of them to congregate, and then even less time to find the second grow patch.

But they'd been under orders to keep info off their radios, so it was Officer Butler who made the call to County.

When the deputy sheriff saw his incoming call was from one of the searchers, he answered quickly. "Sheriff's office. Hunt Terrell speaking."

"This is Officer Butler. We've located two large grow patches of marijuana on the opposite side of the lake from where Graham's body was found. Can't say this has anything to do with what happened to him, but I'd be willing to guess it's part of the story."

"Good work!" Terrell said. "Get pictures. Look for anything that could tell us who is tending them, and put up trail cameras. When they come back to harvest, at least we'll know who it belongs to."

"Yes, sir," Butler said. He disconnected, then turned around. "Who has the trail cams?"

A couple of officers held up their hands. "We do."

"Then distribute what you have. Let's get these up and get out of here. If we're lucky, we'll get an ID."

Within the hour, they had all of the motion-activated trail cameras set up and ready. Then they walked back to where their patrol cars were parked and left as quickly as they'd come.

Millie Powers was talking to a friend when she saw them leaving and proceeded to tell her what she'd seen. It didn't take long for word to spread that the law had been out at Gray Goose Lake.

Chapter 8

OSCAR LANGSTON HAD NEVER PLANNED ON SELLING DRUGS in his midfifties, but he'd never expected to be unemployed for so damn long, either.

Four years ago, he went to work at the oil refinery like always, and by the end of the day, he and everyone on his shift were given a pink slip with a final paycheck. It was five days after his fiftieth birthday. There had been no prior warning. All thirty-four of the men were in shock, and then they found out they were being replaced by machines, which was a double slap in the face.

He had never dreamed he wouldn't be able to find another job in a timely fashion, but it had happened. After his unemployment benefits ran out, his brother-in-law approached him with a business opportunity. At first he was indignant, then four months later he was reluctant, and two more months after that he said yes, and the rest was history.

Now, it was his normal routine. No big deal. Just business. And right now, his business demanded more weed, which meant setting up delivery dates with his suppliers. He hadn't been in contact with the Rankin brothers since Junior told him they were quitting, but he was guessing their other grow patch should be about ready to harvest, and he wanted it. He was at his desk, so he scanned his contact list for Junior Rankin's number and gave him a call.

Junior had Albert up and in his wheelchair, sitting at the kitchen table while he put their breakfast on the table. They were listening to an update on Tropical Storm Fanny with some trepidation as Junior sat down to eat.

Albert frowned. "What do you think, Junior? If it stays on the course it's on now, it'll hit Savannah, which is as good as in our lap."

"I know," Junior said. "We'll have time enough with the warnings to get the herd up to the barn, but there's loose tin on the roof right now, and I reckon I'd better get that fixed."

Albert nodded. "I wish I could help you."

"I know, but I'll get started on it this afternoon, and then we won't have to worry about it later," Junior said. He reached for a piece of toast and buttered it, then began eating the scrambled eggs and sausage that he'd made.

Albert was reaching for a second piece of toast when Junior's phone rang. It was on the table to the left of the butter dish, and when Junior saw the caller ID, he frowned.

"It's Oscar," he muttered.

"I thought you already called him," Albert said.

"I did," he muttered, then answered. "Hello."

"Hey, Junior, it's Oscar. How's that second patch coming along? I'm hoping you had a change of heart."

"Don't know. We quit the business, remember. I reckon it's still there. However, my guess is the county law found it after they found the old man."

Oscar's eyes narrowed. "Out of curiosity, what made you decide to quit?"

"What made me quit? Letting you talk me into killing a man is what made me quit. I don't much like myself anymore, and that's on me. But don't call us again. You hear?" And then he hung up before giving Oscar the opportunity to argue the point.

Albert eyed his brother's expression. He couldn't read him anymore, and it made him sad.

Albert sighed, and Junior heard it. "Don't worry, little brother. I got your back. If anything ever comes to light that pins all this on us, I'm taking the fall. You don't know anything about it. You play dumb and stay that way. There will never be proof you were there."

Albert's eyes filled with tears. "I don't know if I can do that," he said.

Junior slammed his hand down on the table, rattling the ice in the glasses. "You damn sure have to…for Daddy. For the family name, do you hear me?"

Albert shuddered. "I hear you, Junior."

But Junior wasn't satisfied. "Do you promise? Do you swear on our sweet mama's grave?"

Albert choked on a sob. "Yes! Hell, yes, I promise. I swear."

"Okay, then," Junior said. "Now…we're not gonna let that asshole ruin breakfast. Dig in."

"Yes, sir," Albert said. He picked up his napkin, wiped his eyes, and scooped up a bite and stuffed it in his mouth, determined to swallow it even if it gagged him.

As for Oscar, he shrugged it off and made another call. Growers were a dime a dozen. They came and they went, and some went to prison. All he had to do was make a few calls, and he'd be good to go.

The ensuing days passed fast until it was the morning of Patty's leaf-gathering trip at the Leggitt farm. Charlie made her lunch and packed it in her lunch box, adding a bottle of water today since she wouldn't have access to buying milk in the lunchroom.

The day was gray and overcast, so Alice dressed her in blue jeans, a long-sleeved pullover, and a lightweight jacket, and then Charlie put Patty's hair in a ponytail.

Alice watched him patiently brushing and smoothing the hair, despite Patty's squirming and complaining. His face was a study in calm and concentration, and she noticed as he was twisting the band how big his hands were getting. He was going to have long fingers like his grandfather. He already had his height.

"There now," Charlie said.

"Did he do it right, Mama?" Patty asked.

"Of course he did it right," Alice said. "Now tell him thank you."

Patty grinned. "Thank you, Charlie."

He tweaked her nose. "You're welcome. Now sit down with Mama and wait for me to feed Booger before we leave for school."

"Okay," Patty said, and leaned against her mother's shoulder until Alice put her arms around her and scooted her backward into her lap.

"You have to promise Mama you'll be a good girl today and mind everything your teacher says."

"I promise," Patty said.

Their television in the kitchen was on, and in the

background, Alice heard the weatherman giving an update on Tropical Storm Fanny. It was worrisome that it had not changed course in over five days now, but she was holding on to the fact that storms like this often changed course once they neared land. The front edge of the storm was already coming into Savannah, but the eye was still out at sea.

Charlie returned a few minutes later and went straight to the sink to wash his hands. "Hey, Mama, are you going to work today?"

"I told Mr. Bloomer I'd come in for half a day and see how it went. The first football game of the season is tonight, right?"

Charlie beamed. "Yes, ma'am. Will you feel like coming?"

"I wouldn't miss it for the world," she said.

"Me, too!" Patty said.

"Of course, you too," Alice said. "Now…everybody get their backpacks and lunches. It's a work morning for me, remember?"

They scrambled to get their gear and then headed for the door. Once outside, Charlie buckled Patty in the back seat of the car as Alice locked the house and then got in the driver's seat.

"Wish I was old enough to drive for you," Charlie said, then leaned over and buckled his mother's seat belt for her.

"You will be soon enough," she said, resisting the urge to hug and kiss him.

He was trying so hard to be the man of the family that she didn't want to treat him like a kid in public. But if he hugged her, that was a whole other story.

She managed to back out and get the car in drive, and then headed to the elementary school first.

A few clouds were beginning to gather in the pewter-colored sky, and she couldn't help but wonder if they would cancel the field trip, then shrugged it off. She trusted they would make the right call, regardless.

As soon as they reached the elementary school, Charlie got his little sister out with all of her gear and walked her inside. Moments later, as he came running out, Alice wondered if she'd see him running like that tonight out on the football field. This weather might stop a whole lot of plans.

They drove away, and as soon as she reached the middle school, Charlie grabbed his stuff and opened the door. He was halfway out when he looked back. "Love you, Mama. Don't hurt your hand today."

"Love you, too, and yes, I'll be careful," Alice said.

She waited until he was inside and then headed for Main Street. Rain or not, it was time for her to clock in at Bloomer's Hardware.

———

Dan had already received a phone call from Elliot this morning that the staples in his head had been removed, that he was being released and needed a ride home.

So now Dan was on his way to the hospital. He'd missed seeing the old guy out and about and was glad he had healed enough to come home.

Dan glanced up at the sky as he drove, and frowned. This was weather likely related to the incoming front attached to the tropical storm. According to the last report he'd heard, the storm was about to reach hurricane velocity, although the eye was a couple of days away from landfall.

There were some empty rentals he intended to recheck, although he'd already hung storm shutters and had plywood over the windows that didn't have shutters, but that would have to wait until he got Elliot home and settled. As soon as he reached the hospital, he parked near the front entrance, grabbed the bag with a change of clothes for Elliot, and ran inside.

Elliot was sitting on the side of his bed, waiting for the clothes Dan was bringing, and when he saw Dan enter the room with a nurse right behind him, he clapped his hands. "Finally! I'm not accustomed to being without my drawers," he said.

Dan laughed.

"Are those his clothes?" the nurse asked.

"Yes, ma'am," Dan said, and handed them over. "I'll wait outside until—"

"Hogwash!" Elliot said. "This lady has already seen my bare bum far too many times for my liking. I can surely dress in front of another man without losing my composure."

"Yes, sir," Dan said, trying not to laugh, but when Elliot peeled off his hospital gown with such matter-of-fact haste, he grinned.

The nurse began helping him dress, and when he pulled up his underwear, he patted the shorts and sighed.

"I'm finally decent," he said, then pointed at the nurse. "Although too late for your sensibilities."

She chuckled. "Now, Elliot, we've already had this conversation. It's part of a nurse's job and nothing that should cause you to fret."

"I suppose," Elliot said.

A few minutes later, she was putting on his socks and then helped him with his house shoes. "Alrighty now. You are good to go," the nurse said. "You sit a minute while I go get a wheelchair."

Elliot was so relieved to be leaving today that *argue* was not in his vocabulary. He glanced at Dan, who was standing at the window looking out at the view, most of which was the back sides of some of the businesses on Main.

"Dan, are you happy with your decision to stay here?" he asked.

Dan's focus had been on the impending weather, but he stepped away from the window and gave Elliot his full attention. "Yes, sir, I am. In fact, I just sent an offer to buy the rental property business, and Preston's house along with it, to Aidan Payne."

Elliot grinned. "That's wonderful news! Congratulations!"

Dan smiled. "Thank you. I'm happy about it."

Elliot nodded. "Preston's house is a great place to raise a family. Something to think about."

A little tug of pain moved through Dan's chest, and then it was gone.

"Yes, sir," Dan said, and then the nurse was back with the wheelchair and the old man's release papers.

"I'll be bringing him out through the front lobby," she said.

Dan nodded. "I'll run down and drive my truck up to the front door. That way I'll be waiting when you come outside. See you downstairs."

Elliot gave him a thumbs-up and then took a seat

in the wheelchair and began signing the papers so he could go home. He frowned as the nurse informed him he would be having a home health nurse checking on his welfare for the following week until his doctor was satisfied he was capable of taking care of himself, but it was a small price to pay for his independence.

A few minutes later they were in an elevator and heading down to the lobby.

Mrs. Milam was in the principal's office, discussing whether or not the field trip should be canceled. The deciding factor became the close proximity of the farm to town. If it did begin to rain, they were only two miles from Blessings, and all the roads there and back were paved. They'd just load up the children and bring them back.

At that point, the field trip was on.

The school bus was parked in the school oval and the driver patiently waiting. Either they'd cancel and call him, or they'd continue as planned and the children would show up as planned. And he was right. Within ten minutes of the final school bell, the front doors opened and Mrs. Milam and her second-grade class emerged, marching in a line down the sidewalk to the bus.

The driver opened the door and got out, then stood at the door to help little ones up the steps. Some of them cut their eyes up at him and grinned. A few of them looked over their shoulders to see where their teacher was, then giggled as he helped them up. A couple of them spoke, then got shushed by the teacher.

"No talking, remember?" Mrs. Milam said.

Instant silence outside, but inside the bus, the kids were talking and laughing.

Patty Conroy was next to the last in line and already dragging her feet. She'd had no trouble incorporating into first grade when they'd come to town, but this year she was in second grade and the girls in her class had begun pairing off and leaving her alone on the playground. Today was no different. She hadn't mentioned it to Mama or Charlie, because she was certain the other girls would soon like her like they had in first grade.

Connie Milam was well aware this was happening, but her eighteen years of teaching experience had taught her that letting kids work stuff like this out on their own was best, unless bullying or complete ostracizing occurred. At that point, she interfered in a way that usually left the conspirators in tears.

Today, she was going to take a step in interfering and ask to sit with Patty. Getting to sit with teacher was a coveted spot on any trip. Maybe this would lead some of the little ringleaders in class to behave more kindly toward Patty.

Connie was the last to board the bus. She shushed the children again and then began a head count to make sure she had all the class on the bus before it left. She counted nineteen little heads and then gave the driver a thumbs-up.

"This is all of us," she said, and then turned around and tapped Patty on the shoulder. The little blond looked up at her and smiled. "May I sit with you?" Connie asked.

Patty's eyes widened, and so did her smile. "Yes, ma'am," she said, and scooted over, wiggling with joy.

Connie didn't have to look behind her to know this decision had made an impact, because she could hear an undertone of murmuring run through the bus. She raised her hand, and the murmuring stopped as the driver took off.

Outside, the clouds were still there. No more than before, but certainly not dissipating.

Connie enjoyed the chatty little girl more than she'd expected and learned all about how her mother had hurt her hand, and what the bedspread looked like in her room, and how their dog, Booger, could find people who got lost. Patty talked and talked, and by the time they arrived at the Leggitt farm, Connie Milam had fallen a little bit in love. As soon as the bus stopped, she stood up.

"Alright, children, remember we search for our leaves in teams. Do not take your lunches. They'll stay on the bus. Bring the sack with you that you brought to gather your leaves. I'll divide you up into teams as soon as we are all off the bus. Now follow me, and quietly please."

Connie stood up, stepped into the aisle, and then waited for Patty to be first in line. The last one on was the first one to get off. So she marched them off the bus to where Frank Leggitt was waiting with some members of his family. He had roped off the part of the woods in which they would search. It wasn't a large area, and it would serve to keep them together.

As soon as they were all out of the bus, Mrs. Milam got out her list. "I'm going to put you in teams of four, except the last team, which will have only three students. When I call your name, go stand by your teammates. Patty Conroy, stand by Mr. Leggitt. And the next three names I call will join her. You will be team number one."

Patty was beside herself that she was first, and with her chin up and her leaf sack clutched tightly in her hand, she marched over to where the farmer was standing.

The next three names were girls: Judy Rowland, Ruthie Wells, and Carlene Treat. Connie had debated about the wisdom of this, but was hoping this would be the icebreaker Patty needed. As soon as the first team was formed, they stepped aside and waited until all of the students were on a team.

At that point, Mr. Leggitt said his piece about staying within the roped-off area and if they had any problems, to call out and he would come running. Then he introduced his wife, Gertie, and two grown sons, Ron and Archie, who would also be adults along with the teams of the class.

Patty was excited and began talking to the girls, but they either ignored her questions and comments or talked among themselves as if she wasn't there.

Connie Milam was watching their interaction closely and was disappointed when it began in such a fashion. But the day had just begun. There was always a chance for change.

The teams marched into the search area with Frank Leggitt in the lead. He showed them all the big yellow rope he'd used to designate the area and told them not to go beyond the rope or they might get lost.

All of the children nodded, and then as the teams dispersed, an adult went with each of them. Frank had passed out handheld radios to each adult, so if there were any emergencies, there would be no delay in getting assistance.

Connie Milam chose to go with team number one, in hopes of being the bridge that started a friendship. As they moved into the woods, the girls began looking for leaves on the ground.

"Remember, you are looking for different leaves, so don't gather up a whole bunch from beneath the same tree. And if you find one that looks like one you already have, just leave it and keep searching."

Patty nodded. "I know some trees, Mrs. Milam. We lived in the woods before we moved here, and my brother, Charlie, taught me stuff."

Judy snickered. "You lived in the woods? Like animals?"

Patty frowned. "No, we had a house, but it was in the—"

Judy rolled her eyes and interrupted. "Whatever. Come on, girls. I see some good leaves over here."

Patty picked up her sack and followed.

Connie wanted to turn all three of those hateful little girls over her knee, but unfortunately, those days were long gone for teachers. And like Patty, she followed, bringing up the rear.

They moved about the search area and, as time passed, often ran into members of other teams who were laughing and talking among themselves. It was about an hour and a half into the search when Connie heard a bloodcurdling scream from somewhere behind her and grabbed her radio.

"This is Connie. What's wrong? Over."

"This is Gertie Leggitt. A little boy named David fell and cut his head and has a nosebleed. Over."

Connie's heart skipped a beat. "What is your location? Over."

"We are a little to the left of the entrance. Follow the rope, and it'll take you right to us. Over."

Connie turned to her team. "Grab your sacks and follow me!" she said, then lined them up with Patty behind her and then Ruthie, Carlene, and Judy. "Stay right behind me. David got hurt so we need to go help him, okay?"

"Yes, ma'am," they said in unison.

The girls had heard the shriek, and when their teacher started walking out toward the rope, they all began running to keep up with her, Patty included. As soon as Connie saw the rope, she oriented herself to the direction of the entrance and then turned to the girls again.

"Each one of you stay behind me. I have to hurry, so just follow the rope with me."

"Yes, ma'am," Patty said. She was starting to fall into step right behind her teacher again, when Ruthie pushed her aside and took her place. Each girl followed Ruthie's lead until Patty was at the end of their line.

Patty's feelings were hurt, and although her eyes were filled with tears, she was trying not to cry. Everything in front of her was a tear-filled blur as she hurried to catch up. Once she lost sight of Judy and panicked.

"Judy! Wait!"

Then she saw a flash of yellow and knew it was Judy's jacket and ran to catch up. Judy looked over her shoulder when she heard Patty running up behind her and stuck out her tongue.

Startled, Patty stumbled, then without looking where she was going, stepped on a rock that rolled beneath her shoe, turning her ankle. Pain shot up her leg as she lost her balance, and before she knew what was happening, she was falling backward. She fell over the rope and began sliding down the slope of the land on her back.

"Help, Judy, help!" she cried.

Judy heard her and stopped, saw Patty falling very fast, and then turned around and kept running without saying a word.

Patty was grabbing at trees and bushes, trying to slow down. She finally managed to get herself turned onto her side, and the moment that happened, she began rolling down the hill. She cried out once as she rolled into a tree and then suddenly disappeared from view.

Unaware of what had happened, Connie Milam arrived on the scene to find David sitting down with a little cut on his head and a bloody nose.

"Oh, honey! My goodness!" she cried as she dropped down to her knees beside him. Then she turned around to make sure her girls were all there and frowned. "Where's Patty? She was right behind me!"

The girls looked a little nervous.

"I can run faster, so I got in front of her," Ruthie said.

"She was behind Judy," Carlene said.

Connie glanced at the little boy, then stood. "Mrs. Leggitt, I would appreciate it if you would sit with David until I get back."

"Of course, Connie. He's not hurt much. Ron went to get the first aid kit. We'll clean him up and put something on his cut."

Connie glared at the little girls. "So, Judy, where's Patty?"

Judy shrugged. "She fell down, too."

Connie grabbed her by both shoulders. "And you didn't see fit to tell me?"

"My mama says that girl's family are drug dealers. She says we need to stay away from her," Judy said.

"That's what my mama says, too," Carlene said.

"Mine, too," Ruthie said.

Connie was horrified. "All of you. Sit down right now. I'll deal with this when I get back with Patty."

"There comes Ron with the first aid kit. We'll see to the kids," Mrs. Leggitt said. "Archie, you go with Connie."

Archie Leggitt took off at a trot behind Connie Milam. Connie was already on the phone with the principal as she left the group. "Mrs. Winston, this is Connie. We are having an issue out here on the farm. David Walters had a fall. He has a little cut on his forehead, small enough for a Band-Aid, and a bloody nose, but Mrs. Leggitt is dealing with that."

"Oh dear, I'll have to call David's mother," Arlene said.

"Not yet. We have a bigger issue brewing. Patty Conroy has been bullied and ostracized by some of her classmates ever since school began, but I couldn't figure out why. I thought today when I teamed Judy Rowland, Ruthie Wells, and Carlene Treat with her, they would get to know each other a little better and that would solve the problem. But then David got hurt, and as we were all running to join the group to check on David, the other three girls shoved Patty to the back of the team after I had her right behind me, and when we got here, she was missing. Judy Rowland just informed me that she saw her fall and didn't bother to tell me. Archie Leggitt and I are going back to get her, and then we're loading up and returning to school. I would appreciate it if you would have those girls' parents in the office when we get there."

Arlene Winston sighed. "I don't like the sound of this."

"That's not the worst of it," Connie said. "All three of the girls on her team advised me that their mothers told them not to have anything to do with Patty because her family deals drugs."

"Oh my Lord!" Arlene muttered. She had visions of the incident a couple of years back with the Pine brothers. That mess had wound up in court, and three of their students had been put on probation for what they had done to Johnny Pine's younger brother, Beep, and all because the Pine family lived on the wrong side of town and their daddy was in prison. "Just let me know how Patty is before you start back. I'll need to call her mother, too."

"Yes, ma'am," Connie said, then put her phone in her pocket and started running, following the boundary rope back to where she guessed Patty would be waiting. But to her horror, Patty was nowhere to be seen, and Connie Milam could tell by the landmarks she'd noted that she and Archie should have already found her. "This is already farther than where we started from," Connie said.

"Maybe she got turned around after she fell and followed the rope the wrong way," Archie said. "I'll keep going that way, and once I find her, I'll give you a call."

"Okay," Connie said. "But in the meantime, I'm going

to retrace my steps back the way we came. Maybe we were moving too fast and overlooked an obvious clue."

"Deal," Archie said, and took off at a lope, while Connie turned around and began retracing her steps, only this time she was calling Patty's name. She walked and called, and then stopped to listen, all the way back to the entrance where the group was seated.

Her heart was pounding, and the look she gave the three girls finally made them realize they were in big trouble.

"You didn't find her?" Mrs. Leggitt asked.

"No. Archie is following the rope in the other direction, assuming she got turned around and went the wrong way. When he finds her, he'll bring her here."

"There he comes now," Mrs. Leggitt said, pointing. "But he's alone."

"No!" Connie moaned, and ran up to him. "Nothing?"

"Not a sign," Archie said, and then glanced up at the sky. "It looks like it's going to rain."

Connie turned on the three girls again. "Judy! You saw her fall?"

Judy Rowland nodded.

"Where did she fall? What did you see last?"

"She was sliding down into the trees," Judy said.

"And you didn't think that was important enough to tell me?" Connie shrieked, and then took a slow breath. "What if that had been you? Would you want all of us to just go back to school and pretend you didn't exist?"

Judy's chin quivered. "No, but—"

"Never mind! I'll deal with you later," she said. "Mr. Leggitt! Is there a place that steep? Where someone might fall off this big hill?"

"Several places," he said. "It's why I always rope it off."

Connie was in tears. "I need to get these kids back to school, but I can't leave a child behind."

All of the Leggitts were gathered at the entrance, scared that a child had gotten lost on their property—under their watch.

"We'll call Chief Pittman right now and get a search party out here," Frank Leggitt said. "In the meantime, I'd advise you to call her parents."

Connie nodded. "Yes, we will, but as soon as I get the kids back to school, I'm coming back to help search."

"Yes, ma'am," Ron said. "Just keep your radio, then. You'll likely need it to locate us."

Frank Leggitt was pale and shaken. "This has never happened before. I don't understand."

"It's not your fault, Mr. Leggitt. I'm afraid Patty's teammates are to blame for this." Then Connie pointed at the children. "Stand up. Take your leaf bags with you and march straight to the bus."

"But we didn't get to have our picnic!" Judy cried.

"And you and Ruthie and Carlene are to blame. Get in line, all of you."

The bus driver was standing at the entrance, aware something had happened, but he could not have imagined this. "What's wrong?" he asked as he walked beside Connie on the way to the bus.

"Patty Conroy is missing. One of her teammates saw her falling down a slope and didn't see fit to tell anybody. I fear it's a long, ugly story that is going to get worse before it gets better."

He shook his head as he loaded up the students.

Connie stepped on board, then stood at the front of the bus and began to count heads. "Eighteen," she muttered, then tapped the driver on the shoulder. "That's it. Get us back to school ASAP."

Then she sat down in a seat, picked up the phone, and called Arlene Winston again. When she was finished, she covered her face and started to cry.

Chapter 9

ALICE WAS CHECKING A CUSTOMER OUT WHEN HER CELL phone rang. When she saw it was from the elementary school, she stifled a moment of panic.

"Thank you," she said as she dropped the receipt into her customer's sack and then answered the phone as the customer went out the door. "Hello. This is Alice."

"Mrs. Conroy, this is Arlene Winston."

Alice stifled a moan. She knew in her heart this wasn't going to be good news. "What's wrong? What happened to Patty?"

The principal took a deep breath. "This is most distressing, but I have to tell you that Patty is lost at the Leggitt farm. We're looking for her right now, but of course wanted you to be immediately aware."

"Oh my God! I trusted my baby with you. How did you lose her?"

"At this point, all we know for certain is that one girl saw her fall, and then by the time she told, we couldn't find her. I'm sure we'll—"

"Tell me exactly where this farm is located," Alice snapped.

Arlene gave her explicit directions, then added, "I don't want you to panic. We're—"

"You're the one who should be panicking," Alice said. "You better pray to God my baby is safe and unhurt when she's found." Then she hung up in the principal's

ear and got back on the phone and called the middle
school, then waited for the secretary to answer.

"Blessings Middle School."

"Ma'am, this is Alice Conroy. We have a family
emergency, and I am on my way to the school to pick up
my son, Charlie. Please have him waiting in the office
when I get there."

"Yes, of course," the secretary said.

Alice ran to the back room where Fred was eating
lunch. "Fred, the school just called. Patty's class was
on a field trip out to Leggitt's farm, and they lost her."

Fred stood abruptly. "Are you serious?"

Alice nodded, and then burst into tears. "I have to
go."

"Of course you do! Are you going alone?"

"No. Charlie will be with me," she said. Then she
ran to her locker, grabbed her purse and her jacket, and
dashed out of the store.

She was shaking so hard she could barely drive and
didn't have time to baby her sore hand. She sped down
Main Street, taking a right just before the Curl Up and
Dye, and drove toward the middle school, praying with
every beat of her heart. As soon as she reached the
school, she came to a sliding halt and got out on the run.

She could see Charlie standing in the office, and
when he saw her running toward it, he turned white as a
sheet and opened the door and ran to meet her.

"Mama! What's wrong?"

"They lost Patty somewhere on the Leggitt farm
during the field trip. We're going to get Booger," she
said, and then ran into the office. "My daughter is missing on a school trip. Where do I sign him out?"

"Go! I'll sign him out!" the secretary said, and two seconds later, mother and son were out the door and running toward the car.

"I can't believe they let that happen!" Charlie said as they drove through the neighborhood toward their house.

"Neither can I," Alice said. "They said some girl saw her fall but didn't tell anyone when it happened, and by the time she told, they couldn't find Patty."

Charlie frowned. "Probably one of those girls who have been mean to her," he said. "Did she say anything to you about that?"

Alice was horrified. "No! Not once! Are you serious?"

"Yes. Sometimes when I go by the elementary to get her before we walk home, she's either sitting by herself or girls are standing around picking on her. I tell them to get lost and leave her alone, but they aren't scared of me. Girls are mean to each other, I don't care how old they are," he muttered.

"I wish one of you had told me about this," Alice said.

Charlie felt like he'd let both of them down. "I assumed she had talked to you."

"Well, she hadn't," Alice said, and then pulled up into their drive and ran to unlock the front door. "You go get Booger. I'm going to get Patty's nightgown. She just took it off this morning. It'll be good scent for tracking."

"Yes, ma'am," Charlie said, and dumped his backpack and headed through the house. A couple of minutes later, he was back with the big bloodhound on a leash.

Alice met him at the door. "Load him up," she said.

"We don't have any time to waste. The sky is clouding up. If it rains, it will be harder for Booger to stay on track."

"Yes, ma'am," Charlie said, and put the big dog in the back of their car.

Alice backed out, then left rubber on the pavement as she took off out of town.

—⁓⁓—

The bus pulled up to the front of the school, and when it did, Connie Milam stood up. "As you know, we have an emergency! One of your classmates is lost, so I don't have time for foolishness. You can help me and Patty by lining up quietly and going straight to the principal's office without talking. I'll be right behind you."

The children were pale and wide-eyed as they stood up, imagining being the one who got lost. When the troublesome trio stood up, Connie pointed. "You three will walk with me. Everyone…get all of your things off the bus. Don't leave anything behind."

Moments later, they were heading in line up the walk, and when they entered the building, they walked straight into the front office.

Arlene Winston was waiting for Connie Milam to take her students back to class, and as soon as Connie came in last with the three girls in question, the principal pointed at the girls. "All of you, in my office now."

They ducked their heads as tears continued to roll.

Connie stepped up. "Are their parents here yet?"

"Not yet," Arlene said.

Connie frowned. "I want to speak to them first, and then I'll leave the mess to you. But as soon as I'm through, I'm going back to the search site. I had to leave a child behind to get these back, and I didn't like how that felt," she said.

Arlene turned to her secretary. "Mavis, find a teacher who's on her planning period and tell her to come to the office and take these children back to Mrs. Milam's room."

"Yes, ma'am," Mavis said, and began checking teacher schedules.

A couple of minutes later, one of the teachers came running, horrified that a child was lost. She couldn't help search, but she could gladly help with this and took the children back to their class.

At that point, the parents began arriving, but Connie Milam was already in the principal's office with the girls, so Mrs. Winston escorted them into her office as well.

When the parents saw their girls in tears, they started to rush toward them, but the principal asked them to sit instead.

Judy Rowland's father got angry. "What's going on here, and why is my daughter crying?"

The two mothers chimed in, demanding answers.

Mrs. Winston pointed at Connie. "I'm going to let their teacher fill you in. Mrs. Milam, the floor is yours."

Connie stood up. "These girls have been bullying one of their classmates, a little girl named Patty Conroy. I've been aware of the behavior and have redirected them several times since class began this year, thinking it would smooth itself out. Today, I put them on the same team, with me as their leader, as we went to search for leaves. To make a long, horrible story short, they continued to be rude, even hateful. And before I could deal with any of that, we had a small emergency. One of the children fell and bumped his head and got a bloody nose, so we all started back to the main group together.

"I lined the girls up, with Patty behind me, but Ruthie took it upon herself to shove her out of line, and she wound up at the back without my knowledge. When we got to the injured boy, I turned around to tell them where to sit and found Patty was not there. Reluctantly, Judy finally decided to inform me that Patty had fallen. In fact, Judy saw her rolling down a steep slope and didn't think it important enough to tell me, because you all told your children not to play with Patty Conroy because her family sells drugs!"

All three parents turned pale, and then Ruthie's mother, Charlotte, got angry. "Well, it's the truth and—"

Arlene Winston hit her desk with the flat of her hand. "No! That's not the truth. You all heard gossip and passed it on to your children, and now all of you are responsible for the fact that Patty Conroy is missing!"

"What do you mean? Maybe she just ran off!" Mrs. Rowland said.

"By rolling off a mountain? Seriously?" Connie shouted.

"Patty wasn't guilty of anything. Unlike you and your children, she had nothing to hide," Mrs. Winston said. "God only knows where Patty is now, but you better hope she's not dead. A storm is coming. A child is lost. And when you take your girls out of here to the safety of their homes, you can all go with the knowledge that one little girl is not safe at home with her mother because of you. Now I'm going back to help look for her, just as

I would have done had it been one of yours. Just know this isn't over by a long shot."

Then she strode out of the room without looking back.

Fred Bloomer was at the front counter and looked up as the doorbell jingled and Dan Amos walked in.

"Morning, Dan. How can I help you?"

"I just stopped by to see how Alice was doing on her first day back at work," Dan said.

"She's not here," Fred said. "She just got a call from school that her little girl was on some field trip and got lost from the group. Alice took off out of here on the run."

Dan's heart sank. "Where did this happen, and how can I get there?"

"Frank Leggitt's farm, two miles east of town. You can't miss it. It's right on the blacktop. White two-story house. Big red barn behind it."

Dan was out the door and back in his truck within seconds. He couldn't imagine how frightened Patty must be, or how terrified Alice likely was, but he needed to help find her.

He drove with a knot in his gut, hoping by the time he got out there she would already be found. Instead, when he reached the location, Alice's car was parked a short distance from the house, along with a half-dozen other cars, including two from the Blessings PD, and there was one woman on-site. Frank Leggitt's wife.

"Where are they searching for Patty Conroy?" Dan asked.

She pointed. "Follow that yellow rope. You'll run right into them. They're about five minutes ahead of you."

Dan tossed his hat in the truck and took off running. As he did, he could hear people's voices and a dog somewhere within the area, and he wondered if it was Charlie's dog.

After a couple of minutes, he ran up on the search party coming out of the woods to his right. He saw police, Alice, Charlie with his dog, another woman, and a few men he didn't know. The old bloodhound was moving at a lope with his nose near the ground, and Charlie was right behind him, hanging on to the leash with all his strength.

Charlie saw him at the same time Dan saw Charlie. It moved him to see the relief pass across Charlie's face. And then Alice saw him and ran straight into his arms.

In the middle of their reunion, Booger bayed and bolted under the rope.

"Stop him!" Chief Pittman shouted. "That's a steep slope to be running on!"

Charlie pulled Booger back. "Halt, Booger! Halt!"

The dog obeyed, but was trembling and whining. His instinct to finish the hunt was strong, but not as strong as the hold Charlie had on the leash.

"I don't know how you found out, but I'm glad you're here," Alice said.

Dan hugged her close. "I'm glad I'm here, too."

Chief Pittman had already seen Booger in action months earlier. Now that the dog had keyed in on the direction Patty had taken, he grabbed his cell phone. "There's a rescue team coming here from County. Let me check their ETA," he said, and then walked a few feet away to make the call.

They couldn't hear him talking, but they were watching the expressions on his face, and when he came back, they weren't encouraged. "The team is still at least thirty minutes out," he said.

Alice moaned. "No. What if Patty's life depends on timing? That storm is getting closer. Those thirty minutes could be the difference between life or death for her."

Dan turned Alice loose and stepped forward. "I am good at climbing and rappelling. I used to pay people to let me do that for fun. Let me help."

"What do you need?" Lon asked.

"Well, climbing equipment, which I don't suppose you have?"

Lon shook his head. "No, we don't."

Dan nodded. "Then, since we're doing this on the fly, I'll take a long length of rope, a pair of leather gloves, and one of your radios."

Frank Leggitt took the gloves out of his jacket pocket and handed them to Dan, then pointed at the yellow nylon rope in front of them.

"There's your rope. Boys, go untie it and bring it back, ASAP." His sons left the group on the run as Frank kept talking. "You can cut any length you need, mister, or use it all with my blessing. I'm just sick that this happened on our place."

As Frank's sons ran off to collect the rope, Connie Milam stepped forward. "None of this was his fault. They were in my care. I knew Patty was having a few problems with the kids, which is why I made sure I was the adult on her team, but I had no idea the girls were capable of such callous behavior."

"What's going on?" Dan asked.

Alice was so angry she was shaking. "This is Connie Milam, Patty's teacher. The girls on Patty's team have been making fun of her and shunning her."

Connie nodded. "We had another child get hurt, so all of the teams quit searching and met up at the entrance. I took my team that way as well. The moment I realized Patty wasn't with our group, I asked the girls where she was."

Alice interrupted, still so angry she was shaking. "One of them told the teacher she saw Patty fall…in fact, saw her sliding down a slope, but she didn't call out to warn her and didn't even say what she'd seen until they got back to the group."

Connie put her arms around Alice as she picked up the story again. "That's true, and when I confronted her, and then the other two as well, they said that their parents told them not to play with Patty because her family sells drugs. Patty never told me or her mother."

Dan's eyes narrowed angrily as his focus shifted to the teacher. "I haven't practiced criminal law in years, but I'm still a lawyer, and I can put the fear of God in those parents if the need arises."

"I'll keep that in mind," Connie said.

Booger was still pulling on his leash and whining, and when Charlie's focus shifted to the adult conversation, the old dog felt the tension ease on his leash and bolted.

"No! Booger! Come back!" Charlie yelled. He was starting to go after the dog when Dan grabbed him.

"Wait, Charlie! Look! They're bringing me the rope. I'll get her, and when I do, your dog will be there with her, right?"

Charlie's shoulders slumped. He'd lost his sister. He didn't want to lose Booger, too. But Dan was right. "Yes, sir. He can find Patty, and he won't leave her."

"Then let me do this," Dan said.

Charlie looked at his mama and then nodded.

Dan gave him a man-size thump on the back. "Just take care of your mama. Booger will find Patty, and I'll get the both of them back for you."

Charlie turned away to wipe his eyes. He didn't want anyone to know he'd finally given in to tears.

The Leggitt sons arrived at the same time but from separate directions, each with a huge coil of rope on their shoulders that was actually one entire length.

"Tie one end of this off to that tree," Dan said, pointing to a sturdy pine on the downhill slope.

The brothers went down together and did as he asked, leaving the rest of the rope in a coil on the ground.

Chief Pittman handed Dan a radio. "You sure you can handle this?" he asked.

"I wouldn't have volunteered otherwise," Dan said. "Just trust me."

Then he slipped and scooted his way down to the pine tree. He grabbed the loose end of the coil, picked it up and slung it down the slope, watching as it uncoiled in midair. Then he pulled the leather gloves up snug on his hands, grabbed the other coil, played some of it out and wrapped it around his waist. He gripped the rope tied to the tree, wrapped it loosely three times around his forearm, then pulled it behind his back with his other hand, using one to control the length he was letting out, and the other hand to control the speed of his descent. He started down the slope backward, letting the rope play out as he dropped farther and farther until he dropped out of sight in the undergrowth.

"Oh dear God," Alice said, and then went to her knees, too shaky to stand.

———

Dan kept glancing behind him as he descended to make sure he didn't back into a tree. He would have given a lot for the climbing rig that went with this sport, but emergencies call for making do, and this was a definite emergency.

He was still backing down when he paused a moment and looked up to see how far he'd come. Then he pushed through some heavy brush and ran out of solid ground. One moment he was on the slope, and then it was gone and he was hanging out into space and gripping the rope with both hands.

"No, God, no," he whispered, afraid to look down again and see Patty's little body broken on the rocks below.

And then he heard a dog whine. Booger was on a ledge less than six feet down, and Patty was beside him, looking up.

"Thank you, God," Dan said softly, and carefully lowered himself the rest of the way down. He could see tear tracks on Patty's cheeks, and her eyes were still shiny with unshed tears. "Hey, baby girl. Are you alright? Do you hurt anywhere?"

She nodded, rubbing her leg. "I turned my ankle. It made me fall."

He could see it was swollen beneath her sock.

"Does your head hurt anywhere?"

"A little bit."

There was no blood, but he tunneled his fingers carefully through her hair, searching for lumps, and felt nothing urgent. "Can you move your foot?" he asked.

"A little, but it hurts," she said.

"Do you hurt anywhere else? How about your arms?"

She lifted them over her head, but winced a bit.

"How about your back? Can you move your legs?"

She nodded and then showed him by scissoring them back and forth. "I hurt a little bit all over," she said.

"Does it hurt to breathe?" he asked.

She patted her little chest. "No," she said, and breathed in and out to show him.

"That is so awesome," he said, and then rubbed the old dog's head. He was uncertain whether the dog had jumped or fallen, but he seemed to be okay, too. "Way to go, Booger Conroy. You are an amazing fellow."

Then to his surprise, Patty got up on her knees and crawled into his lap, put her arms around his neck, and started to cry. It broke his heart. "You're okay, honey, you're okay. Mama and Charlie and a bunch of people are up at the top of the slope. Even your teacher is looking for you. You just hang on to me. I need to tell them I found you." He scooted backward until they were beneath the overhang and as far away from the ledge as they could get.

When he moved, Booger moved with them. He sniffed Patty once, then sniffed Dan before flopping down beside them.

Dan patted Booger's head again and then unhooked the handheld radio from his waistband and keyed in. "This is Dan. I found them both. They're okay. Over."

Alice heard his voice and started to cry. Connie Milam was sitting beside her and cried along with her.

"Thank God, thank God," Connie said, and kept patting Alice's hand.

Relief swept through Charlie as well, listening as the chief keyed up his radio.

"This is Pittman. A rescue crew is due here soon. What do we need to get all of you back up? Over."

Dan thought about it a moment. "We are on a ledge about six feet down from the end of that slope. She turned her ankle, which is what made her fall, so she can't walk back up. Tell them to bring a litter and strap her in. Over."

"Ten-four. Do you have any resources to get yourself off the ledge? Over."

"Negative. The dog and I are here until the rescue crew figures something out. Tell them to bring a bottle of water for Patty. Over," Dan said.

"Ten-four. Will advise rescue. Over and out."

Dan laid the radio aside and gave Patty a quick hug. "Help is coming, honey, okay?"

She nodded, and when Booger whined, she reached for him. Moments later, the hound was in Dan's lap, too, lying over his legs. Dan patted the dog's head, and then settled Patty against his chest. This was the best outcome possible for such a serious event, and when she laid her head against his shoulder, he closed his eyes. It was almost like holding his son again.

They weren't there long before Dan felt the wind

shift. Now it was blowing in his face. He looked up. The clouds were gathering, and the sky was growing darker.

Come on, guys. We need to be gone before the storm hits.

No sooner had he thought that than he began to hear voices. The rescue crew was on the way down.

"Down here!" he shouted. "Watch for the drop-off!"

Moments later, he saw a rope dangling over the edge, followed by a man in red coveralls, who dropped right into their midst.

Booger woofed.

"Easy, boy. They're here to help," Dan said, and then a litter came over the edge. The man from the rescue squad grabbed it and situated it in front of them.

"I'm Matt," he said, eyeing Patty. "Are you Patty?"

She nodded.

He opened a bottle of water and handed it to her. She reached for it with both hands and drank greedily in huge gulps while the excess ran out both corners of her mouth and down the front of her shirt. She paused once to take a breath, and then took another drink before handing it back. The EMT put the lid back on it and handed it to Dan.

"Okay, Patty. I brought you an easy way to get back up the slope. Are you ready to take a ride back up to your mama?"

She looked at Dan, and when he gave her a thumbs-up, she relaxed. "Yes, I'm ready. Are you gonna bring Dan and Booger, too?"

"You bet, but one at a time, and you get to go first because you've been waiting the longest, okay?"

"Yes, okay," she said, but was still reluctant to let

go of Dan. "You promise you can help get Booger back up?" she asked.

"I promise," Dan said. "You tell Charlie to wait up there for us."

"Okay," Patty said.

"See this soft blanket?" Matt asked, as he spread it over the bottom of the long basket. "I'm going to lay you down in this litter. It's like a little bed. Then I'm going to cover you up so you won't be cold, because the wind is really starting to blow, isn't it? And because you are so special to everyone who loves you, I'll strap you in tight so you can't fall out of your bed, okay?"

"Okay," Patty said.

Dan laid her down in the litter, then Matt began to pull the blankets over her and strap her in. "We're going to start pulling you up now, Patty, so if you want, just close your eyes, and then you open them when you hear your mama's voice," Dan said.

"Okay," Patty said.

Dan knelt over the litter. "See you up top," he said, and then leaned down and kissed her on the forehead. "You are doing great, and thank you for being very brave."

Patty's eyes were fixed upon his face as Matt was radioing the rescue crew to start the lift. First, they pulled Matt up off the ledge so he could help grab the litter, and once he was up, they began pulling Patty up next.

Dan was tall enough so that when he stood, he was easily able to keep the basket from swinging beneath the overhang, and as soon as she was up and out of sight, he sat back down with the dog.

"It's just me and you, boy. May as well make the best

of it. Let's scoot back under the ledge. I'm pretty sure we're gonna get wet before we get back home."

The bloodhound was anxious, both because Patty was out of his sight, and because of the incoming thunderstorm, but after Dan poured the rest of the water into his hand for Booger to drink, he settled back down with Dan.

———

When the searchers above realized the rescue crew was bringing Patty up, they leaped to their feet. An ambulance was back at the entrance, waiting, and when the driver received the news via radio, they were ready to receive their patient.

Charlie was holding his mama's hand when they saw the men in red coveralls emerging through the trees, and then they saw the litter they were carrying between them.

It was all Alice could do to stand still.

Connie Milam was praying, thanking God for answering this prayer.

It felt like forever, watching them work their way up on the steep slope, then all of a sudden, the five-man rescue team had the litter at their feet on level ground.

When Alice saw Patty lying there with her eyes closed, she almost panicked. "Patty! Baby?"

Patty's eyes popped open, and when she saw her mother and Charlie, her expression shifted to one of relief. "Dan said I could open my eyes when I heard your voice," Patty said, and then started to cry.

"Please, sir, can I carry my little sister out of here?" Charlie asked.

Pittman glanced at the EMTs. "The ambulance is

on-site. If she's able to be moved that way, let him. I want Dan and the dog up on solid ground before that storm hits."

They unfastened the straps holding the girl down, and Charlie picked her up.

The rescue team went back down with the litter as Charlie held Patty close to his heart. Alice was hugging the both of them. "I'm so sorry this happened, Pitty-Pat. We're going straight to the doctor," she said.

"Booger found me, Mama, and Dan found us."

"I know," Alice said. "Dan is a very special, very brave man, isn't he?"

Patty nodded. "I think we should keep him as our friend forever."

Alice sighed. *Out of the mouths of babes*.

And then Patty saw her teacher. "Mrs. Milam! You came back for me! Did Judy tell you I fell?" Patty asked.

"Not when she should have. But you don't worry about Judy," Connie said as she gave Patty a quick hug. "In fact, you don't worry about any of those girls anymore. I know what they've been doing, and it's going to stop, okay?"

Patty's lower lip quivered. "They liked me last year. I don't know what I did wrong," she said, and started to cry.

"You did nothing wrong!" Alice said. "Charlie, let's go."

Patty nestled against her brother's chest as he cradled her against him, then they followed the Leggitt brothers, who led the way out.

As they were walking, Patty suddenly remembered. "Charlie, Dan said to tell you to wait up top for them, and he'd make sure Booger got back safe to you."

"Okay, honey," Charlie said.

By the time they walked out, the wind had turned into a blowing mist. The EMTs loaded Patty into the ambulance, and with Alice's promises that she'd be right behind them, Patty Conroy gave herself up to strangers once more.

"Let's go!" Alice said to Charlie.

"You go on, Mama. I'm gonna wait for Dan and Booger. I need to make sure they get up safe, too. I'll see you at the hospital or at home."

Alice frowned. "Are you sure?"

"I have to, Mama. I brought Booger out here. I'm the one who should bring him back. Dan will bring us home."

"Yes, okay," Alice said, then watched him loping back into the woods.

Another gust of wind came, and with it raindrops. She got into her car and headed for Blessings.

Chapter 10

IT WAS RAINING WHEN CHARLIE GOT BACK TO THE rescue site, and just in time. From what he could hear on the radio traffic, they were bringing Booger up, and the old dog hadn't wanted that ride. He'd gone down on his own and obviously wanted to go back the same way.

He hoped Booger hadn't tried to bite anyone. He never had before, but he was stuck on that ledge with strangers. Charlie didn't know how he would behave. So he watched anxiously, trying to see through the downpour. When he finally saw the litter coming up, he dared to relax. And when they brought Booger up to Charlie on his leash, Charlie dropped to his knees and threw his arms around the old dog's neck.

"Way to go, boy! Way to go! You found Patty, didn't you?"

Booger leaned against Charlie's chest and laid his head on his shoulder. It was obvious he was glad to be back with his boy.

"He's quite a dog," Chief Pittman said.

"Yes, sir," Charlie said, then shuddered as the wind blew cold rain down the back of his neck. "Are they going after Dan next? It's going to get really dangerous coming up in this rain," he said.

"Yes. They're taking some regular climbing equipment down to him first, which will help them get him up. Don't worry, Charlie. Dan Amos is, in many aspects, proving himself to be a very remarkable man."

Charlie nodded. "Yes, sir."

"You sure you don't want to wait in one of the cruisers back up at the entrance?"

"No, sir. I'm already wet clear through, so we'll wait here for Dan. He deserves to be met by family, too, and right now me and Booger are all he has."

"It's your call," the chief said, then moved back under some trees for shelter as his cell phone began to ring.

For Dan, the weather had turned his rescue into a very dangerous game of Russian roulette. Between the wind, the downpour, and the periodic flashes of lightning, it was a toss-up whether he would get off this ledge in one piece. Going up was going to be damn hard, but he'd do it all over again just knowing Patty was no longer trapped on this ledge.

It felt like forever that he'd been standing beneath the overhang when he heard someone shouting his name. They were back! Thank God. He walked out into the rain and looked up. A different guy than the one from before was looking down at him.

"Hey, Dan, I'm Roscoe. We brought some climbing gear. Do you know how to put this on?"

Dan saw what the man was dangling over the edge and gave him a thumbs-up. When Roscoe dropped it into his hands, Dan stepped back beneath the ledge to get the rig on, then came out into view again.

"Let's do this!" he shouted.

He wasn't looking forward to this, because to get him

up top, they were going to have to lift him off the ledge, and for a short period of time, he would be swinging in midair, buffeted by the storm, with no protection and no way to brace himself to aid in the climb.

When his feet left solid ground, he gripped the rope and held on as they began to pull him up. A bolt of lightning shot through the gap between the hills below, splintering the pine tree it hit. Dan gritted his teeth, thinking how close that had come to hitting him, and kept his focus on what was above and not below.

He was eye level with the overhang when he saw hands reaching for him. He turned loose of the rope and grabbed them. In a superhuman effort, they pulled him up and onto the slope. His heart was pounding, and his body was so cold his muscles kept knotting, but he'd never been so glad to feel solid ground beneath him.

"Dan? Are you okay?" Roscoe asked.

"I'm okay," Dan said, then grabbed on to the rope again, and pulled himself upright. After adjusting his climbing gear, they began the climb up what had truly become a slippery slope.

Charlie was thinking about the football game they had been scheduled to play tonight. First game of the season, and it had been canceled by Tropical Storm Fanny. He wondered if Mama and Patty were still at the hospital ER, or if they were home.

Thunder rumbled overhead, followed by the blast of a lightning bolt hitting far too close to where they were sitting. The rain and wind were constant. He hadn't been this cold and uncomfortable since they'd first come to Blessings and run out of money for utilities in their rented house. They'd been down to a couple of slices of bread and a little bit of peanut butter when the people of Blessings had rescued them. He took a slow, shuddering breath, trying not to cry, but it was very emotional for him to know the townspeople had rescued his family again when they needed it most. Now all he wanted was to see Dan coming up that slope.

When Booger stood up and started whining, Charlie stood up, too, peering intently through the rain and the trees. At first, he saw nothing but the shape of ghostly trees barely visible through the rain. Then he saw the men in red coveralls, but where was Dan? *Oh God, please don't let them be coming up without him! Please let him be okay!*

Then another man appeared, seemingly out of nowhere. Taller than the rest and not in red coveralls. It was Dan! Charlie could see him straining against the incline of the slope as he climbed, and was so relieved that he started to cry. This made twice in one day, but it wouldn't matter. No one would know tears from raindrops in this storm.

"Yes! Yes!" he shouted, and leaped into the air with a fist pump to God. "Thank you, Lord, thank you!"

Dan was so tired that it was all he could do to put one foot in front of the other. He glanced up, trying to judge how much farther he had to go, and saw Charlie in the distance, jumping and laughing. Dan lifted one fist into the air in a gesture of victory and kept moving toward the top.

When he finally made it up, Charlie was there with open arms. "You did it, Dan! You did it!" he cried.

Lon Pittman was still there. Like Charlie, he wasn't going anywhere until he escorted Dan Amos to his truck. "Way to go, man!" Lon said, and thumped Dan soundly on the back. "Are you okay to walk out to your truck?"

Dan slid an arm around Charlie's shoulders. "If I get shaky, I'll lean on my main man here," he said.

"I've got you," Charlie said. He wrapped Booger's leash around his wrist and then slid his other arm around Dan's waist. "Let's get out of this weather!"

Frank Leggitt was still there as well. He wouldn't, in good conscience, leave the scene until everyone was safely off his property, but he was so relieved the last person in danger had been rescued that, even in the deluge, he was smiling. "Follow me," he said, and led the way for Charlie and Dan, with Booger trotting along beside them.

Lon would be the last one to leave and was standing in the downpour watching Dan Amos as they walked away. Unless he was mistaken, Charlie Conroy had himself a hero—and maybe a man who could finally help the boy put his father's sordid reputation to rest.

Unaware of Pittman's gaze, Dan was concentrating on putting one foot in front of the other and more than grateful for Charlie's presence. His legs were turning to rubber by the time he saw the entrance gate through the trees.

Renewed by the thought of getting out of the rain, he gave Charlie's shoulder a squeeze and pointed to his truck. "We did it," he said.

Charlie nodded.

Frank Leggitt paused at the entrance. "Say, mister, are you able to drive?" he asked.

"Call me Dan, and yes, I'll be fine. Thank you for your help."

"I just wish this had never happened," Frank said. He shook their hands, and trudged back into the woods.

"Load up your dog," Dan said. "The truck's not locked."

Charlie loped to the passenger side, taking Booger with him. He put his dog on the back seat floorboard and got into the front seat as Dan slid in behind the steering wheel.

The sudden shelter from the storm was startling. They could see the storm but were no longer a part of it.

Dan put the key into the ignition and then paused, looking first over his shoulder to the big hound lying on the floorboard and then straight into Charlie's eyes. "You did good today, son. You are going to be one hell of a man one day. I hope I'm around to see it."

"I hope you are, too," Charlie said. "When I grow up, I want to be like you."

Dan felt the pain of that remark but was honored. "Thank you, Charlie. Now let's go home."

"Can I call Mama?" Charlie asked.

Dan pointed to the console between them. "My cell phone is in there. Help yourself." Then he started the engine, backed up, and drove away from the Leggitt farm and straight into Blessings.

⁓

Alice was standing in their living room, watching the storm from the windows and trying not to worry. She glanced over her shoulder to where Patty was asleep on the sofa. Except for scratches and bruising and a swollen ankle, her baby was fine. She couldn't help but wonder what had gone on at the principal's office at the elementary school, but from what Connie Milam had said when they parted company at the hospital, this incident was far from over. Then Alice had shrugged it off. Right now, all she wanted was everyone back safe and sound.

She was still standing at the window when her phone rang. She dug it out of her pocket, saw it was from Dan, and was so happy she wanted to cry.

"Hello!" she said.

"Mama, it's me! We're on our way home."

"Oh, thank the sweet Lord," Alice said. "You must both be freezing. This storm is terrible. Is Dan okay?"

"Yes, ma'am. We're just wet and cold, and I know Dan is tired. Coming up in that storm was hard…very hard."

Then she heard a pause and voices speaking in undertones before Charlie was back on the line. "Dan says to tell you he's fine, and wants to know about Patty. Is she okay?"

"Oh…yes, nothing broken. She has a swollen ankle. She's scratched up some and is beginning to show bruises."

Charlie relayed the message to Dan.

"I'm so happy to know there were no serious injuries," Dan said. "Tell her we're back within the city limits and that you will be home in just a few minutes."

Charlie relayed that message as well and then hung up.

Alice laid her phone down and then ran to unlock the front door. She already had extra throw rugs at the front door to catch the mud on their feet and the water dripping off of their clothes. And she had the big towel they used for Booger's baths hanging on the hat rack beside the door.

When she saw Dan's truck turn off the street and come up the drive, she opened the door and ran out onto the wide porch with Booger's towel, waiting for them to get out.

"There's Mama," Charlie said, and then grinned. "Hey, Booger, there's Mama with your bath towel. We're gonna get you all dry and fed. You get to sleep in the house tonight, for sure."

When Dan parked and killed the engine, Booger got to his feet.

"You get the dog," Dan said. "I'll help your mama dry him off enough to go inside."

"I'll dry him off," Charlie said. "You've done enough for us for one day."

Still, Dan got out, unwilling to go home until he was sure Alice and Patty didn't need anything more.

Booger leaped up the steps and then stood with his head down, as if anticipating a good rubdown. Charlie took the towel and got to work, and as soon as he had the dog's feet clean and dry, he took him inside to finish, leaving the adults on the porch.

Alice saw the weariness on Dan's face. He'd put his life in danger today because of them. "I will never be able to thank you enough," she said, and ignoring the fact that he was sopping wet, she put her arms around his neck and kissed him.

When her warm lips settled on his cold mouth, he sighed, then pulled her closer and returned the kiss.

Alice had already learned to be at peace with the fact that she was very attracted to Dan Amos, but this day and the fact that he was kissing her back changed attraction to want, and want to need.

For Dan, it felt like coming home, but ever mindful of her reputation and the neighbors, he stopped far sooner that he would have liked. "That was the best thank-you I've ever received, but now your clothes are both wet and muddy."

"They'll wash," she said. "I owe you. So much."

He leaned down and whispered against her ear. "I'll collect another day. Go get Charlie in a hot shower, and tell Patty I'm proud of her."

"I will, but there's something you need to know," Alice said, and dumped some unwanted news into Dan's lap. "As you know, all this wind and rain is part of the tropical storm. But it's now been upgraded to a hurricane, and the latest predication is the eye will hit landfall sometime in the next two or three days."

"Damn it. Where do they say it'll make landfall first?"

"Unless it changes course, Savannah and points north and south for about a hundred miles in either direction."

His eyes widened. "Oh, hell no! Then I don't want you all staying here by yourselves. I'm going to bring Elliot to my house to come stay with me. Preston Williams's house has withstood many storms in its lifetime, and it's on an elevation that shouldn't flood. I have reason to believe it's got a few more storms left in it, and I need to know you guys are safe, too. Say yes, pack your bags tonight with at least four or five days' worth of clothes, and I'll come pick all of you up in the morning."

Alice didn't bother to hide her relief. "Seriously? I have been so worried. That would be wonderful, but I can drive us over."

"There's no shelter for your car over there. At least here you have the garage. I know it's an open one, but it shelters your car on three sides."

"Yes, okay," Alice said. "Just give me a call tomorrow when you head this way. I'll pack tonight, and thank you."

"You're welcome, and if you are so inclined, you can thank me with another kiss tomorrow."

Alice blushed, but she was smiling.

Dan laughed, gave her a brief hug, and then ran back out into the storm and drove away.

Alice went back inside, relieved and grateful that she would not be facing this hurricane alone with her kids.

—⁓—

Albert Rankin was in his wheelchair, nervously watching the weather reports while Junior and his dad did the evening chores. They'd already brought their small cattle herd up through the corrals and into the barn to get them out of the storm. He was worried, but there was nothing they could do but pray that the hurricane shifted course.

—⁓—

Twenty miles outside of Blessings, and up in the hills where Alice Conroy had grown up, the Gatlin family was also preparing to weather the storm. Beulah had put up her chickens, and Moses and J. B. were securing sheds and doors to shelter their assortment of livestock. The one hog they were fattening to butcher had his own little lean-to in the sty. There were a couple of goats Beulah milked every day that they sheltered in their barn.

Beulah had her storm bag all packed. It was just a small duffel bag that she used to carry their important papers and keepsakes into the cellar during the spring storms, and this hurricane was no different. If they were going to blow away, at least when they found her, they'd be able to identify the body.

On impulse, she packed Patty's rag doll into the bottom of the bag, then covered it with a change of clothes and their papers on top of that.

She was baking up some food that would keep without refrigeration, and J. B. was filling some of their old milk cans with water from their well. If they ran out, they could always drink from the creek up above their house.

As she was taking pans of hot, light bread out of the oven, she couldn't help but think of Alice and the kids, hoping they were someplace safe.

And then her sons came in the back door, dripping wet as they struggled to close the door against the storm. As soon as she saw them, Beulah let go of the family she'd thrown away to focus on the one she'd kept.

As night fell, they all sat in the living room, glued to the constant weather updates, and like everyone else, praying landfall would be somewhere other than Savannah.

Chapter 11

DAN WAS OUT OF THE SHOWER, CLEAN, WARM, AND DRY. The sweats he was wearing were soft and very old. Part of his life from before.

He'd talked to Elliot earlier, inviting him to come over to stay through the hurricane and adding a little reminder that since he'd just gotten out of the hospital, he really shouldn't stay alone. Dan suspected Elliot was secretly glad, but the old fellow had had to maintain the appearance of independence by fussing just a bit before he'd agreed. Dan told him he was picking up the Conroy family to bring them to his house in the morning, and as soon as he got them settled, he'd get Elliot.

"I will have two bags," Elliot said. "One is clothes. One will be my keepsakes."

"You can bring as much as you want," Dan said. "I'm going to pick you up in the car anyway. It might still be raining."

"Oh…yes, of course, I didn't think of that," Elliot said, and then chuckled. "I am blaming that on being hit on the head and not old age."

Dan grinned. "Good call, Elliot. If you need anything between now and then, don't hesitate to call me. Otherwise, I'll see you in the morning."

"Yes, and thank you," Elliot said, and hung up.

Dan was still smiling as he headed for the kitchen.

A short while later, he was heating up a can of soup

to go with the grilled cheese sandwich he'd just made
and thinking how fortuitous it was that he'd had Laurel
Lorde attend to his upstairs guest rooms last week when
she came to clean.

Tomorrow he would get in more food and water. The
first aid shelf was well stocked, and he'd already located
plenty of batteries for the Civil Defense radio in the
pantry, as well as a stock of large candles and matches,
although this house had a huge generator wired into the
power. If the lights went out, the generator the former
owner had installed automatically kicked in to maintain
them. His admiration for Preston Williams's foresight
continued to grow. He wished he'd had the opportunity
to meet him.

Dan took the soup off the stove and poured it into a
bowl and sat down to eat. As he did, he noticed a text
message from one of his brothers and guessed it was
another "be safe" message. His parents had called him
earlier, begging him to come home before the hurricane
hit, but doing that had never crossed his mind and he
rejected the offer. The roots he was putting down in
Blessings had grown too deep. Besides, he was still the
rental manager until his offer to buy was accepted, and
it was his job to be available to the renters.

Arlene Winston, the elementary principal, had been on
a conference call for the past hour with their lawyer,
Peanut Butterman, and with the superintendent of
schools, and the president of the school board.

She'd explained what had been happening within
Mrs. Milam's second-grade class, and how it had played

out today on the field trip. They discussed the fact that Alice Conroy *could* choose to prosecute the families for defamation of character *or* sue the school district for not addressing a bullying situation.

But after listening to the evidence, Peanut answered their concerns. "So if those are all of the facts, then this is my advice, since this school year has been in session less than a month and there isn't enough evidence to prove you were even aware of the bullying. Patty Conroy never talked to her teacher about it, is that correct?"

"That's correct," Arlene said. "Her teacher, Mrs. Milam, suspected a level of discord but believed that as time passed, they'd work all that out as children often do. Patty never talked to her teacher or her mother."

"There are no precedents to support a lawsuit like this," Peanut said. "It is my opinion that the Blessings School District would never be found guilty in a court of law. The school year had just started. And unless there was a prior issue from the previous school year, awareness of these behaviors would not likely surface this soon. As for Alice Conroy suing the families or not, that would be her decision." Peanut hesitated, then added, "And personally, I wouldn't blame her if she did."

"Then my concerns have been answered," Arlene said.

"I'm fine with our lawyer's assessment," the superintendent said, and the school board president agreed.

That ended the call, and Arlene's concerns.

However, what the children had done on this field trip and what they'd been saying to Patty Conroy at school was on her watch. It was her right, and her job, to issue any punishment she deemed necessary to the children.

Judy Rowland, who had witnessed the accident and

purposefully neglected to tell their teacher immediately, was going to be suspended from school for a week.

Carlene Treat and Ruthie Wells were losing recess privileges for the same amount of time and were going to spend their school week on in-house suspension. School was going to be shut down until the hurricane had passed, and maybe longer depending on the amount of damage they incurred. But Arlene was going to send those letters to their parents tonight before Blessings lost power, notifying the girls and their parents as to what would be awaiting them when school resumed. She was also going to remind them that while this punishment would end the trouble from the school's perspective, Alice Conroy was completely within her rights to sue them for a multitude of charges, not the least of which was defamation of character.

After a quick glance at the hurricane updates running across a scroll at the bottom of the TV show she had muted, she headed for her home office to get the job done.

⁓

Because Charlie had used Dan's phone to call his mother, Dan now had Alice's number, and before he went to bed, he wanted to hear her voice and make sure she and the kids were okay.

He glanced at the clock. It was just after 8:00 p.m. when he made the call.

⁓

Both of the kids' bags were packed for the stay at Dan's, and Alice had just started packing hers when her cell phone rang. She knew it wasn't her boss because he'd already called—first to ask about Patty, and then to tell her he was closing the store until after the storm had passed. But then she saw the caller ID and answered a little breathlessly.

"Hello."

Dan sighed. Even the sound of her voice made him smile. "Hello, you. Everything okay?" he asked.

"Mostly. The kids are anxious about the hurricane."

"What about you? Are you anxious, too?" Dan asked.

Alice tossed the handful of lingerie she was holding into the suitcase and sat down on the side of the bed. "Not like I was when I thought I was going to be on my own with them. I really appreciate your invitation."

"I'm sorry it took a hurricane to be able to spend more time with you guys, but I'm grateful for the opportunity. I'm going to get Elliot over here after I get you guys settled in."

"How is he doing?" Alice asked.

"Actually, quite well, considering."

"And they still have no idea who did that to him?" Alice asked.

"Not to my knowledge," Dan said. "Say, are you or the kids allergic to any food in particular, or is there something they absolutely refuse to eat?"

"No. They're not a bit picky, and none of us have food allergies," Alice said.

"Awesome," Dan said. "Elliot is good to go as well, but I do know he likes his fruits and yogurts."

"But what if the power goes out and you can't refrigerate stuff like that?" Alice asked.

"Thanks to Preston Williams's foresight, there is a

built-in generator in this house, and it makes more than enough power to keep freezers and refrigerators running. I just need to make sure there's enough fuel on-site to keep it running."

"Really? That is likely to come in very helpful if this storm stalls out over land."

"I'm counting on that not happening," Dan muttered.

Alice sighed. "I know, but I learned a long time ago not to count on anything. Maybe some of your optimism will rub off on me."

"You already have a powerhouse under your roof. His name is Charlie," Dan said.

There was a moment of silence, and then Alice agreed. "You're right. Charlie is rock steady, even when he's scared. I say it all the time, but it's true. He's so much like my grandpa, and for that I'm grateful."

"There's not a damn thing wrong with you," Dan said. "You are a survivor, Alice. I know what that means, and it's not an easy road to walk, okay?"

"Okay, and thank you." Then the power flickered a little, and she gasped. "Oh, power surges here. Lights flickered. I need to finish packing while I can still see," she said. "We'll be ready whenever you get here. I hope it's okay that we bring Booger. He and Charlie are inseparable."

"Are you kidding?" Dan said. "Booger is my hero. Of course it's okay. Take care. Call if you need me."

"Bye, Dan. I'm glad you called," Alice said.

"I'm glad I did, too," Dan said, and reluctantly broke the connection.

But now that he'd thought about extra fuel, he decided to put on a slicker and his boots and go get it tonight. Before the power did go out. Before the gas stations could no longer pump gas.

—◇◇◇—

Power flickered again at Alice's house. That wind was blowing power lines hard enough to break them. She had to finish packing and try to get the kids to sleep, although she couldn't blame them for being uneasy. This wasn't a regular thunderstorm. The wind in this storm was just a pale version of what was coming.

—◇◇◇—

County Sheriff Joe Ryman was home from the hospital and resting comfortably in his recliner, while Deputy Sheriff Terrell and a good number of his officers had spent the day assisting the Georgia Highway Patrol in a car chase through Georgia. They had been trying to catch a man from Florida who'd kidnapped his own kids, and do it without getting anyone hurt. They'd finally caught him after he ran out of gas on an interstate in central Georgia.

But Ryman was still focused on the Elliot Graham case. They'd been working that one blind. The only clue related to criminal activity that his deputy and officers had found at the lake search were two grow sites of marijuana. They'd installed trail cameras, certain they'd catch who was tending the sites, but even that proved futile. They were beginning to believe the patches had been abandoned and had reported as much to Ryman once he was home.

It was almost as if the attack on Elliot Graham had triggered something in the attacker that sent him on the run. Ryman was halfway convinced the attacker was a transient long gone from the area. They didn't have proof that the existence of the marijuana patches had anything to do with the attack. So being a part of getting two frightened children back to their mother today went a long way in easing the deputy sheriff's frustration.

He still wanted to interview Big Tom Rankin and hear the story of how Albert was hurt for himself, but it was going to have to wait. At the moment, they had a hurricane breathing down their necks that was taking priority over everything.

After one last check with the night dispatcher, the jailer on duty, and the three prisoners they had in holding cells, Terrell hung up the phone. Wonderful aromas were coming from the kitchen. His wife, Nell, obviously had something good cooking for supper.

Judy Rowland's father, Barton, was working in his office after their supper when his computer dinged, notifying him of new email. He was expecting one regarding his work, so he quickly opened it. But it wasn't related to work. It was from the principal at his daughter's school, and he was sick to his stomach as he read it, then read it again. He'd been at the meeting at the school, but had never imagined it would morph into this.

He then kicked back in his chair, blindly staring at a picture on the wall without actually seeing it. What he already knew about this issue was that he and his wife were completely responsible. They were the ones who'd judged Alice Conroy. They were the ones who'd let Judy get away with selfish, spoiled-little-girl behavior at home, and in the end, all of that had resulted in her being cruel to an innocent child.

According to the letter, Patty Conroy had fallen over a cliff onto a ledge below. He groaned. She could have died. Judy hadn't pushed her, but she also hadn't helped try to save her. How could he make her understand how heinous her behavior had been, and that she'd played a part in endangering a little girl's life? If Patty's fall had been fatal, Judy would have grown up with a horrible blot on her soul. He glanced at the letter again, then printed it off and carried it to the living room and showed his wife.

As expected, her first instinct was to explain away Judy's actions, and then she started in on the Conroys' reputation again. That's when he stopped her.

"Shut up, Renée. The little girl could have died. She fell off a cliff onto a ledge below it. I don't like knowing my child is turning into a bitchy female like her mother."

Renée gasped. "Are you calling me a bitch?"

"Yes. I don't know what drives you, but I'm not proud of either one of us. As parents, we are, at the moment, total failures. I did some checking after Judy and I left the principal's office this afternoon. Alice Conroy does not have a single blemish on her name or reputation. Her husband wasn't always involved in drugs, but like your cousin Jazz, he tried it and got hooked. Now you better pray we don't wind up being sued for defamation of character. Patty Conroy's mother has the right and the evidence. So you will shut the hell up. Judy will be suspended from school for a week, and regarding home, she's losing privileges until after Christmas. I never thought we'd have a child who would be one of those 'mean girls' at school."

Renée shrugged and then looked away. She had no answer to his accusation. What he didn't know was that Judy was just like her. Growing up, Renée had been a mean girl, and no one had ever called her on it. Until now.

"Go get Judy," Barton said.

"Oh, Barton, let's wait until tomorrow. This will surely disturb her rest."

"If Patty Conroy had died, Judy's rest would have been the least of our troubles."

———

Ruthie Wells's father, Jack, had only heard of the incident from his wife's point of view and didn't give it much thought. It was just kids fussing at school, and they would get over it.

And then he got Mrs. Winston's letter, and the roar of rage that came out of his office scared his wife and all three of his kids.

Charlotte came running. "Jack! Jack! What on earth is wrong with you? Keep your voice down. The neighbors will hear."

"All anyone can hear is that damn storm, and you know it," he said, then pointed at the sofa. "Sit."

Beau and True, their tenth-grade twins, came running. "Dad! Dad! What's wrong?" they cried.

He pointed at the sofa. "Sit. You'll both find out soon enough, and where the hell is Ruthie?"

Charlotte's heart skipped. *Oh no. This must have to do with the incident at school.* "Now Jack, don't—"

Jack spun around, pointed a finger at her, and then shook his head.

Charlotte was so shocked by his behavior that she dropped back on the sofa without saying anything more.

"Ruthie! Get in here now!" Jack roared.

Ruthie came slinking up the hall, carrying the baby blanket she still slept with.

Jack yanked it out of her arms as she passed. "You aren't a baby anymore," he said. "Not even close to one. Go sit over there! No, not by your mother. By yourself. In my chair."

Ruthie gave her mother a pleading look. When her mother looked away, she guessed this family meeting wasn't going to bode well for her.

Jack tossed the blanket on a hall table and then strode into the living room. "Ruthie! I just received a letter from your principal, Mrs. Winston. Is it true you and your friends have been calling Patty Conroy bad names?"

Ruthie shrugged.

"That is not an answer," Jack said. "Talk, and don't lie, because I already know what you've done. I just want to hear it come out of your mouth."

Ruthie scooted to the edge of the chair. "We did what Mama told us to do. She said Patty's family sold drugs and not to play with her. Judy and Carlene's mamas told them the same thing."

Charlotte tried a glare, but she didn't have the guts to hold it.

"So, Charlotte, did you really say that, and where did you get this information?"

Charlotte shifted in her seat and then rolled her eyes toward their children.

Jack snorted softly. "Sorry, we're sheltering no one in

this family, because they need to be prepared. Everyone in town is going to know about this."

"Know what, Dad?" Beau asked.

"Know that Mama has been bad-mouthing the Conroys," his sister, True, muttered.

"You knew?" Jack asked.

She shrugged. "Dad! You're never here. You don't know half of what's going on under this roof."

Jack turned and looked at his wife as if she were a stranger. "Enlighten me, Charlotte."

"Why is everyone going to know this?" Charlotte asked.

Jack lit into her. "According to the principal's email, Ruthie and Carlene are going to be on in-house suspension for a week when school resumes, and they will lose recess privileges during that time as well. Judy will be completely suspended from school for an entire week, and it will go on her permanent school record, just like it will go on the others'."

"No!" Ruthie wailed, and started to cry.

Charlotte was starting to go to her when Jack stopped her. "You're the one who turned her into a little bully. You keep your seat."

"Oh my God, Dad! What did she do?" True asked.

Jack turned around, staring straight at Ruthie as he spoke. "Her mother told her not to play with Patty Conroy because their family deals drugs…which, by the way, is a lie. Then Ruthie and her friends not only told everyone else that lie, but they have been bullying her. Today, Patty Conroy fell off a cliff while on the field trip. Judy saw her fall and didn't tell."

Ruthie looked up. "It wasn't me! I didn't see her fall."

"Have you been mean to her?"

Still snuffling, Ruthie shrugged.

Jack sighed. "I have never been as disappointed in one of my children as I am now. I never imagined you capable of doing this. Just know that you are losing every privilege you have in this house, and that includes all of the things you play with. Now go to bed. Your mother will tuck you in later."

"I want my blankie, Daddy. I can't sleep without my blankie."

"Well, you aren't getting it. As far as I'm concerned, you can lie awake all night thinking about Patty Conroy and all the times you made her cry at school."

Ruthie wailed. "My blankie… I want my blankie."

"Go! Now!" Jack said.

"Are we in trouble, Dad?" Beau asked.

"Not unless you've been telling the same story," Jack said.

"I don't even know who those people are. I never heard of them, but I would not have done that," he said, and got up and left the room.

True stood up, but she was looking at her mother in disgust. "Thanks, Mom. Now everybody will be thinking we're freaks. I can't believe you did that. Ruthie is a kid. She still believes what you say," she said, and then she walked out of the room.

Jack was shocked. "Charlotte, what is she talking about? What's going on between you two?"

Charlotte shoved a hand through her long, blond hair. "Nothing. It's just a silly misunderstanding."

"I want to know what that misunderstanding is about. Now."

"Oh, her boyfriend, Grayson, was over here off and on all summer, as you know. She says he's developed this silly little crush on me, and that I knew it and encouraged it. Have you ever heard anything so ridiculous?"

It was the last thing Jack expected to hear. He stared at her in disbelief and knew within seconds she was lying. She had done the unforgiveable. It wasn't just about flirting with other men outside their marriage, which he witnessed time and again, but she'd done it with someone their daughter loved.

"Since I've watched you do that with other men throughout our married life, I don't doubt once that you did it. And for the record, flirting with your daughter's boyfriend is unforgivable."

He walked out of the room, taking Ruthie's blanket with him.

———

A few blocks over, in a neat, two-story house near the city park, the Treat family was in crisis mode. Lance Treat had come home late from his bread delivery route, tired and worried about the incoming hurricane, only to find his wife in tears and their daughter, Carlene, sitting on the stairs howling like a banshee.

He thought someone had died.

"Deidre! Sweetheart! What happened?" he said as his wife walked into his arms. He was trying to console her and still get answers. "Is Carlene okay? Is she hurt? What's happening?"

Deidre wiped her eyes and blew her nose as she stepped out of his arms and then showed him the letter she'd printed off their computer.

Lance scanned it, then gasped and read it again, this time slowly. When he looked up, the shock in his eyes was evident. He walked over to the foot of the stairs and looked up at his daughter.

"Carlene, is this true?"

Carlene upped the volume on her wail.

Lance was familiar with this stunt and in no mood to pander to it or her. "Carlene! Stop crying this instant and answer my question!" he shouted.

Carlene choked on a wail. Daddy never yelled at her. "What question?" she asked and blew her nose on the tail of her T-shirt.

"Is this letter true?" he asked. "Have you been bullying a girl in your class?"

Carlene sidestepped the question with her own version of an answer. "I never touched her. I didn't see her fall."

Lance went up the stairs, grabbed her by the arm, and escorted her downstairs before she knew what was happening, then sat her down in a chair in the living room. "That's not the right answer," he said.

Carlene blinked. He was really quiet. She'd never seen him like this. "I don't know what 'bullying' means," she muttered.

Lance glared at the two of them. "Have you been mean to her? More than once? With Judy and Ruthie?"

Carlene looked at her mother. "I did what you said. You told me not to play with her, so I didn't. Why is everyone mad?"

Lance reeled as if he'd been gut punched, then slowly turned to his wife. "What in God's name have you done? Why would you ever tell her something like that?"

Deidre was crying now, too. "Renée and Charlotte said Patty's family sells drugs. They told their girls not to play with her. You know they're my best friends, so I told Carlene the same thing."

"And now, according to this letter, you know it was a lie. A little girl could have died from that lie, and you and your best friends have opened all of us up to being sued." He pointed at Carlene. "Your mother told you something that wasn't true, and now our family is in trouble. Not Patty's family. Ours. How do you think it's going to feel having people point fingers at us and call us names?"

Carlene started to cry again. "I don't know," she wailed.

"Well, you're both about to find out. And you better pray Mrs. Conroy doesn't sue us, because we would have to sell our house to pay for it."

"I'm sorry, Lance!" Deidre cried.

His shoulders slumped. "So am I, Deidre. So am I."

—◆◆◆—

Unaware of all the ensuing drama after her fall, Patty Conroy limped out of her room and into her mother's room.

Alice was only half asleep and not the least bit surprised to see her baby's silhouette in the doorway. "What's wrong, baby? Are you scared?"

Patty nodded. "Can I sleep with you?"

When Alice threw back the covers and patted the mattress, Patty limped to the bed.

It hurt Alice to see her daughter hurt. She was still too thin, even though their life was better off than it had been in years, and when she curled up on her side, Alice pulled her close against her belly and covered them up. Patty wiggled a little and then settled. Alice fell asleep with the sweet smell of Patty's shampoo filling the room.

Down the hall, Booger was curled up on the rug beside Charlie's bed and whined after a particularly loud crack of thunder.

Charlie rolled over and reached off the side of the bed until he found his dog and then patted him. "It's okay, Booger. It's just the wind."

A few minutes later, the house was quiet inside, while the wind continued to blow, and the rain kept coming down.

The night passed, and the new day dawned just the way last night had ended. In wind and rain.

Chapter 12

I<small>T WAS</small> 7:00 <small>A.M., AND THE PARKING LOT AT THE</small> P<small>IGGLY</small> Wiggly was full of cars. Everybody was there for the same reason Dan was, although he had actually shopped for himself four days ago when the tropical storm had not swayed from its course. But he hadn't thought about bringing in company then, so he hoped there was still enough on the shelves to feed four more.

He grabbed an empty shopping cart out in the parking lot and ran to get out of the rain, pushing it as he went. Once he was inside the teeming store, he headed for the canned food aisles. He hadn't eaten this stuff in years, but he'd grown up on it. Vienna sausages, Spam, tuna in foil packets, potted meats, and then he moved on to the deli area, where he tossed in some rolls and bread wraps that were still on the shelves and got some prepackaged sandwich meats and several varieties of cheese, plus yogurt for Elliot. He moved up the bread and cracker aisle, which was nearly cleaned out except for the old-fashioned saltine crackers. He put some of them in the basket, then headed to the soup aisle, then to the canned fruit. He knew he could cook on the camp stove he had in his truck if he had to so he tossed in a twenty-pound bag of potatoes. There weren't any eggs, but he had several dozen at home. The only milk still on the shelves was a few gallons of skim milk. He took three and left the rest for others

in need. There were three cases of bottled water. He
took two and then added canned juices to supplement.
Next, he headed for the aisle with paper products and
tossed in three giant packs of toilet paper, then swung
by the pharmacy for extra bottles of alcohol and some
over-the-counter painkillers.

One of his renters saw him in the aisle, looked at his
basket, and frowned, thinking Dan was taking all that
for himself. "You taking in boarders or something?"
he drawled.

"Four and a dog so far," Dan said, and walked on,
leaving the man with an embarrassed look on his face.

It was seven forty-five by the time Dan got checked
out and all the purchases loaded in his truck. He drove
home through the rain in haste, unloaded everything,
and put up only the deli meats and cheeses that needed
refrigeration. He'd deal with the rest when he got back.

His phone beeped, signaling a weather update. He
read it, then gave Alice a call. She answered so quickly,
he guessed she'd been waiting for it.

"Hello?"

"It's me," Dan said. "Are you all ready?"

"Yes," she said.

"Then I'm heading your way. See you in a few."

He locked the house on the way out the door and
then set the alarm. He hadn't done that in the daytime
since he'd moved in, but people do strange things in
hard times, and he had no doubt there were people who
would go hungry when this happened for lack of money
to stock up. Some would leave to stay with friends or
family, and some would steal.

The wind was beginning to pick up a bit as Dan got

back in his truck. By the time he reached Alice's house, it was hard to walk against it.

They came out in haste with Charlie in the lead carrying all three bags and Alice holding Booger's leash.

Dan took the bags and put them in the back seat of the truck, then went back to carry Patty and put her in the back seat. When Alice sat down in the front, he handed her the box of food to hold.

Charlie ran back and came out with a big bag of dog food, locking the door behind him and then bolting toward the back seat. "That's everything," he said.

Alice's whole demeanor was one of calm. "Everything that matters," she said, pointing to her family in the back.

"Then hang on," Dan said. "I want to get you guys inside before it blows us off our feet."

He caught a glimpse of Patty's face as he was looking in the rearview mirror to back out. She was staring intently at the back of his head. He smiled at her, then winked, and she put a hand over her mouth to stifle a giggle. When he reached the street and shifted gears, he glanced at Alice. Her profile was in repose, her hands loosely gripping the box of food.

"How's your hand?" he asked.

She lifted her hand and wiggled her fingers. "Healing, I do believe. I never made it back to the doctor's office. We are so grateful to be staying with you, aren't we, kids?"

"Yes, ma'am," Charlie said.

"Me, too," Patty said.

"And me, three," Alice said.

"And me, four," Dan said, which made Patty laugh.

When Booger suddenly woofed, they all laughed.

Even the old dog had to have his say. Dan turned the windshield wipers on high and accelerated.

They reached the house, and he disarmed the security system as they were driving beneath the portico, then let them in the house through the kitchen. He grabbed the bags from the back seat of his pickup truck as Charlie got his dog and the rest of his family out and into the house. Then Charlie went back for the sack of dog food as Dan went back for the box of food they'd brought to share.

Dan carried the bags with their clothes up to the top of the stairs and then set them down and pointed down the upstairs hall.

"My bedroom is the master. It's the last one at the end of the hall on the right. I'm going to put Elliot in the one next to me on the right. You guys take your pick of the other four as to where you want to stay. Alice, I will tell you now that the one at the far end just across from my bedroom is the next largest and also has a king-size bed, if you want to keep Miss Patricia with you."

Patty beamed. "Mama! He called me Patricia."

"I heard that," she said.

"I'm going to leave Charlie in charge of moving your bags so I can go get Elliot. Is that okay, Charlie?"

"Absolutely!" Charlie said. He handed Booger's leash to Patty and picked up the bags as Dan took off downstairs.

Alice watched him go, then followed her kids down the hall as Dan slammed the kitchen door shut and headed across the street to Elliot's house with his windshield wipers on high.

—⁓—

Lovey had debated with herself about even opening Granny's up this morning, but she felt like there were too many people in town who depended on her for breakfast, and so she'd opened, but there was a 10:00 a.m. closing sign on the door, which was a warning to customers to eat fast and go home the same way.

Mercy had come to work when Lon did. It was 5:00 a.m., but she'd need every bit of that time to get biscuits mixed and baked, since Lovey usually opened at 6:00 a.m.

At 7:00 a.m. three men drove up from different directions, parked, and then walked in together.

"Table for three," Barton Rowland said, then followed Lovey to their table. As soon as she was gone, Jack Wells and Lance Treat picked up their menus. They scanned the choices, and the moment the waitress came by with coffee and then took their orders, their conversation began in hushed voices.

Barton took the lead, because he was the one who'd organized this meeting. "So how do you guys feel about the principal's letter?" he asked.

Jack Wells ducked his head. "Ashamed."

Lance nodded. "Pretty much the same way," he said.

"Then we are all on the same page," Barton said. "I have to admit I was aware my wife had told Judy not to play with a girl at school, but I didn't realize the girls had taken that to a whole other level."

Jack sighed. "I didn't know any of this was going on. I'm taking part of the blame for being a workaholic. When I'm home, I now realize I don't pay enough attention to my family."

Lance nodded. "Same here. Totally shocked, ashamed,

and horrified pretty much sum up my feelings. I have no issues with the girls' school punishments, but I read my wife the riot act for letting her friendships influence her decisions."

Jack glanced at Barton. "Mrs. Winston warned us that Mrs. Conroy had the right to sue us on several counts if she wished it. I think the biggest one would be defamation of character," he said.

Barton shoved a shaky hand through his hair. "I think we should talk to Mrs. Conroy. Not only express our horror and regret that this ever happened, but assure her our girls will never harass her daughter again."

"I guess," Lance said. "But when? This is hardly the time, and we don't have any contact information for her, so we can't call."

"I'll get the information," Barton said. "I think we should call her now, while this horror she lived through yesterday is fresh in her mind, to prove our sincerity. If we wait, it would seem to me that we did it as an afterthought."

"I think you're right," Jack said. "You get me a number and I'll call her, gladly. Later on, we can have a group meeting with our wives and daughters and make them apologize to the little girl and her mother in person."

"Oh, I'm definitely for that," Barton said.

"Me, too," Lance added.

"Then it's decided?" Barton asked.

They gave him a thumbs-up, and then their breakfasts arrived. Conscious of the rising wind, they quickly ate, over-tipped their waitress for coming to work in this weather just to serve their meals, and then headed home.

The moment Barton Rowland got inside his house and into his office, he called Arlene Winston's residence. When he asked her for Alice Conroy's phone number, she refused.

"No. I will not give out one parent's private number to another parent without permission. And I'm not going to even call and ask if she wants to speak with you until you tell me why you're calling her. I won't stand for any more harassment from any of you."

"Oh, no! No! I didn't explain myself properly," Barton said. "We are horrified by what happened. All three of our daughters have lost all of their privileges at home for months to come. We support your decision and choices of punishment. We have also expressed huge displeasure to our wives about what their hateful gossip has caused. There will be group apologies from our wives and daughters, too, but not until after the storm has passed. However, Lance, Jack, and I feel like something needs to be said to Mrs. Conroy immediately to express how horrified we are. If we left it for later, it would seem to us as just an afterthought."

"I see," Arlene said. "Well, here's what I can do. I will call Alice Conroy, and if she wishes, I will give you three men *only* her phone number. But if she says no, I expect you to honor her wish."

"Yes, yes, that's fair, and thank you so much," Barton said. "I'll await your call."

Arlene disconnected, then got on her laptop, accessed her school records, and got Alice's number and made the call.

It was just after 10:00 a.m.

—∿∿∿—

By ten, the crew at Granny's was dividing up the leftover biscuits and baked goods that wouldn't survive power outages. Lovey had a small generator that was wired in to the walk-in freezer. Elvis, the fry cook, made sure it was filled up, and then they left, anxious to get home.

Lovey paused in the doorway and looked back into the dining area.

"Please God, let this still be here when the storm is gone," she said softly, then locked the door and ran toward her car.

All around Blessings, other businesses were already dark. The neon Open signs were off, the night-lights on. And store after store on both sides of Main had been boarded up with Closed signs posted.

Blessings was as ready as she could be for what was coming.

—∿∿∿—

Dan saw Elliot watching from the side door of his two-story brick home and made a U-turn in the drive, then parked so that Elliot didn't have more than fifteen feet to walk from his house to Dan's truck, but he hated that Elliot was going to have to walk in the rain. So he hurried to the door and knocked.

Elliot answered immediately. "I'm ready. I have a good supply of food here already boxed up. Shall we take it?"

Dan saw loaves of bread and many cans of soup and canned meats and smiled. This would definitely bolster up what he'd purchased that morning. "This is great.

We'll use it if we need it, okay? Now are these two suitcases all you're taking?"

"Yes," Elliot said, and buttoned his raincoat and then pulled the hood up over his head.

"Let's get you inside the truck first," Dan said, and went out the door, then held on to Elliot's elbow as he walked him to the truck and settled him in the passenger seat.

"These are my house keys," Elliot said. "As soon as you have everything loaded, would you please lock the door? It's a dead bolt, so you'll need the blue key."

"Yes, sir," Dan said, and palmed the keys as he headed back to the house.

Dan got both bags in one trip and put them on the back floorboard, then loaded the box of food into the back seat before going back to lock the door.

"Here are your keys," he said, and dropped them into Elliot's outstretched hand before starting up the engine.

Elliot set his security system from the truck seat, and then Dan drove back across the street. This time when he parked beneath the portico, Charlie was at the door, waiting to help.

Dan got Elliot out, and then the older man waved both of them away.

"I'll get myself into the house and wait for you by the door," he said, leaving Dan and Charlie to carry all his things inside in one load.

When Charlie picked up the box of food, Dan patted him on the shoulder. "You have an amazing work ethic, Charlie. I sure appreciate the help."

"You're welcome," Charlie said, and hurried inside.

Dan followed up with the two bags. Once inside, he

locked his truck from the steps and then shut and locked
the kitchen door as he went inside.

Elliot was standing in the middle of the kitchen
floor, looking all around at the familiar furnishings.
"Everything is still here but Preston," he said, and then
sighed. "Ah well, such is life. Where do you want me to
go?" he asked.

"How do you feel about stairs?" Dan asked.

Elliot smiled. "I feel just fine about them. My bedroom is upstairs at home. I will have no problem."

"Awesome," Dan said. "Charlie, just set the box of
food on the kitchen counter. I'll deal with it later. Elliot,
follow me."

"Let me carry a bag," Charlie said, and then took one
out of Dan's hand and started toward the stairs while
Dan paced himself to Elliot's stride.

———

Alice and Patty had taken Dan's advice and chosen the
bedroom across the hall from his. It had a king-size bed
and an en suite bathroom as well.

Charlie's room had a full-size bed and a smaller bath,
but both rooms had interior storm shutters somewhat
hidden beneath curtains and drapes. Being able to close
them from inside the house was a safety feature for the
upstairs windows.

They set their suitcases against a wall and quickly
headed downstairs. Patty was carrying her doll, and
Charlie was carrying her as they descended. Until the
swelling in her ankle went down some, stairs were not
a good idea. Alice had the blanket they'd brought from
home that Booger liked to lie on. As soon as they got into

the living room, Charlie set Patty on the sofa, then made Booger's bed in the living room next to a heating vent.

The old dog sniffed the blanket, felt the nearby warmth, and despite the strange surroundings, flopped down on the blanket and stretched out.

Patty immediately started playing house behind the sofa, crawling about on her knees or scooting from one place to another on the seat of her pants, while Charlie and his mama headed for the kitchen.

"I think Dan's back," Charlie said, then looked out and saw them pulling up. "Mama, I'm going to help get Mr. Graham's things inside."

"Then I'm going to go back and stay with Patty. I'd just be in the way here with only one good hand."

She was on her way out of the kitchen when her phone began to ring. She glanced at the caller ID. It was Patty's principal. Lord, she hoped there was nothing else for them to deal with and answered cautiously.

"Hello?"

"Alice, this is Arlene Winston. Sorry to bother you at home, but I've had a request from Judy Rowland's father. He has asked me for your phone number. He assures me it's strictly to apologize to you and Patty. I think he's sincere. I've known him for several years, but it's totally your call."

Alice sighed. "I guess it's okay."

"Then I'll let him know," Arlene said. "Are you and the children going to be alright? Do you need any assistance?"

"We're fine. Dan Amos has invited us to stay with him, and he's invited his elderly neighbor, Mr. Graham, to stay here as well. I'll be honest, I was really anxious about being at home alone with my kids, but I do feel easier now."

"That's wonderful," Arlene said. "Mr. Amos is quite the hero."

"He is to us," Alice said. "I have Patty back with nothing worse than bumps, bruises, and a swollen ankle."

"Of course," Arlene said. "So, now that I have your okay, I'll be passing your number to Mr. Rowland. Oh, by the way, his name is Barton."

"Okay," Alice said, and dropped her phone into her pocket as she went back to Patty.

Dan was upstairs getting Elliott settled in his room when Alice's phone rang again. When she saw the caller ID, her heart skipped a beat. Instead of going back to where Patty was playing, she returned to the unoccupied kitchen to answer.

"Hello," she said.

"Mrs. Conroy, this is Barton Rowland. Thank you for allowing me to call. I couldn't spend another night without talking to you and telling you how horrified I am by what my wife did, telling our daughter to ostracize your little girl, and even more by what she and her friends have been doing at school."

Alice sighed. "Yes, well…thank you."

Barton could tell she was less than impressed, and he couldn't blame her. "I want you to know that Judy has lost all privileges here at home until after Christmas. I also want you to know that I consider my wife's behavior nothing short of disgusting. It won't be happening again, and when this storm has passed and life has settled a bit, my wife and daughter will be apologizing to you in person."

"They need to apologize to Patty as well," Alice said.

"Yes! Absolutely…and they will. So, I won't keep you, and I thank you for being so courteous when you didn't have to be. Stay safe, and don't be surprised if Carlene and Ruthie's fathers call you as well. We had a meeting this morning and agreed that the first order of business to this mess our children made needs to be apologies."

Alice was surprised. And it appeared she would get two more calls. "Thank you," she said.

"One last thing," Barton asked. "How is your daughter? We were told she hurt her ankle."

"She is alive, which is a miracle. Her ankle isn't broken, but it's swollen, and she's scratched and bruised from falling off the mountain onto that ledge."

Barton shuddered. "Again, I'm so sorry."

Alice disconnected. She was through talking to him, and she didn't much care what he thought about her hanging up in his ear.

Barton, however, wasn't very encouraged. He swallowed past the lump in his throat as he made the call to Lance and Jack.

Within minutes, Alice received another call, this one from Jack Wells, and directly after his call, Lance Treat made his apology, with a third vow that their wives and daughters would apology to Patty and to her in person.

She thanked them for calling and let it go. Right now, surviving this hurricane was on the top of her list.

Dan had gone to the kitchen to begin putting away the groceries, then saw her on the phone and left to give her privacy. She'd seen him leave, and as soon as she'd hung up, she went looking for him and found him sitting in the living room listening to the constant weather updates.

"Dan, I'd gladly help you put groceries away if you'd tell me where they go."

"That would be great," he said as he got up and headed back to the kitchen with her. "I started to do it earlier and then didn't want to interrupt your calls. Is everything alright?"

She shrugged. "Those were all calls from the girls' fathers. If they're to be believed, they are horrified by their wives' and daughters' behavior. They all apologized profusely. And after the storm is over, their wives and daughters will be apologizing to us all face-to-face."

Dan listened without comment. This was all her rodeo, but he would make sure no one changed the rules on her.

Then Alice picked up packs of toilet paper. "Do these go in the pantry?"

"Yes. Paper products on the shelf to your right," he said, and together, they got everything put away.

While they were working, they could hear laughter coming from the living room, which made Dan smile. There hadn't been laughter in this house since he'd moved in.

"When they're having that much fun, I better see what's going on," Alice said, and left him on his own.

The kitchen was quiet now, and too still. Pretty Alice had taken the energy with her.

Dan was still smiling as he turned up the volume on the television in the kitchen to get a new weather update, and then was glad he did. For the first time since the storm had formed out in the Atlantic, it appeared to be

changing course. The closer the eye moved toward land,
the more it veered to the north. Right now, the new pre-
dictions for landfall were for the central storm surge to
hit both the Carolinas. This didn't leave Georgia out of
danger by any means, but having the eye further up the
coast was great news. The bad news was that the eye
was still two days away from landfall.

Dan felt the weight of responsibility. There was no
way to predict how long this kind of weather would
last, but it most certainly would leave Blessings without
power, and it remained to be seen how much flooding
they would endure. Savannah would certainly suffer
flooding, but Blessings was an hour or so southwest and
on land much higher than along the coast. Still, it felt
like a reprieve as he went into the living room. There
was far too much fun going on in here without him being
a part of it.

Lon Pittman was still at the police station. He'd stay on
the job throughout this storm until rescues were out of
the question, even though he was anxious to get home to
Mercy. He'd sent everyone home, even the dispatchers. As
of now, there was only one other deputy on duty with him.

Harold and Myra Franklin had the plate-glass windows of their florist shop boarded up and were huddled
around their television at home, watching all of the news
and updates.

Johnny and Dori Pine were safe inside their new
home while their three boys were in the den playing.
Dori knew that whatever Johnny's younger brothers,
Marshall and Beep, were playing, Luther, their toddler,

was probably messing it all up. But the boys didn't care. They thought everything Luther did was funny. Johnny, as usual, was taking good care of them all. Their house was as sound and storm-proofed as he could make it, so Dori's only concern was the storm itself.

Mike and LilyAnn Dalton had shut down their gym and day spa yesterday. Rachel Goodhope and her husband had shut down their bed-and-breakfast until the storm passed. Outside of town, Jake and Laurel Lorde were riding out the hurricane inside the house with their daughter, Bonnie, and her pet chicken, Lavonne, who was residing inside an empty dog kennel Jake had brought up from the barn.

Peanut and Ruby Butterman were as ready as they'd ever be for what was coming.

The girls from the Curl Up and Dye were scattered. The manicurist, Mabel Jean Doolittle, had driven to Atlanta two days ago to stay with family. Vesta and Vera Conklin, the other two stylists in the shop, had driven all the way to Tulsa, Oklahoma, to stay with their older sister and her husband.

Lovey Cooper was hunkered down in her home, a little anxious, but it was far from being her first hurricane.

Melissa Dean was so grateful for the big two-story brick home she had inherited, and her storm preparations had been done two days earlier.

Everyone in Blessings was ready.

Main Street in Blessings, Georgia, looked like a ghost town. If it wasn't for the lights still on in some of the houses, it would look like the whole town had been abandoned.

As for the farms and houses in the surrounding countryside, their owners had done their due diligence, too.

Big Tom Rankin and his son Junior were inside with younger son Albert, who was still using a wheelchair. Their animals were in shelters, but if the winds got bad, Big Tom didn't think they'd all hold. He'd called to check on his girlfriend, Ethel Shook, only to find out her son had come after her yesterday and taken her back to his home farther inland. Big Tom felt fairly safe in their house, but part of the farm was in a place prone to floods.

And twenty miles farther inland from Blessings, Beulah Gatlin and her boys, Moses and J. B., had all the shutters shut on the house, the outbuildings shored up, and all of their livestock under shelter.

Now it was just a waiting game.

Chapter 13

It shouldn't have been dark this early, but the rain was blowing sideways, obliterating everything, including a sunset.

Residents of Blessings were on lockdown. Babies were crying, unable to sleep from the roar of the wind and rain. Older children were trying to play games to ignore the storm, and teenagers were still texting their friends, admitting to them how scared they were but pretending nothing was happening in front of their parents.

A portable shed in the backyard of the house where Ruby Dye used to live before she married Peanut Butterman had lost the roof over an hour ago, and once that was gone, the shed collapsed and blew through a neighbor's fence and into the back of their brick house.

Signs had blown off of businesses.

Lights were flickering on and off in neighborhoods.

A car that had been parked out in the open had been rolled over onto its side and slid down the driveway and into the street, blocking it from both directions.

Privacy fences were gone. Trees were down, and Main Street in Blessings had a river of water that was curb high and spreading outward.

In Judy Rowland's home, supper was served in silence, and Judy, eyes swollen from crying, was certain that the raging storm was just part of the punishment coming down on her head.

In Ruthie Wells's home, her father was madder at her mama than he was at her, and Ruthie wasn't sure why.

Carlene Treat couldn't quit crying. She was so humiliated and horrified by the outcome of their behavior that she didn't ever want to go back to school again. Deidre was also in the doghouse for being one of the instigators who got the girls in trouble, and had nothing more to say to anyone.

Carlene sat in her chair at supper, her head down on the table as she continued to sob until the salad wilted and the gravy on her mashed potatoes cooled and congealed on her plate. Lance was heartsick for his daughter and angry at his wife. Finally, he picked Carlene up from the supper table and sat down with her in his recliner in the living room. She was still in his arms when he began to rock, talking to her in a soft, low voice, explaining in simple words that he still loved her. That he would never stop loving her, but that she could never be mean like that to anyone again.

She listened, and her eyes grew heavy as he continued to rock, and when she finally fell asleep in his arms, he closed his eyes and cried with her.

Across town, everyone under Dan's roof was in the kitchen, eating hot soup and cold sandwiches and pretending they didn't hear what was going on outside.

Alice had brought over two pies from her freezer, and one cherry pie had already been reheated in the oven and was cooling on the counter, ready to be eaten. In the utility room just off the kitchen, they could hear a steady crunch as Booger ate his kibble.

They were all laughing and talking when Alice noticed Patty had suddenly gone quiet. Afraid she was hurting, Alice reached for her. "Patty? Are you okay? Do you feel bad, honey?"

Patty shook her head, but now everyone was silent. She looked at her mother, then at Charlie, and then her gaze rested on Dan. "Daddy said you were coming."

Dan felt the blood running out of his face. He looked first at Alice, and then back at Patty in disbelief.

Alice slid a hand across Patty's shoulders. "What did you say, honey?"

Patty leaned back in her chair, her gaze fixed on Dan's face. "I woke up in Daddy's arms," she said. "He told me not to be afraid because you were coming to get me."

"Sweet Jesus," Dan whispered, remembering how calm she'd been when he first saw her.

"You didn't tell us that you knocked yourself out when you fell," Alice said.

Patty shrugged. "I was just asleep, and then I woke up in Daddy's arms."

"Were you awake when Booger got to you?" Dan asked.

Patty nodded. "He barked at me from up, and then jumped down to me."

Dan sighed. "I wondered."

Alice glanced at Charlie. He was sitting so still he didn't appear to be breathing. He'd been so angry with his father for so long that she wondered what he was thinking.

"You were just dreaming," Charlie muttered.

Patty frowned. "No. I woke up before I talked to

Daddy. He said you were mad at him, but that it was okay. He said he was sorry he hurt you."

Charlie shuddered. He wanted to run, but his legs wouldn't move. When he felt the tears running down his face, he quickly wiped them away.

Patty was still looking at Dan, waiting for a response.

Dan glanced at Patty and then made himself smile. "I'll bet that made you feel better, knowing there were people who were coming to help you."

She nodded.

Charlie's eyes narrowed. "You wouldn't be saying all that if you'd known him."

Dan shook his head. "Maybe…maybe not. But I know one thing for a fact. It's all forgiven now."

"What do you mean?" Charlie asked.

Alice groaned. "Charlie, just let this be. There's been enough drama in the family today to last a lifetime, and from the sounds of that storm, it is far from over."

Charlie ducked his head. "Sorry."

Dan stood and began gathering up their plates. "Charlie, help me clean the table so we can cut into your mama's pie. I even have ice cream to cool it off."

The moment passed as Patty clapped her hands. "Pielamodel. Yay."

Elliot had been silent up until now, but hearing Patty mispronounce pie à la mode struck his funny bone. He chuckled, and then he laughed aloud. "I'll have some of that pielamodel, too, if you please."

Alice watched her son as he began gathering up the plates, and then when he set them in the sink, there was a moment when Dan said something to Charlie. She didn't know what it was, but Charlie ducked his head, and when he looked up, his shoulders straightened as if a burden had been lifted.

Then Dan turned to his dinner guests. "Who wants pie straight up, and who wants a scoop of vanilla ice cream on it? I already have Elliot and Patty's preferences. Miss Alice, what is your pleasure?" he asked.

She almost said *My pleasure is you*, but caught herself. "I'll have what everyone is having, please."

By now, Charlie was into the moment with them. "Pielamodel for me, with two scoops, if you please."

Dan laughed. "And I'll take three. I'll cut the pie. Charlie, if you would, do the honors with the ice cream."

"Yes, sir," he said, and took it from the freezer. At that moment, the lights flickered but never went out.

"I guess we better eat fast, or we'll be dining in the dark," Elliot said.

"You forget Preston's built-in generator," Dan said.

Elliot's eyebrows arched. "Yes! Yes, I did forget, but just for a moment. Let me tell you how handy that generator was years back during the college playoffs. It was just after Christmas, and we were all in the living room watching the Alabama–Georgia game. It was the last four minutes of the game. They were tied when the power went off. I swear you could hear the groans all over town. Except Preston's generator kicked right in, and there we were. The only house in town with wired-in power and the ability to watch the end of the game."

"Who won?" Charlie asked.

Elliot rolled his eyes. "Oh, that bunch of Bama boys. By a field goal. It was a terrible thing to see," he said, which made everyone laugh. He patted his stomach as

Charlie served the first dessert to him. "Why, thank you, boy," Elliot said.

Alice smiled. She'd taught her children to serve elders first, and he'd done it without a reminder from her.

The kitchen got quiet as everyone dug into dessert.

Dan looked up and winked at Patty. "I'm gonna eat all my pie like this from now on," he said.

She wiggled with delight, and the evening passed.

Later, when Alice was upstairs with her kids and tucking them into bed, she pulled the covers up to Charlie's chest and then sat down on the side of his mattress. "You were a man today, Son, in every sense of the word. I just want you to know how proud I am of you."

Charlie closed his eyes, and when he opened them again, they were full of unshed tears.

"That's what Dan said. That Daddy was surely very proud of the man I was becoming, and that one day when enough time had passed, I would be able to see that, too. He said it was always okay to be angry if I needed to be, but that I couldn't waste my life by staying that way."

There was a lump in Alice's throat that felt too big to swallow, but when she opened her mouth, it melted away. "Dan is a very wise man, I think," she said.

Charlie nodded. "I like him, Mama. A lot. It would be okay with me if you guys ever went out, like on a date."

Alice blushed and was grateful the room was in shadows. "Then, should the need arise, I thank you for the support."

He smiled. "You're welcome, Mama. I just want us all to be happy."

She leaned over and kissed his forehead. "Just so you know, Dan lost his wife and son in an explosion, too."

Charlie's eyes widened. "Why?"

Alice shrugged. "He used to practice criminal law. I think he put a bad man in jail who wanted to get even. He put a bomb in Dan's car, but his wife and son drove it first and they're the ones who died."

Now Charlie was whispering. "Is that why he has that scar on his face?"

She nodded. "Now go to sleep, quit worrying about grown-ups, and be a kid like you're supposed to be, okay?"

Charlie grabbed her arm. "I love you, Mama."

"I love you, too, Charlie Conroy. More than you will ever know."

"Is the storm going to blow us away?" he asked.

"I think we're as safe here as we could ever be to ride this out. Just have faith. Sleep well, Son. If you get scared, I'm right next door, okay?"

He nodded.

"Want the night-light left on?" she asked as she glanced up at the open door to his bathroom.

"Might as well, so I can see to get around."

"Did you take Booger out earlier?"

"Yes. Dan showed me a good place out of the wind and rain that's attached to the house."

"Okay, then. Sleep tight."

"And don't let the bed bugs bite," Charlie said as she closed the door behind her.

Alice smiled, then walked a few steps down to her room and went in. As usual, Patty was asleep on two-thirds of the bed, so Alice pulled her over to her own side and then got in and covered them both. She looked down at the shadows on her baby's face and tried to wrap her mind around the fact that Marty's spirit had been with her on that ledge. It would be a while before she would fall asleep, and then when she did, she dreamed they were drowning.

The power had gone off in the night, because when Dan woke up the next morning and went down to make coffee, he could hear the generator running. It was a massive one and would run for a lot of hours before he needed to refill it.

"Thank you, Preston," he said as he put water in the reservoir, filled the filter with coffee, and put it on to brew.

The wind was no longer a howl. It was a roar, but with all the windows shuttered, the house felt gloomy. He couldn't see out, even though that was for their own protection. He sat down at the kitchen table and turned on the television for an update.

"…clocked at one hundred twenty miles an hour, and the brunt of the storm continues to bear slightly north. Latest prediction is that the eye will make landfall within the next twenty-four hours. Flooding along the coastal region of Georgia is already happening, and water will continue to rise. People are advised to stay indoors. If you travel, it is at your own risk. Emergency services are not available for anyone."

"Is that the new storm path?" Alice asked as she entered the kitchen.

Dan's heart skipped at the sound of her voice. It was

hard to believe that she was in his house, in his kitchen, at the beginning of a new day. "Good morning, Alice. Yes, that's the new path."

"That's good, right? I mean, the worst has moved north, hasn't it?"

Dan got up and pulled out a chair for her to sit. "Yes, that's good news for us, hurricane-wise. But the side drafts of that circling monster often cause their own versions of hell. Massive tornadoes, hard, straight winds... and the floods. We'll see what nature has in store for us in the next twenty-four hours. That's when the eye should make landfall."

The coffee had finished brewing, and he poured them each a cup and sat back down.

"Umm, thank you," she said.

"Were you able to sleep?" he asked.

She rolled her eyes. "Not much, but not because of the storm. Sleeping with Patty is like sleeping with a little lamb. You know how they jump and hop and flop all over the place?"

Dan laughed. "That bad, is she?"

Alice nodded. "Yes, and while we're talking, what's that sound?"

"Oh…that's the generator. The power is off. Probably all over the area. Not just in town."

Alice shuddered at the sound of rattling shutters. "God, I pray everything holds together."

Dan reached across the table and grasped her hand. "Whatever breaks can be fixed or replaced. We focus only on staying safe…staying alive, okay?"

"Yes. Okay," she said, and blew on her coffee to cool it, because it was still too hot to drink.

"Hey, while that's cooling, I want to see what's happening," Dan said. "Want to take a walk with me upstairs to look out? We can open the shutters from inside."

She nodded.

They got up together, and as they left the kitchen and crossed the hall to get to the staircase, without thinking, he laid a hand in the middle of her back as if he were a blind man and she was his eyes, leading him through the pitfalls.

Alice liked the feeling of his hand on her back. It made her think there was a tether between them. It would be wonderful to be attached to a man like Dan, knowing that no matter what came, they faced it together.

They climbed the steps to the second floor in tandem and then went straight into the first bedroom on the left, because the windows in that room faced the street.

The wind seemed louder here—higher up. They moved to the windows in total silence, and just before Dan opened the shutters, he paused. "Step back, honey. Let me make sure it's safe enough to do this."

She moved aside, but her eyes were widened with anxiety, watching as Dan turned the latches and then swung one shutter against the wall. "Sweet Lord," he whispered, as he pushed the second shutter aside as well.

"Let me see," Alice said, and snuck under his arm to look out.

The visibility was about fifty yards. After that, the wall of rain obliterated whatever was beyond that. He could just see Elliot's house, but nothing beyond. As they were watching, a huge piece of red corrugated iron blew past so fast they couldn't read the writing that was on it.

Alice flinched and jumped back, right into the solid rock of Dan's chest.

"Oh! I'm sorry," she said. "That startled me."

Dan quickly fastened the shutters closed and then put his hands on her shoulders. When she didn't pull away, he slid them down her arms and pulled her close.

Alice relaxed, letting her body weight rest against him.

"If this feels like a bad idea, just tell me no. I won't be offended," Dan said.

"What do I say if it feels like a good idea?" Alice whispered, and then heard the soft rumble of what might have been a laugh.

"For starters, I'd settle for a yes."

Then Alice turned within his embrace to face him. With the light from the window blocked, they were in shadows again, but the glimmer in her eyes and the slight part in her lips were like beacons. He cupped her cheeks and lowered his head.

At first, the kiss was warm and gentle, but it soon turned to hard and hungry. The thought crossed Dan's mind that this should have felt awkward, but it didn't. It just felt right.

It had been two years since a man's lips had been on hers like this, and Dan was only the second man ever to kiss her. That first kiss at the hardware store had startled both of them, but this one they'd seen coming, and neither one had stopped it.

When they finally stopped, Dan wrapped his arms around her. "Please tell me you felt that as much as I did," he said.

"You mean the part where the fuse lit and sent the rocket straight through the top of my head?"

"Yeah, that part," he whispered, and kissed her again, but quicker and purposefully less potently.

Alice sighed. "I think we need to start breakfast or something."

"Oh, we already started something, so breakfast should be next," he said.

Alice laughed, wrapped her arms around his waist, and hugged him. "I love how you make me feel," she said. "Like I'm real again."

Then they left the bedroom and hurried back down the stairs. Within a few minutes, Elliot joined them, and soon afterward, Charlie came down, carrying Patty. As soon as they reached the kitchen, he put her down in one of the chairs.

"Good morning," Dan said, as he set a plate of toast on the table between the butter and the jelly.

"Morning, Dan," Charlie said.

Patty was quiet, listening. "What is that sound?" she asked.

Elliot was sipping coffee and full of life today. He leaned across the table, whispering to Patty. "Do you mean the one that sounds like a dragon's roar, or the sound like a little clown car driving back and forth through the house, looking for a place to park?"

Patty collapsed into giggles. "Dragons aren't real," she said.

Elliot slapped his leg in mock surprise. "Then it must be the clown car looking for a place to park."

She giggled. "Cars can't drive in houses."

Elliot's dark, bushy eyebrows arched. "Then what on earth could it be?"

Alice carried bowls to the table, and Dan brought cereal and milk. "It's the generator, Patty. That's a big motor that keeps the electricity running in this house."

Patty frowned. She still wanted to play. "I think it might be a giant's empty tummy growling."

"Then you better eat your breakfast before yours starts growling as loud as his," Charlie said, pointing to the two boxes on the table. "What kind of cereal do you want? This one, or that one?"

"The one with three elves," she said.

"Snap, Crackle, and Pop," Elliot said. "I know them well. Funny chaps, but definitely a noisy lot."

Patty was enchanted.

And so the meal progressed. It was good there was so much silliness to begin a day that was bound to get worse.

Charlie watched his mother and Dan as they cleaned up the kitchen, and then smiled to himself. They liked each other. It was a start.

Elliot was anxious about his house, so Dan took him back upstairs and opened the shutters again so the old man could look out.

"Still in one piece!" he crowed. "She's a strong old gal, like this one. We'll be safe."

But Dan was focused more on the streets. It wasn't at flood stage, but the water was up to the curbs. *Please God, don't let it get any higher.*

Chief Pittman had taken all the officers off duty and sent them home before midnight last night, but now he was pacing the floor at home, worrying about the people in his town. They'd lost power with everyone else in town but were unaware of it until morning.

Mercy woke up first and tiptoed through the house, her long, bare legs moving quickly as she went to the kitchen to see what was in the freezer above the refrigerator and carried it all to the chest freezer in the utility room. All of that would stay frozen longer. The house was chilly, and she wished she'd at least put on some jeans but was afraid she'd wake Lon.

On a good day, she would have started coffee and breakfast, but the best she could hope for today was to get in bed to stay warm.

Lon had all of their windows boarded up, so she had no way to see what was going on outside, and she was scared. As soon as she got the food put up, she hurried to bed and slipped under the covers to stay warm.

Lon turned over in his sleep. Reaching for her was pure instinct.

Mercy closed her eyes and snuggled against him, grateful he'd made the decision to stop all emergency services until it was safe to be outside. She thought of Elliot at home on his own, but had to believe he would weather this storm as he had all of the others in his life.

She was thinking of her sister, Hope, and her husband, Jack, and his brother, Duke, all out on the family farm in their beautiful two-story home. Wondering how they were faring, and all of the animals they had to care for. She was wondering how well cattle could swim when she finally fell back asleep.

Chapter 14

THE FIRST HOUSE TO GO DOWN IN BLESSINGS WAS ACROSS the street from the Blue Ivy Bar. It so happened to be the one Alice and her kids had moved into when they'd first come to Blessings. The big trees in the yard went down, uprooted by the hurricane. One slammed into the house, blown by the wind, while another tree fell on it. The fact that it was empty was fortuitous, because no one would have been able to get to anyone inside, had it been occupied. And power poles were down all over Blessings, and windows that weren't boarded up were gone.

Lovey was at home alone, wishing she'd accepted Ruby's invitation to go stay with her and Peanut. She had a bathroom window that hadn't gotten boarded up, so she stood in the bathtub, crying helplessly as she watched their wonderful town breaking apart. It occurred to her that she shouldn't be standing there, but before she could move, a nearby tree broke off from its roots and slammed into the side of her house. The impact of the blow broke the glass in front of her, and part of the tree was now inside her house. She'd been thrown out of the tub, hitting the side of her face on the sink as she fell and then landing on the floor between the tub and commode, with her right arm awkwardly bent beneath her.

She had felt the bones snap, but the pain was sharp

and so intense that she passed out in the broken glass, unaware of the rain being blown into the bathroom, or that the bathroom door had blown shut from the force of the wind and rain coming through the opening over the tub. Once she came to long enough that she tried to get up, but the moment she moved, she passed out again from the pain.

All of the lights were out in Dan's house to save generator power, except the one in the living room. Elliot had gone upstairs to nap, and both of Alice's kids were belly down in front of the television when Booger let out a quiet woof.

Charlie jumped to his feet. "Booger needs to go out. Dan, is it still safe to take him out through the old servants' quarters?"

"I'll go with you to make sure," Dan said, and gave Alice's knee a quick pat as he got up.

Patty rolled over on her back and watched them leave, then crawled across the floor and up onto the sofa where she scooted up beneath Alice's arm.

Alice snuggled her close and kissed the top of her head as Patty leaned against her. "What are you thinking about?" Alice asked.

Patty shrugged. "Just stuff, Mama."

"Stuff like school?"

Patty nodded.

"You don't have a thing to worry about," Alice said. "Your days of being bullied are over. Trust me."

"Really?" Patty said.

Alice smiled. "Yes, really."

Patty sighed. Alice felt her body relaxing.

A few moments later, the men were back. Booger circled his blanket and then flopped down on it.

Charlie flopped back down on the floor, not unlike his dog, and Dan sat back down on the sofa. Patty opened her eyes. Dan winked at her, and before Alice knew what was happening, Patty rolled over on her knees and crawled up in Dan's lap and tucked her head beneath his chin.

Alice watched Dan pull the afghan from the back of the sofa and cover her up. Then he wrapped his arms around her and sighed.

She felt like she should say something, but Dan seemed to read her mind and shook his head. "I imagine it's the storm. This is how we sat while we were waiting to be rescued. I know she was scared, but she trusted me. I think she's scared again, but I make her feel safe. And the weird thing is…she makes me feel safe, too, because I already know how to do this…and I've missed it. So much."

Charlie had been listening without letting on, but when Dan said that, he rolled over and sat up. "What did you mean? About knowing how to do this. Do what?"

Dan shrugged. "I already know how to love kids."

Charlie stared—first at Dan, and then at his mama. "So, do you know how to love their mama, too?"

Alice's face flushed.

But Dan grinned. "Yes, I know how, but that's only half the battle. Mamas also like to be in charge of who they do or don't love, so your opinion is good, but it isn't enough. Just leave all that to grown-ups, okay?"

Alice relaxed, but she gave Charlie a look. He grinned

and then rolled back over onto his belly. Within a few minutes, he'd dozed off, too.

Alice started to get up and then bumped her bandaged hand. "Dang it. I will be so glad when this gets well. I'm afraid we'll still be dealing with this hurricane when the time comes to get the stitches removed."

"I can take them out. Don't worry about that," Dan said.

Alice laughed. "Well, of course you can. What's the matter with me?"

Dan looked a little sheepish. "I didn't mean for it to sound like an all-knowing *that*."

Alice poked his arm. "You mean…climbed down from the mountain to perform another miracle 'that'?"

He grinned. "More like climbed off my horse to get the job done, but your words, not mine."

Alice scooted closer and rolled over onto her side with her head against Dan's thigh, where she curled up and closed her eyes.

The emotion welling up in Dan couldn't be denied. All of these people beneath his roof. A hurricane raging outside, and they trusted him enough to fall asleep. They'd done what he hadn't been able to do on his own. A man needed purpose, and he needed to be needed. And the best part of it all—they needed him, too.

He looked down at the little girl in his arms, then at the long-legged boy stretched out on the floor at his feet. And then he reached for Alice. Her hair was soft against his palm. He already knew what it felt like to kiss her. He wanted to know what it was like to make love with her, to sink deep into her warmth. To come apart with her beneath him. She'd given him a reason to live—really live—again. And knowing that much about her already, she would also know what it took to fix a really broken heart.

Upstairs, Elliot woke with a start. He sat up in bed, his heart pounding. He'd seen it so clearly that he knew it was not a dream. The woman was alone—trapped in a small room—and badly hurt. And he knew her.

He got up from the bed on shaky legs and stumbled to the window before opening the shutters just enough to check weather conditions. When he saw the rain blowing sideways, and the downed trees, and the water moving across the grass like the current in a river, he shook his head. Rescue was next to impossible.

"I say, Lord, if You're not going to show me a way to help, then You have no business showing me those in need, okay? So I'm asking for an answer, and time is not on our side."

With that, he made a quick trip to wash up, then put on his house shoes and went downstairs. When he walked into the living room and saw everyone asleep, he turned around and went to the kitchen instead.

Elliot liked his sweets, and he'd already seen the yogurt. He chose a little one-serve carton of peach-flavored yogurt, peeled back the top, and grabbed a spoon from the drawer.

The remote to the kitchen television was on the table. He turned it on and ate his yogurt while watching updates on the storm.

Lovey came to lying in water and in excruciating pain.

The roar of the wind coming in through the broken window was not only deafening, but so strong it took her breath away.

"Help! Help!" she cried, and couldn't even hear her own voice. "Oh my God, please don't let this be how I die."

She needed to get up out of the glass and water, but was afraid to move for fear she'd pass out again. She needed to roll off her broken arm. It was the only chance she had of getting up, but dear God, she was so afraid.

Finally, she found a way to move by pushing her feet against the tub, and then rolled onto her back, screaming with every breath until she choked on the rain now blowing on her face.

Okay girl, you have to get up now before you drown, but how? Then she sighed. She'd gotten herself down here. So now she had to get up. Grateful she still did sit-ups on a semi-regular basis, she used her good arm to steady the broken one and sat up.

Then the moment she did, the room started to spin. She dropped her chin to her chest and closed her eyes until the spinning stopped, then tried it again. She was dizzy, but not as much as before. It occurred to her that she might have suffered a concussion when she hit the sink, and she felt along the side of her head and cheek. There was a huge knot on her cheekbone, along with what felt like dozens of shards of glass in her face, yet with all the rain, she couldn't tell how much she'd been bleeding. But she was halfway to her goal of standing up, and she needed to get out of this room, so she had to move.

Without thinking about how to do it, she just reached

for the tub, pulled herself as close to it as she could get, and then leaned into it, headfirst. When she felt the weight of her body shift, it shifted the broken bones as well. By the time she was on her knees, she was sobbing.

"God help me!" she screamed, and used her good arm to lever herself up.

The moment she stood up, the blast of the wind coming through the window nearly blew her down again. In a panic, she reached for the doorknob to get out of the room and realized she couldn't open the door. The force of the wind had her trapped, and she was getting dizzy again. Afraid she would fall back on the floor, she sat down on the lid of the commode and leaned against the wall beside her.

"Lord, help me. Please send help."

———

Dan was in the kitchen cooking hamburgers. Charlie was at the counter beside him, slicing tomatoes and lettuce, while Alice was getting mayo and mustard from the refrigerator. Patty was already seated and chattering away to anyone who would listen, but this time, it was Elliot who was silent.

Dan noticed it, but hesitated to say anything. But as soon as he finished cooking the last burgers, he added them to the platter and carried them to the table.

Elliot looked up at him and smiled, but Dan could tell he was preoccupied.

"What's up?" Dan asked.

"Someone is hurt and in serious need of help, but no one can get to her yet."

Dan frowned. "Who's hurt?"

"The woman who owns Granny's Country Kitchen."

Alice overheard what they were saying and gasped. "Lovey? Are you talking about Lovey Cooper?"

Elliot nodded.

"What happened to her?" Dan asked.

"She was looking out a window when something blew against her house and broke the window. I don't know details, but she has multiple cuts, a concussion, and a broken arm."

"Oh no," Dan said. "That means wind and rain are coming in that broken window, too."

Elliot looked off into space as if he was watching what was happening to Lovey play out.

"She's trapped in the room. She can't get out," he said.

"Why not?" Alice asked.

"The wind slammed the door shut, and she doesn't have the strength to open it to let herself out. There are several inches of water on the floor, and the roar of the wind is so loud no one will hear her."

"We have to do something," Dan said. "I need to call Chief Pittman, and as soon as it's safe enough, he'll get her and take her to the ER."

"How long before the eye makes landfall?" Alice asked.

"Not sure," Dan said. "Hey, Miss Patricia, would you please turn on the TV?"

Patty grabbed the remote, happy to help, and moments later, they were watching film of different places along the coast and the damage they had already suffered. But there was a bit of good news. The eye was going to make landfall before morning. When that happened, the wind would lay, and if the streets weren't too flooded, they would be able to get to Lovey and get her to the ER before the back side of the hurricane hit the shore.

"I'm going to call the chief. Start without me. I won't be long."

"We'll wait," Alice said, and sat down at the table as Dan left the room.

—⁓—

Mercy Pittman was in their garage with her cell phone plugged in to the charger in the car, talking to her sister, Hope, making sure they were all okay.

Lon was sitting in the living room, listening to storm updates on his battery-powered radio, when his cell phone rang. It was the first call he'd gotten since everything shut down, and when he saw Dan Amos's ID, he quickly answered.

"Hey, Dan. This is Lon. What's up?"

"So, Elliot Graham is staying here with me, along with the Conroy family, and he just dropped a basket of bad news."

"What's wrong?" Lon asked.

"You know he knows stuff, right?" Dan said.

"Yes. I don't really get how he does that, but I also don't belittle something I don't understand. What did he tell you?" Lon asked.

"I'll make this short. Lovey Cooper is trapped in a room inside her house. The storm blew something against her house. It broke the window in the room she was in and, and blew the door shut. She's cut up, likely has a concussion and a broken arm."

Lon groaned. "This is my worst nightmare. I don't have even one vehicle heavy enough to take out in this storm."

"Well, that's not all. There's too much pressure against the door for her to get herself out. She's trapped."

"No, no, no," Lon said. "I have to figure something out. Thank you for letting me know."

"Yes, you're welcome, but here's a thought. If you can get it organized, maybe you can rescue her when the eye makes landfall…"

"Yes. If the streets aren't flooded, we can easily send fire and ambulance, but if they are, I need to figure out plan B."

"We have power. Preston Williams had a huge generator wired into this house, and I have plenty of fuel to keep it running. If you and Mercy need shelter, I have some extra bedrooms."

"Oh, that's good," Lon said, "and thanks. So far we're good, and thanks for letting me know about Lovey. I'll figure this out. You guys stay safe, and tell Elliot I said thank you."

"Will do," Dan said, and then disconnected. He went back into the kitchen, rubbing his hands. "Message delivered. The chief says thank you, Elliot."

"He is most welcome," Elliot said.

"Can we eat now?" Patty asked.

"Yes, we can eat now," Dan said, then they all joined hands.

Alice listened to the soft rise and fall of Dan's voice as he blessed their meal and knew from the ease with which he was doing it that he'd grown up in this way. He added a special blessing of protection for Lovey and ended with an amen.

"Amen," Elliot echoed, and then tucked his napkin into the neck of his shirt.

Patty giggled, but then did hers the same way.

Alice wasn't going to argue that point. It was probably right where it needed to be for Patty. Hamburgers had a tendency to drip, and Patty only wanted ketchup on her burger, which made her supper tonight an accident waiting to happen.

Booger had finished his kibble while Dan was on the phone, and now he lay in the doorway, watching them eat.

The whole time Dan was putting his burger together, he couldn't help but think about Lovey, trapped and in a terrible situation. She'd spent so many years feeding the people of Blessings, and when she needed help, no one could get to her. He said an extra prayer for her, hoping the chief figured out a way to perform the rescue.

———

Lon's phone battery was fading, and he needed to make some calls, so he headed to the car, moving through the house with a flashlight. When he opened the door, Mercy jumped and squealed, which alerted her sister, Hope.

"What's wrong?" Hope asked.

"Oh my gosh, Lon just scared me," Mercy said, and then looked at Lon's face. "Hope, hang on a second. What's wrong?" she asked.

And then he told her, knowing it was going to hit her hard.

Mercy was in tears and put the phone on speaker so her sister could hear. "Hope, did you hear all that?"

"Yes, I did," Hope said. "I can't bear to think of her trapped like that with no medical attention."

Mercy reached for Lon's arm. "What can you do? We can't just leave her there."

"Right now, there isn't a vehicle in Blessings that could get out of a driveway, let alone drive across town. But when the eye passes over land, there will be a lull. Even if it's not passing directly over us anymore, the wind will decrease. We'll get her then."

"How long is that?" she asked.

"At least four hours," Lon said.

"Oh my God," Mercy moaned. "Poor Lovey. She must be in horrible pain. I can't believe this is happening."

"Hey, Lon," Hope said. "Jack and Duke are standing here, too. Jack wants to tell you something."

"Sure. I'm here," Lon said.

"Hey, Lon… This is Jack. You said there aren't any vehicles that would get you around until the wind lays, but that's not entirely true. A big dozer—even one of the oversize farm tractors—could easily drive through deeper water and would not be as impacted by the wind as regular vehicles. Especially a really big dozer. Just an FYI," he said.

"Good call, Jack. Thanks for the info. I'll talk to you later. My battery is about to die."

"Oh! Use my phone!" Mercy said. "It has eighty-five percent power right now. Hope, I'll check in with you later. Be safe." Then she hung up and handed Lon her phone. "Do you need privacy? Do I need to leave?" she asked.

"No, not at all. Unless you want to go back in the house, you're fine."

"I'm staying, then," Mercy said. "Do we know anyone with a dozer?"

"Yes, we do," Lon said, and plugged his cell phone into the charger and googled the phone number for Pine's Dozer Service.

—⁓—

Johnny and Dori Pine were busy trying to get their three boys settled down for the night. The boys were scared and had been ever since the wind and rain began, so they'd made pallets in the master bedroom for Johnny's two younger brothers, Marshall and Beep, and their toddler, Luther, would be sleeping with them.

Dori was in the utility room getting a flashlight apiece for the boys to have in bed with them, and she and Johnny had their flashlight on the table beside the bed.

Johnny was on the floor reading to the boys by flashlight as Dori came back into the bedroom. She handed one light to each boy, and the delight on their faces was obvious as they turned them on and lit up the book Johnny was reading like it was under a spotlight.

Dori grinned.

And then Johnny's cell phone rang. "Hey, honey, see who's calling, okay?"

Dori circled the bed on the run. "Hello? Yes, he's right here. Just a moment," she said, and then handed the phone back to Johnny. "It's Chief Pittman."

"Trade places with me," he said, and took his phone as Dori sat down to finish the story. "This is Johnny," he said as he walked out into the hall.

"Johnny, this is Lon Pittman. I need to ask you a question, and then maybe a favor."

"Ask away," Johnny said.

"Do you have any of your dozers at your house? Not

down the street. Not a half block away in some storage unit. At your house."

"Yes, I do. I unloaded it in the backyard two days ago because I guessed it might be needed for cleanup in Blessings after the hurricane passed. Why?"

"We just received word that Lovey Cooper has been injured. It's reported she may have a concussion, multiple cuts, and a broken arm. And she's trapped in a room with the full blast of the hurricane wind and rain blowing in on her."

"Oh no!" Johnny said. "Why can't she get out? Is the door blocked by debris?"

"It's the force of the wind. She can't get it open. Here's what I want to do, if you're willing to help. In about four hours or so, the wind is supposed to decrease when the eye makes landfall. For a time, it will be safe enough to get out. I thought that would be our best chance to get to her, but I'm not sure how the flooding is going to be."

"I can take a dozer through pretty deep water. The engine sits high…almost above the tracks."

"That's what I was hoping for," Lon said.

"But four hours, Chief? That could be the difference between saving her or recovering a body," Johnny said.

"I know, but—"

"Chief, I have a big cab on that dozer. She doesn't live more than five blocks from me. I can get to her. I can chop a hole in that door and get her out that way. I can get her to the hospital in that dozer. I can, Chief. I can do that."

"You have a young family, Johnny. What if that wind stops you… What if it rolls you over?"

"No, sir. That's not gonna happen, because the one that's here weighs over five tons. What's the top wind speed right now?"

"Maybe a hundred and twenty-five miles an hour. Maybe more."

"Five tons, Chief. That wind isn't going to blow it anywhere. I'll let you know when I get her into the cab, then you let the people at the hospital know I'm bringing her in to the ER. Tell them to get the biggest, strongest people they have working there to meet me. No trying to load her on a gurney. Just carry her inside out of the wind."

"I don't like this. It's totally against my better judgment," Lon said. "If you get stranded, there is absolutely no one who can come help you or come get you."

"Yes, the hurricane is a monster storm, but I drive monster rigs. It will be okay," Johnny said. He hung up, but when he turned around, Dori was standing in the doorway to their bedroom with a look of terror on her face.

"Oh, Johnny, what did you just promise to do?"

"Lovey is hurt. She's trapped in a room in her own house. She's cut up, possible concussion, and a broken arm. And the storm slammed the door shut, and there's no way she can open it to get out. She's hurt and trapped, with a hurricane swirling around her head, Dori. I have to go. I can do it. And you know the big Cat can make the trip." Then he wrapped his arms around her. "Lovey did a lot for us, remember?"

"Yes, I remember," Dori said.

"Now it's time to help her," Johnny said.

Facing the inevitable, Dori turned loose of her fears.

"Get your slicker. Take the big spotlight lantern. Take an ax. Don't forget your cell, even though we could lose cell power at any minute."

"Thank you, baby. I'll be back. I promise."

"I know you will," Dori said. "Just get her to the ER, and tell her we're praying for her."

Johnny nodded, ran into the bedroom to put on his work boots, got a heavy jacket with a hood and the lantern flashlight, and then dug around in the garage until he found the ax he used to chop firewood for their fireplace. The last thing he put on was his hooded slicker, and Dori was still at his heels. He turned around and grabbed her by the shoulders.

"I'm going out now. I'll shut the door. You go back to the boys and tell them I'll be alright."

"I will," she said, then threw her arms around his neck and kissed him. "I love you, Johnny Pine. You come back to us in one piece. You hear?"

"I hear you. I will be okay. I promise. I wouldn't offer to do this if I didn't have my Cat D9 here at the house. You know how big and strong those dozers are, right? Now go. I'm not opening this door until you're out of the kitchen."

She ran out of the room.

Then he grabbed the ax and the spotlight, and out the door he went. He had to push to get it open, then push harder to get it shut, and he could see Dori's cookbooks flying off the shelf. Even though the brunt of the storm was hitting the front of their house, the wind was everywhere.

Johnny knew it was bad out, but he wasn't prepared for the wind's true force as he climbed up onto the dozer with the ax and the big lantern. Once inside the cab, he got the key from under the mat and started the dozer up. The sound was almost lost in the storm, but he could feel the vibration of the engine beneath his feet as he put it in gear.

Within a couple of minutes, he was out of their driveway and making his way up the street. The water was at least six inches deep, but the wind in no way slowed down his progress. The things Johnny had to watch for were downed lines and flying debris. When he finally reached Lovey Cooper's house and saw most of a tree up against the front of her house, he guessed there were limbs inside it, too.

He tensed as he rolled up into the drive and then around to the back side of her house. He would have to force the back door to get in, but damage to her house had already happened. He just needed to get her out of it.

He parked the dozer as close to her back patio as he could get, then pocketed a couple of screwdrivers from his toolbox, grabbed the ax and the spotlight, and got out of the cab. As he did, he was hit with a wind so strong that it nearly blew him off the dozer tracks on which he was standing. He crouched down and held on as he crawled off, then ran to her back door. He grabbed his largest screwdriver and jimmied open her back door. Seconds later, he was inside. He struggled to push the door shut, but to his relief, it caught. Then he pocketed his tools, took the ax and the light and began moving through the unfamiliar layout, shouting Lovey's name.

Lovey was going in and out of consciousness. Her biggest fear was that she'd wind up back on the floor, and if she did, she'd never have the strength to get up again.

The water was up around her ankles, and she could only imagine where else it was spreading inside her house. She was partially shielded from the wind, but she was feeling faint. Just as she was about to slide off the toilet, she caught herself, bumping her broken arm in the process. She screamed—a shrill, high-pitched scream that Johnny heard. It made the hair stand up on the back of his neck, and then he was running toward the sound and calling her name.

At the same time, Lovey thought she could hear someone shouting. She started crying again. No one knew she was trapped. They didn't even know she was hurt. It had to be the wind.

Help me, Lord, help me!

Then she thought she heard a noise—like someone pounding on the bathroom door. And then she very faintly heard a man shouting her name.

"In here!" she screamed. "I'm in here!"

"Get away from the door," he shouted. "Did you hear me? Get away from the door."

"Yes, yes!" she cried, and then held on to the sink for stability, watching as the bathroom door suddenly splintered, and then splintered again and again until she realized someone was chopping a hole in the door that was big enough to get her out.

When she saw a man's hand reach in and start pulling away huge chunks of the door, she started to cry. "Thank you, Lord, thank you."

The man kept chopping and pulling and chopping

and pulling away shards until the middle part of the door was gone.

Now the hole had given the wind another place to blow, and she could see the man fighting against it as he leaned in to assess her situation. And that's when she saw his face.

"Johnny? Johnny Pine?"

He saw her mouth moving, but he couldn't hear her. Her broken arm dangled, but when he reached in to grab her, she locked her good arm around his neck and held on.

Lovey buried her face against his cheek, and somehow, they wound up in her hall. "Thank you, oh thank you," she kept saying.

"You're welcome, darlin'," Johnny said, then laid his ax and the spotlight on a hall table and swung her up in his arms, which elicited another shriek of pain.

He left the ax and grabbed the spotlight as he took off down the hall and into her kitchen. He set her back on her feet long enough to get them out onto the patio. The wind and rain were as shocking here as they had been in her bathroom, but out here there was more.

Lovey held on to Johnny as he struggled to pull her door shut, then he leaned close to her ear so she could hear him. "I'm likely to hurt you getting you into the cab," he said.

She gave him a nod that she understood and gritted her teeth as he picked her up again. When they came out from under the patio, the blast from the elements was shocking. As he began climbing up and into the cab, she grabbed on to her arm to keep it as immobile as possible. His climb up was far more difficult. Not only was he holding on to the dozer to keep from being blown away, but he had to hold on to her as well. The wind and the constant lurch of his body to and fro was true torture for her.

"I'm sorry, I'm so sorry," Johnny kept saying as he struggled until finally they were all the way up to the cab. Finally, he opened the door with one hand and then leaned in and set her down in his seat long enough to close the door and shut them in.

The watertight cab muted the sounds, and for the first time since she was injured, Lovey could hear her own voice. "How did you know? How did you find me?" she asked.

"It's a long story, Miss Lovey. Right now I need to get you to the ER, okay? And that means I need my seat back."

"Where do you need me to be?" Lovey said.

"I think you'll be safest if we start out with you tucked up in the floor beside me."

"Whatever you say. You have no idea how grateful I am for you."

Johnny took off his slicker and his jacket, spread them on the floor, and then pulled her up out of the seat, then eased her back down onto the pallet he'd made for her.

"Okay?" he asked.

Lovey was crying again, but they were tears of relief. "Yes, yes, I'm okay. I just thought I would die there."

Johnny touched her head, felt shards of glass beneath his fingers and flinched. She'd come damn close to making that happen, he thought, then got down to business and started up the engine one more time before he made that call back to the chief.

The call rang twice, and then Johnny heard Lon's voice. "Hello? Johnny?"

"Yeah, it's me, Chief. I've got her in the cab. We're headed to the hospital, which is a good distance away, but tell them we're coming."

Lon let out a whoop that made Johnny grin. "Johnny Pine, you are one heck of a man!" Lon said. "Be safe, and call me again when you get home."

"Yes, sir, I will, if we still have service."

"It is a freaking miracle that we do," Lon said. "And if Hurricane Fanny hadn't taken that turn north, we'd be in a whole lot more trouble."

"Yes, sir. I'm hanging up now." Then Johnny put the dozer in gear, and down the driveway they went, turning left onto the street as he headed for Main.

Chapter 15

"Whoa," Johnny said to himself, as he reached an intersection.

"What's wrong?" Lovey asked.

"There is a tree down across Laurel Avenue, but it's not a problem, honey," Johnny said. "We'll just jog a block east and then get back to Main that way. Are you okay?"

She was shaking, but didn't know if it was from pain or from being wet for so long. "I'm alive. I'll be okay later," Lovey said. "You don't worry about me. I'm happy to ride."

"Yes, ma'am," Johnny said, and slowly, they made their way onto Main Street, then started north toward the hospital. "We're on Main. It won't be long now," he said.

Lovey moaned an acknowledgment. Now that she was out of the wind and rain, she could concentrate on something besides blowing away. And when she did, the first bit of cognizance was the pain. She touched her face and felt glass shards protruding from the flesh and moaned again.

Johnny knew talking wouldn't help, so he stayed quiet and just kept driving the Cat forward, eyeing the strength of the water current in the streets and the low-hanging power lines. When he drove past Granny's Country Kitchen, he didn't mention that her big sign on the roof was gone. But he could see the windows were still boarded up, and unless the roof had suffered damage, she was still good to go. The water was deeper through here. At least a foot of water on the streets and more in the low spots, but it didn't affect him or their mode of travel. The big dozer sat so high up off the ground that they were in no danger of flooding out.

When he finally reached the street that led down to the hospital, he slowed down to turn. "Feel that turn? We're five blocks from getting you some help."

Lovey reached out and clasped his forearm. "You saved me, Johnny. You saved my life."

"Thank you, Miss Lovey, but I didn't do this by myself. God rode shotgun all the way here."

She was sobbing quietly as he pulled up beneath the covered drive-through in front of the ER. Through the rain, he could see four very large men standing inside at the entrance. They'd been watching for their arrival.

"Stay seated a minute, Miss Lovey," Johnny said, and got up and opened up the cab as the men came running out.

One immediately climbed up on the dozer and grabbed hold of the door and leaned in a bit to be heard. "We're going to relay her down," he said.

"She's hurt bad," Johnny said, shouting above the wind to be heard. "And be real careful of her right arm. It's broken in at least two places that I could see."

The orderly nodded, watching as Johnny Pine positioned himself just right, and then squatted down and picked her up. Just before he handed her off, he gently kissed the side of her cheek.

"I'm passing you off to the experts, Miss Lovey,"

he said, and stepped outside the cab with her still in his arms, then lowered her down to the first orderly.

As soon as the orderly had Lovey in a safe position, he turned around to pass her to the next one, who was standing lower down on the dozer. As he did, he was nearly blown off his feet. If it hadn't been for Johnny, who was still hanging on to them, they would be gone.

Then that orderly turned and gave her to the last one. As soon as she was in his arms, they all came down off the dozer and ran for the entrance.

Johnny watched from inside the cab until he couldn't see them anymore, sent a text to Chief Pittman that read "package delivered," and headed home.

It wasn't until he saw his house that he began to breathe easy. He drove up their driveway through the flood of water washing down it and then parked all the way up to the back patio where he'd had the dozer before. He killed the engine, put the keys back under the mat, and then put all of his weather gear back on. He grabbed the spotlight and then out the door he went, scrambling from handhold to porch post.

He climbed up the steps and ran for the back door. The knob turned beneath his hands, and then he was inside and using all of his strength to shut and relock the door.

He began shedding the poncho and heavy jacket, then pulled off his heavy-duty boots. He was down to the wet Levi's when Dori appeared with a flashlight and one of the blankets off their king-size bed. "The kids are asleep. My prayers have been answered. Wrap yourself up in this, and come to bed. You won't get warm any other way."

It wasn't until she came closer that he could tell she'd been crying. He pulled the blanket around himself, welcoming the softness and the warmth, then opened his arms and pulled her close, covering her up with him.

"Oh, honey... Dori, I am sorry I scared you, but she was alive. She's at the ER, and it was worth it."

Dori just nodded and kept hugging him, then led him to bed and held him close while he told her everything. He fell asleep talking about the arm Lovey had broken in two places and the glass he'd felt in her face and hair.

———

Lon Pittman sent a text to Danner Amos just after midnight. All he said was that Lovey was in the hospital and to tell Elliot that he'd saved her life.

"Thank God," Dan said to himself, and then got up and put on some pants and a pair of shoes. It was time to check the fuel gauge on the generator.

———

Two doctors stood, one on either side of an operating table under lights lit by a generator, picking glass out of their patient's face, while two nurses stood on either side of her head, gently cutting away her hair clump by clump, revealing the glass the doctors then pulled from her scalp. They'd reset the broken bones in her arm with titanium rods and screws, holding the shattered bones in place.

They'd used precious power to run the CT scan, making sure there was no internal bleeding from the blow she'd sustained to the side of her head and face, and eventually, Lovey Cooper would heal.

But she'd never be the same. She'd lost hearing in one ear, and her arm would never have the mobility or agility it had before. The scars on her face would fade from her skin, but the memory—the nightmare—would never fade. She would hear that wind for the rest of her life.

It was daylight by the time they pulled the last shard of glass from her neck.

The wind had laid.

The eye had made landfall.

False calm.

Nothing to count on.

Haste lent panic as people opened doors, squinting against a light that wouldn't last.

Water was knee deep. Many houses had flooded, and now was the time the residents could get out. They were wading through water with what they could carry on their backs, trying to get to higher ground, to friends' houses, into the school, into the churches…anywhere that offered shelter.

It wasn't over.

Dan came out the front door of his house to look at the storm damage. Alice stepped out behind him and then reached for the small of his back, taking comfort in the strength beneath her palm.

Charlie stepped out, carrying Patty to protect her healing ankle. Elliot came out last but quickly moved to the front. If Dan hadn't stopped him, he would have waded his way home.

"Not yet, Elliot," Dan said.

"Thought I might just check for damage," Elliot said.

"It looks fine from here, while the back of your head is still healing."

Elliot sighed, then nodded. "Yes, yes, of course you're right."

He stepped back, but Dan saw the longing in his eyes and knew he'd have to watch him.

As they stood, a family of six came wading down the street in front of them. The woman had a bandage on her head. One of the kids had a bandage on his arm. They appeared to be in a stupor.

"Hey! Are you guys okay?" Dan asked.

The man paused. "Tree fell on our house," he said. "We're going to the Baptist church. We heard they're taking in displaced residents."

All of a sudden, Elliot pulled out his key ring. "My garage apartment. It's never gonna flood. No power, but safe and dry. Tell them, Dan. Tell them they can stay there. Here's the key."

He pulled a separate fob off of the key ring and pointed to the two black keys. "Two keys. Give it to them."

Dan took the keys and then shouted at the family who was already moving on. "Hey! Hey!"

The man stopped and turned. "What?"

Dan pointed to the garage apartment across the street. "Mr. Elliot is offering you his garage apartment. It won't flood. There's no power, but it's safe and dry and fully furnished."

The man started back, his arm already outstretched.

Dan turned around and yelled at Charlie. "Go get food in one of those boxes. Nothing that has to be heated or refrigerated. Peanut butter, crackers, canned meats, bread."

Charlie handed Patty to his mother and turned around and ran as Dan waded out into the water to meet the man.

"Here's the key. I know you'll take as good of care of Mr. Graham's property as possible, considering the situation."

The man clutched the key Dan put in his hand and then put it in an inner pocket of the jacket he was wearing. "My name is Ellis Martin. I'm a plumber by trade, but right now out of work. We sure appreciate this," he said, smiling and waving at Elliot.

"Uh…Charlie is bringing you some food. If you'll wait a second, he'll bring it to you."

"That's wonderful!" Ellis said. "Thank you, bless you, mister."

"I'm Dan Amos. I manage about twenty rental houses here in Blessings. When all this mess is over, come back and talk. I could use an on-call plumber if you're interested."

Ellis Martin stared. "We thought we'd lost everything. This is a miracle. I prayed for a miracle, and this is it."

Charlie came running with the box. "The water isn't deep, Dan. I'd be happy to carry it for them."

"I'll carry it for them," Dan said. "You don't want to stress your mama out and get yourself hurt, too."

Charlie glanced over his shoulder. Dan was right. Mama already looked nervous. "Yes, you're right. Good call," he said, and handed the box to Dan.

"Now go back and get two cases of that water, and don't come any farther than here. I'll come back for it."

"Yes, sir," Charlie said, and started running back to the house, sloshing through the ankle-deep water.

Dan waved at Alice. "I'll be right back. In the meantime, you're in charge."

Alice grinned.

Dan laughed. "Okay, Ellis. Let's go. You round up your family and head them toward that garage apartment directly across the street."

Ellis pushed through the water as fast as he could. Dan saw him talking to his wife, who started to cry. He gave her a hug and then began leading the way to their new shelter.

Elliot watched from the porch, smiling to himself. They were happy, which made him happy he'd had something to share. He watched Dan herd them all up the stairs, then set the box halfway up the stairs and start back for the water.

Charlie was waiting, and as soon as he handed over the two cases, he went back to where his mama was standing, while Dan carried the water to the family and set the two cases on the steps as well.

Ellis had already carried in the food, and Dan could hear the family talking. He set the two cases of water up high on the steps and yelled at Ellis.

"Don't forget the water!"

Ellis popped his head out, gave Dan a thumbs-up, and he and his oldest boy came out and carried the cases inside as Dan started back across the street.

He was almost to the place where the curb should be and had slowed down to make sure he didn't trip on it going up when he saw a small plastic tub floating past. Then he caught a glimpse of something in it and turned and grabbed it before it floated past. It was a pint-size canning jar with a piece of paper inside. He let the plastic tub go, but carried the jar back to the house, climbed up the steps, and then sat down on the top step to take off his shoes.

"What's that?" Alice asked as she came out and sat down beside him.

"I don't know. It was inside a plastic tub and floating down the street. I think there's writing on the paper." Dan unscrewed the lid, pulled out the paper, and handed it to her. "What's it say?" he said as he began pulling off his wet socks.

Alice scanned it, then gasped. "Oh my gosh, Dan! It's a message! Someone needs help. There's a name and an address."

Dan reached for his cell phone. There was no signal. "Damn it," he said.

"What's wrong?" Alice asked.

"No signal. It was bound to happen."

Elliot sat down on the other side of Dan and pointed to his house. "I have a CB radio at my house. I listen to truckers all the time. If the police dispatch radio is on, I know how to find their signal."

Dan sighed. "You were bound and determined to get back to your house, regardless, weren't you?"

"You can go with me, of course," Elliot said.

"Of course," Dan said, and put the wet socks back on and then the boots. "Way easier to get these off," he muttered, then glanced up at the sky. "We have to hurry, and no dawdling through your house."

"No dawdling," Elliot said.

Alice patted Dan's knee. "I know. I'm in charge again until you two get back. Just make sure you do."

Dan leaned over and kissed her square on the mouth

before she knew it was coming. "We will hurry," he said.

"I don't hurry much anymore," Elliot said.

"You're going to be riding piggyback, mister, so don't complain."

The old man's eyes widened. "Well now, I can do that, of course. Are you sure I won't be too heavy?"

Dan grinned. "I'm sure. Put your arms around my neck now, and when I stand up, I'll grab your legs. Just lock them around my waist and hang on."

Elliot was grinning. "I haven't done this in years," he said, and as Dan was getting up, Elliot put his arms around his neck. By the time Dan was completely upright, he had Elliot safely secured.

"Here we go," he said. "Alice, put that paper in my shirt pocket, please."

Alice tucked it safely into his shirt pocket. "Be careful, you two, and just so you know, I'm watching the both of you all the way across."

Dan took off down the driveway so he wouldn't have to search for the curb below the water and then waded into the street. They made it across without seeing any more people afoot, and then he put Elliot down on the front steps. They hurried to the front door. Elliot aimed his security remote and disarmed the alarm, then unlocked the door and hurried inside. Dan was starting to take off his shoes when Elliot stopped him.

"They're fine. Follow me. The CB radio is in my library. It's down the main hall on the right."

Dan followed him through the house, then into the library.

"I thought you needed an antenna to send and receive," Dan said.

Elliott nodded. "It's up in the attic on the third floor. If I need to raise it, I can do it by hand. Have a seat. If I can get through, this won't take long. May I have the paper, please?"

Dan handed him the message and then sat down to watch. In no time, Elliot made contact with the day dispatcher, Avery Ames. "He has a CB at his home," Elliot said. "We talk at night sometimes."

Dan just shook his head and sat back and listened. He soon found out that Avery had an old stripped-down Hummer that he could use to get to the chief's house. The axle height on those vehicles was plenty tall enough to get through the water in the streets. Elliot read the note to Avery, then read it again as Avery wrote everything down.

"I know them. Message will be delivered. Straight-Aim over and out."

"Why is he Straight-Aim?" Dan asked as Avery signed off.

Elliot grinned. "His last name is Ames. So, Ames, Aim. And he works at the police station, so I guess he thought the handle was suitable. Every CBer has to have a handle."

"So, what's your handle?" Dan asked.

"Paint-Job. Fitting, of course."

Dan grinned. "Of course."

Elliot turned everything off and stood. "That's done. Now if you don't mind, I'll just take a quick look through the rooms. If something is leaking, I can at least put buckets beneath the leaks."

"I'll help," Dan said.

Within a few minutes, they'd been through the whole house, and the verdict was good.

"No leaks," Dan said.

Elliot nodded as he patted the nearest wall. "She's a fine old gal and has held up well. I'm not the least surprised."

"So, let's get out of here," Dan said. "This calm won't last much longer. In fact, I think the wind has picked up some already."

"Then let's go," Elliot said, and led the way out the front door. Again, he set the security alarm with the remote.

Dan walked down the first two steps. "Okay, Elliot. I'm used to being the cowboy, but today I'm happy to be the horse. Hop on."

And he did.

They crossed the street again and then headed back up Dan's driveway. He didn't set Elliot down until they reached the front porch.

"Whoa, Silver! Whoa, big boy!" Elliot said.

Dan was still laughing when Elliot dismounted and took himself inside the house.

Dan sat down on the top step again and removed his shoes and socks, then carried them inside. He left them in the back room to dry, then headed up to his room to change.

Alice met him at the top of the stairs. "Everything okay?" she asked.

"We got the message delivered to the police dispatcher, who was on his way to deliver it to the chief when we left the house. Our job there is done," he said, and picked her up in his arms as he reached the top, and kissed her.

She wrapped her arms around his neck and leaned into the kiss, which turned into much more than a greeting. By the time he turned her loose, her cheeks were flushed and her lips still parted.

He grinned. "What was that I said? Oh yeah… 'My job here is done.'"

Alice wrapped her arms around his waist and leaned back just enough to meet his gaze. "So, would I be playing with fire if I told you how utterly sexy you are?" she whispered.

The smile slid off Dan's face. The desire to take her to bed was so strong and so sudden that it made him ache. When he looked down into the sky-blue color of her eyes, he saw his own reflection. It was like looking at the ghost of his soul trapped within her magic, as she had already stolen his heart. Only he didn't feel trapped. He felt blessed that he had been given a chance to fall in love again.

"I don't play games, so you won't get burned. But it's only fair you know that when I want something, I go after it, and I already know I want you."

Alice sighed. "I wonder how long it would have taken us to get to this place if it hadn't been for a hurricane."

"It would have happened anyway. What we've learned about each other is that when we're faced with threat or danger, we don't run away."

Alice lifted a hand to his cheek, lightly tracing the shape of his scar. "Life gives us scars. Some are visible, some are not, but we honor the warrior, regardless."

Dan clasped her hand, then lifted it to his lips and

kissed it. "I don't want to rush you into something you're not ready for. I know it hasn't even been a year since you were widowed and—"

Alice frowned. "That's not true. I was widowed three years ago when I lost Marty to drugs. Just because he was still breathing and we were still living under the same roof didn't mean anything. I was there because of a vow…not from love."

The poignancy in her story was heartbreaking. "You mean the ''til death do us part'?" Dan asked.

Alice's eyes flashed. He couldn't tell if it was anger or regret.

"Enough about that," she said. "Go change clothes. Get dry and comfortable again, and when you're done, would you please help me undo these bandages?" She held up the hand with the stitches. "I haven't looked at it once since the doctor put the bandage on. I was supposed to go back in three days and let him look at it and put a new bandage on it. But of course, that didn't happen. I need to make sure it's okay."

Dan frowned. "That's not good. Yes, of course I'll help. Give me a couple of minutes, and I'll meet you down in the kitchen with the first aid kit."

Chapter 16

THE CHIEF READ THE NOTE AVERY BROUGHT, THEN THEY went together in Avery's Hummer to the home of Pearl Patton. She'd sent the SOS note Dan Amos had found floating in the floodwaters.

Avery pulled up into her drive first and got out. Chief Pittman was right behind him, carrying a big flashlight as they waded through water up to her bottom step. After that, it was dry all the way to her front door.

"Good thing this house was built with a crawl space beneath," Avery said. "Otherwise it would have flooded."

"There are a lot of houses like that in Blessings. The older houses all have crawl spaces, and some even have basements," Lon said, and then knocked.

There was a long moment of silence, then he knocked again.

This time he heard footsteps and the sound of a woman crying.

He tensed. It was never good when a woman was crying.

The door opened, and the old woman came out of the house with a flashlight in one hand and a pistol in the other.

Lon flinched. "Uh...Miss Pearl, is that gun loaded?"

"Well, yes, I should hope so. How else am I gonna kill that snake? It's in the hall bathroom. Dang hurricane probably floated it under my house and it found a way in. I got it trapped in there, but I'm afraid to go in, and I surely do need to pee."

Lon stifled a grin. "Yes, ma'am. We'll see what we can do. Just let me have the gun, and you wait right here."

She handed him the pistol, sat down on the sofa, then jumped up and got down on her knees to look under it. Once she was satisfied there were no snakes hiding in the sofa, she sat back down.

"Do you know what kind of snake it is?" Lon asked.

"It's a big ole ugly cottonmouth. Last time I saw it, it was behind my bathtub. I need it gone, or I won't ever sleep in this house again," she said, and started to cry in earnest.

"Which is the bathroom?" Lon asked.

"Down the hall. First door on the right."

Lon and Avery started down the hall. The eye had brought momentary calm, but the boarded-up windows in the house made it dark. They swept the corners with their flashlights and, as they reached the door, opened it slowly, then slipped inside. There was a linen closet just to the right. Lon opened it up, flashed his light, and saw a folded stack of bedsheets and a stack of pillowcases.

"Grab one of the cases," Lon said. "It would be better to carry the snake out of here in a bag than to shoot a hole in her floor trying to kill it."

"I'm sure scared of snakes," Avery said.

"So am I," Lon said. "Just hang on to the pillowcase and get ready to open it."

"Yes, sir," Avery said. "There are very few places that snake can hide in here, and she said it was behind her bathtub."

They both stood there staring at the old claw-foot tub and then backed up and peeked under it.

"Oh shit," Avery said. "There it is, Chief. Under the tub, not behind it, and that's one big-ass snake. He's as big around as my arm."

"And as long," Lon said. He looked around for something to flush it out, saw a toilet plunger behind the toilet, unscrewed the handle from the rubber head, and then poked the handle beneath the tub.

The snake slithered backward, hissing.

"Oh man, oh man, oh man, I hate snakes," Avery said.

Lon climbed into the tub, waited a few moments, and then poked the handle down between the wall and the back of the tub.

"Got it!" Lon said.

"Got what?" Avery said.

"I got the head pinned. Now if I can just... Oh shit! There it goes!" Lon shouted.

Avery screamed and leaped up onto the closed lid of the commode as the water moccasin shot out from beneath the tub.

Lon leaped out of the tub, coming down on the back of the snake with his big boot, and reached down and grabbed it right behind the head.

"Open the pillowcase!" Lon cried.

Avery popped it open and held it out as far away from him as he could.

Lon dropped the snake into the depths and then grabbed the case from Avery and tied the top into a knot.

"Okay, we got it," Lon said, grinning. "You can get down off the toilet now."

Avery glared. "I done told you I don't like snakes."

"Yes, yes you did," Lon said. "Now let's get before that storm starts back up."

"Yes, sir," Avery said.

They came out of the bathroom carrying the snake in the bag. Miss Pearl was curled up in a ball on her sofa, wide-eyed and shaking. "Who screamed?" she asked.

Avery ducked his head. "Uh, that would be me."

"Did he bite you?" she asked.

"No, ma'am. I'm fine."

"We got your snake," Lon said. "And we have it in one of your pillowcases. I'll get it back to you in a couple of days."

"I don't want it back," she said. "I'd never be able to sleep, knowing a snake had been inside it."

"Yes, ma'am," Lon said. "We'll be going now. You're safe."

"Thank you!" Pearl cried.

"You're welcome, Miss Pearl. Stay inside. That other half of the storm will be churning back up any time now."

"Yes, yes, I will," she said. "But first, thank you all so much."

And she ran to let them out, then slammed the door in their faces. They could hear her running as they came down off the steps.

"She needed to pee. Remember, Chief?" Avery said.

Lon chuckled. "So she did."

"What are we going to do with that snake?" Avery asked.

"Let it out down at the edge of town. That's the direction the floodwaters are running. It'll wash on down with the current."

They took off in that direction, and as soon as they

reached a good spot, Lon jumped out, untied the pillowcase, and dumped the snake in the swiftly flowing
water, watching as it floated out of sight.

Avery took the chief home and let him out in his
drive.

Lon gave him a quick pat on the shoulder. "Go home,
Avery, and thank you for helping."

"Yes sir," Avery said, and took off through the water,
anxious to get back to his house, while the chief went up
the drive and back into his house to get his truck keys.
He'd seen the water's depths, and there was one person
he needed to check up on, and one more notification he
felt he needed to make.

Peanut was outside putting some extra nails in the plywood over one window when Chief Pittman pulled up
into his drive. One of the pluses of the location of his
house was the hill on which it was located. There was
water running in the streets, but not anywhere close to
his house.

"Hey, Peanut, where's Ruby?" Lon asked.

Peanut frowned. "Inside. What's wrong?"

"Lovey is in surgery."

Peanut's heart jumped. "What the hell happened?"

"She got injured in some way by the storm, then
trapped in a room in her house."

"Oh, Jesus," Peanut whispered. "Ruby is going to
lose it. How on earth did you find her? How did you
get her out?"

Lon wasn't about to start a rumor about Elliot
Graham, so he skipped that part. "It's a long story, but

the bottom line is I called Johnny Pine to ask if we could use one of his dozers to get her out when the eye made landfall, but he wouldn't wait. He had a five-ton Cat in his backyard with a big cab over it and got out in the storm and went after her. He took an ax to her bathroom door and chopped a hole big enough to get her out, then drove the dozer all the way to the ER through that storm. I just came from the hospital. She's still in surgery."

"Can I get up the street in my Jeep? It can take some high water. How deep is it?"

"About a foot. It's slowly going down, but that won't last when the eye passes."

"Well, I know where we're going to be spending the last half of the storm, so I guess we better get moving," Peanut said. "Thank you for letting us know. Lovey is like a sister to Ruby."

"I know," Lon said. "Just be careful, and hurry."

Peanut drove the last nail into the wood and grabbed his tools as the chief backed out into the moving water and slowly drove away. He ran into the house calling Ruby's name.

She came out of the hall carrying some extra blankets because the wind had made the house so cold.

"What's wrong?" Ruby asked.

"Lovey is in surgery. I'll explain everything as we go."

Ruby dropped the blankets and ran back to their bedroom. She changed her house slippers for boots, grabbed an all-weather coat and her purse, and was at the door waiting for him to go out onto the portico to get in the car.

"No. I'm getting the Jeep out of the garage. Just wait

on the portico," he said. "And we have to hurry. We need to get to the hospital before the calm passes. We'll have to stay there, you know."

"I wouldn't leave Lovey anyway. You can drop me off and come back home, if you want."

Peanut swept her up into his arms and kissed her long and hard. "Nothing separates us again. Not even a damn hurricane. Wait here. I'll pick you up in the Jeep."

Ruby's lips were still tingling when Peanut came roaring up to the house. She jumped into the front seat, buckled up, and held on as Peanut rolled down the drive and then made his way through the water-filled streets, explaining what the chief had told him.

"We're halfway there," he said as he took a left turn onto Main. "Say a prayer there are no surprises beneath this water."

Ruby gasped. "Surprises? What kind of surprises?"

"The kind where the street has washed away, leaving a hole big enough to hide this Jeep in."

"Oh my God," Ruby muttered, and prayed all the way up Main, then down to the hospital.

Peanut circled around to the ER, let her out where the water had gone down, then parked a few yards away. He got out on the run, splashing water as he went, and they went into the ER together.

Once they found out Lovey was still in surgery but would be on the second floor when it was over, they ran up the stairwell.

Ruby got all the way to the nurses' desk, saw the skeleton staff and the drawn expressions on their faces, and could see how exhausted they were.

"How long have y'all been on duty?" she asked.

"Thirty-six hours," one said.

"We volunteered. We're here because we don't have kids or husbands at home," another added.

"God bless you," Ruby said. "What can you tell me about Lovey Cooper's status?"

"Are you family?" one of them asked.

"I'm all the family she has in this world," Ruby said. "Now tell me what you know, and let her surgeon know she has family on this floor."

Fifteen minutes later, Peanut and Ruby were sitting together on a sofa, holding hands without talking. All the talking had been done at the nurses' station. Now they were trying to absorb the horror of what they'd been told.

Finally, Ruby laid her head against Peanut's shoulder. "It doesn't matter if she winds up deaf in one ear."

Peanut nodded. "And it doesn't matter if her arm never regains full strength."

"Hair will grow," Ruby added.

"And scars will fade," Peanut said.

"At least I'll still have her," Ruby whispered.

That's when they heard the rain. "It's back," Peanut said.

Ruby's hands curled into fists. Her eyes were flashing through unshed tears. "Damn Hurricane Fanny. If she was a real woman, I'd shave her head bald, too."

Peanut laughed, then leaned over and kissed her again. "I just love you," he said.

Ruby sighed. "I love you, too. I wonder what's going to happen to Granny's."

"I suspect not a damn thing," Peanut said. "They'll hold it together for her until she's well enough to come back. You just wait and see."

About an hour later, a doctor came into the waiting room, saw Peanut and Ruby, and stopped short. "Hello, Peanut. They said Lovey Cooper's family was here."

Ruby stood. "We're all the family she has, Dr. Quick. How is she?"

With that, he began to explain, and ended with an upbeat note. "She came through the surgery much better than we expected. Despite the issues I just discussed, Lovey will still be able to work all she wants and do what she's been doing for the past thirty years. Just not until she heals."

"When can we see her?" Ruby asked.

"She's still in recovery, but I'll leave word at the nurses' station to come get you once she's in her room."

"Thank you. Thank you so much," Ruby said.

"You know you're stuck here until the hurricane has passed, don't you?" he added.

"I wouldn't want to be anywhere else," Ruby said.

"We'll be fine," Peanut said.

"Then I'm going to clean up and try to catch up on some sleep. I'm sure we'll talk again," the doctor said, and walked out.

"My poor Lovey," Ruby said.

Peanut put his arm around her shoulders. "She's still here, and the doctor said she is going to heal. That's all good. Now come sit with me. It will be at least another hour before they bring her out of recovery."

Ruby sat.

Peanut sat beside her and tucked her beneath his arm. "Just listen to that storm."

"Lovey is only one victim. I wonder how many others

there will be. Oh, Peanut, what if there are others that don't get rescued in time?"

"Ruby, darlin', don't borrow trouble."

"Yes, you're right. Think positive. I'll think positive, like how great it will be when we get cell phone service back."

———✳———

Alice was in the kitchen waiting for Dan and decided to start a fresh pot of coffee. She peeked in the cookie jar, saw the Oreos, and took one before replacing the lid. She had just taken a bite when Dan hurried into the room with an armful of first aid items.

"Cookie break?" he said.

"Wanna bite?" she asked.

"Not right now," he said. "I want a look at your hand. Now that I know it hasn't been tended since the day it happened, I'm concerned."

"It doesn't hurt, and I haven't felt sick," she said.

"Sit down at the table and let's take a look, anyway," he said.

Alice sat, and Dan had just begun to cut away the bandage when Patty wandered into the kitchen with her baby doll tucked under her arm.

"Whatcha' doin', Mama?" she asked.

"Come sit in the chair beside me and watch," Alice said.

Charlie was only a few steps behind Patty. "Dan, is it okay if I get a Pepsi?"

"Sure, and you don't have to ask," Dan reminded him as he began unwinding the gauze.

"Charlie, can I have a drink of your pop?" Patty asked.

"You can have your own glass if you want," he said.

"Yes, please," Patty said, and then leaned across the table toward Dan. "Charlie always gives me my drink in a special glass, 'cause he says I backwash in his."

Dan glanced up at Charlie, who shrugged and then grimaced. Then he looked back at Patty and grinned. "Backwash, huh? Filing that away for future reference," he said.

Alice laughed at her daughter. "I just love you, child, and thank you, my son, for being such a generous big brother."

Charlie grinned. "Yes, ma'am."

"I love you, too, Mama," Patty said, and leaned her head against her mother's shoulder for a closer look, just as Dan pulled off the last fold of gauze, revealing the stitches across the palm of her hand.

Patty gasped in horror. "Mama! What is that in your hand?"

"Those are the stitches. I cut it deep, so the doctor sewed the skin back together to help it heal."

Patty's voice was shaking. "Stitches like when you sew the hem back on my dress?"

"Sort of," Alice said.

"But these stitches don't stay in your mama's hand," Dan said. "When her hand heals, the doctor will just take a little pair of scissors and snip the stitch and then pull it out. There will be a little scar on Mama's hand, like the one here on my face, but much, much smaller, okay?"

Patty looked intently at Dan's scar, and then at her mama's hand, but Alice was focused on Dan's opinion. "What do you think?" she asked.

Dan turned her hand toward the light, pushing gently

on areas around the sutures. "When I do that, does it hurt?"

"Not much," Alice said.

Charlie came over with his sister's glass of Pepsi and set it down in front of her before leaning over Alice's shoulder. "Let me see, Mama."

She held up her hand.

"Dang, that's gonna be a cool scar," Charlie said.

"Cool, huh? Awesome," she drawled.

And this time Dan laughed. "Okay, Miss Alice. It is my opinion that your hand is healing well. I don't see anything that looks infected. It's still really red around the stitches, but that's normal. Come over to the sink. I'd rather just pour the alcohol on it and let it dry than swab the surface."

Alice followed Dan to the sink, leaving Charlie with Patty.

"I sure hope this doesn't hurt," Dan said as he poured a small but steady stream of alcohol over the cut.

"There's a slight burn, but only in one spot," Alice said.

"Okay, let that air-dry. No towel or paper towels, and then I'll put a new bandage on it."

"Thank you, Dr. Amos," Alice said, and then keyed back in on her children's conversation and realized it was still about backwash.

"Charlie, I took a drink, and I don't see no backwash in my pop," Patty muttered.

"Good for you," Charlie said, and handed her a cookie.

She grinned, took a big bite and chewed, then washed it down with another drink of her pop.

Charlie leaned over and looked in her glass. "What's that in your pop?" he asked.

Patty looked and frowned. "That's some of my cookie."

"Right. Backwash," Charlie said.

"But it's just cookie," Patty said.

Charlie tweaked her nose. "Your cookie…not mine. I'm not drinking your chewed-up cookie in my pop, understand?"

Patty nodded, and when Alice came and sat back down beside her, she held up her little glass. "Want a drink, Mama?"

Alice sighed. "Maybe just a sip," she said.

Charlie laughed. "Ew! Mama!"

Alice gave him a look. "How do you think you learned to drink from a glass?"

"Uh…I don't know… I guess you gave us little drinks."

"Bingo," Alice said. "At which time you were no better at it than Patty."

Charlie's eyes widened. "I never thought of that."

By now, Dan was laughing out loud. "Makes me wonder what me and my brothers shared with Mom," he said.

"I bet she and I could share some stories," Alice said.

"She's going to love you," Dan said. "Is your hand dry yet?"

Alice was still reeling from the thought of meeting his parents when he shifted his focus at lightning speed. Now she was giving *him* that look. "Is that how you tripped people up on the stand and got them to incriminate themselves?"

He grinned. "You're never going to fall for that, are you?" he said, and reached for fresh bandages.

"Not likely, and yes, it's dry," she said.

Elliot wandered into the kitchen and wanted to see

the wound, too, so she showed it off one last time. "Looks good," he said. "Healing nicely, too, like my head wound."

Dan frowned. "Except that Alice accidentally hurt herself." Then he lowered his voice so Patty didn't hear. "And someone tried to kill you."

Elliot shrugged.

Alice glanced up. "How is it that you know all kinds of stuff without seeing it happen, and yet you don't know what happened to you?"

"People like me can't see our own lives and dangers...only what happens to others," he said.

"Well, that has to suck," Dan said.

Elliot chuckled. "Yes, I suppose that's a way to look at it." Then he glanced at the kids. "Is it snack time?"

"Yes, sir," Charlie said.

"Watch out for the backwash," Dan whispered.

Elliot looked confused. "The what?"

Alice laughed. "You're safe. Patty's glass is empty."

And while they were chatting, they heard rain falling and realized that the wind had begun to blow again. Dan finished up the bandage quickly and ran to check the generator.

Alice felt a moment of panic. This brief calm had lulled them into a false sense of safety. She so dreaded what was coming.

"Charlie, when did you last take Booger out?"

"Just before I came in here, Mama. He's good for quite a while."

"Good job," she said. "So you can hear the storm now, right? That means no more running in and out of the house. Not until Dan or I tell you it's okay."

"We won't, Mama. Can we watch some television?"

"Wait and see what Dan says. He's checking the generator right now."

Dan came back, walking slower than he had when he left.

"Is everything okay?" Alice asked.

"Yes."

"Is it okay if the kids watch television for a bit?"

"Absolutely," Dan said.

Elliot reached for a cookie to take with him. "I'll go with them. Hey, guys, can we watch old TV shows like we did yesterday?"

Patty sighed. "Sorry, Elliot. Today is my turn to choose. Tomorrow is Charlie's. You get the day after that."

"Oh, alright," Elliot said. "What are we watching today?"

"*My Little Pony*," Patty said, and skipped out of the kitchen with a smile on her face.

"Oh dear. Well then," Elliot mumbled. "That calls for two cookies *and* a Pepsi that I am not to share."

"You do have a television in your bedroom," Dan said.

"I know," Elliot said. "But I haven't been around children in such a long time. I am really enjoying the experience."

And then he was gone.

Alice shook her head. "He's enjoying the experience. That is the kindest way of putting that I've ever heard."

Before Dan could answer, there was a huge thud outside the back door that was loud enough to be heard over the wind.

"Oh my Lord, Dan! What was that?" she cried.

Dan was already running for the closest window with indoor shutters. "It sounded like one of the big trees at the back of the property," he said. "I need to see where it fell. Hopefully not against the house."

Alice followed him into the butler's pantry. There was an exterior window with shutters that shut from inside near the old servants' quarters.

"Stay back," Dan said. "We don't want to wind up like Lovey."

Alice froze. "Oh, Dan. Be careful."

He unlatched the shutters, then slowly opened one side. The window was still intact, so he took a chance and swung both shutters back. One of the biggest live oaks was down less than twenty yards from the back of the house. He gave the yard a quick look to check for downed lines, then shut and latched the shutters again.

"What was that?" Alice asked.

"The largest live oak is down. It came way too close to the house."

Alice shuddered. "I'm going to go sit with my kids."

"And I'm coming to sit with you," Dan said. "Don't be scared, sweetheart. We're together, and we're safe. That's enough."

—⁓—

"Lovey! Lovey! Can you hear me?"

Lovey moaned. "Hear," she said.

The nurse patted Lovey's arm. "Wake up, darling. Can you open your eyes for me?"

Lovey's voice faded. "Stop talking."

The nurse laughed. "I can't. It's my job to get you to open your eyes."

Lovey sighed. Maybe if she did, the nurse would go away, so she started to look, and then moaned.

"Stuck," she said.

"Your eyes are stuck?" the nurse asked.

"Stuck," Lovey said.

The nurse tore open a packet of sterile gauze and began wiping it gently across Lovey's eyes.

"Try again," the nurse said. "Open your eyes for me."

And she did. "I know you," Lovey said. "Sorghum on biscuits."

The nurse smiled. "My name is Pauletta, but I do love sorghum on my biscuits. Now, tell me your name."

"Lovey Nell Cooper."

"Great, Lovey. Do you know where you are?"

"Hospital?"

"Do you remember what happened?" Pauletta asked.

Tears rolled down Lovey's face. "Trapped. Hurt."

"But you're safe now. We'll be moving you to a room soon."

"Yes, soon," Lovey whispered, and let herself roll back into a painless void.

Chapter 17

THERE WAS A HUGE RIPPING SOUND OVER THE WAITING room ceiling, loud enough that it made both Peanut and Ruby leap to their feet. At the same time, a nurse came to the doorway.

"Lovey is in her room now."

"Did you hear that?" Peanut said, pointing to the ceiling.

The nurse nodded. "Probably another part of the roof. That's why we've moved all of our patients onto the second floor. It leaves two floors above empty, which should protect the ones that are still here from waking up with rainwater in their beds."

"What a mess," Peanut said.

Ruby grabbed Peanut's hand and started pulling him toward the door.

"What room is she in?" Ruby asked.

"Room 210, right across from the nurses' station. Follow me." When they arrived, she pointed to the room. "She's in and out of consciousness, and she needs to rest. You're both welcome to sit with her for as long as you want, but keep talking to a minimum for today."

"Yes, ma'am," Ruby said.

Peanut squeezed her hand and then opened the door.

Ruby's demeanor was calm, her steps sure and steady. But inside, she was shaking. When they got to

Lovey's bed, **Ruby** moved to one side and Peanut took the other.

They were both silent, taking in the sight. Lovey's hair was gone, leaving visible the bloody cuts in her scalp and face where all the glass had been.

Ruby heard Peanut take a deep breath and then exhale slowly. He was as shocked by the extent of Lovey's injuries as she was. Then Ruby noticed a place next to Lovey's eye with three stitches and wondered if the ear in which she'd lost hearing was on the same side.

"Where she hit her face on the sink," Peanut whispered.

Ruby nodded, eyeing the hard cast on her friend's arm and wondering how many rods and screws they'd had to use to reset the two breaks.

When Lovey exhaled on a moan, Ruby touched her shoulder. "Lovey, darling, this is Ruby. Peanut and I are here."

Lovey opened her eyes. "Ruby. Sister...how—"

"We'll talk about all that later," Ruby said. "I just wanted you to know you're not in here alone."

A tear rolled from the corner of Lovey's eye onto her pillow. "So scared. Trapped... Couldn't—"

"I know, darling. I know. But you're safe now. Just rest. I'll be here when you wake up again."

"Safe," Lovey said, and let the pain meds pull her under.

Peanut pulled up the chairs to her bedside, and then they sat. They looked at each other in disbelief, then Peanut leaned forward, kissed the side of Ruby's cheek, and whispered in her ear.

"Now you know how I felt when you were

kidnapped and came back all cut and beat up. You survived, and so will she. Just rest. If she wakes up again, you'll know."

Ruby nodded, but rest wasn't happening. She was already planning who to put in charge at Granny's until Lovey was able to go back to work. Mercy Pittman was the first name that popped up, and Ruby decided to keep her in mind. There were already two employees Mercy had trained that knew how to make her biscuits and pies, so they could pick up the slack if Mercy moved up to the front for a while.

Peanut was watching Ruby's face. He could almost see the wheels turning in her head. She was working on a project, and if he was a betting man, he'd bet it had to do with Lovey and her café.

When the calm moved over Big Tom Rankin's farm, he and Junior hurried out to the barn to check on the animals. Their machine shed had lost part of the roof. The windows they'd boarded up on the garage were still covered, but something had hit one of them so hard from the outside that the glass it was covering had still broken. The shards were all over the concrete floor.

Junior was a few yards ahead of his dad and was the first to see that the back side of the corral was gone, obviously washed away because the creek just below the barn had flooded and was up where the corral used to be.

"Daddy! Look!" Junior yelled, and Big Tom came running.

"Well. Dang it," Big Tom said. "That's gonna be a

job repairing all that. Hope it hasn't washed dirt away beneath the creek bank as well. We'd have to reconfigure the corral if it did."

Junior took off his cap, scratching his head as he began eyeing the sight before him, then heard a calf bawling and turned around. The calf was just outside the barn and by itself.

"What in the world? Daddy! The cattle are gone! They were inside the barn, and now they're not."

Big Tom looked down for tracks, but they'd been rained out.

"Dang it. There's no telling where they went in that storm. It's likely to take days to round them up if they're not already dead. But right now, I'm going to put the calf up."

Junior pointed downstream. "I'm gonna walk a little ways down to look around."

"No. Let it be. We don't want to be too far away from the house when the second wave hits."

"I won't go far," Junior promised.

"Then I'll be right behind you," Big Tom said, and hurried toward the barn, shooing the calf back into shelter as he went.

Junior glanced up at the sky, then headed downstream at a trot. He could hear his daddy grumbling and cursing as he ran the calf back into the barn, but his focus was on the water and the trees in front of him.

"Dumbass cattle," Junior muttered. "You had a safe place to be, and what did you do? Stampeded off into a storm. One of you even left your baby behind. What the hell were you thinking?"

Back in the barn, Big Tom was just about to fasten

the calf up in one of the old horse stalls when he heard a squall and then a hiss that stopped his heart.

He reached for the pitchfork just inside an open granary as he spun around, only to come face-to-face with a cougar that had chosen the barn to take refuge from the storm.

The cat was on a stack of hay bales and at eye level with Big Tom, with less than ten feet separating them. The only way out of the barn was the opening behind the man.

Big Tom's head was spinning, trying to think of a way to get out of this confrontation. One of the few times he'd left his rifle in the house when going out to check livestock, and this was the result. He started backing out, yelling for help as he went.

Albert was in the kitchen, watching out the back door from his wheelchair as his daddy and his brother walked from building to building and wishing he was out there with them. He hated feeling so helpless. Then when he saw Junior take off from the barn and walk downstream at the creek and disappear, he frowned, wondering what was going on.

He sat for a few moments, eyeing the downed trees and broken limbs, hoping their roof was in better shape than what he could see of the barn roof, when he heard someone shout. He couldn't tell what they'd said, but the tone of voice sounded panicked.

He leaned forward and opened the storm door and rolled the wheelchair out onto the porch. Then he heard the sound again. It was Daddy, screaming…shouting…

Albert leaned forward in the wheelchair. Where the heck was Junior? Then he saw his daddy backing out of the barn with a pitchfork in his hands. He didn't know what or who was after him, and it didn't matter. His daddy was in danger.

Without thinking of consequences, he got out of the wheelchair and, ignoring the pain, ran into the house, grabbed a rifle off the gun rack, checked to make sure it was loaded, then ran outside toward the barn. Within seconds, he saw the cougar emerge from the barn, and it wasn't running away. It looked like it was about to leap at Big Tom.

"Daddy!" Albert screamed, and pulled the trigger.

The big cat leaped straight up into the air and came down screaming and writhing.

Albert shot one more time, and then it was down. The gunshot was still echoing in his head when he began feeling the pain on the bottoms of his feet.

Junior was about a hundred yards away when he thought he heard someone shout. He stopped, tilting his head to listen, but the rush of the flooded water was too loud to distinguish what he'd heard. And then he heard it again and again and turned back toward the barn and starting running.

The top of the barn had just come into view when he heard the first gunshot. Now he was really worried and ran faster without looking where he was going. When the second gunshot went off, he'd just come out of the trees. He could see his daddy, and he saw Albert with a rifle in his hands.

"What happened?" he yelled.

Big Tom turned around, saw Junior running out of

the trees, and then to his horror saw the ground go out from under Junior's feet. As he'd feared, the ground had been undercut by the rush of floodwaters.

"Noooo!" Big Tom screamed as he watched his son fall backward, down into the flood. He started running, screaming Junior's name and waiting for him to surface.

Only he never did.

Big Tom ran until he felt the wind beginning to rise and knew he had a choice to make. Die with this son, or go back and save the other. He turned around, this time running faster and faster. He could feel rain in the wind now and cut through a wooded area and ran straight up a hill. It was steeper, but a much shorter way home. By the time he ran out of the trees and headed up to the house, the wind was pushing him.

He could see Albert standing on the back porch and hanging on to a post to keep from being blown against the house. When Big Tom saw the relief on his younger son's face, it was the impetus he needed to keep moving.

It seemed like forever before he reached the steps, but when he did, he lunged toward a porch post and fell straight into Albert's arms. With the force of the hurricane at their backs, it took both of them to get the storm door open, and when they did, they fell into the kitchen just as the wind blew the storm door shut behind them so hard it vibrated on its hinges.

"Shut the door, Daddy! Shut the door!" Albert screamed.

Big Tom rolled over onto his knees to get up, then grabbed the heavy wooden door and threw all of his weight against it to slam it shut. He locked it, dropped his work coat onto the washing machine, and kicked off his boots, and then slid down the wall and started to wail.

Albert didn't know what had happened, but the fact that Junior hadn't come back with Big Tom said enough.

"Daddy, what happened to Junior?" he asked.

Big Tom put his hands over his face and kept shaking his head as he sobbed and sobbed.

Albert knew the answer now, but he had to hear it. He kicked the bottom of Big Tom's foot and screamed.

"Daddy! What happened? Where's Junior?"

Big Tom lifted his head. "Drowned. Gone. The creek is way out of its banks, flooded with rushing water. It collapsed beneath him and threw him into the flood. I ran and ran, but he never came up. The cows are gone. Junior is gone. And I would be gone, too, if you hadn't saved my life."

He crawled over to where Albert was sitting and wrapped him in his arms. "Thank you, Son. Thank you for what you did, and at your expense." Then he wiped away tears as he reached for one of Albert's feet. "Let's look at what you've done to yourself."

Albert lay down, wincing as his dad pulled off the thick socks he'd been wearing.

"I need to go get a flashlight and the first aid kit," Big Tom said. "Don't move, Son. I won't be long."

He made himself get up, then walked back through the house on shaking legs. He'd watched his first son's birth, and he'd witnessed his death. It was a pain too sharp to be borne, and yet it was the living who needed tending.

He got a flashlight from the dining room table, went back to the bathroom to get some bandages and rubbing alcohol, then got a dry pair of his own socks and headed back to the kitchen.

Albert was still crying, but he hadn't moved.

Big Tom sat back down and gave both feet the once-over before he started cleaning them up. "Sorry if this hurts."

"It's okay, Daddy. We're both hurting. Just clean me up so I don't get anything infected," Albert said.

"I'll do my best," Big Tom said, and then laid a large, folded-up bath towel beneath Albert's feet and started cleaning them with alcohol and then over-the-counter antiseptic, talking as he worked.

"I think the cougar took shelter in the barn, and when it did, it spooked the cows. I'm sure now that we lost them, too. They either died in the first wave of the hurricane, or they'll die in this one."

Albert listened without comment, knowing his daddy didn't need answers. He was just talking to keep from screaming. He couldn't quit thinking about Junior, and what he'd said about wanting to dedicate the rest of his life to helping others, but this happened instead. He kept wondering if Junior had brought this karma to himself. If this was his punishment for murder. Granted, the man didn't die, but that had nothing to do with any action Junior had taken. He'd walked away, thinking the man was dead.

Finally, he heard his daddy say "All done" and pat the side of his leg.

"Where's your chair?" Big Tom asked.

"I gave it a shove inside when the wind started to blow. It's here in the kitchen somewhere," Albert said.

Big Tom swung the flashlight around the corners of

the room and saw that the chair had rolled up to the table. "There it is."

He got up, grabbed the wheelchair, and pushed it back to where Albert was lying.

Albert slowly sat up. He started to pull himself into the chair when Big Tom just bent over and lifted him up, then eased both his feet onto the footrests.

"There you are. Let me clean all this up, and then I'll find your pain meds."

"They're on the table beside my bed," Albert said, too shaken to move.

He couldn't escape the thought of Junior's body being bounced and slammed down through the flood-waters. What if they never found him?

I'm so sorry, Brother. I'm so sorry this happened, but I'm going to let myself believe that you're no longer living with that burden on your heart. God forgives, and I'm going to spend the rest of my life trying to forget we ever went down that path to easy money.

He heard his daddy's footsteps and wiped his eyes as Big Tom came back with two pills in his hand and the water that had been left in the bottle by Albert's bed.

"Here you go, Son."

"Thank you, Daddy," Albert said, and downed them.

"Now you need to eat something, or those pain pills will make you sick on an empty belly," Big Tom said.

Albert looked up at his dad as his eyes welled. "I don't know if I can get anything down without it coming back up."

Big Tom laid a hand on Albert's head and felt the heat from his scalp and the springy texture of his hair. Life. He still had one son left.

"Then we'll eat something together. I'm choosing a can of Vienna sausages and some crackers."

Albert nodded. "Yes, okay. I'll eat some with you."

Big Tom pulled a couple of paper towels off the roll on the cabinet and laid them down for plates, then got two small cans of Vienna sausages and a box of saltine crackers out of the pantry. He opened the cans, drained off the water in which the sausages had been canned, and then turned them both out on a paper plate and set them on the table.

"Want pickles?" Big Tom asked.

Instant tears welled in Albert's eyes. Junior was the one who liked pickles with his, but he wasn't going to remind his father.

"Dills if we have any, Daddy."

"We have them," Big Tom said and set them on the table, laying a small fork beside the jar to help get them out.

Albert reached for one of the little sausages, put it on a cracker, then took a bite. Big Tom forked out a couple of pickles, and they sat and ate without speaking another word.

Once Big Tom excused himself to get fresh water they had stored in the refrigerator, even though it wasn't getting anything cold. Albert knew his daddy used that moment to wipe his eyes, and then he was back with a new bottle of water.

Albert ate a total of five sausages before he quit. "Daddy, I just can't eat any more. I'm sorry I'm wasting food."

"You aren't. I've got a little dry ice in the smallest cooler. I'll set the meat in there."

Albert rolled himself out of the kitchen and went down the hall to the bathroom while the wind roared and the rain came down on the roof over his head. The sound was deafening, and knowing Junior was lost out there only made it worse.

He wasn't in there long, and when he came out, he went to his room and managed to pull off his dirty clothes and put on clean ones before he lay down. The pain pills made him sleepy enough that it didn't take him long to fall asleep, but his dreams were filled with horror. And when he woke up, he sadly realized the worst of what he'd been dreaming had already come true.

Dan had just come back from refueling the generator when Charlie appeared in the kitchen with Booger.

"I need to take him out," Charlie said.

Dan reached down and patted the old dog's head, then scratched behind one of those big, floppy ears. "I'll go with you," Dan said. "Just for safety's sake."

"I appreciate it," Charlie said, and together they went through the old servants' quarters and then out to what had once been a dogtrot between two buildings. It had been bricked up a little over a hundred years ago to make it look like another wing of the house, but that dogtrot was still nothing but a glorified hall that would be easy enough to clean when the hurricane was gone.

As soon as the dog had done his business, they headed back into the main part of the house. Even as they were coming through the kitchen, they could hear some kind of uproar.

Charlie looked anxious, but Dan was already running.

"What's wrong?" Dan asked as he ran into the living room.

"We can't find Patty," Alice said. "She was here in the living room, and now she's not."

"Where was she playing?" Dan asked.

Elliot pointed. "Over by the fireplace. She didn't leave the room, or I would have seen her."

Alice was in tears.

Dan walked toward the fireplace, frowning, and then saw her doll on the floor beside the bookshelves and immediately knew where she'd gone.

"Don't cry," Dan said. "I know exactly where she's at. She got herself in there, and now she can't figure out how to get out."

"Out of what?" Alice cried.

"This house used to be on a route for the Underground Railroad. There is a room behind this bookcase where they hid the runaway slaves," Dan said, and went straight to the bookshelves, squatted down, and pressed on a decorative scroll that had been carved into the wood on both ends of the shelves.

Immediately, a door about five feet high swung inward. Patty was sitting in several layers of dirt, with tears on her cheeks.

Dan reached in and pulled her out, then hugged her. "Bless your heart, honey. Why didn't you call out?"

"I was afraid Mama would get mad because I got so dirty," she said.

Alice dropped to her knees. "Child, you are going to make my hair gray long before its time. Since when have I ever been mad at you for getting dirty?"

Patty sniffled. "Since never, I guess."

Alice started to pick her up, when Dan did it for her. "Don't want to get your clean bandage dirty. We'll follow. You lead the way."

"Oh, right!" Alice said. "I guess to the bathroom in our bedroom."

Patty hid her face against Dan's neck all the way up the stairs and into the bedroom she shared with her mother.

"You're okay," Dan whispered. "No one's mad, honey. You just scared us."

"I'm sorry," she said. "I didn't mean to get stuck."

He patted her back and then set her down on the closed lid of the commode.

The whine of the storm was more evident up here, and it made Alice shudder. "I cannot imagine how hard and how frightening this would be if the kids and I were at Hope House alone. This house feels like a fortress, and you are the guardian at the gate. Thank you for counting us in."

Dan was so touched by what she'd said. He slid a hand beneath the thick fall of her dark hair and brushed a kiss across her forehead.

"Alice Conroy, you and your children have given me more joy in the last couple of days than I've had in ten years and have given my life purpose. Believe me, you are very welcome. Now, do you need anything else?"

"We can manage the rest. Thank you, again. I swear, when this is over, you're never going to want to see us again."

Dan cupped the side of her cheek. "That's far from true. I don't want to think about anyone leaving. If you need anything, I'll be downstairs."

Alice nodded.

He could hear her talking as he walked out of the bathroom. Something about getting a leash for Patty like the one they used for Booger, which made Patty giggle. He smiled.

They had the television on in the kitchen while they were making supper to listen to weather updates. The fact that the newscasters were finally talking about the hurricane weakening as it moved farther inland was reason to celebrate. And with no cell phone service, conversation had its own kind of revival at the table as they ate.

For Dan, it had begun to feel like this was his little family, and because of the storm and the limitation on the generator, a light was on only in the room in which they'd gathered, and when they moved from room to room, they turned everything off as they went. It gave intimacy and a sense of safety to have light in the darkness, and every time he went to refuel the generator, Dan thanked Preston Williams for the foresight to have this done.

Tonight they were having stew made from hamburger meat, onions, potatoes, and a big bag of mixed vegetables. It was plain food, but it was hearty and it was warm. Elliot tasted it as he gave it a stir and added a tiny bit more salt. When Alice stirred it later, then tasted, she added a bay leaf. Dan came by later, tasted it, added a couple of tablespoons of Worcestershire sauce, stirred it up, tasted it again, and took it off the heat.

Alice called her children to the table. Bowls were filled. Cheese and crackers were served on the side, and water was the beverage of choice.

It wasn't long after the kitchen was cleaned up before

Alice took Patty upstairs and put her to bed. After having a bath only a couple of hours earlier, she tucked her doll under her chin and fell asleep.

Charlie was tired and willingly took Booger upstairs to watch TV.

Elliot got a book from the library and went to his room, leaving Dan and Alice alone. It was just after 9:00 p.m. and they were sitting in the shadows with only the television for light, watching one weather update after another, waiting for the one when the forecasters began talking about the storm losing force as it moved farther inland.

Even though Alice felt safe here with Dan, watching what was happening farther along the coast made her anxious. There was so much devastation, and so many lives would be forever changed. Finally, she'd had enough.

Alice looked at Dan. "Are you sleepy?"

"No. Are you?" he said.

She shook her head.

"What do you want to do?" he asked.

She shrugged. "What do you want to do?"

"Make love to you," he said softly.

Alice's eyes widened.

"Did that scare you?" he asked.

"No. I'm hardly an innocent or a virgin. Does it scare you?" she asked.

"No. I'm hardly an innocent or a virgin, either," he said. "So what do you think?"

Alice hesitated. Saying this might change the tenuous grasp they had on their very new relationship, but he'd asked, and she wasn't going to lie. "I think making love with you might mean more to me than it does to you, and I don't want to be a convenient attraction."

Dan leaned across the sofa and pulled her into his arms. "I haven't felt like this for a woman since my wife died. I'm not a player, sweetheart."

"Neither am I, and for obvious reasons," Alice said.

Dan traced the shape of her cheek with the back of his hand. "For your children."

She nodded. "We're still in the middle of being tagged as drug dealers. The last thing I want is to be considered 'an available woman.'"

Dan brushed a kiss across her lips. "But if we were together, then you would obviously be unavailable."

She sighed. "Why do I feel like I'm on the stand and about to confess to your desires?"

He laughed softly. "I'm not trying to sell you anything but me. I want to give this relationship a chance. I want you…all of you…in my life."

"Can you make love on mute?" Alice asked.

"Uh…not sure what you're getting at," he said.

"Surely you remember making love with kids next door."

He laughed out loud. "Ah…on mute. I love that." Then his laughter shifted to a quiet smile. "Of course I remember. Give me a chance, and I'll prove it."

She got up and started walking away.

"Hey! Where are you going?" he asked.

She paused, then turned around. "Upstairs. I'm an equal opportunity employer, but you need to show me what you've got. I don't take anyone's word without a little proof to go with it. Are you coming?"

"Not yet. I'm a ladies-first man," Dan said, and bounced up from the sofa.

Chapter 18

ALICE HEARD THE TELEVISION IN CHARLIE'S ROOM AS THEY passed by the door.

Elliot's room was quiet but the light was still on, and Alice's room was quiet, which meant Patty was still asleep.

Dan held her hand all the way up the stairs and was still holding it when they went inside his room and locked the door. The night-light in the bathroom shed all the light they needed. But there was an element of risk to making love during a hurricane.

"I know there's a lot to be said for foreplay, but I'd say it's a chancy move tonight, considering the number of factors that could bring this whole event to a halt," Dan said softly.

She gave him a thumbs-up and took off her shoes and socks, then pulled her shirt over her head.

Dan slid his arms around her waist, pulled her close, and kissed her. Her heart was racing as she reached for his belt buckle, and then he unfastened her bra and pulled it off.

"Take it off, Amos," Alice whispered, eyeing his shirt as she unsnapped her jeans and began struggling to get them off with only one good hand.

He was out of his clothes within seconds and then took hers off as well. For a few moments, they were motionless, looking at the shapes and sizes of each other, then their gazes met.

Alice sighed. "Just so you know, you are only the second man I've ever made love to, so I don't have any tricks to fall back on."

"None needed," he said.

He cupped the fullness of her breasts, ran his hands down the sides of her very small waist, and then followed the flare of her hips as he picked her up and laid her down in his bed.

The wind blew something against the brickwork near his windows that shattered upon impact. She jumped. Dan rose up on one elbow just long enough to look into her eyes…to make sure she was still on board.

"No, I have not changed my mind," she whispered.

"Neither have I," he said, and kissed her long and hard, while the world outside came apart around them.

Being with Dan felt like a dream. The only thing that made it real for Alice was the building heat deep in her belly and the need to feel him inside her. When he finally slid between her legs, she rose up to meet him, following his lead as if they'd been dancing together for years. Their passion, coupled with the overhead storm, was an aphrodisiac they hadn't expected.

One moment Alice was riding the high, and then another gust of wind slammed something else against the house, and when it did, the climax slammed into her as well. She was shaking in every muscle as the contractions moved through her, and while she was still riding the afterglow, Dan finally let go. He fell into the climax as wave after wave of pleasure moved through him.

It took a couple of minutes for hearts to stop racing and pulses to go back into steady rhythm. The silence between them was from the total satisfaction of what just happened.

"Sweet bird of youth. That was nothing but pure beauty," Alice whispered.

Dan rose up on his elbows and looked down into her face. Dark hair tousled. Eyelids at half-mast. Lips the tiniest bit swollen. And he could still feel the rhythm of her heartbeat.

"I guess you know I'm gonna want to do this again," he said.

She ran her thumb along the edge of his lower lip. "I will be looking forward to it," she said. "But my instinct tells me I need to get dressed."

He sighed. "Duly noted," he whispered, and gave her one last kiss before she got out of bed.

He watched as she began gathering up her clothes, but when she started toward the bathroom to dress, she suddenly stopped and turned her head, as if trying to look at the back side of her hip.

"What are you looking for?" he asked.

"Your brand. It's still burning," she said, then gave him a slow, sexy smile before she closed the door.

Dan couldn't get the smile off his face as he got up and started dressing, and within five minutes, they were on their way downstairs. It was time for him to check the fuel gauge on the generator while Alice began to put away the games the kids had been playing.

Because of the kissing and hugging that went on between tasks, it took far longer than it should have to bring an end to the day.

―⁓―

Big Tom and Albert were still up when daybreak came.

Big Tom wouldn't go to bed because every time he closed his eyes, he saw Junior falling backward into the floodwaters.

Albert had dozed off once or twice, but the winds would either blow something against the house or blow something off of it, and it kept him awake wondering if they would still have a house when this was over.

After the second time he woke up, he stayed awake for his dad. They spent the rest of the night talking and crying and talking some more, remembering their favorite stories about Junior, and all the while, Albert had the burden on his heart of knowing what they had done and how far Junior had fallen from the way he'd been raised.

———

The storm was battering Beulah Gatlin's old two-story house, snapping trees like matchsticks and tossing them about. One had already landed on the porch, taking out the porch posts and the roof that covered it, which scared the family to the point of moving into the back of the house.

Moses and J. B. paced like caged animals, while Beulah lay in her bed fully dressed, with that baby doll clutched close to her chest.

Every time her sons came to check on her, she'd send them away. She didn't want company. She was busy taking the rage in her heart for how her life had turned out and turning it into pity for herself. By the time she finally dozed off, she'd found a way to turn her sins into heroic gestures and convinced herself that sending

Marty's family away had been necessary to eradicate the memory of his fall from grace.

—⁓—

At Ruby's insistence, Peanut had finally taken his long, tall self back to the waiting room, where he'd stretched out on the sofa and gone to sleep.

As for Ruby, she was up and down all night and way into the early-morning hours comforting Lovey, getting a drink, covering her up because she was cold, holding her hand as she breathed through excruciating pain while waiting for pain meds to kick in, or turning on the light over her bed and calming her when she woke up screaming for help, dreaming that she was still trapped.

By morning, Ruby knew the details of everything that happened—from the time Lovey was standing at the window looking out to the moment she saw Johnny Pine's face as he chopped a hole in the door to rescue her.

Lovey talked about the ride to the ER in some kind of giant bulldozer and how strong a man Johnny turned out to be. She cried quiet tears when she talked about dying and was somewhat surprised to still be here.

Ruby was shocked by how much of the hurricane Lovey had been subjected to and knew now that she'd lost hearing in one ear not because of an injury, but from the blast of the wind itself as she lay helpless on the bathroom floor.

Once when Lovey drifted off to sleep, Ruby ran back down the hall to the waiting room, dropped to her knees beside the sofa where Peanut lay sleeping, and put her head down on his chest and cried.

He woke up thinking Lovey had died, only to find out Ruby was simply overwhelmed by what her friend had endured. He sat her down on the sofa and headed to the vending machines, returning with cold pop, sweet chocolate, and a bag of salty chips. They sat together in silence, sharing food as they were learning to share their lives, grateful to still have each other.

Just after daylight, one of the nurses came in to give Lovey another dose of pain meds. She injected it into the IV, refilled the water pitcher, and added some ice before helping ready Lovey for breakfast, while Ruby watched in silence.

"The meals are minimal in choices, but we won't let anyone go hungry," the nurse said. "Oh…and a bit of good news. The latest hurricane update is that it's moving farther inland, weakening in intensity as it goes."

"Oh thank God," Ruby said. "I'm going to go tell Peanut."

"I don't think it's safe to drive outside just yet," the nurse said. "We can bring cold cereal and hot coffee for both of you when we bring Lovey's breakfast."

Ruby smiled. "That would be much appreciated. Thank you so much."

"We're the ones who are grateful. We're all pretty tired here on the floor, and you took almost all of the care Lovey needed last night onto your shoulders."

"She's the sister I never had, and that's what family does for each other," Ruby said. "Lovey, I'm going up to the waiting room to get Peanut. I'll be right back."

Lovey nodded. She closed her eyes and took deep breaths, praying for that pain shot to take effect again. For a while, she was measuring her life by how long she could go from pain shot to pain shot. By the time Ruby and Peanut returned, she had fallen back to sleep. But things were looking up.

When an orderly brought breakfast to the room a short while later, he was smiling. "The wind isn't as strong as it was. Maybe there's going to be something left of Blessings after all."

—*m*—

Alice woke up beside Patty, thought of last night, and shivered with anticipation. It marked the first step into the possibility of a new life—a full life—with a pretty special man. She rolled over onto her back and stretched, and as she did, realized something was drastically different.

The wind wasn't as strong. The rain didn't sound like a deluge. What if this was the beginning of the end for Hurricane Fanny? She jumped up, covered her bandaged hand with a plastic bag and tied it down around her wrist with a strip of masking tape, then showered and dressed in the same jeans she'd worn yesterday. She put on a clean shirt and some socks and shoes, then gave her hair a good brushing and left it down around her shoulders.

She laid out some clean clothes for Patty and then headed downstairs to start the coffee. The hum of the generator had become the heartbeat of the home. Alice knew all too well how fortunate they were not to have been without city water, without sewers, and without heat or lights for all these days.

She wondered, as she measured out the coffee, how the family was doing who'd taken shelter in Elliot's garage apartment. They had no home, and they'd lost all of their belongings. Normally, the people of Blessings would have come together as they always did and donated food and clothing to get them back on their feet. But there was no way to know if this was even possible until Blessings regained power. There was no way to know how many people's homes had flooded and how many people besides Lovey Cooper had been injured. It was a frightening time for the whole town.

Dan came into the kitchen with a smile on his face and kissed the back of her neck. "You smell good," he said. "Like lavender."

"Your nice bath soap," Alice said, and then turned to face him and gave him a proper good-morning kiss.

"My sweet Alice, you tempt a man beyond good sense. I'm going to check the fuel in the generator. I'll help make breakfast when I get back."

Alice put bacon on to cook because they had it, and then mixed up some pancake batter and set it aside.

Charlie came into the kitchen with Booger on a leash. "I'm taking him out. Be back in a jiffy," he said.

"Is Patty awake?" Alice asked.

"I heard her singing, so yes, she's awake. Is she getting dressed? I have no idea," he said, and then loped down the back hall with Booger on his heels.

Alice started making pancakes, and each time she had a stack ready, she put them in the warming oven. Charlie came back and put out Booger's food in the utility room.

"Did you make pancakes?" he asked.

She nodded.

"I'll go get Patty," he said, and gave her a thumbs-up as he loped out of the kitchen.

Alice rolled her eyes. "Walk, Charlie. Once in a while, it's okay to walk."

Within a few minutes, the kitchen was full of chatter and laughing. Alice was still making pancakes as fast as she could, and eating from her plate in between flipping them over.

Dan got up to refill his coffee and then set it down by the stove and moved Alice and her plate to the table. "You sit. I'll finish cooking up the last of the batter."

"Thank you," she said, and added some syrup to her short stack, then finished it off.

"Who wants more?" Dan asked.

Elliot held up his hand, and so did Charlie. Patty happened to look up, saw their hands raised, and shot hers into the air, too.

"Patty, you still have pancakes on your plate. Why did you raise your hand?" Alice asked.

The look of indignation on her face was hard to miss. "They did," she said, pointing. "Why can't I?"

Alice grinned. "Do you know why their hands are up?" she asked.

Patty frowned. "No."

"They were asking for more pancakes."

Patty gasped and then began waving her hand back and forth above her head.

"What's that mean?" Alice asked.

"I'm erasing my yes," Patty said.

Dan laughed.

Elliot reached over and patted her head. "Delightful child, but I'm not erasing my request."

"I'm not either," Charlie said.

Dan set the platter on the table between them. There

were three pancakes. "That's the last. Figure it out between you," he said.

Charlie reached for the platter first, and just when Alice was about to scold him, he handed it to Elliot. "You first, sir," Charlie said.

Elliot smiled. "Why, thank you, Charlie." He took one and handed the platter back to Charlie, who immediately slid the remaining two onto his plate.

"Mama, can I go play now? I'm full."

"Wipe your mouth, and yes."

Patty swiped and then jumped up.

"Patty! Wait!" Alice said. "Do you remember what we talked about yesterday afternoon when I was giving you a bath?"

Patty nodded her head, but Alice had seen that ruse before. "What did I say?" she asked.

"Not to play on the railroad tracks again?"

Dan laughed before he could stop himself.

Alice stifled a giggle. "No, I said…do not *ever* go into that secret room again, and you know it."

"And you said it was a railroad under the ground, too," Patty said. "I promise! I will not go there again."

Alice frowned. "Charlie—"

"I'm going, Mama. I'm going. Come on, squirt. Want to play Chutes and Ladders again?"

Patty nodded and took her big brother's hand as they left the room.

Dan was still smiling when Elliot brought a stack of dirty dishes to the counter. "I'm going to go to my room for a bit and listen to weather updates. It really sounds like today is the day that it finally fizzles out here. And none too soon, I say. Miss Alice, thank you for that wonderful breakfast. I am going to be so spoiled that by the time I get back into my own house, I won't want to lift a finger to help myself."

As soon as they were alone, Dan and Alice took one look at each other and burst into laughter.

"Oh my God…the railroad tracks. I'm sorry…but I lost it."

"Yes…my lesson about the Underground Railroad might have been a couple of years too soon," Alice said, wiping her eyes. "You have no idea how hard it is to keep a straight face with that kid."

Dan wrapped his arms around her and gave her a big hug. "All this time I've been thinking I would never be happy again if you weren't falling for me like I was for you, and now that I know you are, I also realize what a bonus your kids are, bringing so much joy into my life."

Alice's vision blurred, her voice just above a whisper. "I can't believe this is really happening."

Dan's heart skipped a beat. "What are you talking about? I adore you. I adore your kids. What did I say wrong?"

"No, no, that's not what I meant. Before you came here, I was the woman whose world went up in smoke. I buried my husband after he burned down everything we owned, and within a week, we were abandoned on a street corner here in Blessings by his family with not even enough money to make one month's rent. And it was still cold weather here. We had no clothes but what we were wearing. No food in the house, and I was sick. I thought I was going to die and leave my children orphans."

Dan just put his arms around her and let her talk.

"Charlie saved us. He put out flyers all over town about having a dog for hire. 'If you lost it, Booger can find it,' the flyer said. And he was charging twenty-five dollars for the service."

A cold chill ran up the middle of Dan's back. "You aren't serious."

"Yes. I am. He was twelve years old, and he took it upon himself to become the man of the house. As fate would have it, the police chief had seen the flyer, and when an old woman went missing from the senior citizens center, he came after Charlie and his dog."

"Did they find her?" Dan asked.

"Yes. She lived a day or so afterward, but then she passed. But that called attention to us and our situation, and before we knew it, we began receiving food and clothes, and the chief got our utilities turned on, and Peanut Butterman got us signed up on welfare. I enrolled the kids in school and on my way home saw a Help Wanted sign in the window of Bloomer's Hardware, and you know the rest. What I'm getting at is I went from a hardship charity case to now...and all this...and you."

"I see you as so special. I see you as a woman who didn't quit on herself or her kids. I see a woman so easy to love. You are what my mother would call a woman with 'don't quit' in her blood. I admire everything about you."

"Thank you," Alice said. "You are my knight in shining armor. I dreamed of them as a little girl, but never knew one...until you."

Dan put his arm around her shoulder. "My work here is done. Shall we sit among the court jesters, m'lady?"

Alice laughed, which was exactly what he wanted her

to do, and she was still smiling when he turned the light out in the kitchen and they went to find her kids.

—–∿∿∿—–

The hurricane winds were waning by the hour. The rain was no longer blinding, and there was a hint of clearing skies in the south.

Big Tom opened the front door and walked out onto the porch. He could hear the rush of water in the flooded creek and winced.

Albert rolled his wheelchair to the open doorway and looked out. "What are you thinking, Daddy?"

"I'm thinking it's time to go notify the county sheriff about what happened to Junior. That way people can be looking for him downstream."

"Can I go with you?" Albert asked.

Before, Big Tom would have insisted his younger son stay behind. He wasn't healed. If Tom had troubles, Albert might not be able to walk out, but yesterday had turned Big Tom's way of thinking. He'd seen Albert as a man, not just as his son. And if Albert believed he could handle the ride, then that was enough for him.

"You sure can," Big Tom said. "We might not be able to get all the way through, but we're gonna try. I promise I won't drive into any deep water. There's no telling whether the road is washed out beneath it or not, but let's give it a go."

"I'll go get my things. I won't be long."

"I'm going to get the old four-by-four dually out of the shop. It'll ride higher, which might come in handy," Big Tom said. "I'll wait for you at the kitchen door. It's easier to get you and the chair loaded up there."

"Yes, sir," Albert said, and wheeled himself down the hall to his bedroom.

Big Tom grabbed his things, got the keys that went with the Dually, and headed out the back door to the shop. He checked the fuel, then drove the truck out of the shop to the big tanks of farm fuel and filled it up with diesel, the same fuel he used for his tractor. He stopped by the barn to check on the calf. It was bawling. It ate the same feed he fed the others, and it was big enough to be weaned.

"Tough way to get weaned, little buddy," Big Tom said, then put some feed in the stall and got a bucket of rainwater from the barrel outside and left it in the stall as well.

He stopped up at the back door and helped Albert into that high-riding rig, folded up his wheelchair and put it on the back floorboard between the seats.

"You good to go? Need pain meds or anything, Son?"

"I took some this morning. I'll be good until evening."

With that, Big Tom jumped in behind the wheel. The windshield wipers were whipping back and forth like the hips of a hula dancer. It was a risky trip, but there was a big reason to make it, and Albert wasn't about to let his daddy make it alone.

Their first roadblock was a tree down over the road, but Big Tom was prepared. He got out, pulled his chain saw out of the truck bed, and dealt with the blockage before moving on.

They passed a side road with a sign that read Bridge Out. It occurred to Albert that the water that ran under that bridge came down from the creek on their farm. When he looked at his daddy, he realized the thought was in his head as well.

As they topped a small hill, they could see water across the road below.

"It doesn't look deep," Big Tom said.

"At least drive down. We can tell once we get there," Albert said, so they did, and realized as they got closer that it wasn't deep, just moving swiftly. They drove right through it.

One mile ran into another and then another, until they were in Hinesville, the county seat of Liberty County. Hinesville looked deserted. There was flood debris along the curbs, and all kinds of storm debris lying about.

"Wait here and let me see if they're even open," Big Tom said, but before he could turn around, they both watched a man come out of the building, get in his truck, and drive away.

"I reckon they're open, Daddy," Albert said.

"Yes. Sit tight. I'll get your chair out of the back."

Albert unlocked his seat belt, then opened the door to wait. Moments later, his daddy had the chair set up and ready.

Big Tom lifted Albert out, settled him into his chair, and then locked their truck. "Hang on," Big Tom said, and pulled Albert and his chair up onto the street backward, then pushed him toward the police station.

The moment they were inside, Big Tom's demeanor changed. He was teary and nervous again as he had been at home. Albert guessed it had to do with having to tell the story again.

"Sit down, Daddy. I can do this much," Albert said, and rolled his chair up to the counter.

"Good morning, how can we help you?" the clerk asked.

"We need to speak to the sheriff."

"What is your name?" she asked.

"I'm Albert Rankin, and this is my daddy, Big Tom Rankin."

"What is your business?" she asked, and then added, "Sorry for being so slow. Our computers are still down, so we're taking all information by hand."

"We're here to report a death."

The woman looked up, first at Albert, then over his shoulder to the big man behind him.

"What's the name of the deceased, and what was the cause of death?" she asked.

"We called him Junior, but he was named for Daddy. His name was Thomas Ray Rankin. The cause of death… he fell into a flooded creek while they were looking for our cattle. He went under and never came up."

"I'm sorry for your loss," the clerk said. "Please wait here. I need to see if Deputy Sheriff Terrell is available."

"What happened to Sheriff Ryman?" Big Tom asked.

"He had surgery before the hurricane. He's still recovering at home. One moment, please."

She hurried down a hallway, then returned almost immediately. "Follow me," she said.

Big Tom got up and pushed Albert down the hall and into the second office on the left.

"Deputy Terrell, this is Tom Rankin and his son, Albert."

Hunt Terrell got up and came around the desk to shake their hands. "I'm Deputy Sheriff Hunt Terrell. My sympathics on the loss of your son. Take a seat, sir. Since we're operating on small generators, computers are down. I'll take down the pertinent info on paper, so bear with me. Now, tell me what happened."

Big Tom's head dropped.

Albert laid his hand on his daddy's arm and gave it a squeeze. "You can do this, Daddy."

Big Tom nodded, then took a deep breath and started talking.

Chapter 19

BY MIDAFTERNOON, THE WIND WAS BLOWING AT LESS than thirty miles per hour and the rain was intermittent. Elliot wanted to go home, and then Dan reminded him he'd be there without power.

"Ah...that's right," Elliot said. "I've been so comfortable here that I forgot. So, I'll gladly accept your hospitality until Blessings gets power again."

"Good," Dan said. "We've been inside your home since all this began, but Alice has not checked on hers, so we're going to see if we can get to that part of town. There's no way of telling if the streets are clear, but either way, we won't be long."

Elliot nodded. "Then I'm going up to rest a bit. If I fall asleep, wake me when supper's ready."

Alice smiled. "We won't forget you," she said, then went to check on the kids. Charlie was on babysitting duty until they got back, and happily so, because Dan had popped some popcorn for them and they were sharing another Pepsi as they settled in to watch a Disney movie.

"We won't be long," Alice said. "Patty, you be good for Charlie, okay?"

Patty nodded. "I'm always good for Charlie. I love him so much," she said.

Charlie's cheeks flushed, but Alice could tell he was secretly pleased.

"No going outside."

"It's okay, Mama. I got this," Charlie said.

Alice gave them both a thumbs-up and then followed Dan out the side door to the portico. He settled his Stetson firmly on his head, helped her up into the passenger seat, and buckled her up. As he did, Alice leaned over and kissed the side of his cheek.

"I've been wanting to do that for days," she said.

"Then I'm really glad you followed through," he said, and kissed her squarely on the mouth. "That's my contribution to impulse." Then he circled the truck and got in. "Here goes nothin', darlin'. Let's go take a look at Blessings."

"I'm nervous," Alice said. "I'm praying the house didn't flood and that our belongings are okay. I so don't want to have to start over again."

"There's no starting over going on around here. No matter what happens, we're not going back, we're moving forward, right?"

She glanced at his profile—dark hair, that big cowboy hat, a straight nose, a strong chin, and very kissable lips—and thought, *Damn straight we're moving forward.*

They hadn't driven more than five blocks when Dan glanced to his right and then pointed. "Hey, look, that whole house is destroyed. Trees fell on it from both ways."

"I wonder if the house belongs to that family who's staying in Elliot's garage apartment. Didn't he say they lost everything when trees fell on their house?"

"Yes, he did. That's rough," Dan said, eyeing the remnants of shredded curtains hanging out of a broken window and glimpses of a sofa, and beyond that, what was left of a kitchen.

"They're fortunate that didn't kill them all," Alice said, and rode in silence, contemplating what might await her, until they were close to her neighborhood. That's when she scooted to the edge of her seat.

She could see how high up the water had gotten, since the waterline was visible because of the debris. But she couldn't see any sign of water getting high enough to come into the house.

"So far, so good," she said, and then Dan turned the corner and she saw the roof of her house. "The roof is still on the front of the house. The garage is still standing."

He pulled up in the drive and parked behind her car. "Your car is fine," he said. "The attached garage held up, and your windows are still boarded up. Let's go inside and see if you have any leaks."

Alice unbuckled her seat belt, and Dan helped her down. "Got your key?" he asked.

She unlocked the security alarm, then Dan unlocked the door and stepped aside for her to enter. Even as she was walking in, she could feel the balance. Nothing had been disturbed.

"Everything is okay in here," she said, and then went from room to room, checking for signs of a leaking roof or broken windows. She walked through it twice, just to make sure she hadn't missed anything, and then sat down in the living room with a sigh of relief. "There is a crack in the window in the utility room, but it's still boarded up. Other than that, all is well."

"It won't take much to replace the glass," Dan said. "I can do it easily." Then there was a knock at her door, and Julia, her neighbor from across the street, peeked in.

"I saw you walk in. I just wanted to check on you and the kids. I knew you weren't home, but I was worried."

"That is so sweet of you," Alice said. "We have been Mr. Amos's guests throughout the storm. He also sheltered his elderly neighbor from across the street. Julia, do you know Dan Amos?"

"Only by reputation. One of my aunts rents one of the properties you manage. I'm Julia Youngman. Nice to meet you."

"Ms. Youngman, it's my pleasure," Dan said.

Alice stood up. "We were just about to leave. I told the kids we wouldn't be gone long, so thank you for thinking of us."

"Of course," Julia said. She gave Dan one last lingering smile, and then she was gone.

Alice grinned. "You made a conquest."

"It's the hat," he said, and then stole a quick kiss before they left.

Once they were back in the truck, Dan headed toward Main, curious what might have happened to it. There was still water in the streets, but only a few inches.

"Look at all the flood debris," Alice said, then gasped. "Oh no! The Piggly Wiggly sign is gone. And the sign at Granny's is gone, too. Part of the roof at the travel agency has been damaged. Looks like it was hit by some kind of flying debris."

"None of that is permanent, and so far, we haven't heard of any fatalities. That's the miracle."

"You're right," Alice said.

"Let's check Bloomer's Hardware," Dan suggested,

and drove a little farther up Main. "Looks okay, unless Fred had roof damage, too."

"Once we get power back up, we're likely to be very busy for a few months as people start fixing or rebuilding what was destroyed," Alice said.

"It all looks pretty sad right now, but it will get fixed. Nothing is open, so are you ready to go home?"

She nodded, thinking how easily she'd thought of the big house when he said *home*, then realized it wasn't the house, it was Dan who made it home.

Albert watched his daddy's face as they drove out of Hinesville and saw something he never thought he'd see. His daddy was a broken man. Witnessing his son's death had hurt him to the core.

Big Tom cleared his throat. "What if they never find Junior? What if—"

"Daddy! Don't!" Albert said. "Junior is with the Lord now, and with Mama. He's not suffering anymore. He's home. We're the ones who are sad. We're the ones who will have to figure out how to make the rest of our lives matter without him in them."

"But—"

"No buts, Daddy! Sailors are buried at sea, so losing his body in a flood only means we won't be digging a hole and putting him in it later. What happens to a body once someone dies doesn't change a thing. The deceased don't care now. Don't you see? No matter how family chooses to put their loved ones to rest, it's never for the ones they've lost. It's always for the ones left behind. We'll figure it out day by day."

Big Tom sighed. "How did you get so smart?"

Albert shrugged. "That's not being smart. That's just knowing what I know."

Big Tom reached across the console and gave Albert a pat on the shoulder. "Thank you for coming with me today. This would have been twice as hard if I'd come on my own."

Albert nodded. "Staying home alone would have been worse for me, too." Then he pointed. "Look, Daddy! Look toward the west where the clouds are thinning out. It's a rainbow!"

The sight made Big Tom's heart a little bit lighter.

"It's a sign, isn't it? That's Junior telling us he's okay," Albert said.

His father looked up. "I don't know if it's Junior, but someone is telling us that eventually it will be okay."

―⁓―

Chief Pittman was on a mission to get repair crews to Blessings. He'd been able to contact utility companies to let them know there were some ongoing life-or-death situations with people who used oxygen tanks, and power companies to get them to assess Blessings and replace power poles. He knew they were only one of many small towns on a list with cities in the same shape, but Blessings was his responsibility, and he'd do anything to keep it and the people safe and well.

―⁓―

Moses Gatlin was standing quietly in the front room of their farmhouse. He'd been listening for some time now and was convinced that the wind wasn't blowing as hard as it had been. He took a chance and opened the front door to look out, then breathed a quiet sigh of relief. The rain was falling, but gently, not in a blowing gale.

Thank you, Lord.

They didn't have a battery-powered radio to verify what he thought, but he was guessing this was the hurricane in its death throes.

J. B. came up behind him and gave him a pat on the back. "Looks like we made it, Moses. There were a couple of times this past week when I wasn't sure we would."

Moses nodded. "I hear you. I'll go tell Mama. This will perk her right up."

"Something needs to," J. B. muttered. "She's been as cranky as an old bear."

Moses nodded as he shut the door, then went down the hall to her room. He knocked, and when she didn't answer, he peeked in. She was on her side facing the door, staring at the wall.

"Mama! The storm is passing! Winds are dying. It's still raining a bit, but not bad. It'll feel good to get out of the house. Want to come with us? We're going to go check on the livestock and buildings."

"Close the door and leave me be," Beulah Gatlin said.

"Mama, what's wrong?" Moses asked. "Are you ailing? Do you need to see a doctor?"

"Get out! Get out! Get out!" Beulah screamed, and grabbed a coffee cup from the side table and threw it at him.

Moses ducked and slammed the door shut just before the cup hit him in the head, then yelled at her from the hall. "What's the matter with you?"

She threw something else at the door as an answer.

J. B. came running. "What's happening? Was that you shouting?"

Moses shoved a shaky hand through his hair. "It was both of us. I don't know what's wrong with Mama, but she's losing it."

"Are we still going out to check on the livestock?" J. B. asked.

Moses nodded. "Someone has to keep their shit together. I guess it's gonna be us."

They got on their work boots and rain gear and headed out the door. They found a fence down, a door at the hen house blown off its hinges, and all of the chickens drowned. It was a depressing sight, and Moses was glad his mother had stayed in the house after all.

It took over two hours to bury the chickens and repair the doors, before they had time to go check on their goats and the roof on the hay barn. The reality of their situation was that what was left of their livestock needed tending, and their mama did not. So they kept on working.

———

Beulah was angry. Marty wouldn't leave her alone. He showed up when she was asleep and stared at her without talking, and when she was awake, she could hear his voice in her head.

I thought you loved me, Mama, but when my family needed you most, you threw them away.

She'd started out trying to explain why, but it didn't stop him. He was digging at her daily, picking off the scab on her conscience. And there was the wind that blew and blew and never stopped, and the rain that kept falling and still didn't wash away her sins.

She had been staring at the wall, waiting for the wind to blow it down on top of her and put an end to her misery, but instead, Number Two son was telling her the wind was easing—that the hurricane was coming to an end.

Too soon! Too soon! she screamed, and then realized the scream was just in her head. And there was Marty again, sitting on the foot of her bed.

"Go away! You don't belong here anymore."

I thought you loved me.

"I did. You ruined everything with the meth. It's your fault," Beulah said, and covered her face with her hands.

If it was my fault, then why did you punish my family? Why didn't you say something to me, instead?

"She was your wife! She should have been the one strong enough to change you. It's her fault, too!" Beulah cried, and then sat up on the side of the bed. "Go away! Go away! You aren't allowed to be here anymore."

I can be anywhere I want now, Mama. You have no power here.

Beulah stood up, then laid the old rag doll she'd been holding back down on the pillow and walked out of the bedroom.

I know where you're going, Mama. You're going to hell.

Tears were rolling down Beulah's face as she staggered up the hall. "Don't talk. Stop talking."

Coward. You are a coward, Mama. You want to die, but you want something or someone to make it happen to you. No wall is going to fall on you. No hurricane is going to blow you away. No flood is going to wash you away. You will live with this memory for the rest of your life.

Beulah moaned. "No, no, no," she said, and then got all the way to the kitchen.

She stood for a few moments, weighing her options. There was no thought in her mind but to escape. But how? Then she looked at the propane cookstove and sighed. *Yes. Yes. This would work.* She reached for the controls and turned them on, one burner at a time, then went over to the table and sat, listening to the hiss of escaping gas and thinking of all the meals she'd served at this table. Watching her boys blow out the candles on their birthday cakes here. Teaching Charlie, her first grandson, how to drink from a cup. Feeding Patty her first dish of oatmeal. And watching Alice, with her young girl wiles, taking Marty away from her.

She could smell the gas now. The room was full of it. She stood up, then opened the back door and stood on the threshold looking through the storm door. She wanted her last sight of this earth to be what she loved best.

She could see Moses and J. B. down at the barn. They were far enough away not to be hurt. She took the little matchbox out of her apron pocket, took out a match, and pulled it across the striker. There was a loud and distinct sound of moving air, like a sleeping giant behind her suddenly inhaled, then the flash of flame. The walls in the house blew out into the yard, while the upstairs fell down into the pyre.

Moses was in the barn when he heard the explosion and felt the ground shake beneath his feet.

"What the heck was that?" he asked.

J. B. ran out to look, then started screaming. "Run,

Moses, run. The house blew up! Mama! Oh my God, Mama!"

Moses came out of the barn in long, giant strides, trying to catch up with J. B. as he flew across the muddy ground, knowing as he ran that she was gone.

J. B. had stopped about fifty yards from the house when Moses caught up. He was out of breath and talking in shorthand. "Too hot. No closer."

Moses stopped, then bent over and grabbed his knees to keep from falling facedown. When he could breathe without thinking he was going to pass out, he rose up and stared at the flames eating into the wood and at the smoke spiraling up into the air.

Which part of that is Mama? he wondered, and kept hearing the mad shriek in her voice as she ordered him to get out. He was never going to voice the fear, but he'd bet his last dollar that none of this was an accident.

"Oh my God, Moses! What are we going to do?" J. B. cried.

"This makes no sense. We live through a hurricane and now this?" J. B. was grasping at straws, trying to make sense of it. "Wait! What if it was the hurricane? What if it loosened the propane connection on the cookstove? What if it had been leaking gas, and when Mama went to heat up her coffee, it exploded?"

Moses shook his head. "All I know is we're just as homeless now as Alice and the kids were when Marty set their house on fire. That's God paying us back," he whispered, and dropped to his knees.

"At least the truck is in the shed," J. B. said.

"And the keys were in the house," Moses added.

J. B. started to cry. "The house is gone, Brother. Mama is gone. What are we gonna do?"

Moses pulled himself up to his feet. "If the extra set of keys isn't in the truck, I'm gonna hot-wire it and drive to Hinesville and tell the sheriff."

"I'm going with you," J. B. said.

"Of course you are. I wouldn't leave you behind," Moses said.

— ~~~ —

Deputy Sheriff Hunt Terrell had just come back from a call and was hanging up his raincoat and shaking the water off his hat when the clerk came to the office door.

"Moses and J. B. Gatlin are up front. They want to talk to you."

Hunt frowned. "Why is that name familiar?"

"Their brother was Marty Conroy."

Hunt snapped his fingers. "That's it! He's the one who blew up his home, himself, and everything he and his family owned the first part of this year, right?"

"Yes, sir."

"Then send them on back. Do we have any news on repair crews in the area?" Hunt asked.

"Not to my knowledge, sir."

"Okay. Just checking. We're lucky to have a generator but it's barely enough to power lights and heat. We need communication up and running."

"Yes, sir," the clerk said, and left the room.

Hunt poured himself a cup of hot coffee and was stirring in sugar when the men knocked. "Come in," Hunt said. "Take a seat. Can I offer you a cup of coffee?"

Moses looked at J. B. There was no telling when

they'd have the luxury of making themselves a cup of coffee again.

"Yes, sir, we sure would appreciate it," Moses said, then watched the deputy fill two Styrofoam cups.

"Creamer or sugar?" Hunt asked.

"Black is fine," J. B. said.

Hunt set the coffee down in front of them, then sat down in his chair and took a quick sip of his own. "So, gentlemen, what brings you here?" he asked, then was surprised when they both teared up.

"We came to report our mama's death," Moses said.

Hunt grimaced. "My sympathies. I remember her. What happened?"

"We're not sure," Moses said. "The hurricane has been wearing on her disposition something fierce. The more the wind blew, the more she withdrew. The last couple of days she wouldn't come out of her room except to eat. But this morning, when the wind began to die back some and the rain was just rain, J. B. and I told her we were going out to check the property, check our livestock and outbuildings to see how they all weathered. I tried to get her to go with us, but she didn't want to, so me and J. B. went on out."

Hunt was listening without comment but making notes. And when Moses Gatlin paused for a moment, his brother picked up the story.

"We found a door blown off the chicken house and all of the hens had drowned. Took us a good two hours to bury all the carcasses and repair the door. We had just gone into the barn to look for roof leaks when we heard a horrible explosion. The ground actually shook beneath our feet. I ran out to look and saw our house was on fire. I shouted at Moses and then took off running."

"And I was right behind him," Moses said as he picked up the story again. "We couldn't get close. The fire was so hot. But we knew Mama was gone. We don't know what happened. Only that something blew up."

"Did you have power?" Hunt asked.

"No, sir. We haven't had lights or water for days," Moses said.

"But we did have an old propane cookstove," J. B. added.

"Didn't your brother die earlier this year from his house exploding?" Hunt asked.

Moses's heart sank. It was too much of a coincidence for two members of a family to both die in the same way, but months apart. "Yes, sir, he did. But he was high on meth when it happened."

Hunt tapped his pen against his desk as he looked down at his notes, and then looked up. "Did your mother do drugs?"

Moses gasped. "No, sir! She didn't even smoke or chew or drink alcohol."

"So what do you think caused the explosion?" Hunt asked.

"I thought maybe the hurricane damaged something. Like maybe the fitting connecting the stove to the propane coming in the house?"

"How did you light your stove? Did it have an electric timer, or—"

"No," Moses said, then wiped his eyes and blew his nose. "I mentioned it was older. We just turned on the burner and lit a match to it."

Hunt made another note. "I'll notify the medical examiner. In the meantime, where can you be reached?"

"We don't have any place to stay. Everything we owned is gone. I reckon for now, we'll be sleeping in the barn…either on the hay or in our truck."

"Did you have insurance on the house?" Hunt asked.

"A small policy. Nothing that will replace what we lost."

"Alright," Hunt said. "I think I have enough to get the investigation started. Don't move or clean up anything. Leave it all where it lies until the crime scene team collects all the evidence."

J. B. paled. "Crime scene? There is no crime scene. Just what's left of our lives."

"I'm sorry," Hunt said. "But when anyone dies in an unexplained accident, it has to be investigated to prove there was no foul play. You should have remembered that from when your brother Marty blew his home up."

Moses wiped a shaky hand over his face. "Yes, sir. I just didn't think. We'll be there. Do you think it will be today when they show up?"

"Yes," Hunt said. "It will be today."

"Then as soon as we find something to eat and get a few supplies, we'll be on our way home."

"There's a shelter set up at the Baptist church here in Hinesville. Go down there and tell Preacher Jordan that Hunt Terrell said you needed a little help and something to eat. There aren't any stores open as yet, so that's the closest place around here you'll find for a meal."

"Thank you," Moses said.

"Yes, thanks," J. B. added.

"I'll walk you out," Hunt said, and led the way up the hall to the front lobby, then watched them leave. As soon as they were gone, he turned to the clerk. "I'm going to the ME's office. Notify my crime scene team by handheld radio. Tell them to meet me here at the office, and that we have a death at an explosion. They'll know what to do."

"Yes, sir. Will do," she said, and reached for the walkie-talkie on her desk as he left through the back door.

Chapter 20

MOSES AND J. B. WERE NUMB. TALKING TO THE LAW ABOUT what had happened had seemed surreal—like they were talking about someone else's life. And they were both silently wondering how this second explosion on the same property was going to play out, since both had resulted in a death.

They found the church and sat down to chili cooked over camp stoves, made from meat that had been donated by the local grocer. The shelter didn't have food to give away, but the Gatlin brothers were grateful for what they had in their bellies when they left.

As they drove out of Hinesville, Moses glanced over at his brother. "Do you think we should try to find Alice and the kids and tell them about Mama?"

J. B. didn't bother to hide his surprise. "Why?"

Moses sighed. "I don't know. It just seems like the right thing to do."

"We didn't once do the right thing by them when Marty died. She's not gonna want to see our faces. And this isn't the best time to go hunting her down. Go home. We got cops coming."

"Yeah, I guess you're right," Moses said, and let go of the impulse.

Ruby was feeding Lovey her lunch when Peanut came

into the room with a smile on his face. "The hurricane has been downgraded to a tropical storm and is moving inland. I don't know how long it will take to get power back, but the good news is that the process can begin today," he said.

"That's wonderful!" Ruby said, and spooned another bite of soup into Lovey's mouth that she quickly chewed and swallowed.

"It's sure good news," Lovey said. "This means I will be able to start cleanup and rebuilding on my house."

"Is there anything I can do to aid in that process?" Peanut asked.

"Just find me a good building crew," Lovey said.

"I'll see what I can do about that," Peanut said.

Ruby spooned another bite into Lovey's mouth, then chased it with a sip of sweet tea. "Honey, as soon as Lovey finishes lunch, I want to go home, clean up, and sleep a bit, because I'm spending the night here with her again."

Lovey frowned. "No, I don't need you to do that. I'm mostly sleeping off pain meds, anyway, and if I need something, I can buzz a nurse. They were able to get enough people in here this morning to change shifts."

Ruby started to argue, but Lovey shook her head.

"Nope. I'm serious. You were a lifesaver last night, but I had just come out of surgery and was loopy as all get out. Go home. Rest. Come see me tomorrow."

"Really?" Ruby asked.

Lovey smiled. "Yes, really. And just for the record, I don't want company, so if anyone asks, tell them I'm not ready for that yet. Once people find out what happened, they'll just want to come and stare at me out of curiosity.

I'm not ready to share the bald head and cuts. I look like Freddy Krueger paid me a visit."

Ruby laughed. "Okay, but right now, you need to get through dessert. It's pudding."

"I wish it was a piece of one of Mercy's pies," Lovey muttered.

"There'll be time enough for them in the days to come," Ruby said. "Today, it's pudding."

———

Instead of going straight home from the sheriff's office, Big Tom and Albert headed for Blessings. With no other way to communicate with his boss, Big Tom needed to find out when he planned to open up again.

As they came into town, it was both shocking and sad to see the devastation. It was obvious some homes had flooded, because they could see the watermarks on the outside walls. And the wind had done a number on quite a few of the fine old trees that lined the streets.

Big Tom noticed, as they passed, that the police station was open and decided to stop in and let Chief Pittman know what had happened to Junior. The streets were virtually empty, so he made a U-turn and parked.

"Want to get out, Albert?"

"Yes sir. We're in this together."

So again, Tom dealt with the wheelchair, and then getting Albert in it, before they went inside.

———

Chief Pittman was standing at the front desk talking to Avery when the door opened, and when he saw who it was, and that Albert was with Big Tom, Lon was surprised. The very two people he'd wanted to speak with about Elliot's attack.

"Good afternoon," Lon said. "Albert...how are you doing?" he added.

Albert shrugged. "It's been a hard day, sir."

Big Tom added. "We need to talk to you, if you have the time."

"Sure do. Come on back," Lon said, and led the way.

As soon as they were seated, Big Tom started talking. "We just came from the sheriff's office and were coming here to talk to my boss about work when it occurred to me that I should probably notify you as well."

"Notify me about what?" Lon asked.

Big Tom leaned back in his chair, as if bracing himself for the g-force of what he was going to say. "We lost Junior yesterday during the calm."

Lon leaned forward, startled by the news. "I'm so sorry, sir. What happened?"

Tom felt another breakdown coming. He'd thought he could handle it, but he'd obviously been wrong as he choked on a sob.

Albert reached for his daddy's arm. "Let me, Daddy."

Big Tom nodded, swallowing back tears as Albert began to explain what had happened, all the way from finding the creek out of its banks, the back of the corral gone, and all of the cattle missing. Then he went on to explain about the cougar and what had happened to Junior on his way back.

"So you witnessed this happening?" Lon said.

"Daddy saw it. From where I was standing, I never did see Junior...only Daddy's reaction."

Big Tom nodded. "I was looking straight at him when

the bank caved in. He fell backward into the flood and never surfaced. I ran after him but never even had a glimpse, and then the hurricane amped back up and I had to run to get home. I knew Albert needed me, and there was nothing more I could ever do for Junior. I'm telling you this on the off chance someone shows up here with a story about finding a body."

Lon's heart went out to Big Tom. He remembered all too well nearly losing Mercy in floodwaters. "That is a horrible thing to witness, and my sympathies for your loss," he said, then glanced at Albert. "I heard a bit about how you injured your feet. So, care to tell me the story?"

Albert's shoulders slumped. "To tell you the truth, Chief, the past few days have all been a blur, and that seems like a lifetime ago. The bottom line is I was on the dock. Junior was out on the lake in our boat. I was messing around pulling in my stringer and getting ready to leave when I fell in. I got myself out and pulled off my shoes and socks. I was dumping water out of my shoes when a black bear got between me and my truck. It challenged me, and I panicked like a little girl. I threw my catch of fish at it and did the one thing Daddy always told us not to do. I turned around and ran." He wiped a shaky hand over his face.

"It was the dumbest thing I've ever done, and I'm paying for it now. If I hadn't been hurt, I would have been outside with Daddy and Junior. I can't help thinking that might have made the difference. Maybe I would have been able to grab Junior's arm as he was falling. Maybe we would have taken a different route besides right along the floodwaters. But maybe doesn't change facts. My feet are a mess, and Junior is gone. If you hear anything, we would appreciate the information."

"Certainly," Lon said, and led the way out for them.

He thought about Albert's story even more after going back to his office, but hearing it from the victim himself made a difference in his first opinion of what Dan Amos had overheard. Albert straight up admitted it had been stupid. People make stupid mistakes when they're scared. The man with bad feet had had nothing to do with an attack on a man on the other side of the lake, and the only one who had been in the boat was now deceased.

Lon crossed off that lead and decided to go by Dan Amos's house and check up on Elliot. Maybe he'd remembered something else.

——

The rain was down to a drizzle when Chief Pittman arrived at Dan's house. As he got out, he heard the sound of a motor running, saw lights inside the house, and remembered they had a generator running. He climbed up the steps and rang the bell.

A few moments later, Dan opened the door. "Morning, Chief. Come in!"

Lon stopped on the doormat. "My shoes are wet. I'll deliver my message here."

Dan grinned and pointed behind him. Patty was lying on the floor, using Booger as a pillow, and Charlie was flat on the floor watching TV. Elliot was reading, and Alice was coming from the kitchen, wiping her hands on a towel.

"Wet shoes are not an issue here. Come sit, unless you need privacy. If so, we can go to the kitchen."

"The kitchen would be ideal, and Elliot needs to join us."

Elliot looked up. "Did someone say my name?"

"Yes, sir," Dan said. "The chief requests your presence in the kitchen."

"Of course," Elliot said, and followed them, then joined them at the table.

"So what's up?" Dan asked.

"Regarding what you overheard Big Tom Rankin talking about at Lovey's last week… You were wondering if his sons could have had anything to do with Elliot's attack, or if they might have witnessed something."

"Oh yes," Dan said. "Did you ever get to talk to him?"

"No. The hurricane hit too fast, but oddly enough, he and his younger son, Albert, came into the station this morning. The older son, Junior, died yesterday during the calm. They were out checking livestock. A creek had flooded behind their barn, and Junior was standing too close to the edge. The ground on which he was standing suddenly collapsed, throwing him backward into the floodwaters. He went under and never surfaced. Big Tom witnessed it."

"Oh my!" Elliot said. "Poor chap!"

Dan's empathy for the man was instant. He knew exactly what it felt like to witness the tragic, unexpected death of someone you loved.

"To cut this short, I did question Albert about what had happened to him, and I came closer to believing the incident than I had before. And Junior, the one closest to where Elliot was found, is dead. So, right now I have no more leads as to who hurt you, Elliot, but that doesn't mean I'm stopping the investigation."

"It feels over," Elliot said. "I won't lose sleep about it."

Lon watched the old man's face and, not for the first time, wondered how his head worked. He was certainly one of a kind in Blessings. "Okay then. I just wanted to update you with what we know."

"Thanks," Dan said. "Is there anything you know about the power outages? I'm sure the utility companies are overwhelmed, but I thought I'd ask."

"Haven't heard anything definite, but then our communication systems are down to handheld radios."

"I have a CB radio at my house," Elliot offered. "If you have vital info you need to share anywhere, come and get me, and I'll gladly open my house to the police. Your day dispatcher, Avery Ames, has one, too. He is one of my CB friends. We talk some late at night."

"That's much appreciated, but if needed, we'll just have Avery relay messages for us." Then he got up. "I'd better get back to the station."

Dan walked him back to the door, and after Lon left, he sat down and quietly told Alice what was going on.

"Hurricane Fanny has caused so much tragedy. I thank God every night for you and Patty. You both came far too close to being early victims," Alice said.

"Thank Booger and Charlie," Dan said. "They found her. I just helped with the rescue." Then he kissed the back of her hand and changed the subject. "I checked the fuel gauge on the generator. We're good for hours here, but I need to get out and check the rental properties and assess damages. I know there will be repairs needed on some, if not all. I hate going anywhere and being unable for us to contact each other, but this has to be done."

"Take your cell phone, in case we do get cell coverage

again. And in the meantime, we'll be just fine. Go do what you have to do. I found stew meat in your freezer. Are you okay with me using it?"

"I'm okay with you doing whatever you want to do here, and stew would be great. I'll get back as soon as I can," he said, and this time he leaned over and kissed her. He picked up his phone as he went out the side door and then drove away.

Alice went straight to the kitchen to get out the stew meat. It felt good to be useful again.

———∿∿∿———

When Dan returned later that afternoon, the mailman had finally made his route. Dan spent part of the evening going through mail, then sat down to a full meal of beef stew and corn bread, and said a prayer of thanks for the passing of the storm.

———∿∿∿———

It was the middle of the night two days later when Dan's phone suddenly signaled a text. He woke abruptly and turned on the light. "We have a signal…and bars," he said, then rolled over to sit on the side of his bed and read the message.

It was the latest in a series of very anxious messages from his family. Several were from his parents, and then others from both of his brothers. He immediately sent back texts letting them know all was well and that the cell coverage had just this moment returned. He promised to stay in touch and then hit Send.

It was an uplifting moment to know things were finally being repaired, and Dan was too amped to go back to sleep, so he decided to check on the generator and get something to drink.

He slipped into a pair of sweatpants and an old long-sleeved T-shirt and went out into the hall. The first thing he noticed was that the door to Alice's room was open, and then he saw Patty curled up in the hall a few yards away. He darted into Alice's room and flipped on the light.

"Alice!" he said sharply.

She sat straight up in bed. "What? What's wrong?" And then realized Patty wasn't there. "Patty? Where's Patty?"

Dan motioned for her to come. "She's out here."

Alice flew out of bed without reaching for a robe and came running, her dark hair disheveled and her eyes wide with panic.

Dan grabbed her arm. "Don't scare her," he whispered.

Alice nodded and was grateful for Dan's hand on her shoulder as they hurried down the hall. She dropped to her knees beside Patty and felt of her forehead. It was cool. Her arms were cold, and her little feet were freezing.

"She's so cold," Alice said.

"Let me," he said, and scooped her up, cradling her in his arms before following Alice back to their room. As he sat down on the side of the bed, Patty slowly opened her eyes.

"I'm cold," she said.

Dan put her in Alice's arms and then covered both of them up with the blanket at the foot of the bed.

Alice gently brushed the hair from her eyes. "Patty, darling, were you dreaming?"

Patty shrugged. "Maybe."

"What about?" Alice asked.

"Bad Grandma," she whispered.

"Oh my Lord," Alice said, and began rocking her where she sat. "You're okay, sweetheart. We don't ever have to see her again, and she can't hurt you. She's a long ways away."

Dan frowned. "Who is this woman?"

"Marty's mother," Alice said.

"Oh! The one who—?" Then he stopped when Alice nodded. "So what was Bad Grandma doing in your dream?" Dan asked.

"Just looking at me," Patty said, and then burst into tears. "She wouldn't go away, so I ran."

"I'm so sorry she scared you," Dan said, and then remembered a night when his little boy had a bad dream about being teased at school, and what he'd seen Holly do to console him.

Alice was angry all over again, remembering the shock they'd all endured when they were rejected by their family. She'd had no idea how deeply it had affected Patty and had never heard her use the description *bad grandma* before.

"I know how to make Bad Grandma go away," Dan said.

Patty swiped away tears. "Really?"

He nodded. "We have to do this together. You, Mama, and me."

Alice was intrigued. "What do we need to do?"

"What was her name?"

"Beulah," Alice said.

"Okay, now all of us hold hands. Then we need to close our eyes. Picture Bad Grandma's face and keep looking. I'm going to say a prayer for her to be happy, and you watch and see if she begins to smile. When she smiles at you, then Bad Grandma is gone and Happy Grandma is back. Are you ready? Okay, now close your eyes."

Dan watched Alice and Patty's eyes shut and was moved by the fact that both of them immediately frowned. Bad Grandma must have been a real headache. Then he closed his eyes, too, trying to paraphrase what Holly had said.

"Something has made Beulah sad and angry, Lord. We're asking you to look in her heart and find the little girl she used to be, and then whisper in her ear that she is loved."

He heard Alice's swift intake of breath and knew it had moved her, but he kept talking. "Remind Beulah how to be happy, and please tell her no one is mad at her. Isn't this right, girls?"

Alice's voice shook, but she didn't hesitate. "I'm not mad at you anymore, Beulah."

Then Patty piped up. "I'm not mad, Grandma."

All of a sudden they heard movement in the door behind them. "I'm not mad, either," Charlie said.

Dan motioned for him to join them, and pulled Charlie into the circle. "Okay, Lord, Beulah knows she is forgiven. Tell her to go in peace and be happy." Then Dan whispered, "Now we wait until you see her smile."

Alice was the first. "I see it. She's smiling at me."

"I see your smile, Grandma," Charlie said.

"Grandma is laughing," Patty said.

"Then it's done," Dan said. "She won't be sad anymore."

Patty crawled out of her mother's lap and into Dan's arms. "Thank you for taking Bad Grandma away."

"I didn't do it. You and Mama and Charlie did it."

"Thanks, Dan," Charlie said.

"Group hug," Dan said, and Alice didn't hesitate to join in. He looked at her over the heads of her children and saw tears in her eyes, but she was smiling. He'd take that as an affirmation.

"Okay, kids, let's try to get back to sleep," Alice said.

"Not sleepy yet, Mama," Patty said.

"I'm not sleepy anymore, either," Charlie said.

But Dan knew it was because of what had just happened. "Well, I hate to brag, but I also know how to fix this," and he winked at Alice. "If it's okay with Mama, I think this might be the perfect time for an ice cream raid."

"Mama says that's a great idea," Alice said.

"Yay!" Patty said, and bailed out of Dan's lap.

"Robe and house shoes!" Alice said. "And for me, as well."

"What about Elliot?" Patty asked.

"I think Elliot needs sleep worse than he needs ice cream," Dan said. "And we need to be quiet so we don't wake him as we go downstairs."

A few minutes later, they were at the kitchen table eating ice cream and laughing and talking. By the time the ice cream was gone, so were the memories of the dream. The kids were running ahead of them up the stairs when Alice reached for Dan's hand.

"Just when I think I've seen the best there is of you, you turn around and show me a new and wonderful facet. You are an amazing person, a wonderful man, and forever my hero."

Dan was so moved that he kissed her there, without caring that the kids might turn around and see them, and knowing he would spend the rest of the night awake and wanting her.

But it was worth it.

———∼∼∼———

The next day dawned with a nearly clear sky and no sign of rain. The street and garbage crews were making rounds for the first time in days, picking up limbs, cleaning up flood debris, pulling Blessings back together one street at a time.

Charlie spent some time cleaning up the dogtrot, with Booger nearby. Alice and Patty were doing a load of laundry, and Dan was outside using a chain saw on the trees he'd lost in the back of the house.

Elliot went across the street to talk to the Martin family who was living in the garage apartment, and then later Dan saw Ellis Martin outside with Elliot, removing the shutters and taking down the boards from the windows.

At the same time all that was going on, Alice received a phone call from Barton Rowland. She answered without looking at caller ID, and then her heart skipped a beat when she heard his voice. "Hello?"

"Mrs. Conroy, this is Barton Rowland. I hope you and your family have fared safely during the hurricane?"

Alice's heart was racing. She hated confrontations of all kinds, even if she was on the receiving end of apologies. "Yes, we are all fine."

"Wonderful. The reason I'm calling is to ask permission for our wives and daughters to come apologize to you and Patty in person. Would this afternoon be okay, or would you prefer another time?"

"No, this afternoon is fine."

"Are you okay with two o'clock?" he asked.

"Yes, I can make that work, but we're not at home. We have been guests of Dan Amos during the hurricane and will likely be here until power is restored. Do you know where he lives?"

"Yes, that's Preston Williams's old estate, right?"

"Yes."

"We're all coming together so this isn't a long intrusion into your day."

"We'll be waiting," Alice said, and hung up.

She sat thinking about the afternoon ahead, then sighed. "May as well get this over with," she said, then got up and took a cold bottle of water outside to Dan.

He saw her coming and killed the chain saw. "Hey, beautiful. Is that for me?"

She nodded and handed him the water, watching as he drank in long, thirsty gulps.

"Thank you," he said, and then sat down on the trunk of the tree and pulled her between his legs. "So, what's going on?"

"How do you know anything is going on?" she asked.

He put his finger on the space between her eyebrows. "Because when you're bothered, there are four little frown lines right here, even when you're pretending it's all good. So confess."

"The three girls and their mothers are coming here this afternoon at two to make their apologies to Patty and to me. I am begging for your attendance."

"You couldn't keep me away," he said. "I would hug you, but I'm too sweaty and dirty."

She put her arms around his neck and leaned against him anyway. "Thank you," she said.

"Thank you? I'm not doing you a favor, my darling Alice. There's something I don't think you have completely grasped. I love you. With all my heart. I felt it before we made love, but I *knew* it afterward. We belong."

Alice leaned back. "I love you, too, Danner Amos. So much."

"Then we're on the same page. Yes?"

She nodded.

Dan smiled. "When you have trouble, I'm your go-to, yes?"

"Yes."

"And you will always be my touchstone. No secrets between us from this day forward," he added.

Tears were running down her cheeks. "Deal."

Dan wiped away her tears. "Best deal I ever made, too," he said, and sealed it with a kiss.

Chapter 21

PATTY'S LONG BLOND HAIR WAS SHINY CLEAN AND CURLY, and Alice had dressed her in jeans, a little yellow blouse, and tennis shoes. She was sitting primly beside her mother, who was wearing almost the same thing, except Alice's shirt was blue-and-white plaid, and her thick, dark hair was hanging loose around her face. She still had the bandage on her right hand, and after a futile attempt to put makeup on with her left hand, she'd washed it all off and settled for a little lipstick.

Charlie was sitting nearby with Booger lying at his feet, and Dan was just coming down the stairs when the doorbell rang. "I'll get it," he said as he strode past the living room on his way to the front door.

Alice was so caught up in the black jeans and long-sleeved white shirt he was wearing that she forgot to be anxious about who was on the other side of the door. Then she felt Patty scoot a little closer and reached for her hand.

"We've got this," she whispered, and winked.

Patty relaxed and then smiled.

But the three families at the door weren't smiling, and when they saw Dan's imposing figure in the doorway of an equally imposing home, their anxiety rose.

"Good afternoon," Dan said. "Come in. We've been waiting for you." And just like that, he not only took control of their presence, but let them know Alice and

Patty were not facing this alone. As soon as he shut the door, he gestured. "Follow me," he said, and led them into the living room, well aware that it was the most imposing room in the house.

The massive fireplace at the end of the room and the rich cherrywood paneling on the walls was a nod to old elegance. But the oxblood red of the leather chairs and sofas, the gold sconces on the walls, the ancient andirons at the fireplace, along with the massive crystal chandelier hanging from the thirty-foot ceiling above the seating area, were ostentatious and anything but subtle.

"Seat yourselves," Dan said as he took a seat on the arm of the sofa beside Alice and then casually rested his hand on her shoulder.

The men saw it as a reminder that he would back her on whatever she chose to do. The women saw it as the gesture of a man who'd already staked his claim.

Their attention moved to Alice Conroy, sitting calmly in all that glamour, wearing jeans and a plaid shirt, with only a swipe of lipstick. A true example of the old saying that "Less is more," and she was still the prettiest woman in the room.

Alice saw them staring and judging, and decided to take control of this meeting.

"I'm Alice Conroy. This is my daughter, Patty, and my son, Charlie. I'm assuming you know Danner Amos. I know none of you. Not even your daughters, which makes this meeting all the more shocking to me. I've already spoken to your husbands, so I have no need to hear anything more from them. Will the rest of you please stand when you introduce yourselves, then say what you came to say."

The women were dumbfounded. They had expected a hillbilly. Instead, they got a queen wearing plaid.

Renée Rowland spoke first. "I'm Renée Rowland, and—"

"She asked you to stand," Dan said.

Renée blinked, stood, and made Judy stand up beside her. "I'm Renée Rowland, and this is my daughter, Judy. I am so terribly embarrassed about all of this. I hope you accept my apology. I should not listen to gossip and certainly should not have passed it on as fact to my daughter."

Renée poked her daughter, then nodded.

Judy looked down at the floor and before she even opened her mouth, Dan spoke again.

"Young lady, you did not offend the floor. Patty is waiting for your apology. You look at her."

Renée paled, thinking of the lengths to which all of this could still go. "Do what he said, Judy."

Judy was pasty-faced as she looked at Patty. "I did a bad thing. Mama told me not to play with you, but she didn't tell me to be mean to you. I saw you fall. I am so sorry I didn't tell Teacher right then. I didn't want you to get hurt. I just wanted Teacher to myself. I'm sorry. Really sorry." And then she started to cry.

Patty shrank back against her mama's arm. Listening to what Judy had been thinking about her made her sad.

Charlotte Wells stood up next, with her daughter Ruthie at her side. "This is all so horribly upsetting. I don't know what to say."

"'I'm sorry' would be a good way to begin," Dan said.

Charlotte's expression blanked. "Uh…yes, of course. I'm so sorry, Miss Conroy, I—"

"Mrs. I'm a widow," Alice said shortly.

Charlotte was pissed she had to do this. It was so demeaning. But she was far more nervous about what her husband was going to do to her than about all of this. She feared he was going to ask for a divorce, and that didn't fit into how she envisioned her future.

"I'm Charlotte Wells, and this is my daughter Ruthie. I'm so very sorry I was a part of this. I'm even sorrier that your daughter was hurt. It was certainly never our goal to have anyone hurt."

Alice interrupted. "You had a goal? Regarding me? What exactly did you hope to achieve?"

Charlotte moaned. "I didn't mean it like that. There wasn't a specific goal, just making sure we weren't harboring drug dealers, you see."

Alice's heart was starting to pound. The woman wasn't just mean. She was stupid, too. "So, your point is that people with a family member who gets hooked on drugs are also dealers?"

Jack Wells tapped his wife on the back of her head. "Charlotte, do us all a favor. Apologize and then shut the hell up."

"Pleaseforgiveme," she muttered, then pushed Ruthie forward.

Ruthie was confused. Judy was the one who hadn't told their teacher that Patty had fallen, and she didn't understand why she was in all this trouble. But she knew what her daddy was going to do to her if she didn't do this right. He'd already taken away her blankie and electronics until Christmas, and it was only September. So she took a deep breath and repeated what she'd practiced to say, and said it with a big, happy smile on her face, thinking that looking friendly would be proper.

"I'm sorry, Patty. I'm sorry you were hurt. I'm sorry we were mean to you at school. I promise never to do that again."

Charlotte and Ruthie sat down.

Dan kept watching Jack Wells's face. The man was livid, but not at the situation. It was all directed at his wife and daughter.

And then Deidre and her daughter stood up. "I'm Deidre Treat, and this is my daughter, Carlene. I am so ashamed of myself right now that it's hard to talk. I let myself be influenced because I wanted these two ladies to like me. I went along to get along, as my granny used to say, and it was my mistake. I am disgusted with myself that I spread gossip. In my mind, that's the same thing as lying, and yet I did it. The horrifying part is that I actually told my daughter not to play with your sweet child. I did it because I wanted these two women to like me, without thinking about how it would hurt Patty. I don't deserve your forgiveness, but I sure do want it. I'm sorry, Alice. I'm as sorry as a woman can be and still be breathing." Then she patted Carlene's back. "Your turn, sweetie."

Carlene was already crying. "I'm sorry, Patty. I should never have said bad things about you. I should have played with you when you wanted to play. If you ever want to play with me again, I will say yes, a thousand times. And I am so sorry you got hurt. Please don't be mad at me. I won't be mean to you or anyone else as long as I live," she said, and then she burst into tears.

Before Alice knew what was happening, Patty was off the sofa and hugging Carlene. "It's okay," she said.

"I'm not mad at you. I was never mad at any of you. I just wanted you to like me."

Alice dropped to her knees and pulled both little girls up to her, hugging them tight. Then she stood. "Thank you, Carlene. We accept your apologies. Thank you."

"What about mine?" Renée asked.

Alice shifted her gaze to the woman without blinking. "So, Renée, the first words out of your mouth were that you were embarrassed. You lost me after that, but I heard you out. Your daughter is a child. I hope you teach her how to be a better person, or by the time she's grown and happens to see you in need of rescue, you're gonna be up shit creek.

"As for you, Mrs. Wells, you and I both know that wasn't an apology. When school begins again, just know that if this gossip hasn't stopped, and if you haven't curbed your daughter's behavior toward mine, then I will turn the entire matter over to my attorney, Danner Amos. Dan, would you care to have a word with them before they leave?"

Dan stood up, started to speak, and then stopped. "Charlie, would you please take your sister to the kitchen for a little snack? Maybe share another Pepsi and some cookies?"

"Yes, sir," Charlie said, and took Patty by the hand and left the room, with Booger at their heels.

As soon as they were out of hearing distance, Dan lit into the three families.

"In my other life, before I came here, I was the most effective prosecutor in Dallas, Texas. I was on a first-name basis with most of the big shots in that city, and trust me, there are a lot of them. In my whole career, I tried hundreds of cases and put a lot of criminals in prison for a long time. So if you think I'm going to let all this slide just because everyone said 'I'm sorry,' then you'd better think again. One word from Alice, and you'll be selling everything you own to get out from under the money you'll be paying for her pain and suffering and the defamation of her character, not to mention the physical and emotional trauma that little girl incurred because of what your daughters did…on your orders.

"Because of what you said and did, a little girl almost died. That will make national news. Your names and faces will be plastered all over social media and news stations across the country. So when school starts again, you'd better make sure that the gossip and lies you spread are over and your daughters have learned what it means to be kind. If you don't…if you and yours are still messing with her, I'll be messing with you. Do we all understand each other now?"

The men were pale. The women were in shock.

"Time's up," Dan said, and showed them to the door.

When they were gone, the air in the room felt lighter.

Dan walked back into the living room. "Well, was I scary enough?"

Alice walked into his arms. "Forever my hero."

When he pulled her close and felt her trembling, he was mad all over again. "The only sincere apology was the last one. Even her little girl seemed sorry. There's hope for them."

Alice looked up, saw the flash of want in his eyes, and then lowered her voice. "I'm so glad this is over."

"So am I," Dan said. "I knew you were dreading it for Patty, but sweetheart, you were amazing. You nailed them to the wall and called them on their bullshit in the most ladylike manner I've ever seen. I'm so proud of you."

"Thank you. And I'm giving you fair warning... I have reason to believe you might get lucky tonight."

Dan's smile began in his eyes, spread to his lips, and erupted into a laugh of such joy that he couldn't hold back, and then he kissed her with such passion that she lost her breath.

"I have such a hunger for you," Dan whispered. "But I'll settle for pop and cookies now, and you for dessert tonight."

"Deal," Alice said.

When they let go of each other, it was with reluctance, but the distant sound of Elliot's laughter from another room was the punctuation needed to shift their thoughts to the children and what they might be doing that made him laugh.

"Uh-oh," Alice said. "Time to make an appearance."

"Whatever it is, it's funny, and I could use a good laugh," Dan said. "Let's go see."

At the same time, Elliot was in the kitchen having cookies with the crew, which is how he thought of them, the body of Junior Rankin was discovered floating among flood debris more than eight miles from where he fell in.

While Elliot was dunking his cookie in a glass of milk and thinking about how he would paint the picture of Charlie and his dog, Junior's body was being put into a body bag and taken to the medical examiner's office.

Hunt Terrell got the news via cell phone that one of the rescuers had known Junior well enough to tentatively identify the body, but that meant Hunt was now going to have to make that call. He hated death notifications worse than any other part of his job but was thankful cell service had been restored, because it saved him a long drive out to the Rankin farm. He sat down behind his desk, got the phone number from the report they had filed, and made the call.

Albert was in the kitchen looking for a fresh bottle of water when one of the two cell phones on the sideboard began to ring. He wheeled himself over to answer, surprised that service had been restored, and saw it was his daddy's phone. But Big Tom was at the barn feeding their surviving calf, so he answered.

"Hello, Albert Rankin speaking."

"Hello, Albert. This is Deputy Sheriff Terrell. May I speak to your father?"

"Well, sir, he's down at the barn feeding a calf. It's the only head of livestock we have left, and he's a little partial about wanting to save it. Can I take a message?"

"Yes, I can give you the message, but I need your daddy to call me when he can. Your brother's body was found this morning about eight miles downriver from where he fell in. He was taken to the ME's office around noon and will be there until after the autopsy. Even though it was a tentative ID made by someone who knew him, we need an official verification by family. I am so sorry for your loss."

Albert was shaking all over again. "Yes, yes, I'll tell

him, and we're sure grateful he was found. This will ease my daddy's heart. I'll have Daddy call as soon as he gets back to the house."

"Thank you," Hunt said. "Again, I'm sorry for your loss."

Albert disconnected, then laid the phone down on the kitchen table and rolled himself out to the back porch. He sat there for a few moments to collect himself and his breath, and then let out an ear-piercing whistle.

Within seconds, Big Tom had stepped out of the barn and was looking toward the house. Albert raised his arm and motioned for him to come. Big Tom went into the barn and a couple of minutes later came back out, running toward the house. He arrived wild-eyed and out of breath. "What's wrong?" he asked.

"Deputy Terrell just called. They found Junior's body. Although he's tentatively been identified, they want family to verify the identification."

"Oh Lord! Thank you, Lord!" Big Tom said softly, then hugged Albert. "He won't be lost anymore."

"That's right, Daddy. Junior is no longer lost," Albert said. "Do you want to go now?"

"Yes, but let me go change clothes. I was worried about that little bull calf, but now I think he's gonna make it. He ate real good, and I'll feed him a bottle of milk supplement before bedtime."

Big Tom was still talking about the blessing of finding his boy when he went to change clothes. All Albert could do was cry.

As they drove off to the county seat, the jubilation of having Junior found was slowly turning to the realization of seeing him and the condition he was in.

Their arrival later was even quieter. The deputy had told Big Tom where the ME's office was and to call him when they got into town and he'd meet them there. So when they drove into town, Albert called.

Fifteen minutes later, they were in the outer office of the morgue, waiting for the viewing. After the long trip, and all the calls back and forth to make this happen, they were finally ushered into a small room with one big curtained window in it. A voice came over an intercom, asking Deputy Terrell if they were ready.

He looked at the Rankins, and when they nodded, he said, "Yes, we're ready."

The Rankins were watching the window when the curtain was pulled back, and there lay Junior, covered up except for his neck and head. He was almost unrecognizable. If it hadn't been for his red hair and those big, wide shoulders beneath the sheet...

"Oh Lord," Big Tom said, and then turned away and burst into hard, ugly sobs.

Albert wheeled himself straight up to the window, pulled himself upright, and stood as close to the glass as he could get, mapping every piece of that face until he knew he would never forget. Never forget that this was what karma could do. No one ever got away with sin. Not really. Then he turned around and looked straight into Hunt Terrell's eyes.

"Yes, that's my brother. That's Junior."

Hunt nodded. "Thank you. I'm sorry this was necessary. I know it wasn't easy."

"No, sir, it wasn't," Albert said. "But lots of things in life aren't easy. If that's all, we'll be going now."

"Reckon your daddy is fit to drive?" Hunt asked.

"It won't matter. I'm driving home," Albert said, then patted Tom's knee. "Daddy, come push me out onto the street. We're going home now."

Big Tom did as he was told and was in enough shock that it didn't even occur to him that Albert shouldn't drive. He just knew he couldn't.

—·——

Beulah Gatlin would have been mad as a wet hen at all the lawmen meddling around her place if she hadn't gone and blown herself up. But if she hadn't done that, then they wouldn't be here, so the point was moot.

There were a goodly number of vehicles and even more officers of the law walking all over the mountain where her house used to stand. They were bagging evidence, taking pictures, and every so often glancing over at the Gatlin brothers, who'd parked out by the family cemetery at the edge of the clearing and were sitting on the tailgate, watching the process unfold.

Moses glanced at the cemetery and then back at the blast site. "I don't suppose they'll find enough of Mama to bury," he said.

J. B. ducked his head and wiped his eyes. "That's hard to think about."

"I know, Brother. But a fact is a fact. However, if they do, we know where to put her, right beside Marty and his daddy. The spots open on either side of Daddy are for us," Moses said.

"I don't want to think about that, either," J. B. said. "I'm tired of people we love dying. I'm even more tired of talking about it. When all of this is over, let's leave. I don't want to rebuild anything up here. There's nothing here but bad memories."

Moses put his arm around J. B. and gave him a quick hug. "Maybe we should leave. Maybe you're right. I'll think on it some."

———～～———

It was midnight, the witching hour, when Alice slipped out of bed and across the hall into Dan's bedroom, then stopped, staring into the shadows and trying to find him, because he wasn't in his bed.

But when the lock suddenly clicked on the door behind her and she felt his hands and then his lips on the back of her neck, she shivered. And when his hands slid around her body and cupped the weight of her breasts, she sighed.

Seconds later, her nightgown was off and she was in his arms and in the bed. When he laid her down, she felt the crisp coolness of the sheets and then the heat of his body as he joined her. He traced the shape of her lower lip with his thumb and then kissed the hollow at the base of her throat.

"You're in my blood. I hear your voice even when you're nowhere to be seen. Every time I close my eyes, I see your face. I love you, Alice. I don't want you to move away from me. I want to know that your clothes are in the closet next to mine. I want to hear the laughter of your children in this house, and I need to know that every night when I go to bed, you are in the bed next to me. You set my clock. You give light to my life. Please don't leave after the power comes back on."

Alice's heart was racing. Some would think this

had happened too fast, but she didn't care what anyone thought or worry if they didn't understand. His every word was a love song. Every touch of his hands on her body felt so familiar, as if they'd done this countless times through many lifetimes and still hadn't had enough. And then he said them—the words that made this right.

"Marry me, Alice. Love me as much as I love you."

"Yes," she said. "Yes, yes, yes, and I already do."

They made love in the darkness without saying a word, following nothing but the soft gasps and quiet moans to let them know they were in the zone. One minute passed, and then another, and they were moving mindlessly with the heat flowing through their blood when it suddenly turned into that jolt of perfect passion, followed by a downhill slide of lust.

They lay motionless afterward, holding on to each other until their hearts began to beat at a normal rhythm.

Alice put her hand on his chest, feeling the heartbeat beneath her palm. "This all really happened, right? You did say you loved me. You did propose."

"Yes, yes, and yes," Dan said.

Her eyes welled, but she was smiling. "Right now, I'm as happy as I've ever been, and I can't believe I have to get dressed and leave you."

"Hey…that doesn't matter. You're mine, no matter where you lay your head."

Alice glanced at the clock, then jumped out of bed and grabbed her gown, pulling it over her head. "Love you," she whispered. She unlocked the door, and slipped out of his room and into her bathroom, just as Patty turned over and muttered something in her sleep.

When she came out, she crawled into bed beside her baby and pulled her close. "Miracles happen when you least expect them," she said softly, and pulled up the covers. Within minutes, they were both asleep.

Across the hall, Dan was lying on his back, thinking about the future and, for the first time since he'd lost his family, looking forward to the years to come.

——————

Just before daylight the next morning, a half-dozen big trucks from electric companies all over the state rolled into town. The manager of the power plant in Blessings met them in the parking lot of the Piggly Wiggly, discussed what was needed and where to start, and off they went.

The first grid to be restored was at the hospital, and the jubilant shouts that went up when the normal lighting came on were heard all over the building. After that, they moved to restoring power at gas stations and the nursing home, then the businesses up and down Main. By afternoon the trucks had headed into the residential areas. Half of the trucks went to work on one side of the railroad tracks, while the rest of the trucks worked on the other.

Johnny Pine went up to Lovcy's house with his work crew, removed the downed tree, and boarded up the hole in the outer wall until she was well enough to deal with repairs.

——————

Back at Dan's house, Alice removed the bandage from her hand to check on the healing, then went through the house looking for Dan. She found him in his office, at his computer paying bills.

"Dan, do you have a minute?" she asked.

He pushed away from the computer and swiveled around. "For you, I have forever. What do you need, sweetheart?"

She held out her hand. "Doesn't this look well enough to you to remove the stitches?"

He turned her hand palm up and tilted it toward his desk lamp. The edges of the cut had healed, and there wasn't any puffiness or redness.

"Does this hurt?" he asked as he gently pressed on different places on her hand.

Alice shook her head.

"It looks good to me. Want to make a quick trip up to the ER and get the stitches removed?"

"No, I want you to take them out."

He grinned. "Then let's go get the first aid kit, some scissors, and some tweezers."

By the time he got back with what he needed, he'd brought an audience with him. Elliot saw him getting the first aid kit. Charlie overheard the conversation about stitches coming out, and he brought Patty so he could keep an eye on her.

Alice saw them all coming and laughed. "I should have set up a concession and sold popcorn for the event."

"We're having popcorn?" Patty said.

Alice laughed. "No, and I should have known better than to assume you'd let that pass. So, everyone gather 'round. Get the best seats possible, and then please sit still."

It took Dan a couple of minutes to get set up, and then he paused. "You still sure you want me to do this?"

"I've trusted you with far more important and

difficult things than this, and you came through with flying colors. Proceed, Dr. Amos. I promise not to cry."

She laughed, but Dan couldn't. Being the one to cause her pain wasn't something he wanted on his conscience, no matter how innocent the act. So he turned her chair just a bit to the right, clipped stitches, and then pulled them out, one by one, with the tweezers. Alice never flinched.

"Done!" he said, and wiped an alcohol-soaked gauze pad all over the palm of her hand.

"What a relief!" Alice said, and then made a fist a couple of times. "Other than a little tender where it was cut, it feels so good to get rid of the stitches and bandages."

Patty leaned against her mama's shoulder and patted her leg. "Now you'll feel all better."

Alice hugged her. "Yes, I do feel better."

The generator went silent right in the middle of their celebration, but the lights were still on.

"The power must be back on!" Dan said, and took off to check.

"Oh, what wonderful news!" Elliot said. "I can go home! I can sleep in my own bed tonight! Not that I didn't appreciate being a guest here, but we all want to go home. I'm going to pack up my stuff and go check on the Martin family. They don't have a home to go back to. I need to make sure they understand they're welcome to stay where they are for the time being."

"You pack. I'll carry your bags over for you," Charlie said, and a short while later, he and Dan moved Elliot home.

When they returned, Dan went down the hall to his office and the room suddenly went silent.

Patty got quiet, and Charlie looked everywhere but at his mother.

"Hey! What's wrong with you two?" Alice asked.

Charlie shrugged. "I guess I got used to having Dan part of us," he said.

"I don't want to leave my Dan," Patty said, and started to cry.

"Oh my goodness," Alice said. "Come here to me. You, too, Charlie. You're not too big to hug your mama." She put her arms around them.

Dan walked in on the tears and sad faces and stopped. "What happened? What's wrong?"

Patty tore out of her mama's arms and ran to him, sobbing. As he picked her up, she wrapped her arms around his neck. "I don't want to go home without you," she said, and hid her face in the curve of his neck.

Dan looked at Alice, who was still comforting Charlie. "Him, too?"

She nodded.

"Then this seems like the time to ask them the same thing I asked you last night. Is it okay?"

She nodded again as her eyes blurred with tears.

He sat down at the table, with Patty in his lap. "Charlie, sit with us for a minute, okay?"

Charlie sat, his shoulders slumped and his gaze focused on the floor.

"So here's the deal," Dan said. "Last night I asked your mama to marry me, and she said yes."

Both kids looked at their mother in shock.

"Mama! The best news ever and you didn't tell us?" Charlie said.

Patty's eyes grew wide in wonder. "We're getting married?" she asked.

"Yes, we are," Alice said. "I was just waiting for the right time to bring it up."

Charlie was staring at Dan in disbelief. He leaned forward on the table and then buried his face in his arms. They could tell he was crying, but they didn't know why.

Dan transferred Patty to her mother's lap and got up, ready to tackle another problem. "What's wrong, Bud? If you think I'm trying to take your daddy's place, then don't worry. I would never try to—"

Charlie's head came up. His eyes were swimming with tears, but there was no mistaking the fire in his voice. "You are the kind of man I wished mine had been. This is the best news ever. I like you so much, and just knowing you're going to be around to help Mama make decisions now, instead of me trying to figure them out, is such a relief. Most of the time I didn't know what I was doing, but I couldn't let Mama down. Thank you for always being there for us, and thank you for loving our mama as much as we do. I will be proud to be your stepson."

Dan was both moved and elated. "You are a good man, Charlie. You make me proud. I'm the one who's happy. So happy that all of you are ready to trust me and to let me love you. I was lost for a really long time, and now I feel whole again. I'm the one who's grateful. I'm the one who's blessed. Group hug," he said, and pulled all of them into his embrace.

Having power again meant many things to many people.

Dan had hired Ellis Martin full time as a handyman-plumber and had a full work crew doing repairs on the rental properties.

Ruby organized a meeting with all of the employees at Granny's. A cleaning crew was set up to clean out all of the freezers and refrigerators, throw away any remaining food, and reorder.

Mercy agreed to run the front just until Lovey was able to come back to work, and the two bakers she'd trained were officially moved from part-time to full-time employees.

Elvis the fry cook knew what to order in the way of meat and line items. The dishwasher was moved up to bus boy, and one waitress's husband, who had recently retired, volunteered to be temporary dishwasher to help Lovey out.

"Okay then," Ruby said after the meeting was winding down. "Everyone knows their job now. Call in your orders to get this place in working order, and let's start cleaning everything out to make room for the new deliveries. We'll have Granny's back up and running in no time."

"What about Lovey?" Mercy asked. "What about her house?"

"Lovey is coming home with me, and when she's well enough to live on her own again, she can live in my old house while hers is being repaired."

"Awesome," the crew said, and then grabbed trash cans and scrub buckets full of hot, soapy water.

While they were working there, the same thing was going on at the Piggly Wiggly, and down the street the gas stations and the quick stop were getting their businesses up and running once more.

Blessings was finding her own rhythm again, and it was good.

———∿∿∿———

The next morning was all about the move. And once Alice thought about what had to be done, she realized it wasn't that much. They'd moved into Hope House with nothing but the clothes and kitchenware they'd been given, and Alice was leaving everything behind except their clothes. There was no telling what the next family might need, and she was happy to be able to donate to the furnishings, even if that was just with pots and pans.

Alice was in work clothes, ready to go tackle the packing, and Dan was in his office on the computer signing final papers on the purchase of the property, after which he would transfer the agreed-upon amount from an account he still had in Dallas to Aidan Payne's lawyer, who was handling the sale.

They were getting ready to head over to Hope House when the doorbell rang. "I'll get it!" Charlie shouted, and bounded toward the door.

Alice was in the other room and already on her way to the foyer when she heard Charlie shouting. She started running at the same time Dan came flying out of the office. Patty had been in the living room with Charlie and was now peeking around the doorway, on the verge of tears because all the shouting scared her.

When Alice came around the corner and saw the two men at the door, she went from shock to rage. She couldn't get there fast enough, afraid Charlie would do more than shout.

—∿∿—

"Look, Charlie! We didn't come here to cause trouble," Moses Gatlin said. "We just thought you all would want to know—"

"We don't want to know anything about what's happening to you!" Charlie said. "You are nothing to me!"

"Looks like you guys landed on your feet real nice," J. B. added, eyeing the house and what he could see past Charlie's shoulder.

"We landed right where you dumped us!" Charlie said. "No clothes. No car. No food, and just enough money for one month's rent. At that point, Mama got sick. Real sick. Like for weeks, and they turned off our utilities 'cause we couldn't pay, and we lived in a shack behind a bar in cold weather with nothing to eat and no way to stay warm. That's how we landed, you sorry excuse for a man!"

Moses looked sick. "Is that true?" he asked.

But before Charlie could answer, Alice ducked under his arm and found herself face-to-face with the past. "I've got this, Son!" Alice said. "You go get Dan."

"I'm right here," Dan said, and now the Gatlin brothers were wondering if this might have been a mistake. "Say what you need to say, honey," Dan said. "I've got your back."

"I don't know how you found us, but get out!" Alice said.

Moses shuffled from foot to foot. He'd come hoping for some kind of forgiveness from her for what he'd done, but that obviously wasn't happening. Still, he persisted. "I asked around and got directions to find the house. I have something you need to know and—"

Alice took a step forward, and when she did, so did Dan. "You gave us away! You no longer exist in our world! There's nothing I want to hear about any of you."

"Mama is dead," J. B. said. "Our house exploded. She was inside."

"Karma," Charlie yelled.

Charlie's uncles did not disagree.

"So," Alice said, "someone you love died when your house exploded, and now you have no place to live. As you drive away from this house, consider that what you gave to us was returned to you. Mirror-image karma. Go away."

Moses sighed. "I just want you to know I'm sorry."

Alice turned around, grabbed Charlie's arm, picked Patty up in the hall, and walked out of sight.

Dan stepped into the doorway, wearing his court face. "Never do this again," he said softly.

J. B. grabbed Moses by the arm and yanked. They turned around and walked back to their old truck.

Dan followed them out to his bottom step and stood with his arms folded, watching until they drove out of sight before he went inside. He found the Conroys in the kitchen. "They're gone. You guys okay?" he asked.

"We're fine," Alice said. "So, everybody ready to head to Hope House?"

They nodded.

"Then head for the truck," Dan said. "Tonight will be the first night of the rest of our life together. Who's excited besides me?"

And that ended the drama of their unexpected

company for the kids, but Dan knew every time the thought crossed Alice's mind from the expression on her face. He hated that had happened, but thought maybe it had to happen to cut those final ties.

That night, after they were all settled into their own rooms, and Alice was officially moved in with Dan, the house took on a different tone. It felt light and happy, as if it had readied itself for the next generation.

The same night out at the Rankin farm, Albert and Big Tom were in the kitchen making supper. Albert was peeling potatoes and Big Tom was frying up some sausage patties. Once the sausage was done, he'd make a pan of gravy to go with it.

They had temporary plans made to bury Junior at the Blessings Cemetery beside his mother once the county released his body, and tonight they were just grateful their house was still standing and that power was back on.

Big Tom's phone rang, and when he saw it was Ethel, he smiled. "I need to take this, Son. I'll be right back." Then he shoved the skillet full of sausage off the burner and left the room.

The television was on the evening news, and Albert was watching bits and pieces of the storm coverage as he worked. He finished the potato he was peeling and then looked up just as they began scrolling names and faces of victims across the screen. He paused when one face stood out from all the others, and the name beneath it confirmed the man's identification.

Their pot buyer, Oscar Langston, the man who'd told

Junior to take a life, had had his taken instead. He'd died during the hurricane!

Albert shivered, wondering what his fate would have been if he hadn't run away. His feet were healing, but they would be scarred reminders of making the better decision.

"You done with them taters, Son?" Big Tom asked as he came back into the room.

"Almost, Daddy," Albert said, and quickly peeled the last one. "Here you go."

Big Tom took them, washed them, and then sliced them up to cook. "Ethel sends her love to both of us," he said.

Albert nodded. "She seems like a good woman, Daddy. I'm glad she makes you happy."

"Thank you, Albert. Supper will be done in a few minutes."

Albert nodded, but he was still thinking about Oscar Langston. Everyone who'd known what he and Junior were doing was dead. It felt like divine intervention, and whether it was or not, it didn't matter anymore. Tomorrow would be a new day with a new outlook. And soon, he'd be out of this chair and returning to a new way of life—finding a way to move on without a brother.

―∿∿―

A couple of weeks later, the Blessings middle-school football team was getting ready to take the field. It would be Charlie's first time to start as a running back. It was his height, skill, and swiftness that had earned him that right, and no one was prouder than Dan and Alice.

Alice was thinking about the upcoming meeting with Dan's family when she glanced down on the bottom row where Patty was sitting. She slipped her hand beneath Dan's elbow and pointed. "Look at those two," she said, pointing to Patty and her classmate, Carlene. After school resumed, they'd become inseparable.

Dan saw them with their heads together, giggling and pointing at the players out on the field. "Life handed us a little miracle there."

"And a much-needed miracle," Alice said.

Dan rubbed the one-carat diamond on her ring finger and gave her one of those *You. Me. Later* looks.

She arched an eyebrow. "Message received," she whispered. And then the school band started playing, and the team ran out onto the field.

———

Charlie Conroy was living his dream as he looked up into the stands, searching for his mama and Dan. As soon as he saw them, his nerves settled.

Life was happening, and it was good.

———

But not everyone was happy to be in Blessings, especially the man standing in the shadows beneath the stadium. The last thing Bowie James had ever imagined himself doing was coming home. Yet here he was. Damn hurricane. Damn conscience. He hadn't been able to ignore either one.

Keep reading for a sneak peek at the next book in Sharon Sala's Blessings, Georgia series

$\mathcal{A}$ RAINBOW
ABOVE *us*

BOWIE WAS AT THE STATION SIGNING THE VANDALISM complaint when Emmitt Boone burst into the station. Even though the doctor had put a brace over Emmitt's nose to keep it from being bumped and dislocated again, it was too swollen to ignore.

Emmitt took one look at Bowie and turned white as a sheet.

"What's he doing here?"

The chief looked up. "Signing a complaint against your son."

Emmitt gasped. "But you said when you called that he'd been arrested for vandalism. What does he have to do with it?"

Bowie kept writing without looking up. "It was my vehicle he vandalized. Keyed the hell out of it, too. It will cost thousands to get that fixed."

Emmitt groaned.

Bowie slid the complaint across the desk toward the chief.

"If that's all, I'll be leaving now."

"That's all," Lon said.

Emmitt started to grab Bowie's arm, then thought better of it.

"Wait! Wait! Let's talk this out. I don't want my kid having an arrest record."

"You're the one who raised him," Bowie said. "Besides, he's getting off easy from me. When I was his age, you and your brothers beat the hell out of me, and I didn't do anything to any of you. I told you what would happen if you didn't leave me alone. I'll see you in court."

Emmitt cursed beneath his breath as Bowie walked out of the precinct, then turned to the chief. "Can I talk to my boy?"

"I suppose, after I pat you down," Lon said, and confiscated a large pocket knife. "You can have that back when you leave."

"Hell, Chief! You're treating us like common criminals," Emmitt muttered.

Lon shrugged. "Unfortunately, your son is a criminal now. And the cost of the repairs on Mr. James's vehicle will turn this arrest into a felony."

Emmitt's lips parted, then he thought better of arguing.

While Lon took Emmitt back to see his son, Bowie was on his way back to his motor home. He didn't have any sympathy whatsoever for the kid, or for Emmitt. He hadn't been here even twenty-four hours, and he'd been assaulted, and his car vandalized. He could only imagine how the rest of his time here would play out. And, it was already daylight. Time to begin another day.

He hurried inside and changed the sheets on his bed for his girls' arrival, cleaned up the bathroom, and moved most of what he used daily into the other bathroom.

Closet space was limited, so they'd have to manage

with what he had, and hopefully, the renovation would go smoothly, and wouldn't take too long. A half-dozen men from one of his work crews were on their way to Blessings. He'd made reservations for them at a local bed and breakfast, and paid two weeks in advance. After that, he'd pay week by week, until they were done.

Once he had everything neat, clean, and put away, he headed to Granny's for breakfast. It wasn't yet eight o'clock, too early to go visiting at a nursing home. He set the security alarm again, then locked up as he left.

Frank and Jewel were sitting at a little table outside having their morning coffee, and waved at him from the front yard.

He grinned and waved back. Sometimes that was the extent of being neighbors in the life he led.

By the time he got to Granny's, the parking lot was nearly full. He hoped they didn't run out of biscuits before he got his share. They were the best he'd ever eaten. And then it dawned on him that he'd already met the police chief, the man who was married to the baker.

Bowie was thinking about biscuits and gravy when he walked inside. The dining room was packed, but there were a couple of vacant tables, and one empty booth.

Mercy welcomed him back as she took him to a small table.

"Enjoy," she said, and left the menu with him, only Bowie didn't bother picking it up. He already knew what he wanted.

A different waitress showed up with a coffee pot, and filled the empty cup in front of him.

"Good morning, I'm Lila. Do you know what you want, or do you need a few minutes?"

"I want sausage, biscuits, and gravy," he said.

"No eggs to go with them?" Lila asked.

"No eggs," Bowie said.

She smiled. "Coming right up."

Bowie leaned back and took a quick sip of the coffee, then set it aside to cool a bit as he glanced around the room. This morning, the other diners were staring without apologies.

He stared back until they looked away. The news was probably already spreading about the teenager who keyed his car. For the people who knew him growing up, the fact that the boy in jail was Emmitt Boone's son, only made the news juicier.

His phone signaled a text. He read it and grinned. His crew was less than an hour out of Blessings. He sent back a text telling them about Granny's, and to go ahead and get settled in the bed and breakfast before they ate. He'd get in touch with them later.

When his food came, he looked at the plate of browned sausage patties, the basket of hot biscuits, and a bowl of white gravy, and couldn't wait to dig in. The first bite did not disappoint, and he ate two plates full before he stopped. He was finishing up his coffee, when Lila stopped by and left his bill on the table.

Bowie left a tip and headed up front to pay. It was almost nine o'clock now, and he was anxious to go to the nursing home.

He and the girls had stayed in touch for the past twenty years by phone calls, letters, the occasional postcard he would send, and as technology changed, now by face-timing on their phones. And then it just occurred to him that their phone must have fallen victim to the flood, since they hadn't called him about the house, and why they written the letter instead. He'd find out details soon enough.

He was pulling out money to pay, when the entrance door opened behind him. He heard the heavy footsteps, the angry growl of a man's voice, then saw what amounted to panic on Mercy's face.

"Turn around and face me like a man!" the man yelled.

Bowie ignored him, and kept talking to Mercy. "Breakfast was great. Do me a favor and please call the police. Oh, and keep the change," Bowie said, and handed her cash.

The man behind him was obviously impatient, but Bowie already knew who it was, and when Judson Boone grabbed him by the shoulder, and tried to yank him around, he didn't yield.

Bowie shrugged off the hand, turned to face the nemesis from his childhood dreams, and took satisfaction in the shock he saw on Jud's face.

"Like looking in a mirror, and seeing a vision of your younger self, isn't it? Outside," Bowie said quietly, and pointed to the door.

"Like hell! You don't tell me what to do!" Jud shouted, and took a swing at Bowie.

Bowie calmly grabbed his wrist in mid-air and tightened his hold, until the old man grimaced.

"I said, outside," Bowie said softly, and took off for the exit, dragging Jud with him.

Once they were in the parking lot, Bowie turned him loose.

"What's the matter with you, trying to start a fight in there? You truly don't give a shit about anything but yourself, do you?"

Jud was still trying to wrap his head around the fact that the family bastard was his doppelganger, and didn't bother answering the questions. He'd come here to straighten out the mess his family was in, but was beginning to realize it might be harder than he'd expected.

Bowie James was a good four inches taller than him, and bulked up big-time beneath his clothes. He should have brought backup. Instead, he pointed a finger in Bowie's face.

"You broke Emmitt's nose and—"

"Don't do that," Bowie said, and grabbed the finger and pushed it away. "Whatever happened to your little thugs, they brought on themselves. They jumped me in the dark, and both had weapons. They should be ready to take what they were trying to dish out, don't you think?"

Jud didn't know how to respond to this quiet menace, but he was well aware it could go wrong at any moment, and spit out the rest of what he'd come here to say.

"I want my grandson out of jail, and you're gonna drop charges, do you understand?"

"Go home, old man," Bowie said. "I told your boys last night that I didn't want any trouble. I came here to fix my grandma's house, and then I'm leaving. I don't want anything to do with Blessings, and that includes anyone named Boone."

"You don't tell me no! No one tells me, no!" Jud shouted.

Bowie could hear sirens coming up Main. "You want a cell next to your grandson?"

"I want him out!" Jud said, and swung at Bowie again, but Bowie dodged the blow, grabbed his arm, and yanked it behind his back, then pinned him against a van just as a police cruiser pulled up into the parking lot.

Jud was struggling and cursing, and trying to get free.

Bowie recognized Deputy Ralph, as he hurried toward them.

"You again?" Ralph said, eyeing the man Bowie James had pressed up against a van.

"I'm sorry to say, it's just more of the same," Bowie said.

"I'll kill you! I swear to God, I'll see you dead!" Jud screamed.

Bowie just pushed Jud's head a little firmer against the van, and yanked his arm a little higher behind his back.

"Well, that was stupid," Bowie said. "You just threatened my life in front of a policeman."

Deputy Ralph cuffed Jud, and then pulled him around. "You get the cell next to Junior. I think he'll be glad to see you. Jail isn't anything like home."

Jud was so shocked that he was actually in handcuffs, that he began to stumble and stammer.

"Oh, well, ya'll know I didn't mean it. I was just pissed off about Junior being in jail. How about we let bygones be bygones?"

Bowie's eyes narrowed. "Do you remember Mama begging you to stop your sons from beating me?"

Jud's face paled, but Bowie kept talking.

"I remember. I couldn't see you because my eyes were swollen shut, but I heard you laugh and call her a whore."

A couple had come out of Granny's, saw what was happening, and stayed to watch. It was the beginning of the crowd that was gathering.

Jud was embarrassed to be seen in this situation and started shouting again.

"So you're out for revenge?"

Bowie shook his head. "I already told you why I came. And when I'm done with Gran's house, I'll be gone. You started this again without taking one thing into consideration. I was only a kid when you ran me and Mama out of town. I'm not a kid anymore, and you bit off more than you can chew and swallow here, old man. You figure all this out with the judge. Maybe he'll give you and your grandson a bargain…like a two for one deal."

"I didn't touch you," Jud said. "You can't put someone in jail for arguing."

Then Mercy stepped out of the crowd.

"Jud Boone tried to start a fight in Granny's, and this man stopped him, and dragged him out without disturbing any of the diners. I was watching from the window after they left. Jud kept trying to fight, and this man just kept stopping him without fighting back."

Jud glared at her.

"I'll remember that. I can make you sorry you ever opened your mouth," he yelled.

"You just threatened Mr. James, and the police chief's wife in my presence," Deputy Ralph said, and grabbed Jud by the elbow and opened the back door to his cruiser. "Watch your head," he added, then shut the door, and drove off with his prisoner.

Bowie was beginning to doubt his ability to stay out of trouble long enough to finish what he came to do. And the crowd from inside Granny's was staring at him again. He'd had enough.

"Didn't your parents ever tell you it's rude to stare at people? How many of you are thinking about taking a swing at me when my back is turned again?"

Shock spread across their faces, and then they all began talking at once.

"No, never."

"Sorry for staring."

"No, we're sorry."

"It wasn't that!"

Then one old man spoke up.

"I'm sorry, sir. I remember you and your mama…a real sweet girl. But you don't look the same. You look so much like Jud Boone looked when he was young, that I thought I was seeing things."

Bowie shrugged, but at least now he got the reason for the stares. "Think what it's like to be me. I look in a mirror and see the devil."

Then he got in his car and drove out of the parking lot. It was time to get the girls.

———ᴚᴚ———

Ella James was pinning up her mother's long braided into a little doughnut shape at the back of her head. It had turned completely white the year Billie Jo committed suicide, and she'd never been the same. This set-back with the flood had taken her mother all the way down.

Twenty-five year old Rowan Harper, the girl kneeling at Pearl's feet, was also a hurricane refugee who'd lost everything. The county sheriff had picked her up on a road where she'd been walking, and when he heard her story, he called the director of the nursing home in Blessings, to see if he had room for one more refugee. After he was assured there was a room for her, he took her to Blessings and dropped her off where people were sent to die, arriving at her temporary lodgings with nothing but the clothes on her back.

Ella and Pearl had taken to her, and after a week together, they'd become each other's family. This morning, Rowan was tying the laces on Pearl's tennis shoes, while Ella was still working on her mama's hair. It took a village to get the old woman dressed these days. She'd sunk into a depression that no amount of distraction could change.

Rowan rocked back on her heels when she was finished, and patted Pearl's leg.

"Did I get them too tight, honey?"

"No, dear, they're just fine. Thank you," she said.

As Rowan went to make up Pearl's bed, she couldn't help but remember doing this for her father every day. His loss was still fresh and painful, and she kept blinking away tears. Hurricane Fanny had not only washed away their home, but it had taken her daddy with it.

When Pearl and Ella offered her a place to live with them, she cried from the relief. Only right now, everything was on hold, because they had nowhere else to go, either.

Rowan finished with the bed, and was going into the bathroom to clean it, when a man's deep voice interrupted the silence.

"There are my girls," he said.

She heard Ella gasp, and Pearl let out a cry of such joy, and then began to weep.

She only got a glimpse of the giant of a man walking in, before Ella was in his arms. He was laughing and hugging her so tight, that he swung her off her feet.

For a moment, Rowan wondered what it would feel

like to be loved like that, watching Pearl flying out of her chair crying and laughing. "You came, you came! Ella said you would."

Bowie held out one arm. "Come here, Gran. I need a hug from you, too."

Pearl fell into his arms.

So, he's Pearl's grandson.

Rowan could see that he mattered greatly to them, and stood quietly, watching the reunion and their joy, with only a brief flash of envy. Then, as if sensing he was being watched, the man looked up and saw her. She caught a flash of something beyond curiosity, and then it was gone.

Bowie was so happy to see his family, that it took a bit for him to realize there was another woman in the room. He knew he was staring, but didn't look away.

She was young and leggy, like a colt, and with a lot of long hair as dark as her eyes, wearing a pair of worn out shorts, and an a green T-shirt, about two sizes too large. Her feet were bare, and there was a sadness on her face, even though she smiled at him.

Bowie smiled back. "Hey, Aunt Ella, why don't you introduce me to your friend?"

Ella frowned. "Oh, where are my manners? Rowan, this is my nephew, Bowie James. His mother, Billie Jo, was my youngest sister. Bowie, this is Rowan Harper. She's in the same predicament Mama and I are, only she lost her daddy *and* her home, in the flood."

"A pleasure to meet you, Rowan Harper. My condolences on your losses. That hurricane was a bad one."

"Yes, it was," Rowan said. "Thank you for the sympathy. It is a pleasure to meet you, too."

Pearl patted Bowie's arm. "When we get our house fixed, Rowan is coming to live with us. She doesn't have anything, or anybody left, and we have those two extra bedrooms."

Bowie blinked. This certainly added a hitch to his plans, but what the heck. He had the extra sleeping space, and it wouldn't be for that long. He couldn't take the girls and leave her behind.

"That sounds like an answer to everyone's prayers," Bowie said. "So, Gran, I haven't seen the house yet, is it locked?"

Ella nodded. "Yes, wait a second and I'll get the key."

She got her purse from the small closet, dug through the contents, and pulled out a key ring and handed it over.

"It's the gold one, and it's going to take you a while to fix the mess that it's in. Oh…you should also know that right after the flood waters went down, some people from church came to the house and helped Mama and me pack up what hadn't been ruined. We got some clothing, our business papers, the pots and pans, of course, and also my Granny's sideboard and the family silver. It's all in storage here in town. Whatever is still in the house is to be thrown away."

"Good to know. And it's not going to take as long as you think," Bowie said. "I brought one of my best work crews with me. They'll be staying in the local bed and breakfast while we're here, and I am taking all three of you to stay with me in my motor home until we're done. No more nursing home."

When Pearl's eyes welled, Bowie hugged her again. "Don't cry, Gran. I'll fix the house. But you all need to know that there may be some more trouble while I'm here."

Ella frowned. "What do you mean, more trouble?"

Bowie ran a hand through his hair in frustration.

"I only arrived here last night, and in that short length of time, I have had three run-ins with the Boones, so be prepared. As long as I'm here, Jud isn't going to let anything rest, although he'll have to get out of jail to do it."

Ella gasped. "Jud Boone is in jail? What did he do to you?"

"Emmitt's oldest boy is in jail, too, Mel is probably drinking meals for a while, and Emmitt's nose is broken," Bowie said.

Rowan eyed the width of Bowie James's shoulders, the muscles visible beneath his shirt, and the size of his hands, and guessed the Boones, whoever they were, might have come off luckier than they knew.

Pearl wasn't amused. "I won't stand for any of this," she said. "It's Jud's fault Billie Jo took you and ran away in the middle of the night. I never saw her again. I'll be having something to say to him, myself, if he starts this old feud up all over again."

"What feud?" Rowan asked.

Pearl threw up her hands in disgust.

"Oh, it's so stupid, and it began three generations back. My father and Jud's father were sort of friends, but always in competition, and they loved the same girl. The animosity grew when the girl chose my father, instead of Jud's father. And then even though Jud's father later married someone else, the hard feelings grew between them, and he passed it down to his children. Any chance

Mr. Boone had to cause trouble for my daddy, he didn't hesitate to take it."

Bowie stopped her. "You can finish this ugly saga for Rowan later. How about I get you all out of here? How long will it take you to pack?"

"We have one suitcase between Mama and me," Ella said.

"I don't feel right intruding on you," Rowan said. "I accepted these sweet ladies generosity, but it does not mean you should pick up the slack. I'm sure the director will let me stay until you repair the house."

"No, ma'am," Bowie said. "I came to rescue my girls, and the way I look at it, you're the bonus I didn't know was coming. Now I repeat…how long will it take you to pack?"

Rowan felt like Pearl. She wanted to cry from the joy and relief of not being left behind.

"Everything I have will fit in a grocery sack," she said.

"Then let's get crackin'," Bowie said. "I already met with the director and told him you all were leaving, so there's nothing left to do but take you away."

What had begun as just another day, had turned into a rescue, and a family reunion for Ella and Gran.

But for Rowan, it was a whole other thing. It hadn't taken her long to go from curiosity about the stranger, to having something of a crush. She'd always dreamed of the 'knight in shining armor' version of true love, and he was certainly a good example of that. Even though she'd known him less than fifteen minutes, and she'd turned out to be the unexpected guest at the shelter he was offering, she wasn't going to turn down the first ray of hope she'd had since before the storm.

About the Author

Sharon Sala is a member of the Romance Writers of America, as well as the Oklahoma Chapter of RWA. She has over 115 books in print, published in five genres—romance, young adult, Western, general fiction, and women's fiction. First published in 1991, she is an eight-time RITA finalist, winner of the Janet Dailey Award, five-time RT Career Achievement winner, five-time winner of the National Readers' Choice Award, five-time winner of the Colorado Romance Writers' Award of Excellence, and winner of the Heart of Excellence, as well as winner of the Booksellers Best Award. In 2011, she was named RWA's recipient of the Nora Roberts Lifetime Achievement Award. In 2017, RWA presented her with the Centennial Award for recognition of her 100th published novel. Her books are *New York Times* and *USA Today* bestsellers and get great reviews from *Publishers Weekly*. Writing changed her life, her world, and her fate. She lives in Oklahoma, the state where she was born. Visit her at sharonsala.net.

MAGNOLIA BRIDES

These women have marriage on their minds and love in their hearts...and in this small Georgia town, anything is possible

By Lynnette Austin

The Best Laid Wedding Plans

When Jenni Beth Beaumont inherits her family's beautiful antebellum home, her dream of turning it into a wedding destination feels closer than ever. But former crush Cole Bryson plans to buy and tear down the house. Good thing Jenni will do whatever it takes to keep her dream—and protect herself from falling for Cole all over again.

Every Bride Has Her Day

Sam Montgomery thought he'd have no trouble finding peace and quiet in the small Georgia town where he inherited a rundown house. Until his effusively optimistic neighbor, Cricket O'Malley, storms into his life—and his heart.

Picture Perfect Wedding

Beck Elliot thought he'd never again see the woman who broke his heart. But when divorced single mom Tansy Calhoun moves back to Misty Bottoms to open a shop, she's impossible to avoid...and so are his old feelings.

"Lynnette Austin has made her mark on contemporary romance."

—Night Owl Reviews for Picture Perfect Wedding

For more Lynnette Austin, visit:
sourcebooks.com

THE MONTGOMERY BROTHERS

Samantha Chase, *New York Times* and *USA Today* Bestselling Author

Return to You

James Montgomery has achieved everything he'd hoped for in life...except marrying the girl of his dreams. Now Selena Ainsley is back, but how can she face the man she loved and left behind?

Meant for You

Summer Montgomery wants to be taken seriously almost as much as she wants her brother's off-limits best friend, Ethan. But it only takes one night away from watchful eyes to make impossible dreams come true...

I'll Be There

Zach Montgomery lives by his own rules and doesn't answer to anyone. But his assistant, Gabriella Martine, has no intention of backing down.

Until There Was Us

Megan Montgomery can't stop thinking about her sexy hookup with Alex Rebat at her cousin's wedding. Alex can't stop thinking about her—and now that Megan's back in town, Alex hopes she'll take a chance on a future they can only build together.

Also by Sharon Sala